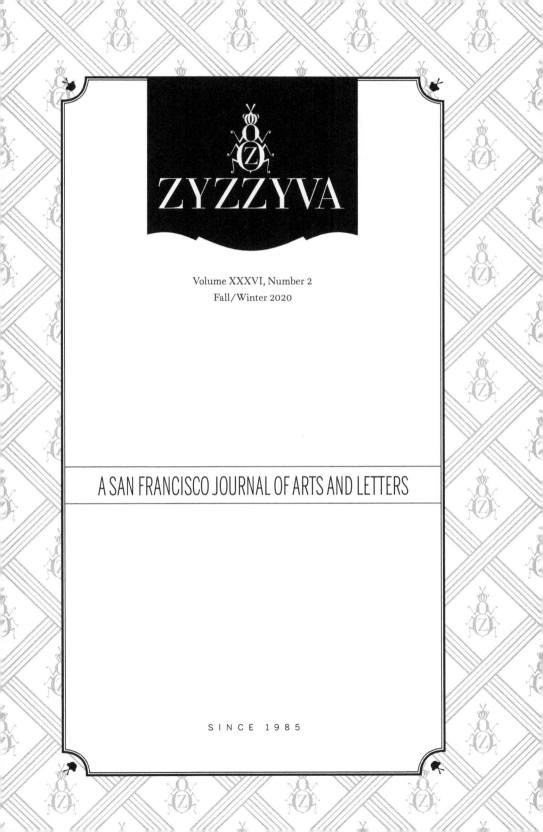

ZYZZYVA

Volume XXXVI, Number 2
Fall/Winter 2020

A SAN FRANCISCO JOURNAL OF ARTS AND LETTERS

SINCE 1985

ZYZZYVA

EDITOR
Laura Cogan

MANAGING EDITOR
Oscar Villalon

EDITORIAL ASSISTANT
Zack Ravas

SALES & MARKETING
Laura Howard

CONTRIBUTING EDITORS
Andrew Altschul, Sam Barry,
Robin Ekiss, John Freeman, Paul Madonna,
Ismail Muhammad, David L. Ulin

COPY EDITOR
Regan McMahon

INTERNS
Jesse Bedayn, Bella Davis, Cade Johnson

BOARD OF DIRECTORS
Warren Lazarow, *President*
Laura Cogan
Patrick Corman
Jane Gillette
Regis McKenna
Barbara Meacham
Jonathan Schmidt

ORIGINAL DESIGN
Three Steps Ahead

TYPE DESIGN
Text font created specially for
ZYZZYVA by Matthew Butterick

PRODUCTION
Josh Korwin

PRINTER
Versa Press, Inc.

DISTRIBUTION
Media Solutions, Small Changes, ANC 365

SUBSCRIPTION SERVICES
EBSCO

ARCHIVES
Bancroft Library, UC Berkeley

CONTACT
57 Post St., #604, San Francisco, CA 94104
E contact@zyzzyva.org
W www.zyzzyva.org

SUBSCRIPTION
$42/four issues; $70/eight issues
Student rate: $30/four issues

ZYZZYVA (19604) is published in April, August, and December by ZYZZYVA,
Inc., a nonprofit, tax-exempt corporation. © 2020 ZYZZYVA, Inc.

CONTENTS

Letter from the Editor 16

FICTION

Ray Bradbury: The Pedestrian. 19

Jonathan Escoffery: Odd Jobs. 58

Francisco González: Panda Express. 106

Perry Janes: This Is Going to Hurt. 168

Siel Ju: People Say They Want Something. 150

Michelle Latiolais: Winter Discounted 96

Kathleen Mackay: Jello Sees 194

Andrés Reconco: This Is How It Happens 222

IN CONVERSATION

But Maybe I Save a Life: A Conversation with **Wanda Coleman** by **Steve Ryfle**: 239

NONFICTION

Tom Bissell: Nabokov's Rocking Chair: *Lolita* at the Movies 263

Joe Donnelly: Messiah Wolf 132

A. Kendra Greene: The Rest You Have to Dust. 25

Wendy C. Ortiz: Alterations 72

Nina Revoyr: Postcard from L.A., April 47

David L. Ulin: Drive. 82

POETRY

Victoria Chang: Dear Father. 231

             Dear Mother. 235

David Hernandez: Uncertain Frontier. 261

             A Life that Doubles-Back on Itself. 262

L.A. Johnson: Twenty-Seven Objects of Explicit Wonder. 44

             Good Behavior. 45

Genevieve Kaplan: Show love to polar bears and earn 1,000 points 165

Douglas Manuel: Humpin' 77

          Mustang Sally 78

Dan Murphy: I Will Be Buried in Canoga Park 90

          Father Prescription 92

Mary Otis: Bodily 127

          Human Sound Station 128

VISUAL ART

Henry Lara, 40 (notes), 42, 56, 70, 80, 88, 94, 104, 130, 148, 166, 192, 220

Mary Frampton, 18 • Rod Bradley, 241

FRONT & BACK COVERS

Cover artwork designed by Josh Korwin.

FORTHCOMING

No. 120 publishes in April 2021.

Zyzzyva.

(ZIZ-zi-va) n. A San Francisco
literary journal; any of various
tropical American weevils of the
genus *Zyzzyva.* The last word in
the Oxford English Dictionary.

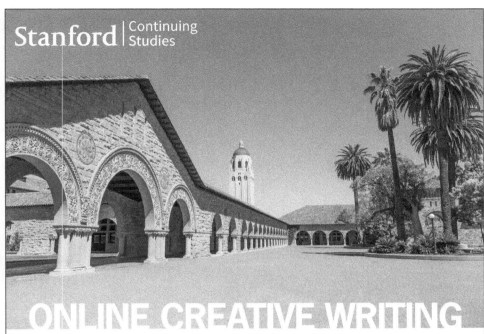

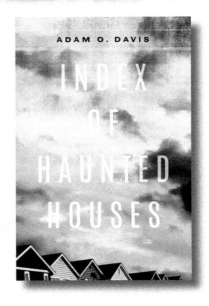

pacificREVIEW
A West Coast Arts Review Annual

pacificreview.sdsu.edu

GIVE THE GIFT
OF
ZYZZYVA

2020 BUNDLE
$30 for 3 issues*

2019 BUNDLE
$30 for all 3 issues

SUBSCRIPTIONS
$42 for 4 issues

2019 BUNDLE INCLUDES:
INTERVIEWS: JIM GAVIN, JORDAN KANTOR, KEVIN KILLIAN & DODIE BELLAMY; PROSE BY CHIA-CHIA LIN, TOMMY ORANGE, DAGOBERTO GILB

2020 BUNDLE INCLUDES:
BOTH OF OUR 35TH ANNIVERSARY ISSUES (Nº 118 & Nº 119) PLUS Nº 111, THE ACCLAIMED ART & RESISTANCE ISSUE

SHOP NOW FOR THE HOLIDAYS
W W W . Z Y Z Z Y V A . O R G

35TH ANNIVERSARY SPONSORS
THANK YOU FOR BEING THERE FOR US

Jeff Albers, Heather Altfeld, Andrew Altschul, Lauren Alwan, Emmerich Anklam, Andy Armendariz, Reagan Arthur, Bethany Ball, Rick Barot, Juliet Bashore, Paul Beatty, Lane Berger, Byron & Judy Bernhard, Stuart Bernstein, Carolyn Bishop, Aiesha Blevins, Emily Brennan, Patrick Brice, Brandi Brooks, Michelle Brower, Michael Brown, Claire Burdett, Nora Rodriguez Camagna, Chris Carosi, Caroline Casey, Xandra Castleton, David Cattin, Malea Chavez, Elizabeth Choi, Olivia Clare, Patrick Coleman, Ingrid Rojas Contreras, Patrick Corman, Nina Costales, Kelly Cressio-Moeller, Ann Cummins, Matt Daughenbaugh, Jeffrey Davis, Morgan Davis, Leticia Del Toro, Joseph Di Prisco, Frances Dinkelspiel, Kira Brunner Don, Joe Donnelly, Sharon Donovan, Robert Edmondson, Robin & Keith Ekiss, Patricia Engel, Charles Faulkner, Mary Fawcett, Yalitza Ferreras, Peter Fish, Wendy Fox, Joan Frank, Laura Fraser, John Freeman, Alejandro Gallegos, Brad Gallien, Darien Hsu Gee, Kathleen Gibbons, Molly Giles, Pacifica Goddard, Sarah Goelet, Glen David Gold, Ann Goldsmith, Susan Goldsmith, Tim Goodman, Ella Martinsen Gorham, Karl Greenfeld, Anisse Gross, Daniel Gumbiner, Rohitha Gunetilleke, Kathleen Hansen, Marcy Harbut, Deborah Harris, Laird Harrison, Peter Hartlaub, Sarah Haufrect, Jonathan Holman, Debra Howard, Laura Howard, Virginia Howard, Vanessa Hua, Irene Huhulea, Huru, Susan Ito, Jory John, Dana

Johnson, Brett Jones, Kenneth Jones, Kathleen Jorgenson, Edward Kamlan, Sydnie Kohara, Alexandra Kontes, Josh Korwin, R.O. Kwon, Lila LaHood, Adair Lara, Paula M. Latiolais, Ashley Levy, Ralph Lewin, Julie Lindow, Lisa Locascio, Valerie Mackintosh, Tara Mesalik Macmahon, Dave Madden, Sunisa Manning, Lisa Margonelli, Lauren Markham, Manjula Martin, Adrien Martinez, Sean McDonald, Therese McKenna, Julie McLaughlin, John McMurtrie, Stephen Melikian, JJ & Andrea Miller, Joseph Miller, Kate Milliken, Caille Millner, Anthony Mohr, Joshua Mohr, Rachel Moore, Izumi Motai, Alden Mudge, Manuel Munoz, Judy Myers, Beth Nguyen, Scott O'Connor, Robin Olivier, Richard Osler, E.C Osondu, Lori Ostlund, Mary Otis, David Paul, Maddy Raskulinecz, Bino Realuyo, Carl Reeverts, Flavia Stefani Resende, Alan Rinzler, Suzanne Rivecca, Catherine Robbins, Jason Roberts, Allison Rodriguez, Kristie Rohner, Dianna Rose, Roy Ruderman, Marcia Schneider, Adam Schorin, DeeDee Serrano, Anne Seymour, Barbara Seymour, Motoyuki Shibata, Susan Shors, Moira Shourie, Jesus Sierra, Maureen Simons, Christine Sneed, Octavio Solis, Stephen Sparks, Justin St. Germain, Peter Steinberg, Joseph Stillwell, Charles Stinson, Tink & Seymour Sumell, Arne Svenson, Chris Svenson, Mary Taugher, Lisa Taylor, Nick Taylor, Gary Thomas, Robert Thomas, Andrew Tonkovich, David Ulin, Ben Vance, Clayton Verbinski, John Vieira, Gracie Villalon-Degnan, Long Vo, Julia Wackenheim, Peter Walker, Meghan Ward, Bryan Washington, Althea Wasow, Don Waters, Jody Weiner, Debbie Weissman, Harry Whitney, Colin Winnette, Christy Wise, Dallas Woodburn, Matthew Woodman, Jenny Xie, Donald Zancanella, Matthew Zapruder, Olga Zilberbourg, Isaac Zisman. ❧

LETTER FROM THE EDITOR

Dear Reader,

Though Los Angeles occupies an outsized space in America's (and even the world's) cultural imagination because of the film and television industries, its literary culture is comparatively overlooked or minimized. Here on the West Coast we are busy enough going about our work that it is easy to forget for long stretches at a time the still significant East Coast bias in publishing. And then every so often someone in New York sends up a flare of disdain, a subtle or overt reminder. But the West Coast in general, and Los Angeles in particular, have nothing to be defensive about, nothing to prove. Our literary culture is evident from the sheer number of immensely talented writers doing their work here. To wit: at 312 pages, this issue spotlighting L.A. writers and artists is our longest yet, and, were the cost of freight not a consideration, we could gladly have included more work. (As it is, we rely entirely on the USPS and its affordable shipping rates to keep sending this journal out into the world—a subject of some concern as I write this in September.)

And while much is made of the cultural differences between ZYZZYVA's hometown and Los Angeles, I'd like to think that such tensions are more generative than they are antagonistic; that the frisson of competition between NorCal and SoCal, while genuine, also sparks creativity and inspiration.

Moreover, in this climate it feels especially urgent to reject the insidious notion that all resources are finite and depleted and we must battle each other fiercely for survival. Today, California is ablaze, with over two million acres charred by wildfires. Meanwhile, our state continues to struggle with the myriad consequences of the pandemic. It's true enough that we are fighting for our lives; natural enough to feel we are, each of us, on our own. But in the shared experience of this prolonged season of peril, our communities are also bonded.

In truth, we are each other's community, each other's audience, each other's readers and subscribers, teachers and students, critics and boosters. No matter the challenges of the literary ecosystem, we should be able to count on each other for generosity of spirit, time, curiosity, and attention.

Representing Los Angeles and SoCal writers has always been part of this journal's mission—as our index of published authors easily attests: for decades we've published writers such as Wanda Coleman, F.X. Toole, Jim Gavin, Lou Mathews, Dana Johnson, Héctor Tobar, and too many others to list here.

For all these reasons, we believe an L.A. issue only makes sense, the perfect duet with our celebration of the Bay Area last winter.

Many of the Bay Area issue's themes harmonize here: abundance and deprivation; loneliness in a crowd; urban beauty in close proximity to human degradation; the agonizing grind of carving out a creative life in a financial center. The variety of voices demonstrates L.A.'s unquestionable depth of talent. Henry Lara's photography and reportage gives us the opportunity to see the faces and hear the stories of the most overlooked Angelenos. Michelle Latiolais captures the poignant quotidian heartaches of trying to live a dignified life in a crass world. A. Kendra Greene takes us on a tour through an idiosyncratic museum of the Holy Land, open by appointment only. Tom Bissell's essay explores the intricacies and limitations of adapting literature for the screen, in general, and doing so with Nabokov's thorniest work in particular. And, to celebrate his centennial, this issue opens with a now-classic story by Ray Bradbury, a short, prescient gem (first published in 1951) that speaks eloquently to so many contemporary concerns.

Whether L.A. is familiar territory or only known to you through the screen or the page, we hope you'll find this time capsule of 2020 Los Angeles writing as diverse, excellent, and creative as that eternally iconic and enigmatic place itself.

L.

PHOTO BY MARY FRAMPTON

Ray Bradbury at UCLA *project to illustrate characters from his science
fiction dramas,* 1964, black & white negative, 2 × 2 inches, courtesy: UCLA
Charles E. Young Research Library Department of Special Collections

THE PEDESTRIAN

RAY BRADBURY

To enter out into that silence that was the city at eight o'clock of a misty evening in November, to put your feet upon that buckling concrete walk, to step over grassy seams and make your way, hands in pockets, through the silences, that was what Mr. Leonard Mead most dearly loved to do. He would stand upon the corner of an intersection and peer down long moonlit avenues of sidewalk in four directions, deciding which way to go, but it really made no difference; he was alone in this world of A.D. 2053, or as good as alone, and with a final decision made, a path selected, he would stride off, sending patterns of frosty air before him like the smoke of a cigar.

Sometimes he would walk for hours and miles and return only at midnight to his house. And on his way he would see the cottages and homes with their dark windows, and it was not unequal to walking through a graveyard where only the faintest glimmers of firefly light appeared in flickers behind the windows. Sudden gray phantoms seemed to manifest upon inner room walls where a curtain was still undrawn against the night, or there were whisperings and murmurs where a window in a tomblike building was still open.

Mr. Leonard Mead would pause, cock his head, listen, look, and march on, his feet making no noise on the lumpy walk. For long ago

20   he had wisely changed to sneakers when strolling at night, because the dogs in intermittent squads would parallel his journey with barkings if he wore hard heels, and lights might click on and faces appear and an entire street be startled by the passing of a lone figure, himself, in the early November evening.

On this particular evening he began his journey in a westerly direction, toward the hidden sea. There was a good crystal frost in the air; it cut the nose and made the lungs blaze like a Christmas tree inside; you could feel the cold light going on and off, all the branches filled with invisible snow. He listened to the faint push of his soft shoes through autumn leaves with satisfaction, and whistled a cold quiet whistle between his teeth, occasionally picking up a leaf as he passed, examining its skeletal pattern in the infrequent lamplights as he went on, smelling its rusty smell.

"Hello, in there," he whispered to every house on every side as he moved. "What's up tonight on Channel 4, Channel 7, Channel 9? Where are the cowboys rushing, and do I see the United States Cavalry over the next hill to the rescue?"

The street was silent and long and empty, with only his shadow moving like the shadow of a hawk in mid-country. If he closed his eyes and stood very still, frozen, he could imagine himself upon the center of a plain, a wintry, windless Arizona desert with no house in a thousand miles, and only dry river beds, the streets, for company.

"What is it now?" he asked the houses, noticing his wrist watch. "Eight-thirty P.M.? Time for a dozen assorted murders? A quiz? A revue? A comedian falling off the stage?"

Was that a murmur of laughter from within a moon-white house? He hesitated, but went on when nothing more happened. He stumbled over a particularly uneven section of sidewalk. The cement was vanishing under flowers and grass. In ten years of walking by night or day, for

thousands of miles, he had never met another person walking, not
once in all that time.

He came to a cloverleaf intersection which stood silent where two main highways crossed the town. During the day it was a thunderous surge of cars, the gas stations open, a great insect rustling and a ceaseless jockeying for position as the scarab beetles, a faint incense puttering from their exhausts, skimmed homeward to the far directions. But now these highways, too, were like streams in a dry season, all stone and bed and moon radiance.

He turned back on a side street, circling around toward his home. He was within a block of his destination when the lone car turned a corner quite suddenly and flashed a fierce white cone of light upon him. He stood entranced, not unlike a night moth, stunned by the illumination, and then drawn toward it.

A metallic voice called to him:

"Stand still. Stay where you are! Don't move!"

He halted.

"Put up your hands!"

"But—" he said.

"Your hands up! Or we'll shoot!"

The police, of course, but what a rare, incredible thing; in a city of three million, there was only one police car left, wasn't that correct? Ever since a year ago, 2052, the election year, the force had been cut down from three cars to one. Crime was ebbing; there was no need now for the police, save for this one lone car wandering and wandering the empty streets.

"Your name?" said the police car in a metallic whisper. He couldn't see the men in it for the bright light in his eyes.

"Leonard Mead," he said.

"Speak up!"

"Leonard Mead!"

"Business or profession?"

"I guess you'd call me a writer."

"No profession," said the police car, as if talking to itself. The light held him fixed, like a museum specimen, needle thrust through chest.

"You might say that," said Mr. Mead. He hadn't written in years. Magazines and books didn't sell any more. Everything went on in the tomblike houses at night now, he thought, continuing his fancy. The tombs, ill-lit by television light, where the people sat like the dead, the gray or multicolored lights touching their faces, but never really touching them.

"No profession," said the phonograph voice, hissing. "What are you doing out?"

"Walking," said Leonard Mead.

"Walking!"

"Just walking," he said simply, but his face felt cold.

"Walking, just walking, walking?"

"Yes, sir."

"Walking where? For what?"

"Walking for air. Walking to see."

"Your address!"

"Eleven South Saint James Street."

"And there is air in your house, you have an air conditioner, Mr. Mead?"

"Yes."

"And you have a viewing screen in your house to see with?"

"No."

"No?" There was a crackling quiet that in itself was an accusation.

"Are you married, Mr. Mead?"

"No."

"Not married," said the police voice behind the fiery beam. The **23**
moon was high and clear among the stars and the houses were gray
and silent.

"Nobody wanted me," said Leonard Mead with a smile.

"Don't speak unless you're spoken to!"

Leonard Mead waited in the cold night.

"Just walking, Mr. Mead?"

"Yes."

"But you haven't explained for what purpose."

"I explained; for air, and to see, and just to walk."

"Have you done this often?"

"Every night for years."

The police car sat in the center of the street with its radio throat
faintly humming.

"Well, Mr. Mead," it said.

"Is that all?" he asked politely.

"Yes," said the voice.

"Here." There was a sigh, a pop. The back door of the police car
sprang wide. "Get in."

"Wait a minute, I haven't done anything!"

"Get in."

"I protest!"

"Mr. Mead."

He walked like a man suddenly drunk. As he passed the front
window of the car he looked in. As he had expected, there was no one
in the front seat, no one in the car at all.

"Get in." He put his hand to the door and peered into the back seat,
which was a little cell, a little black jail with bars. It smelled of riveted
steel. It smelled of harsh antiseptic; it smelled too clean and hard and
metallic. There was nothing soft there.

24   "Now if you had a wife to give you an alibi," said the iron voice. "But—"

"Where are you taking me?"

The car hesitated, or rather gave a faint whirring click, as if information, somewhere, was dropping card by punch-slotted card under electric eyes. "To the Psychiatric Center for Research on Regressive Tendencies."

He got in. The door shut with a soft thud. The police car rolled through the night avenues, flashing its dim lights ahead.

They passed one house on one street a moment later, one house in an entire city of houses that were dark, but this one particular house had all of its electric lights brightly lit, every window a loud yellow illumination, square and warm in the cool darkness.

"That's my house," said Leonard Mead.

No one answered him.

The car moved down the empty riverbed streets and off away, leaving the empty streets with the empty sidewalks, and no sound and no motion all the rest of the chill November night. ❧

. . . .

First published in the August 1951 issue of *The Reporter* © 1951 by the Fortnightly Publishing Company, renewed 1979 by Ray Bradbury. Reprinted by permission of Don Congdon Associates, Inc.

Ray Bradbury authored dozens of books of fiction, poetry, and essays, including Fahrenheit 451, The Martian Chronicles, The Illustrated Man, *and* Something Wicked This Way Comes. *Among his many accolades were the World Fantasy Award for Lifetime Achievement, the National Book Foundation Medal for Distinguished Contribution to American Letters, the National Medal of Arts, and the Commandeur of the Ordre des Arts et des Lettres. This year marks his centennial. He died in Los Angeles in 2012.*

THE REST YOU HAVE TO DUST

A. KENDRA GREENE

A sign says no recording. So Jared leaves the audio recorder in his shirt pocket, switched off. He asks just to be sure, but it's no photographs, no videos, no audio here at the Holy Land Exhibition—even though Karen and her mother, who's the other caretaker living here, both ask after Jared's wife, they've noticed she's already got her figure back, and the new baby, *don't they just change your life,* and the beautiful white dog Jared walks twice a day past the museum, *what's its name again?*

Jared lives half a block up the hill. It's a neighborhood that's all houses and houses divvied up into flats and a network of secret staircases hemmed betwixt property lines and ascending steeply to the skyline. I have no such neighborly in, but though Karen says no recording, Jared introduces me first thing as a writer and apparently that's okay. *Then you'll want these,* Karen says, producing a trifold brochure and biographical half-sheet which I tuck into the back of my notebook. She gives Jared nothing.

Karen doesn't go into it, but a second, more specific No Documenting sign explains that modern devices have no place in the ancient times we are attempting to visit. I imagine the prepared visitor arriving with wax tablets and a stylus, stacks of papyrus and a fresh reed nib. I imagine I should take off my wristwatch and my plastic-soled shoes, but Karen

26   doesn't mention them and, though the entire museum spans only five rooms, the tour takes two hours and we have some ground to cover.

Let us travel. Not to the eight-course dinners of the 1930s. Not to the father teaching a son to weave baskets in Australia, nor to the flagpole-gripping feats-of-strength the son liked to demonstrate in his own old age, his body rigid and nattily dressed and parallel to the ground. Yes, soon to the Hearst newspapers, the old Hollywood biblical movies, the salty heart of Lot's wife, but it is our guide with her handful of keys who will set the pace. *Let us travel to Damascus,* she says, and we fall on her heels as she clips up a staircase, twists the first key, and unlocks the first door.

The Holyland Exhibition is not a church. You could be forgiven for suspecting so. It's a nonprofit, interdenominational organization, still housed in the building purpose-built back in 1924 for "the study of Bible knowledge." *We haven't changed so much as the phone number,* Karen says, and if you can no longer ride the Red Car line to this residential pocket, it borders Highway 2 close enough to hear the traffic. The Exhibition opened in one room in 1928 and has since grown to five, four if you forget to count the gift shop. Karen doesn't mention what they keep in all the other rooms stacked in two white-stucco stories around the off-limits courtyard. She doesn't mention anything about the places we aren't allowed to go, and I don't mention Orchard or Empire or any of the words that used to start Los Angeles phone numbers back in the day—Gladstone to call my grandparents' house, Normandy for this part of Silverlake. Which is to say, the phone number at least *has* changed, but it seems pedantic to clarify and I keep to myself how the phone company didn't switch out the old exchange names for all-numeric calling until 1958.

One wishes for sons. That is what I learn at the gaming table in the middle of the room. Because the inlay is so intricate, never mind the

complicated mechanism of swivel drop twist that reconfigures form
and access, now lifting away the card felt to reveal a chessboard gives
way to backgammon and then all the pockets and drawers for the pieces.
Just the cutting and piecing of so much mother of pearl means this table
will take a lifetime to make. Unless one has sons to help. Daughters
will apprentice other work. And so one wishes for sons.

Antonia Frederick Futterer had neither daughters nor sons. He kept
up the cane and wicker weaving learned from his father, occasionally
whipping up a basket in his seventies to demonstrate what could be
accomplished in a mere forty hours; but he didn't pass on the trade
and Karen says that even the baskets he wove here have been lost, who
knows how? *It's a shame*, Karen says.

Futterer had a niece through his second wife, the girl shown in
a picture in the Auditorium conferring an honor from the Red Cross
on Helen Keller. And children, scads of children, used to come to the
interdenominational Bible school he built this building for. Now children
come to the Holy Land Exhibition as a museum, not a school. *The
field trips come by sixth grade*, Karen says, *if they are going to come at
all.* Sometimes a tour bus pulls up. Once a traveler with a layover at
LAX made the trip over for no other reason than because his last name
was Futterer, too. *No relation*, Karen says, but the man called and he
came and then he caught his flight to Singapore. Explorer Futterer had
neither daughters nor sons, but Karen's mom came to be a caretaker
here, and later Karen, too. *No one invites you*, Karen says. *You have to
know you're supposed to be here.*

In the Damascus Room, I learn that a camel saddle is a piece of
furniture and that the Bible mentions it as such and everything. At the
row of holy books I learn that *the Muslim says God is above us* and *the
Jew says God is above and around us* and *the Christian says God is above
and around and within us. And that does not make the Christians better,*

28 not at all, *but it does make the Christians more responsible, because they know, you see?*

The Holy Land Exhibition is open daily, tours by appointment only. And you have to take the tour. Don't worry: you want to. All two hours of it. You want to because the text in the exhibition case only describes an "Arab burden bearer who carries heavy burdens on their back for a living." Karen says, *would you believe it,* he's carrying a piano. The text says, "The Garden Tomb—a model from the city of Jerusalem." The text says, "Mr. and Mrs. Mattar, caretakers of the garden tomb in Jerusalem from 1952 to 1967." Karen says, *Mrs. Mattar used to live next door.* Karen says, *Mr. Mattar was killed in the Six Day War,* and that during the war *the Mattars hid in the tomb.* It occurs to me later that Karen didn't specify where Mr. Mattar died, that there is ambiguity even in the addendums, that the tomb may have been either Mr. Mattar's shelter or his crypt.

As a general matter, the Holy Land Exhibition keeps text to a minimum. Object labels are reasonably common, but not the big explanatory texts favored by larger institutions. Yet where there is text—text on cream-colored cards and every letter struck by a typewriter key—it borders on exquisite. *Oranges and lemons from place where Peter raised to life Tabitha. Stones from Old Jordan stream collected by A.F. Futterer, explorer. Silver worm found by explorer in Holy Land. Leaves picked from the caves of Engedi (where David hid from King Saul) by Explorer A. F. Futterer. Snake skin from Mt. Olivet found by A. F. Futterer the day after arriving there.*

It's one room, this brief natural history of the Holy Land. The Archaeology and Bible Art Room, to be specific. One room in the grand paradox of museums: particularly attuned to the senses, but with everything behind glass. *Cubes of sugar made in Palestine, 1927. Almonds from Mt. Sinai, 1958. Salt made from the Dead Sea waters, the lowest place on earth. Walnuts from the place where John the Baptist was born. Moss from the place where Jesus was born. Wheat from the place where Christ spent His boyhood days. This piece of thorn is from the same bush it is said from which the crown of thorns was made and put on the head of the Saviour. Part of the 2,000 varieties of wild flowers from all parts of the Holy Land.*

The oranges and lemons have dried almost to black, not shriveled exactly, but desiccated to a dark diminutive state and arranged by decreasing height like a line of Russian nesting dolls. *But the figs and raisins,* Karen says, *are still soft and plump to the touch.* If the point was to display recognizable citrus, one might as well pull lemons off the neighbors' trees, rotate them with oranges fresh from the valley orchards. Indeed California is no stranger to citrus or almonds or walnuts or even moss—I imagine you could make salt from its very own seawater. And I can't for the life of me decide if this is the point: what a similar place, Los Angeles and the Holy Land, you now and all those Bible people then. Or if now has nothing to do with it.

Maybe all the transported fruit and grain is only to bear witness to some undeniable then. Why relate to now when now is changing and adrift? Let us travel, to walls great or wailing. Let us anchor to whatever still persists.

Do you want to hold the top of the Great Pyramid of Egypt? I don't even know how this is possible, but when Karen asks I say yes reflexively because the answer is obvious and I know I will never hear this question again. Certainly no one in a *museum* will pose such a question, not to the public, not on a tour, not in front of everybody. Do you want to heft the Hope Diamond? Do you want the bullet that killed Lincoln to roll around in your hands? Do you want enough moon dust to stuff your mouth and fill the pockets of your cheeks?

Do you want to hold the top of the Great Pyramid? I imagine myself

30 inverted, the tip in my hand like an ice cream cone but the rest of the pyramid still attached, ready to crush me except I'm the one in perilous handstand upside down. Before I can imagine what I've agreed to, my hand is out and a chunk of rock is in it. I would not, per se, know the difference between this chunk of rock and a hunk of concrete broken off a turtarrier in the parking lot. But if its aesthetic value is minor, its symbolic value is too much to take in. I am not up to the scale of the Pyramids. I cannot begin to appreciate their millennia, and I cannot fathom even their mass. Just the last century of this little bit of one of them overwhelms me: the evidence, here in my hand, of how very recently one could muster the carte blanche to chip away at legacy, and steal the crumbs back home.

Am I wrong about this? Was it possible in my grandfather's lifetime but not in mine to believe you saw something in the text everyone else had overlooked and set off halfway around the world to dig up *the Lost Golden Ark of the Covenant*? You could do that in 1926. And, well, if by chance you didn't find the Ark in your two-year hunt, you could still cut stalks of wheat and press wildflowers and start a one-room exhibition when you got back. You could, in fact, hack off a football-sized chunk from the salt pillar reputed to be Lot's luckless wife and mail it home. When people ask what part, Karen says looking at the cloudy yellow crystal, *we tell them the heart. That's what a hard heart looks like.*

She says it in the same tone of voice she will say *and that's where we get the phrase Holy Cow*; and, *that's what I call a first date*; and, *so if your heart isn't changed, you die an old goat.* Really, the hunk of salt crystal is probably just a toe or an ear or a chip off her left shoulder: nothing so vital as a heart, instead one of the vulnerable, superficial bits that's easiest to reach.

There have always been tomb raiders and trophy hunters and antiquities dealers who'd unbind the Audubon birds or a Gutenberg

Bible because the sum of the leaves is worth more than the book intact. **31**
But isn't it curious that this urge is even possible, to dismantle a thing
because you value it when whole? Imagine parceling out a complete
skeleton, one great Tyrannosaurus bone at a time. And then, why even
whole bones when you could shave off slices from the rib bones in
portions paper thin? Take the tiny carpals and break them in half to
make more. We've proved in my grandfather's lifetime that we are a
people to hasten the extinction of a species just to make sure we get a
good specimen before they sell out. *You know man always wants to build
big because it makes him look like something*, Karen says. I want Karen
to tell me not why we build but why we collect. But maybe collections
are built the same as anything else.

When the *American Weekly* described Futterer's quest at the time, it
posited that immortality awaited the discoverer of the Ark. The author
meant that in an everlasting-fame sort of way, but a few decades later a
screenwriter imagined the phrase literally, added a few Nazis and gave
us Indiana Jones. Karen says that happens all the time, writers flipping
through old papers for story ideas, *that's the way it works*. Futterer was
working from an old text, too, and his annotations were direct. When
Explorer Futterer read the land, he was moved to pick up a rock and
record its provenance, in pencil, right on the rock itself: *Mt. Sinai, Where
Moses received the law from God.* I like to imagine that no sooner had he
punctuated this statement than he set the rock back where he'd plucked
it from the landscape, marrying the words to the geology, the thing in its
site. Really, I like to imagine a boulder picking up Futterer and scribbling
in its rock language across the explorer's back: *Cenozoic, When Heat
and Moisture Recede*, but of course neither event was going to happen,
and I can only imagine the alternate histories because that gray-brown
plum-size rock is on display right now, in the room with the Dead Sea
salt and the silver worm, its inscription covering most of one side.

32 There is a fabulous concreteness to the Holy Land collection. A guileless this-is-the-thing-from-the-place curation. Here is the sap that makes frankincense. Here is the sap that makes myrrh. Indeed, for a place I'd expected to positively drip with agenda, it's subtler than most institutions. There are the 300 glass slides in the Archaeology and Bible Art Room retelling the Bible in hand-colored pictures, from Adam in Eden to Paul in Rome, but we barely stop to look. The Holy Land Exhibition is not a place without invention, indeed the centerpiece of the Auditorium is Futterer's Eye-o-Graphic Bible System, *the most rapid, visual system for learning the Bible.* But maybe, on the whole, it's still a museum more of axioms than proofs.

The sarcophagus is real, by the way. It is upright and cedar red and two thousand years old. And the thing about the real sarcophagus is the fake mummy inside it. Explorer Futterer had it made. He felt it was important. Staff call it *the dummy mummy,* and no sooner do they tell you it exists than they tell you it's not real.

Not only is it not real, you can't see it. The closest you'll come to seeing the actual fake mummy is a small, partial, gray-scale picture of the dummy mummy, alongside some text we don't take time to read there in the corner of the Egyptian room.

What else wouldn't I know unless Karen told me? *Television was invented so that every eye might see. The Hollywood sign is the length of the ark: 450 feet. Do you know what letters are in the middle of Jerusalem?* USA. *Did you know there was no Mr. Caucasian? Did you know black babies are born white? The only thing I get from this painting is that these are the guys responsible for everyone going into debt for an education.* For all the things Karen tells me that I can't confirm, this is the one I don't even want to question. She tells me the sarcophagus I can see is real and the mummy I can't see is fake, and this strikes me as so sublime that I believe both things, urgently, even now.

For twenty years, Futterer rented out furniture from the collection to Hollywood movie sets. You can see some of it in *Casablanca*. Or else Jesus with his disciples surrounded by the drapes and rugs and lamps and plates of the explorer's collection. You can see Rudolph Valentino in the movies lean up against a Futterer cabinet or wearing a Futterer "Real gold-threaded sheik's headdress … valued $100 … finest Damascus silk"—or if not Valentino then his double, Rudolph Florentino.

People used to ask: Why do it? Why lend out objects of religious significance to godless Hollywood? *Because,* Futterer used to say, *it's the only way to get them to pay their tithes.* Karen pauses so we can laugh. This was an era when Disneyland provided the camels for the park's annual Holiday Parade, and the Holy Land Exhibition outfitted them. And why not send the collection out into the world rather than wait for the world to come to it? Why not put a real headdress on the fake Valentino? It all worked fine until one day something wasn't returned, and before you could say, "Florentino," that was the end of the loans. Maybe the mystery is why these masters of stagecraft and spectacle and simulacrum came to Futterer at all. What did these storytellers borrow that they could not make themselves?

Karen tips a goat's bell strung along the wall, and then another and another and every sound is different because no two bells are sized alike, and so each rings out in its own metal pitch. It is the same with the ceremonial bells for India's cows and elephants, none the same, even if you got a herd together. *But not so for sheep,* Karen says, and I look and I see how every metal bell cuts the same curve and clanks the same clank *because the sheep are all the same,* Karen says—*aren't we?*

I'm engrossed in the beautiful practicality of knowing by ear which goat has gone beyond the hillock and which has clambered up some rocks, but Karen gives me a look that says we aren't done with the significance of sheep, the perfect humility of interchangeable parts.

34 I see then that I am not meant to admire the goat bells but rather to praise the standard weights and measures that find one soul equal to any other and all of them wanting. This is beautiful too, of course, the repetition, the resonance, the possibility we might respond not to the chime of the individual but more universally to the individual's need, and all need akin. Karen turns to leave the room and I follow her as my shepherd, though it is not the sheep's song that rings in my ears.

The switchable, swappable, exchangeable sheep remind me of the wheat in the adjoining room. Collections generally toe a line between goatly and sheepish ambition, between collecting a spectacular individual or the most typical representative of a notable group. Which is to say, there are things we collect because of their rarity, because there is nothing else like them; and there are things we collect because they so successfully reference something too big to collect. It's not a binary; one cannot separate collections as the shepherd separates goats from sheep. There are times when it matters that it is *this* Degas painting of a ballerina and times when it matters that this is *a* Degas or *a* work of Impressionism—an exemplar of some kind that illuminates something too vast or dispersed or complicated to fit in a room.

The wheat of Christ's boyhood home, those half dozen stems on display, is the tiniest fraction of the millions of stalks of wheat that have been reaped in that rough location in the two millennia since the boyhood or the Christ or the home flickered on this earth. Imagine granaries enough to contain such a harvest. This is not the original or the best or the wheat-iest wheat on display. It's not the wheat ground into the flour and baked into the loaves and turned into the fishes. It's plant life grown within more or less the same cartographical region as a historical event. And that's enough! That mere whiff of anointment, and it goes on display. There is boldness in this meekness. If Futterer had brought back the Ark, it would be a marvel; it would tell its own story.

But the wheat does not tell its own story, it witnesses the long shadow of another, and the very tenuousness of its connection is testament, a measure of how great the distant star must be to pull even this minutiae into its orbit.

We'll travel to the genealogy. That's the best thing here. That and the butterfly alphabet are the only things I care about, Karen says. *The rest you have to dust.* The butterfly alphabet, perhaps you've seen this, documents the shapes of the English alphabet as seen in patterns of color on butterfly wings. Karen shows us in a book of photographs. I wish for other languages. The right angles of Korean. The embroidery of cedillas and umlauts and breves. What of the Arabic sunkūn? The Hebrew niqqud? The Early Cyrillic titlo? But of course that's not the point. The point is that Karen will spend two hours on this tour, will show you the shepherd's sling and the dinner gongs and the Egyptian eyeliner container in the shape of a bird—and all the while the two things she really wants you to see are intangible. They have visual aids, the butterfly alphabet has its book and the genealogy has its diagram, but what Karen wants you to know is that God made our language before we did and you can follow a straight red line sixty-four generations from Adam to Immanuel. Whatever else you see, you should know: there is order and there is sense. Our cleverness predates us. Perhaps our goodness, too.

I associate holy places with relics. This saint's nose. That pope's finger. It's not, I don't think, that we must keep the things in themselves, but we must keep their stories. And so that we don't forget the stories, we keep the things that occasion us to tell them. This, I tend to think, is the basic logic of museums. Maybe, sometimes, the thing itself is the story; maybe sometimes all you need to know is the shape and the finish of *this* bowl. But mostly, isn't it better to know that the missing bit of the bowl was broken on purpose, that the bowl was buried with the dead like a hat and the hole released the soul? If you could have a museum of things or a museum of stories, wouldn't you take the stories?

You should pretend the grape fizz is coffee. The Tazah chocolate wafers go wonderfully with coffee. They taste lousy with grape fizz. As for the apricot mishmash, if you bought it at the bazaar, *you'd buy it by the yard*. I imagine gowns of it, drapes of it, heavy sheets of dried fruit growing sticky in the heat, even as I peel my allotted one-inch square from the bit of waxed paper before me. *I'm going to eat with you because I love this*, Karen says. *Also, you'll know they're okay.*

Here in the Auditorium the wooden school desks are sturdy, polished to bright amber, and make a fine tray for our refreshments. It is rare that a museum will feed you and more's the pity. In a little room above its exhibitions, the Museum of Jurassic Technology will serve you tea and cookies surrounded by portraits of Russian space dogs. Admission to Iceland's Shark Museum wouldn't be complete without a bite of the beast and a shot of alcohol to chase it. I have felt the Great Pyramid scrape against my skin and heard the flock of sheep bells, and why not round out the hour with four kinds of sugar on my tongue?

Plus, it's a study aid. Except that while chewing strawberry lokum, Karen says, *just call it Turkish delight*. I struggle to respond in the right places as Karen prefaces the Rapid 4,000 Year Genealogical Chart from Adam to Immanuel. *And they know because they've seen it with their*, Karen pauses three full beats until I open my mouth and we say together, *eyes*.

I imagine the sound of a class of children filling in the blanks, the rising glee of their chorus because it is so satisfying to know the right answer and to say the right thing, and suddenly I want to apologize to Karen. Perhaps Karen, too, has noticed that I'm bad at this, and she begins to patch over my failures in this call and response with the retorts of visitors past. When Karen explains the inset in the Genealogical

Chart, twenty-six pairs of opposites in a box matching the virtuous and vicious since Cain and Abel, her point is that there are two lineages, and are we from the goodies or the baddies? I get this one flat wrong. The baddies, obviously. Karen herself is guilty of every bad thing there is. A boy following the logic once asked her at this part of the presentation, "Have you killed somebody?" She didn't tell him yes. And she didn't suggest to him, as she did to me, that *hate in one's heart is as bad as murder, you know?* But she didn't tell him no, either. *That's a very personal question.*

If we'd come in the 1930s for the eight-course Bible-themed dinners, there would have been barood to drink, or as the menu at the time described it, "King Solomon's Barood ... Explosion." It was effervescing, you see. *But we've lost the recipe,* Karen says. So no explosions today. Nor any soup. Nor a soup slurping contest, and no prize awarded to whoever slurped the loudest. In the 1930s, as the soup was slurped and the American economy collapsed, Explorer Futterer saw that people would be hungry. *And he decided to feed their minds.* With the proceeds from the fifty-cent eight-course meals, Futterer bought Bibles. Three tons of Bibles. So many that even now you can buy one of those very King James Authorized red letter editions from the gift shop—though a note in the case cautions, "Do not purchase unless you read it." And there's another stipulation. *We only accept cash and check,* Karen says under the real goat-hair tent. *Explorer Futterer never used credit. It promotes bad habits.* Futterer walked three penniless years through the gold fields of western Australia and miracles followed in his wake. He was provided for. *And the day we have to accept credit is the day we close the store,* Karen says. *We owe that to our patrons.* This is a place that will show you the tear jars but not the tears. You are welcome to faith but not credit. And if you want a copy of the butterfly alphabet book, it's not stocked here. You'll have to find it somewhere else.

38   The Rapid 4,000 Year Genealogical Chart is Futterer's legacy. Patented and everything. The chart is white with clean black letters and a bold red line connecting the dots from the first man to God's only son. It's a cloud of names linked in an orderly chain of speech bubbles, all the begats gathered up from their paragraphs and stacked into columns. I learn "Cad" is a Bible name. I learn that in sixty-four generations no one reuses a name. I learn that Mary has a pedigree that branches off with the brother of someone important, Saul maybe, but that you would never record a woman's name in official documents so she doesn't appear—the Blessed Virgin Mary doesn't make the chart— and according to the Rapid 4,000 Year Genealogical Chart, Immanuel is son only to Joseph. One wishes for sons, I guess. Certainly there is work enough to do.

When I google the chart later that night, there is no evidence of it on the Internet. Not in words, not in images. Nor was it reproduced in the handouts Karen gave me first thing when I said I was a writer. And for all the surprise and suspicion and serendipity of the Holy Land Exhibition, this seems the most unlikely thing of all: I have seen something that does not exist on the Internet.

It occurs to me I should have bought one of the posters in the gift shop made up as a Jerusalem bazaar, with its tapestries on the wall and the oil lamps reworked for electricity. I had the cash. I was distracted, however, by the inlaid sign from Damascus arranged to read *Dios Bendiga Este Hogar* in mother-of-pearl, on sale for $11. I'd been contemplating the crowns of thorns from Jerusalem, half a dozen of them on a rack, just $9 apiece. And while I had the urge to introduce everyone I knew to apricot mishmash and chocolate wafers and drinks poured out in one-ounce cups, it wasn't the same buying it prepackaged in a reasonable amount: I wanted either yards of mishmash or a postage stamp's worth. And so, unwilling to commit to reading a remaindered copy of the King

James and unable to determine the acceptable limit of material goods I could buy from an institution devoted to less worldly transactions, I concluded I could virtuously do without any of it. It hadn't occurred to me my access to the Rapid 4,000 Year Genealogical Chart would be chaperoned at best, and then essentially nonexistent until I purchased a copy of my own.

The half sheet Karen gave me reports that Futterer presented his Bible System in over 6,000 churches and organizations nationwide. It was a thing that was meant to be seen. All that exposure then and if I wanted to see it now I'd have to go back and hope someone agreed to let me in. I couldn't even knock at the door; I'd have to call out from the chain strung across the walk to bar entrance, call up the red front steps, wait for Karen or her mother to appear at the landing, weigh my request, and direct me to go around and meet at the side entrance gates.

When we leave, as we walk the half block up the hill all I can say to Jared is, "All babies are born white?" For everything I have been asked to accept, to believe, to take on faith, I pick at this one thing—not even the most unbelievable thing, but the one that makes me the most nervous, the most afraid. As it happens, Jared has recently seen a baby born: his baby, his first.

"I was going to say purple."

His wife and child have slept through these last two hours, will never know how that time passed except for what we tell them. Just as we will never know their dreams. But they should be waking, just about now. And there is still some olive oil cake waiting in the ice box for us, and the yogurt and pistachios to cover it. ❧

A. Kendra Greene is a writer and artist who has worked at the Museum of Contemporary Photography, the Chicago History Museum, the University of Iowa Museum of Natural History, and the Dallas Museum of Art. Her most recent book is The Museum of Whales You Will Never See *(Penguin Books).*

ARTIST'S NOTES

HENRY LARA

I was born and raised in Los Angeles, but most of the stories I've heard about L.A. did not relate to my life here. They were not of the people I was encountering on the streets. I felt most narratives of our city offered a distorted picture of what Los Angeles truly is. Yes, L.A. has its glamour, it has many sunny days, it has beaches and beautiful palm trees, but L.A. is much more than that. L.A. is blue collar. It is back breaking. It is hope. It is homelessness and misery. It is immigrant. It is missed opportunities. It is dark. It is multi-everything.

In 2015 I began taking long walks throughout Los Angeles. Being a natural people watcher, I observed people's behavior and began to snap pictures using my Nikon D750. As I got more comfortable, I began approaching the people that most interested me. This led to long conversations with them. I was in awe of how each person's story had its own signature, its own DNA. Each with its own triumph or failure. The people I photographed reminded me of the kind of people I grew up seeing on street corners, on bus stops, in restaurants, in liquor stores, in my own neighborhood and even in my own family. That same year, I began an Instagram page and called it Angeleno Heart. I wanted everyone to know who these people were. I wanted to give them a voice.

I hit the streets about twice a week on my days off from my regular job. I never have a plan. I just let the day take its course and lead me where it will. Often, I'll make eye contact with someone and an instinct of sorts tells me I should approach them. I find something to complement them on to break the ice and I begin to have a conversation with them. I do not consider them interviews. They are just conversations that take a natural course. Sometimes I get lost in them for hours at a time. Sometimes they are only ten minutes long. Then I tell the person what my intentions are with our conversation. Ninety-nine percent of the time, they're happy to share their story. They open up. It leads to laughter, excitement and sometimes tears. It is a kind of therapy for both of us.

I always make the portrait black-and-white, and I present the story just as it was told to me. It is their voice; I'm just the person typing them up. But I do like to give each story a title. It gives it a signature and identity.

I have spent a third of my time on the streets of Skid Row in downtown L.A. These stories have been the toughest and most eye-opening experiences for me. Although they have been tough, I would like to think that they are beautiful in their own way. In a five-year span—and with the permission of each of the subjects—I have gathered over 260 of these portrait-and-story pairs. This work has helped me become a more understanding human being. It is easy to judge a face or a situation from a distance. But when you simply converse with another being, a mutual understanding about being human develops. Understanding Los Angeles starts with understanding its people. I hope you enjoy these stories. They have changed my life.

....

Henry Lara's work is on Instagram at @angelenoheart.

SMOKES & CHOPS

HENRY LARA

"I'm able to eat very normally at least twice a day. Once in a bit, I'm able to get my hands on a nice lamb loin chop. I'm grateful for many many things. I've been over on the other side, too. I was an electrician for thirty-seven years, had my own business. I've eaten at the best restaurants and have travelled to many countries. I've had nice hounds that have loved me. I've killed in the war. I've been shot at. I've had beautiful women that have loved me and that I've loved back. I've had butterflies, I've been jealous. I've been excited. I've been mad and I've been happy. I have felt sadness. I've been sick and vomited many times. I've cried and I have screamed in joyous moments. I've been to jail and I've been to the doctor many times over. I've been married and divorced. I've had surgery three times. I've been depressed. I've been a father to both a girl and a boy. Homeless? What does that even mean? There's shelter everywhere. There's an endless supply of cover just about anywhere you look. I don't like that word, *homeless*. Animals don't say they're homeless, why should we? Just because we think we have more logic? 'Cause not having a building with amenities means you're homeless? Home is earth. I'd be homeless if I had no one to talk to. Or if I couldn't see people and trees. Like on Mars. Maybe if I was on Mars I'd be homeless. But there's plenty of action here on earth. I don't buy that baloney. I'm in my situation because that's what I've chosen. I don't blame the system or anyone for that matter. I enjoy a good smoke and a good bite. I also enjoy the sounds of the city at six in the morning as it begins its struggles for the day. I could succumb tomorrow and that would be fine with me. I've already felt everything there is to feel."

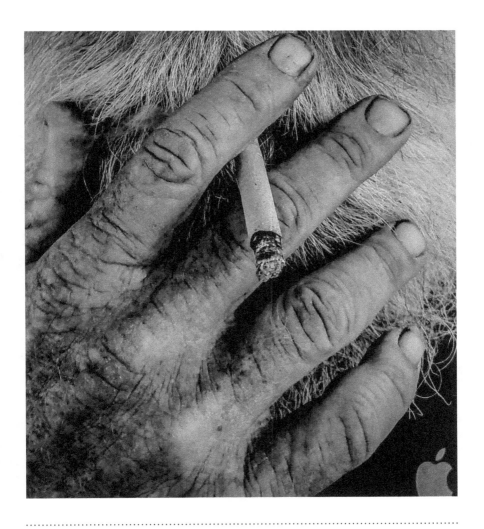

Mikey is a Vietnam veteran. He lives below Dodger Stadium next to the 5 Freeway in Los Angeles. (10/18/19)

TWENTY-SEVEN OBJECTS OF EXPLICIT WONDER

L.A. JOHNSON

1. house with lawn gone yellow
2. no matter which direction, the wind
3. swimming pools and dreams of pools
4. coyotes that shriek like children
5. naked intruders
6. scent of honeysuckle through a sunroof
7. dish, broken, never thrown away
8. half-lidded sentences that ramble on
9. swimsuits drying on balconies
10. water even a seahorse would swim in
11. the clear circles a hawk makes in the air
12. reservoir, with a lover's name
13. confessions heard over the ocean's waves
14. two eggs cracked, each with two yokes
15. fingerprints on mirrors
16. fire danger warning: code red
17. the type of daylight when tarantulas weep
18. oranges peeled over kitchen sinks
19. blue bowls on a porch collecting rainwater
20. flock of green parrots, chattering
21. ice melting in plastic grocery bags
22. laughter in the river lined with concrete
23. sunset, somewhere
24. red lights on mountaintops that blink off and on
25. the splash of water after a dive
26. radios floating music
27. letters, bent from folding

GOOD BEHAVIOR

L.A. JOHNSON

The winds, I tell you,
    are making everyone crazy.

Tension pours out of Santa Ana
    and rattles each open window.

Tonight, a thirst possess me, violent
    with forgotten vow.

A thirst that makes an ocean
    desire water, cold water,

waves that swallow sound. Dangerous
    words fill my mouth that want

for the night to explode electric
    and burn every house down—

because we've left the oven on forever,
    watched clouds pass in stillness

never bothering to shut the blinds.
    How are we supposed to be

good to one another: apologize
    for blue temptation, pocket knives,

nights I changed the radio station
    away from some country twang.

I hold a gun beneath my tongue,
    lies crack my slippery teeth.

46

In the identical apartment
            down the hall, a woman

sobs uncontrollably, shouts
            and gasps into the telephone.

We listen brazenly, our ears pressed
            against the wall. We catch her red

obscenities between muffled appeals
            of *forgive-me-please, I-promise.*

Beyond this room, the hot wind
            blows water out of the pool,

shivers the trees into tremble,
            and we swelter with nausea.

Lover, follow me into the wet grass
            that ripples in the spell of heat.

Find where we can lie together.
            Let our bodies cool in the damp

while the wind whips through us
            and against us, the palms unfurling

their hands like spirals of rapture.
            Let us sweat together on the wild lawn.

L.A. Johnson is a Provost Fellow in the PhD in Creative Writing & Literature program at University of Southern California. Her most recent chapbook is Little Climates *(Bull City Press).*

POSTCARD FROM L.A., APRIL

NINA REVOYR

On every trip into the mountains, there are times when I feel acutely in danger. Sometimes the risk is immediate, as when I've climbed up a frozen slope, ice ax and crampons keeping me attached to the earth, one misstep and I could fall, as I did on Mt. Shasta—sliding forty, fifty, sixty feet down the mountain before I could sink my ice ax into the hardened snow. Sometimes it's a thunderstorm when I'm approaching a peak or pass, the lightning cracking out of dark clouds and striking far too close. But most of the time it's not so much an awareness of danger but rather a healthy respect for the power of the natural world: the bear that might appear out of nowhere, the hypothermia-inducing cold, or just the massive expanse of the mountains. An awkward step off a boulder could snap my ankle or send me flying off a ledge, into a huge, impersonal landscape that existed well before I was born and will continue, unmoved and beautiful, long after I'm gone.

In those moments, on those trips, I am both wholly contained within myself and an indistinct part of the larger order. I'm focused on placing one foot after another, with no room to think of anything else. I am fully *present* in a way I am at no other time. And while part of that is due to fear, I also often feel a sense of exhilaration, even joy. I'm never more aware of being alive.

48   As we enter our fourth week of a stay-at-home order in Los Angeles due to the coronavirus pandemic, I've been thinking about the duality of fear and awareness. I am in a high-risk category—I have adult-onset asthma, and then, a few years ago, I got very sick after being exposed to toxic chemicals. I experienced such severe lung damage that in 2017, after multiple trips to the hospital and a complex regimen of intense medications that enabled me—just barely—to breathe, we had to move away from our beloved but pollution-ridden neighborhood near downtown L.A. to get to better air. No one seeing me now—running through our new neighborhood in Hermosa Beach, working in my high-octane job, or chugging up a 12,000-foot mountain pass with a 40-lb pack on my shoulders—would know this. My blood pressure is normal, my heart rate low, my diet comprised of low-fat proteins, whole grains, and fresh vegetables and fruits. As my primary care doctor told me in January, I'm in "very good health." Except that my particular condition—lung disease, which is now well-controlled but lies dormant and ready to strike—makes me particularly vulnerable to the novel coronavirus.

My wife and I are aware of the dangers, and of course we are nervous. We understood the severity of the situation early on, not least because my company's headquarters is in Seattle, and I was there for several days at the end of February, flying home just a few hours before the report of the first death, in a nursing home just north of our office. The very next day, back home in L.A., I interacted with someone at a crowded community event who I learned later had tested positive for the virus. (Luckily, I passed the fourteen-day mark after both of these events without incident.) My company—like others in Seattle—switched to working at home in the first week of March, which meant that our L.A. office did, too—a full week or two before many others here.

Now, my wife and I assiduously avoid contact with others—not answering the door for deliveries, eschewing the grocery store, walking outside, yes, but giving wide berth to anyone coming toward us. On weeknights, we don't venture out with our dog until 9:30 or 10 P.M., when the only people we encounter are two other late-night dogwalkers, who give us our space. At this point we know people who've fallen very ill—and while no one we know has died, we have friends who've lost loved ones—and we know that we'll lose someone eventually. It's possible that we'll be lost, too—and so, clearheadedly, we are updating our wills, taking care of details, in the event that one or both of us is stricken.

And yet, for the most part, I'm doing just fine. I am not overcome by anxiety. While I certainly feel extreme concern and a healthy sense of amazement that our lives have changed so much and so fast, I got over the *surprise* of it fairly quickly. I check the news and a few key Twitter feeds at midday and in the evening, but I've stopped obsessively watching cable TV. There are foods I wish we had—pad thai, sushi, enchiladas from our favorite Mexican place—and routines, like Sunday morning hikes in the local mountains. (Right now, I should be training for my annual summer backpacking trip, which this year was supposed to be the John Muir Trail.) I miss weekend visits to our favorite restaurants and bars. Instead of running our usual Saturday errands, we now have basic items—as well as prescriptions—delivered, opening cardboard boxes outside and wiping everything down with disinfectant before we bring it in. We don't order takeout food out of an abundance of caution. We wash our hands twenty, thirty, forty times a day. And we hope that this will all be enough.

But I don't feel the encroaching sense of doom so many of our friends do—at least, not yet. I don't share the reactions of some of my younger acquaintances—not the ones who believe they're invulnerable and are flouting social distancing rules, but rather the ones who *do* feel vulnerable, and are shaken to the core at the idea that the world has suddenly turned against them. My wife and I both feel the strain of the situation, but we are neither shocked nor depressed. Our fundamental understanding of things has not been upended.

Part of this is because we are privileged, and know it. We have shelter—a modest but comfortable house, with a bit of outside space. We're both employed, and are likely to stay so for the immediate future. We are able to work from home, and are still getting paid—something that is not the case for a growing number of people we know. And even while I'm stuck at home, my job has kept me extremely busy and interacting with others—both of which have been salves for my mental health. As a bonus, my work has now pivoted almost entirely to addressing the COVID-19 crisis. I work in philanthropy, supporting efforts to increase economic mobility for low-income children and families—work that seems even more critical now, when so many social divides have been exposed and deepened—and so I feel the usefulness of contributing, even if only in small ways, to efforts to help. Our lives are also simpler because we don't have children, and thus do not face the crushing and myriad challenges confronting our friends and colleagues, who are suddenly home-schooling their kids while also trying to keep up some semblance of work. In all of these ways, we have it easier than most. I did not grow up in privilege—I was raised by a single dad, mostly in a small apartment in a gritty part of L.A.—and so I'm very clear about my good fortune now.

We are also well aware that whatever challenges we face pale compared with the desperation of many people we know—folks who aren't sure where their next meals are coming from; or students who are trying to continue their educations without Internet access; or people whose businesses are shuttered with no end in sight; or families who won't be able to afford their rent after the current moratorium on evictions; or undocumented workers who've lost service jobs but aren't eligible for federal relief funds. So many people in our circle were barely scraping by before the crisis—and are being completely pushed over the edge by it now.

Even among our more fortunate friends, we are still probably better off than most. In Los Angeles, where natural disasters seem more common than seasons—where the last year has seen both devastating fires and the biggest earthquakes we've felt in two decades—we've learned our lesson about basic preparedness, and have built up a supply of shelf-stable and dehydrated foods. And because of my backpacking and mountain climbing trips, I already have items like portable stoves and fuel, and water purifying devices—not to mention an array of tents and sleeping bags—if things ever really get out of hand.

But I think the main reason we're doing all right is because we've been through so much crisis already. Three years ago, when my respiratory system deteriorated, it wasn't clear that I would make it. Things devolved to the point that I was coughing up blood; that I could not be in smoggy air—even for a few minutes—without wearing a mask; that the chemical scent of a plug-in air freshener or someone's perfume would trigger an asthma attack; when every day, all day, I struggled for each and every breath.

My doctors think the sudden worsening of my respiratory illness—which itself was likely caused by years of living in terrible air—was the result of sustained exposure to the toxic chemicals and dust of new construction, both at home (five new houses right next to us, which took three years to build) and at work (five massive new skyscrapers going up directly around our office). Soon enough, the VOCs of carpets, faux-wood flooring, paints, and glues were like Kryptonite for me, acting like invisible hands that wrenched my lungs and made it impossible for me to breathe. At the worst of it, after I'd already left my home of eighteen years because I couldn't breathe in the smoggy air, I was sleeping in a tent in the backyard of a rental near the beach. The rental

52 had recently been remodeled, and I couldn't be inside for more than a few minutes because of whatever was emanating from the building materials. So during the very period when I was most ill; when I would fall asleep every night praying that I'd wake up the next morning, I could not be in my own home, nor in the place I'd rented. I could not share a bed with my wife nor be around my dog, who also triggered a reaction.

Even after we found another rental—one that I thankfully recovered in over the next year and half—we never turned on the gas because it aggravated my lungs. This meant that we went without a stove for fifteen months and without heat for two winters—and while February in Southern California is obviously mild compared to other places, going through months on end of morning temperatures in the 40s and 50s without heat, while not traumatic, was also not very fun.

Now, it is totally different. I am off of asthma medications altogether. Most of the time I don't even think about asthma, although I always carry my emergency inhaler, just in case. I got back to my regular lifestyle and athletic pursuits; to my high-elevation backpacking trips in the Sierras. This improvement, this regaining of my health, this restoration to a better baseline, means I am a little less vulnerable than I would have been to getting seriously ill, even if I am infected with coronavirus. At least it gives me a fighting chance.

The respiratory illness was the most dramatic health crisis, but there have also been others, including a cancer scare that consumed the first six weeks of 2020, just before the coronavirus hit.

But the larger point is this: we have already faced direct threats to our lives. And we're already aware of how precarious life is. We have already seen how quickly everything can change; how the things we thought were clear and predictable—our immediate health; how and where we live; our daily routines—are anything but; that it can all fall apart at any minute. We have no illusion that the world is fixed—we know that everything is transient and mutable. Lungs so constricted that it feels like you're trying to draw air in through a mattress? Check. Ambulance ride to the E.R., where they hook you up to breathing machines? Check. Six weeks of uncertainty, biopsies, and surgery before they determine that what you have isn't cancer, at least not yet? Check.

And that doesn't even cover the other traumas and losses we've experienced, separately and together, with parents, and families, and friends taken far too soon. Or the traumas that both of our families have been through, with displacements from war, or struggles with immigration and racism; or efforts, with little more than determination and grit, to feed themselves and their children.

As inconvenient as it is to be stuck in our homes, it's just that: inconvenient. Three years ago, when I was sick, I couldn't be in my house; I couldn't eat or rest or sleep inside. Now I can do all those things, and it feels—well, pretty comfortable. These simple pleasures seem even more poignant when I think of how isolated COVID-19 patients become, many leaving their homes for hospitals, unable to touch or even see their loved ones. In contrast, I'm sheltering with my family. We eat well, work, read, watch lots of movies, and cuddle on the couch with our dog. If this is a sacrifice, it's a sacrifice of luxury. I feel that every day. I'm also well aware of the tens of thousands of people who do not have the benefit of housing, or even quiet yards to sleep in—as well as the many hundreds of thousands more in L.A. alone whose ability to stay in their homes and apartments is now hanging by a thread. And while confirmed cases of the virus in L.A. County, in these early weeks, seem most prevalent in wealthier areas—where people are more likely to have traveled overseas, and where there's more access to testing— it's clear that lower-income communities of color are going to be hit hard—as they have been in other parts of the country—with far fewer resources to help, and less access to health care.

54   But there's even more to my relative sense of well-being. There's something about being in tangible danger that heightens my awareness of everything—my gratitude for being in a house, and in a place where I can breathe clean air; my love for my wife and dog; the satisfaction of our quality—if limited—diet; my appreciation for a meaningful job. (And of course I'm aware that whatever risks we face are nothing compared with what health care professionals, first responders, grocery store employees, and delivery workers are heroically enduring.) I'm aware of the hummingbirds whizzing outside; the growth of new blossoms on the lemon trees; the flowering, all over the neighborhood, of plants in early spring; the drama of the post-rain sky; the incredible double rainbow that appeared over the ocean one morning when we were feeling our very worst. And most of all, and most important, the fact that—whatever awaits us—right now we feel fine, even great, physically; the fact that we're in good health—at least for now.

It is still early—just a few weeks into the outbreak in the U.S., when the numbers of those infected and killed by this virus are still lower than those who die each year of the flu. This will change. I know that. I know that it is highly possible that my wife or I or both of us will eventually get sick—especially after we go back to our physical work places, whenever that may be. And I also know that for both of us, but especially me, the risks that things could get bad are very real.

And so, for now, we are doing the best we can, and hoping it will be enough. We are savoring the beautiful things the world is offering up and feeling grateful for our blessings—not in spite of the danger, but because of it.

As when I'm hiking a narrow trail with a steep drop off beside me; or traversing up an icy slope in crampons, my sense of the precariousness of everything—of the chance of falling to oblivion—makes me even more aware of the now. I am present in my home, my landscape, my family, in a way that's pure and intense; I feel not just relief and gratitude, but also a kind of exhilaration. Tomorrow may be different, but it's not tomorrow yet—and it was never promised, anyway. Today I'm alive, and the world around us is blooming. And wow, is it spectacular. ❧

Nina Revoyr is the author of several novels, including The Age of Dreaming, *which was a finalist for the* Los Angeles Times Book Prize; *Southland, a* Los Angeles Times *best-seller and "Best Book" of 2003;* Wingshooters, *which won an Indie Booksellers Choice Award, and most recently,* A Student of History *(Akashic Books).*

THE STROKES OF GENTRIFICATION

HENRY LARA

"I lost my apartment in Lincoln Heights seven months ago. I lived there for nine years. I've always had stable jobs. I've worked at warehouses and as a brick layer. I also do general mechanic work. I arrived here in 1980 with my wife. We lived a comfortable life and raised two boys. My wife passed away six years ago. I couldn't control my emotions and I fell into depression. Losing my wife was the hardest thing I've ever gone through. I drank heavily for two years after she passed but my boys helped me through it. They were stronger than me. I'm grateful for them. Son hombres buenos. One of my boys works for Metro and my oldest boy has his own landscaping company. My oldest just brought me a granddaughter ten months ago. I cried when she was born; she reminds me of Perla, my wife. I'm going to spoil her as much as possible. I live in my truck now. My boys tell me that I am a victim of this thing called 'gentrification,' and that a lot of people are going through bad times because of it. Unfortunately, it happened to me. My oldest son wants me to move in with him, he has extra space. But you know, I've had a wife with our own place. And although I am his father, having someone else come into your private space is not good for anyone. It brings problems. Yo me las averiguo. I see him almost every day. I help him with landscaping, and he pays me. He knows I'm strong and that things will turn around. On Monday we are all going to get together and celebrate Memorial Day. We are going to grill carne asada, costillas de puerco, frijoles charros, guacamole and a very hot salsa. I'm looking forward to seeing my granddaughter. She is showings signs that she wants to walk. Who knows? Maybe I'll witness her first steps."

Mario was born in Chihuahua, Mexico, in 1960. He became a legal citizen soon after President Reagan signed the Immigration Reform Act of 1986. He says he is proud of what he has contributed to this country and doesn't understand this whole gentrification thing. (5/26/18)

ODD JOBS

JONATHAN ESCOFFERY

The exotic-animals dealer made me kneel on a caiman's tail. The reggaeton video producer paid in medianoches. The caterer forced me to serve poolside in glitter and a Speedo. But the gig that saved me after my father kicked me out was Jelly's. Her Craigslist ad read: *I've never had a black eye...*

> *... and i want one. i need bruises for a photo project but i also want to see what it feels like. i dont need any roiders here or knockouts just a solid sock to the face. thanks.*
>
> *compensation: idk $35-40? i wasnt really gonna pay a lot for this, but we can discuss.*
>
> *must not have ebola or a problem hitting a girl.*
>
> *sorry, no black guys.*

But I responded to her post anyway. I'd reached the point in my starvation where personal ethics and phenotypic traits couldn't deter me.

She'd wanted to meet at a coffee house, but I wrote back, *How am I going to punch you in the face at Starbucks?* The money wasn't much, but after a flurry of email exchanges, I discovered that, of all Greater Miami's sprawling suburban neighborhoods, she lived in Saga Bay, five minutes from where I'd parked my SUV for the last couple of days.

I was anxious to move on from the shopping center, as one of the security officers had begun spiraling the lot in his golf cart, despite my alternating parking spaces every two hours or so. But in my bright red '87 Dodge Raider who was I fooling? I'd backed the Raider into a space in front of the bagel shop, damn near onto the sidewalk, so I could catch their Wi-Fi on my otherwise useless phone. When the guard finally tapped fleshy knuckles against the tinted glass, I wriggled from the Raider's bed into the driver's seat, turned the key in the ignition, and cracked the window.

"My man," he said. "You living out your car, my man?" His head swooped, glimpsing the Raider's contents through the narrow opening. I'd abandoned most of my books and photo albums to my father's garage, along with my bachelor's degree, still enveloped in the cardboard shipping container it had arrived in. There remained the dead giveaways: my kitchenware, and the duvet I'd needed up at college. Clothes piles lumped the Raider's cargo area, doubling as my mattress.

"My lady ran into Publix," I told the guard, maneuvering my head into his line of sight. "She'll be out in a few."

He made the face I'd been receiving more and more lately. The I-don't-care-that-you're-lying-just-don't-infect-me-with-your-poverty face. The if-your-family-let-this-happen-to-you-then-you-probably-deserve-it face. The I-don't-trust-you-around-my-kids face I'd received from my sister-in-law the week before when my brother invited me for dinner, but not to spend the night.

"Hold up." A chuckle bubbled out of the guard's throat. "Trelawny?"

Through the dust-beaten windshield, cars zipped along Old Cutler Road. I could take it north, connect with US-1, then get up to Hollywood Beach or Fort Lauderdale, where next to no one knew my name. South would take me to Florida City then the Keys. If only I had gas money.

"We went to school together, man."

"Yeah, I remember." But he could tell that I didn't. Something like

60 defeat eclipsed his vision; to find himself unremembered wrecked his Tuesday. "Last name Johnson, yeah?"

"St. Pierre," he said. A familiar scar cut through his eyebrow, making me think we had met, had maybe called one another friend, but I remembered high school like I remembered dreams, in waves, with little recall for faces or what they should have meant to me. We watched each other through the crack, neither asking what had landed the other here. "Listen," he said. "I'll give you another hour then you have to bounce. My supervisor's a dick and I can't lose my job over you."

The sixty-minute reprieve St. Pierre offered was as much kindness as I'd received in the two and half months I'd been living out of the Raider. I glanced down at my gas gauge, at the glowering orange light, and did the math. I could probably get the Raider a couple of miles up the road. Wherever it died, the cops would have it ticketed and towed within days, then I would never get it back.

St. Pierre lingered outside my door for some reason. I guess to ask, "Ain't you go away to some bigwig school? Marquette or Notre Dame or someplace? What happened?"

"Graduation."

He laughed, stretching his arms over the Raider's roof before flinching from the heat, drawing them to his sides. His nose brushed the glass, eyes filling the space above. "Them degrees don't do much for people like us, huh? They're going to hold us down either way. 'S'why I didn't bother."

"Smart," I said, wondering what the hell he meant by *people like us*. I *had* bothered, had faithfully followed the upward mobility playbook, to wind up an extraordinary failure. And this asshole wanted us in the same category. I'd experienced similarly artificial camaraderie with fellow second-generation immigrants I met at university, who thought it transgressive that they elected to take literature courses when their parents expected them to go to medical school. "I'm supposed to be a

doctor," they'd say with ease, as though they'd already earned their future prestige and wealth, as if it were there to be plucked from the garden of their parents' devotion and preparation—imagine moving through the world with such confidence! When invited to share the expectations my Jamaican parents held for me, I recalled the last recommendation I'd received from my contractor father and exuberantly explained, "I'm supposed to work at Home Depot."

St. Pierre was saying, "You'll cook yourself like this, with the windows up." He said it like I hadn't noticed I'd been broiling for the last eight hours. "Some lady fricasseed her toddler just last week. Saw it on the news." An ache in his voice made me know he was a father.

"You're trying to son me?" I asked him.

"Say again?" Sweat threatened to spill over the lower rims of his eyes.

"Do I look like a baby, you yappy fassyhole?"

St. Pierre appeared more hurt than I might have intended, and as I could not stomach his expression—an expression that connoted, *I own a mattress and have Tupperwared food refrigerating*—I kicked the engine on and peeled out.

It occurred to me halfway to Jelly's that I might have asked St. Pierre if his dick supervisor was hiring. When my father put me out, back in May, I phoned the warehouse where I'd risen from pallet jack jockey to certified forklift driver before leaving Miami for college, but the manager, citing my degree, deemed me overqualified—he didn't believe I would find job satisfaction loading and unloading shrink-wrapped boxes of imported bananas. I wasn't worth the cost to HR.

But what else was out there for the class of 2009? The 40K-a-year entry-level positions I'd been promised all my life no longer existed post-recession and even the lowliest jobs wanted five-plus years of experience. I graduated with a 4.0 and couldn't get an interview for an unpaid internship.

Thankfully, Jelly hadn't expressed any interest in seeing my resume. Hers was a two-story town house with a vaulted ceiling and a fenced-in yard. She looked surprised when she opened the door, and I thought I might have the wrong house before recalling that I wasn't to have shown up Black. But enough people in Miami claimed they couldn't tell what I was, so I'd learned not to short myself before they did. If she asked, *Aren't you?* I'd answer, *Nope*, and leave her the burden of providing evidence to the contrary. But she didn't ask. Instead, she stretched her bare arms the width of the doorway, blocking my entry.

In her white maxi and gold belt, tousled hair falling down her front and back, she looked as though she'd recently escaped a Grecian urn. Then again, my ability to fixate on faulty associations had grown powerful under the August sun.

There weren't any cars in her driveway, no signs of life beyond her threshold. "Who else is home?" I asked.

"Why?" Jelly said. "You planning to rape me?" On the floor behind her, I spotted no blue tarps or black plastic or anything that suggested I wasn't meant to make it out alive. Still, she might take this opportunity to stand her ground—arguing later that I had reduced her comfort level, or property value, or whatever it is my skinfolk are authorized to be slaughtered for these days.

Jelly didn't appear to be in any particular discomfort, so I asked, "Is this really for a photo project?"

"Does it matter?" She unclenched the doorjamb and leaned her shoulder against it.

"I printed our emails," I lied. "And forwarded them to my brother. Just in case." The latter statement should have been true. But Delano wouldn't have been happy to hear from me, not after the previous week's dinner, not if his wife told him what I'd confessed to her. Plus I didn't need him knowing the depths to which his kid brother had sunk.

Jelly held her elbow in her palm and bit her thumbnail, deciding. I'd caught my reflection in the Raider's darkened windows; I looked more than slightly stepped on. There was no way she was letting me through her door. "You're taller than I might have wanted," she said. "I think it's best if it's straight on. I don't want to be punched from a downward angle. Take your shoes off first."

"You've given this some thought," I said, entering. I kicked off my flip-flops in the foyer and followed her past her heavily air-conditioned dining area. I hadn't felt seventy degrees in what might have been weeks, and the cool air made my damp flesh tingle. I wondered about the odds of her letting me use her shower after.

It's important to build rapport with your employers, so I asked what she'd been up to today, to which she responded, "Besides this? Eating shit." That's Miami for *little else of consequence.*

In the living room, a mammoth flat-screen paralleled a teal sofa. Above the TV, a rash of quinceañera portraits distended the wall. She wore braces in the photographs and looked younger, though not much. "This is your parents' house?" A purple backpack slumped on the floor beside the couch, its unzipped mouth gaping stupidly. I dug my arm in and pulled from its depths Millett's *Sexual Politics.* On the inside cover a stamp declared the book the property of the library at Florida International University. "You're in college then. Class of?"

"Let's skip the chitchat," Jelly said. "Right here in front of the couch is fine. Are you ready?"

But I was shook. Reality began attaching itself to the moment in the form of family photos on the walls and side tables. Young Jelly and her little brother at Epcot Center—at the beach, even younger, clutching a yellow plastic bucket and shovel. Or maybe reality was what I'd been living those months on the streets, this being its opposite: middle-class

64 façade, with its attendant codes of conduct. I dumped the book on the floor and turned for the entrance. "This was a mistake."

Jelly snatched my wrist. "Wait." Her eyes flickered, and I felt she was trying to communicate something profound. "Do you understand the kind of psychotic responses I had to sift through to get you here? The dick pics? The run-on sentences? I can't start over."

"I'm sorry that happened to you." I placed my free hand over hers and removed it from my wrist. "Why don't you revisit your shortlist?"

"I don't understand the problem." Her eyelids wrinkled. "I'm paying you to do it."

"All the same," I said. "I'd recommend seeking a different kind of help."

Jelly yelled, "Shove that paternalistic crap up your ass," which only hastened me down the hall.

"I'd love to avail you," I said over my shoulder. "Theoretically."

That didn't have the soothing effect I'd hoped it would.

Jelly screamed, "Coward," the word shrinking me in the foyer.

I toed my sandal, terrified of what would happen if I reached for the doorknob. All I needed was to get caught fleeing this screaming white woman's house, for some neighbor to decide to play hero.

Jelly must have mistaken my hesitancy for a negotiation tactic, because she said, "Fine. I'll give you eighty. And you don't even have to use closed fists. Just slap me a little."

I'd been back in Miami three months, and the forty she'd originally offered was as much cash as I'd seen in a single day. Eighty dollars was a gold mine. "What time do your parents get home exactly?"

"We've got a solid forty minutes," she assured me.

With the promise of four Jacksons searing into my medulla, I sat Jelly at the edge of the couch. I slipped my forefinger beneath her chin, nudging it upward, and she looked me in the face with these enormous brown eyes, the kind with which—by some evolutionary outcome—people associate innocence. I couldn't do it. I lowered myself to the couch and told her as much.

"You know why you can't?"

I watched the bow of her lip, keen to see if she could name what lingering virtue superseded my instinct for self-preservation.

"Because you're a misogynist. You think that little worm between your thighs means you know what's best for me. You piss-ant."

She had a point, but I didn't like being called names. That's what got me in this mess to begin with. My father, in a drunken fit of honesty, told me my liberal arts education had made me lackadaisical, and that I was a fool to have gone tens of thousands of dollars into debt only to ruin myself for work. Rather than listing the dozens of jobs I'd applied for in the two weeks I'd been home, I asked how it was that he'd given my brother the money to start his tree service yet he hadn't put a dollar into my education. "Because I believe in him," he'd admitted. So I retrieved an ax from his shed, entered the garden where he invested most of his post-retirement labor, and went to work on its centerpiece, the ackee tree my brother gifted him years before.

Jelly asked, "You think you control what happens to my body?"

I told her, "Of course not," but that I had a confession to make, one that would render me ineligible for further participation in her project. "Truth is, I'm a Black guy."

"Figures," she said, exasperated. But I could tell embarrassment was seeping in, a little self-examination. "I don't actually care. It's just … my parents. Their rules are bullshit, but it's still their house." She explained that once, in high school, her older sister brought a Black boy home for a study date and that night caught the beating of her life from their father. Just for bringing him inside.

"You're like the twelfth white woman to have told me that story,"

66   I said.

"I'm Latina," she said. "Brown."

"Point being, I have enough to bear. I don't want to know this stuff." But I couldn't seem to get up off her couch.

"The funny part is, Ravi wasn't even Black. He was South Asian."

"Hilarious," I agreed. But I felt sick with hatred. For her father, yes, but hatred of all fathers, for their propensity for passing down the worst of themselves. How was it that her post hadn't read, *Sorry, no racists? Sorry, no child abusers?*

"If it motivates you," Jelly continued, "you're exactly who he wouldn't want helping me with this."

"Fortuitous. And I'm helping you with what exactly?"

"Uh-uh," she said. "I'm in control. You don't get to ask me that."

Wondering if this was really about her father, or an art project, or if it had to do with deviancy she'd failed to locate in her sexual partners, I stood and told her I would try again. It's not easy slapping someone for the first time, even when they've asked you to. Even when they're paying you. "Look away," I pleaded.

"I want to see it coming."

"Fine." I patted her cheek with four fingers.

She looked at me as a kindergarten teacher might her slowest pupil. "You're going to have to do it harder than that."

My arm felt incapable, already missing mass I'd built at my university's rec center. Incredible, the pace at which your body eats itself when left unfed. I readjusted her chin and inhaled deeply. On my second go at it, Jelly toppled over.

She didn't speak for a while, lying limp atop the couch, which frightened me. Her dark hair fanned over her face and shoulders. From underneath it I could hear clipped pants. Eventually, she said, "Good," her voice the offspring of astonishment and discordance. She pushed herself up, and when she brushed away her hair, a splotch the shape of Minnesota gleamed red from her chin to her cheekbone, but I doubted it would actually bruise. "That was good."

"All right then."

"Do it again. Harder if you want." She scooted to the end of the couch and braced herself against the arm. "Hold on." She tied her hair back in a ponytail. "Okay."

I glanced down the hall toward the front door, wondering what it would take before she'd hand over my payment. I imagined I could have begged an old girlfriend from college to send money; enough of them had expressed ambivalence about their trust funds that this seemed a plausible path down which I might drag myself from homelessness. But I'd have sooner hanged myself. The pity they'd cast my way over the course of four years—it was as though they'd known before I had.

I couldn't trouble my mother: just weeks before graduating, I'd called from my Midwestern apartment to ask, in a tone I hadn't meant to sound accusatory, how she could leave Miami for Kingston when her children were here. "It's for me," she admitted, and she'd never sounded less motherly or more human. I could hear the packing tape unspooling, as she continued filling boxes while we spoke. "Look how long me spent taking care of men. Your father," she said, though they'd divorced back when I was in junior high. "You boys. Who has ever taken care of me?" It was more truth than I'd been ready to hear. Though later, I was glad to have heard it, and vowed to build a life in which I might be a comfort to her, and never again a burden.

And what if I simply rolled up my windows, parked in the unmitigated sunbeams, and waited? The thought had begun gnawing at me, a persistent refrain.

I imagined, too, that I could have returned to my father's and begged him to take me in, despite his promising never to again, not after my

68   outburst. Not after I'd assaulted his precious tree. But even if he did, his incessant disappointment, his *why can't you just*s and *why aren't you more like*s and his *be a man*s assaulted my self-worth more than the hunger. And more than the hunger, and as much as the desperation and shame, the sleep deprivation bore new pathways in my brain, and I'd begun hearing voices and sensing entities that hovered in my peripherals then vanished as I turned to seize them.

I turned to Jelly who sat solid against the couch's arm, expectant. I clutched her ponytail and angled her head back. Diamond studs twinkled in her earlobes. Her mouth opened and I saw beyond her white rabbit teeth down into the pink of her. I raised my palm and clapped her cheek.

"Harder," she said, her voice a grated whisper. The outline of my fingers surfaced before dissolving into her skin. She mouthed, *Harder*, and I tugged her ponytail to expose her unblemished cheek and clapped it. She blinked shut her eyes, nodding.

I straddled her, and she tensed, but did not push me away. Strange, what flooded my senses, pressed close, was the ripeness I'd carried in from the outside world. I rested my hand over her throat then tapped her jaw. Saliva fell out onto her lip and chin. I rubbed the spit away with my thumb and she gazed up at me, and her expression…the intimacy…I slapped her with certitude. She closed her eyes and nodded fiercely. Tears streaked her taut cheeks. I let go and stumbled to my feet. I expected her to demand more, but she just sat there sobbing.

I began to ask if I'd gone further than she'd wanted, but my words came out, "Do *me* now." I didn't know who put them there, but I felt jubilant at those words and jubilant with anticipation. Soon I'd connect with something enlivening I hadn't before, or else something injurious I had.

I'd found zero catharsis striking my father's ackee tree—do you understand how difficult it is to fell a tree with an ax? I'd battered myself against it, spending myself, and still it towered. At dinner that past week, though, my brother reported that the tree's fruit had rotted overnight and it had yet to produce more. *Trauma* was the word he used. My brother is an arborist and so feels qualified to use such a word. When he excused himself to the bathroom, my sister-in-law leaned over her plate to ask if I'd considered that my actions hurt my father *and* my brother, but I doubt she or I expected my honest answer would be, "Good."

Jelly sat firm in the grips of her release, so I went into the kitchen to make myself a sandwich and wait my turn.

You wouldn't believe the options they had on hand: prosciutto, chorizo, smoked kielbasa, maple ham, honey turkey breast, dill pickles, pitted Castelvetrano olives, at least three types of mustard, including Dijon—and that's not to speak of the cheeses. Jesus Christ, the cheeses. That must be why I didn't hear them come in. Crouched in the refrigerator's bowels, I never stood a chance. Likely, they saw her, saw me, and two plus two equaled seven. The mother's heel hacked into my clavicle, sending me sprawling, but the dad's caught up rather impressively. His sole, cannonading against my temple, sparked fireworks in my retinas.

Even the little brother joined in.

It was elegant, almost, the way they worked in unison. If only my family had found me such a unifying force. I recognized it then, like petrichor, or some misplaced scent from childhood, not simply the weight of existence crushing my lungs, but the awakening urge, the exquisite, racking compulsion to survive. ❧

Jonathan Escoffery is the winner of The Paris Review's *2020 Plimpton Prize for Fiction and is the recipient of a 2020 National Endowment for the Arts Fellowship. He currently attends the University of Southern California's PhD. in Creative Writing & Literature Program as a Provost Fellow.*

UNA GUERRA, PAPA!

HENRY LARA

"Nunca dejamos nuestro país porque no lo amamos, lo dejamos por necesidad, por peligro. [We never leave our country because we don't love it, we leave out of necessity, out of danger.] When I was a boy in El Salvador, I used to help my mom gather wood so that she could cook pupusas and make fresh coffee to sell on the streets. My father drove a big truck and delivered roasted coffee beans to distribution centers, but we rarely saw him. One day he simply never returned. To help my mom make ends meet, I began selling a newspaper called *La Prensa Gráfica* for ten cents. I used to go to school barefoot because we didn't have enough money. It's not until I was twelve that I was able to buy my own shoes. I learned my times tables fast because our teachers pulled our ears very hard until we learned them. When I was twenty-three, a detective approached me and asked if I wanted to become a cop. Eight months later after the Academy, I became a proud officer. But in '78 with the civil war going on, many cops were being killed by the guerrillas. Our pay was poor and after a few shooting matches, I resigned. I was scared for my life. I soon became a security officer, but they were killing us, too, so in 1991, I decided to come here to Los Angeles. I had a few friends here who had fled earlier. My way here was treacherous, very hard to talk about. I saw so many bad things coming through Mexico. I almost lost my life, but el coyote was able to bring me here safely. In '98, I graduated from Belmont High and received my GED. I believe in education, it's the true base for any human. I'm proud of the fact that I can read and write English. I've done all types of jobs, but unfortunately, I have fallen on hard times and lost both my apartment and my car. But I'm hopeful, I know things will change. La vida es una guerra, papa!"

Eduardo Martinez says he is scheduled to be sworn in soon as a U.S. citizen. He loves classic rock, especially the Moody Blues. He hopes to reunite with his wife. He lives in this trailer home, which he rents for $200 a month. (12/20/18)

ALTERATIONS

WENDY C. ORTIZ

I'm a knife cutting through the desert in a truck with the windows open, oven air blasting in my face and my curls getting tangled while a beer sweats between my thighs. One hand on the wheel. Time has no hold on me. There's another five beers on the floor next to me and many more drinks ahead when I reach town, the old western town where I've laid my head a few times in the rooms with fake fireplaces, stumbling distance to the bar. The sun bakes my arm that's parked in the open window, my left arm, freckled, scarred, the arm of the hand I write with, and my silver ring glints in the sun.

Wait, should there be a silver ring there?

Yeah, it's fine. I can be partnered and still have this fantasy.

It's my daughter that gets in the way of carrying out such a fantasy. And my career, which would not look kindly on a DUI.

So it remains unspooled. Remains in daydream.

We are at a playgroup at a playground with no fences and I have a bolter. At the moment, though, my toddler isn't bolting but sitting in the sand with another child's doll—oversized head, big doe eyes, and a voice that is disembodied because her mouth doesn't move. I don't even try to listen to what the doll is saying. I don't need to know. My daughter doesn't have much of an interest in dolls but this one is a stranger's doll, and she seems taken with it. I look at the other mother

I'm standing with, trying to carry on a conversation with.

Somehow we start talking about psychedelics.

"I'm kind of a psychedelic girl, myself," she says.

In that moment I'm aware we're heading into territory that's possibly taboo, on this playground, among the mothers in the playgroup, the strangers standing around us in the sandbox. It's a conversation I definitely want to go deeper into, as I, too, am "of the psychedelic variety."

"Yeah," I say. "I know what you mean."

Because it's been years since I've ingested a psychedelic. And it's been years since I've even seriously considered ingesting one. I'm not the fifteen-year-old girl I once was, who looked up the drugs she planned to ingest that night in her health class textbook, dog-earing the page "Designer Drugs." I'm not the nineteen-year-old girl who did her final paper on MDMA for "Drugs and Society" class, complete with an informal case study of her own Ecstasy use. I am also no longer acquainted with the people who made drug ingestion easy, or free, or carefree.

But I still identify.

The pulsing paisley waves still want to overwhelm me. I still long to see plants breathe once in a while, words appear in the sand when the tide goes out, every granule whispering their secret under my feet.

I'm sitting in the sand. Desert again. The place I once wanted to be my home until I remembered the ocean. There is a stillness in the air that almost sounds like the portent of a bomb. I'm waiting for it until I forget about it.

There's the hum in my mouth I can't be sure I'm creating. The sun bakes a point on the top of my head and I lazily lift my arm. I can see where my arm just moved from, the smear of movement, still apparent in the air. I let one arm circle lazily, eyes catching all the trails, until my shoulder surprises me with a small protest.

A lizard traipses by and my breath catches. I laugh out loud. The lizard was asking for it.

Night is still hours away and I have nowhere to be, and no one is looking for me, and I'm safe. Water, food if I want it, simple building blocks of protein and amino acids and nutrients I might require in these circumstances, where my brain is blown to smithereens and I am by my lonesome, recording it and living it, that altered space I am always trying to get back to.

There are several bottles of beer in our refrigerator that seem lodged there, in the back bottom shelf, never really moving until a group of friends is coming. Bottles of wine in our cupboards and living in our wine rack, gathering dust until I wipe one down and transport it in a paper bag to a party or to a dinner as a gift.

Rarely do I find myself with a particular thirst for alcohol in my house. The thirst finds me, though: as I drive down Western Avenue toward the hiking trail in Griffith Park, when I see Frank & Hank's, an old haunt of mine; when a certain song arrives by radio station oracle and there is an afternoon or evening ahead of me with nothing I must do. Always during my twice yearly visits to the dentist, which makes me park somewhere near the Drawing Room, scene of so many previous blasted nights.

Even then, though, the thirst is contained.

The thirst wishes itself into my present, the kind that would have me day-drinking and happy-sloppy. Rarer and rarer, if ever.

I've caught myself telling students about how listening to music, to me, can often feel like ingesting drugs. About how I have to limit my intake, listen under ideal circumstances, because some songs have the ability to pull me under, steal an afternoon, rattle my heart and fuck up my psyche for hours. My only relief is if, in exchange, I'm able to write about it.

But why write about it when I can lose myself in it?

"I am of the psychedelic variety" is code.

My admission to students, to readers, about the power certain music holds over me feels weirdly vulnerable, as though you will find the music and play it to undo me, to liquefy and puddle me.

At age six, my child occasionally stared off into the middle distance and turned off her hearing, transformed into enlarged eyes, wan smile. Whenever I noticed I asked, Are you zoning?

"Zoning" is my code with her for enjoying what is in one's head, what no one else can touch or see or feel, that landscape that is all one's own, limitless. Ultimately unreachable but for the moments when the conditions are perfect to careen around in there while everyone sees your corporeal form upright, eyes glazed. This is my code for checking out.

My child slowly nods if she has even one tendril left tethering her to the earth.

My own "zoning" is composed of the few moments when I can let go of this plane enough to make the internal dive. The structures of my life don't always allow for the complete "zone" experience. The structures of my life don't allow for sweaty afternoons recovering from a pitcher of brunch margaritas. The structures of my life don't allow for me to get in my car right now, point east on the I-10, and land with my head mushrooming under a brutal desert sun.

It might be a consequence of my mid-forties, because I never remember asking myself this before now, but how about making a decision I'll thank myself for tomorrow? The structures of my daily life sigh long and hard but grind on. I amuse myself with a daydream involving camping out at the beach, planting a square bit of paper on my tongue, letting the sunrise destroy me. I ask for the plants to breathe for me, just enough that I can witness. When I switch on the radio it presents a song I can resist, or not.

My doctor notes in my chart that I am a "passive smoker." A passive smoker like me can live for years smoking three, four, maybe five cigarettes a day. I can live with this definition of passive, applied to me.

Smoking cigarettes has never been a linear habit for me: I have gone off and on for years. I rarely smoked in any of my homes as an adult. Like many people, I smoke more when I'm drinking alcohol. Like many people, I smoke more when I'm stressed.

When my father unexpectedly died in 2014, I told myself, You get to smoke for as long as you want. In addition, I went unconscious in many ways.

Years later I look up from where I inhabit what little square footage I take up on this planet and think, It's time. And as a natural purger, I make it happen. I quit.

I write to you, craving. I know there are music and texts I won't gravitate toward in these next few fragile weeks of newness, because they threaten to drive me back to the pleasure, the simple pleasure of lighting this stick of tobacco. The ritual I've agreed to set aside for newer other rituals, still to be determined.

To even write this is to want.

The want of the chemicals that I know will work their weirdness in me. A place to step away to, me and my body, while not leaving completely. (I write, craving.)

It's sometimes a struggle to be as contained as I am expected to be. Supposed to be.

The beers stand sentry in their long-held positions in the fridge. Empty packs of cigarettes with a smattering of loose tobacco in their confines lie at the bottom of the damp trash. Someone is looking for me, needing something. I feel my feet anchored to the ground, crown chakra itching. Something shimmers in the periphery.

I write, craving. ✄

....

Wendy C. Ortiz is the author of Excavation: A Memoir *(Future Tense Books),* Hollywood Notebook *(Writ Large Press), and* Bruja *(CCM).*

HUMPIN'

DOUGLAS MANUEL

The crowd wilding out, lost and caught
    in the snare of the beat, in harmony,
        more like one body, not many—Damon's

the brain running things. *1, 2, 3, 4,*
    leave your worries at the door. 5, 6, 7, 8,
        you better make your booty shake.

His crown not of thorns but beads of sweat
    more precious than diamonds. *Work it,*
        baby, work it, baby, work it. The dance

floor more sanctuary than club, and he's
    the priest. When he was an altar
        boy, his back was always to the crowd.

Not now. Now the strobe lights are
    the whitest thing in the room, and the groove
        is the only god anyone is praying to.

Denise has never loved him more
    than when he's commanding the dance
        floor, but now she sees him as she never has

before: a man cloaked with that much glory,
    surrounded by so many, soaring in that
        much sound, can only end up alone

and back down on the ground.

MUSTANG SALLY

DOUGLAS MANUEL

Always, Denise's daddy was supposed to be

coming: this Sunday at 2 P.M., last Saturday
at 4:30, the Friday before that, the Tuesday

before that, as far back as Denise could
remember. Always, there Denise sat

on the crumbling front porch steps. A little
girl amongst little ruins, the little pink straps

of her backpack securely strapped, waiting
for her father to come back. Between

inspecting big black ants, letting them climb
and scale her hands, she would make believe

each passing car was her father's: that black
Bonneville with the loose and lowered front

bumper looking like a swollen lower lip,
that Pontiac Firebird with the wide, flat hood

spread out like the table Denise saw white folks
eat at on TV, that Skylark the color of night

after rain clouds sigh and leave the sky,
that dusty old gold Pinto rusted around the wheel

wells. Denise saw herself in each passenger seat,
her daddy driving, sometimes she had ice cream

(Blue moon in a cup, not cone, Denise's accident-
prone.), sometimes a brown bag full of penny candy.

If her mood was better than fine, then, Denise
envisioned Fun Dip with its white dipstick. She

couldn't resist it. The only thing consistent, it's just
Denise and her daddy with nothing but open road

ahead of them and enough time to make up
for every time he left her sitting on that porch until

the streetlights announced it was dinner time.

Douglas Manuel is the author of Testify *(Red Hen Press) and* Trouble Funk, *forthcoming from Red Hen Press. He is a recipient of the Dana Gioia Poetry Award and of a fellowship from the Borchard Foundation Center on Literary Art.*

MOONCHILD

HENRY LARA

"We all have dreams. I pursued those dreams. I've always loved singing and dancing. As a young girl, I was inspired by Stevie Wonder. He's my musical godfather. I've been singing since I was four years old. I was always surrounded by music, so singing has always been part of my soul. My father played the saxophone with an Air Force band and that was deep for me, too. I've been on my own since I was a teenager. I started traveling to talent shows all over the States to make ends meet. In time, I made some connections and continued making strides. I've collaborated with great artists such as George Clinton, Ray Parker Jr., Al McKay, Special Ed, and Phyllis Nelson. I loved Phyllis, she became my sister. She died in 1998, her death had a huge effect on me. I once sang at Dionne Warwick's home. In 2005, I sang at the Hippodrome in London. In 2015, I recorded a song named "That's What You Do" and I thought I was on my way to something. But I met some bad people. I wasn't paid and I got introduced to bad things. It's been very difficult since. I just need some help to get back on my feet. I'm willing to try anything. Counseling and therapy are what I really need. I've been on the streets for some time now. It's miserable out here and I ain't using my soul. We all have one, and we need to use it. My soul has been going to waste. I've been doing a lot of bad things out here. I just want change, but I just don't know where or who to turn to. I know I need serious help; I accept that. I'm very grateful to be alive. I can still sing; I have no diseases and I still feel healthy. I'm done with the bells and the whistles. The Lord has given me his testimony. I just need a fine-tuning. I'm a moonchild, I know there is still a chance."

Aidita Gibson has been roaming the streets of Skid Row for some years. She is trying to find her way back to what she lost. She still has a very beautiful singing voice. She struck her signature pose. (5/1/18)

DRIVE

DAVID L. ULIN

The traffic is thick from the moment I pull onto the freeway, up the long ramp at Washington and Fairfax, where a decade or more ago, the bus carrying my son and his fifth grade classmates on a field trip once broke down. This was in the days before cell phones— or before I had a cell phone—and I recall the news spreading as if in a parlor game. One parent saw the bus on her way to work, belching black smoke on the shoulder of the rise. She called another parent, who called a third, and so on and so on and so on … we all know how this goes.

It's been years since I thought about that incident, and in truth, I'm not thinking about it as I'm driving either, although I am compelled by the layers we leave behind. Live long enough in a place and your shadows, your ghosts, thicken everywhere, insistent, pushing, just beneath the surface of the world. Across the street, the pavement where I fell off the curb a year ago, racing to catch a bus. Half a mile west, the preschool where we sent both our children, and half a mile further, the grade school they attended after that. If time is an abstraction, a set of isolated instants, it is also a physical force. I see it three, four times a week, every time I come here, every time I make the turn onto the 10. Even this drive, to teach in the desert…I have done it twice a year or more since 2009. It is rote, almost, a matter of muscle memory; there have been times when I have found myself in the left turn lane at Fairfax, waiting for the arrow, only to realize that this is not where I am headed, that I did not mean to turn onto the freeway in any conscious sense.

Today, it's all intention, Friday afternoon, two-thirty, car newly filled with gas. In the trunk, my suitcase, a week's worth of clothes; in the back seat, my computer and my books. I'm pressing, more than a little, left late, always late, although today later, even, than the norm. As much as I am eager to get there, I find it difficult to leave my house. Or no, not leave, although that's true also, but to make the necessary preparations, bank, dry cleaner, do the laundry, sort through clothes, decide what to take. It's not that I have an embarrassment of riches, just the opposite. I have no nice clothes; this is not self-deprecation or hyperbole, but something closer to (what's that?) unvarnished truth. I do not care most of the time, but it's been so long since I've bought pants, socks, underwear, that even my usual shabby chic has tilted to the threadbare. This morning, putting clothes into my bag, I felt embarrassed (yes, embarrassed) by the state of my shoes, the holes in the seat of my favorite pair of khakis, the buttons missing, sweat stains in the armpits of my tees. Most of it is maskable, still—a long sleeve shirt, untucked, will cover many indignities—but for the first time, it is as if I've hit the tipping point, as if I can see the entropy. One thread peels back to another, to another, to another again. What once was new, whole in the most practical sense, begins to unravel, to return to fibers, chaos, to the residue of its component parts. I am not thinking metaphorically, but standing in my bedroom, transferring my rags in loose piles to the maw of my suitcase, I am confronted by an unavoidable sense of, yes, time again, on the most specific, the most physical, of terms.

Time is the substance of my driving also, the atmosphere through which I move. In optimum conditions—early in the morning, or late on a weekend afternoon—it is two hours, door to door, from my house in the flats of Los Angeles to the resort in Rancho Mirage where I will spend the next ten days working with students, when I am not holed up in my room. That is the baseline, the ticking clock, as it were; any minute beyond two hours that this journey takes is time I have lost. Time as commodity, as resource, doled out like so many coins. And I know this is a useless rubric, that the drive will take as long as it takes. And I know that time is relative, that it is what we do with it, how we engage in it, that matters, rather than the passage itself. When asked to explain the theory of relativity, Einstein responded with a parable. *Put your hand on a hot stove for a minute*, he is reported to have said, *and it seems like an hour. Sit with your beloved for an hour, and it seems like a minute. That's relativity.* The story is likely apocryphal; google it, and several variations appear. But the idea, the idea is at the heart of everything, the whole struggle encapsulated in three sentences, thirty-two words. Time is fluid, he is saying, time is contingent, time is … *relative.*

And yet, how to have such equanimity? This is the question I am asking as I head east on the 10 through downtown, aware of the digital numbers on my dashboard, slipping one unto the next with the implacable rigidity of a clock without a face. Two-thirty-five, two-forty, two-forty-five and I am maneuvering around the traffic, using all my tricks and strategies. Service roads, access ramps, every exit with a lane for through traffic, the split just south of downtown for the 110. This is, in its way, a vernacular of urban living, shortcuts only a resident will know. More time, more history, personal or otherwise, more layers interwoven through the uninflected landscape of the everyday. I buy time by using the experience time has offered, a decade of driving this stretch of road, knowing it as Samuel Clemens knew the Mississippi River in his day. *Know how to run it? Why, I can run it with my eyes shut,* he declares in *Life on the Mississippi.* I, too, can run it with my eyes shut…and what does it say about me that on occasion, I have done exactly that, shutting my own eyes for five seconds here, ten seconds there, as I navigate the concrete river of the freeway, as I try my best to (yes) make time?

The drive grows tight, congested, as I reach the eastern edge of the city, move through El Monte, Glendora, Montclair. Even the carpool lane is stop and start, and on the main road, long stretches of movement so incremental it hardly feels like movement at all. I switch on the radio, satellite, flick through my pre-sets, and again. I pause for Mott the Hoople, then for an ancient live recording of the Grateful Dead performing "That's It for the Other One," these songs I know so well it is as if they are part of my DNA. Ask me a question about American history—the Haymarket riots, say, or the Whiskey Rebellion—and I have to look it up. Ask me, however, to hum the guitar solo, note for note, from "Whole Lotta Love" or Jimi Hendrix's "Fire," and it rolls directly off my tongue. Time again, I suppose, or relativity, the stuff that lingers, stuff that sticks. This is why I don't listen to music as much as I once did (or very much at all, except in select instances); it has long since become encoded within me, something I don't need to think about.

The same, I was hoping, would be true of this drive: two hours, in and out. It's been a long week, a lot of loose ends, preparing for this residency, finishing up a bunch of other work. I like to think of the drive as a kind of re-entry, or more accurately, a transition, a sort of liminal state. In the car, all things are possible: those books, waiting to be read, carefully selected, even though I know that most of them will spend the week unopened on the table beside my bed. I've been looking forward to the time alone, to a kind of quiet, solitude. I've been looking forward to existing in a state of autopilot, to letting the road take care of itself. To drive on a crowded freeway, though, is the opposite of autopilot; it requires your full attention, which is part of what makes

86   it seem so slow. Cars braking, then accelerating, lanes opening for a hundred yards before clamping down again. Around Pomona, I am hit with a wave of exhaustion so deep, I want to pull off the road and go to sleep. Not for five seconds, nor even fifteen, but for an hour, three hours, until darkness descends across the scorched earth of the Inland Empire like a salve. The music, it's only making me more erratic, all this switching between stations, fifteen riffs from songs I can't stand, an ongoing cycle, "Hotel California" yielding to "The Wreck of the Edmund Fitzgerald" yielding to "Fooled Around and Fell in Love." When I first subscribed, it was with the idea (hope?) that the satellite would open me, again, to different music, but as with most things, it has only brought me back, more deeply, to what I already know.

   And what I know is that I dislike driving, or is *hate* too strong a word? And what I know is that this drive is taking forever, every minute an affront or an accusation, every minute an assault. Almost three hours to get to Redlands, three and a half to Beaumont, a drive that generally takes an hour-and-a-half. With each passing milestone, I find myself doing the math, adding and subtracting, seeing how many hours I am behind. There is a faculty meeting at four-thirty, but I'm going to miss that, and the new student orientation at five. Still hoping for the opening reception, at six o'clock, but it is nothing I can control. Finally, east of Banning, the freeway opens, and the lanes begin to thin, grow clear. I crank up the air conditioning, turn off the music, feel the rising hum of anticipation, as elusive as the hissing of my wheels. Cars, or so the trope insists, are freedom; *See the USA in your Chevrolet*, the old slogan goes. Not far from where I grew up, on the Upper East Side of Manhattan, that slogan lingered on an old gas station billboard, first erected in the 1950s or early 1960s, portraying a perfect American family, mom, dad, son, and daughter, white as dust and blond as corn silk, in their red Chevy convertible driving along an open road. Urban detritus, or another set of layers, more elements of time. It was archaic **87** even when I used to live in the neighborhood, thirty years ago. The same, I think, is true of the freeways, relics of another era, of another way of life. And yet, what they tell us is that time is always with us, that it does not pass so much as echo, resonate. *Put your hand on a hot stove for a minute, and it seems like an hour. Sit with your beloved for an hour, and it seems like a minute. That's relativity.* Or better yet: Drive in traffic for four hours and it seems like an eternity, although like everything, this too eventually ends. ❧

David L. Ulin is a contributing editor at ZYZZYVA. He is the author and editor of many books, including The Lost Art of Reading (Sasquatch) and, most recently, the Library of America's volumes on Joan Didion. The second volume of Didion's work, Didion: The 1980s and '90s, will be published in spring 2021.

POOF!

HENRY LARA

"I think the worst thing to go through in life is pain. Whether it's physical pain or emotional pain. Hunger is painful. Being cold is painful. When your heart hurts because your partner smashed it, that's painful, too. Pain is part of life. But you know? There's a pain so strong that only a loving mother is susceptible to, and that's the loss of a child. It's death. If I could tell God to eliminate a feeling he created, it would be to eliminate pain. In 1988 my diabetic son and his girlfriend were arguing. She hit him across the head with a pan and he went into a coma and later died. I've slowly been dying since then. Since his death I've kept busy. I lived in Houston for many years and worked at Sakowitz department store, it's like a Macy's. I packed glassware and other chinaware. I also lived in San Antonio. One thing I decided to do was to separate myself from my sister. She told me I didn't raise my son the right way. Being supportive would have been nice, but she bashed me instead. I'm alone now. I need my own place and getting housing is difficult. I love L.A. but housing here is funky. I try to be upbeat and smile. I try to be around good people. I like to people-watch during the day. It's like the Wild, Wild West here. I imagine what each person's world is like. I also love Chinese food. When my husband and I first got married we used to go out and try different Chinese restaurants. My favorite is egg foo young. For many years I wanted to take my life but my faith in the Lord helped me. I miss reading the Bible with my son. We used to spend an hour a day reading God's word. Although I believe in God, sometimes I wish I could just say 'Poof!' and have all this pain disappear. There's good people in the world but there's also big egos. Egos are powerful. It stops the progress of humanity. They are the cause of all destruction. You don't have to physically hurt someone to kill them. Just remember that today you are here but tomorrow the world may decide to go 'poof' and disappear you from this earth. Be nice to people."

Joanne S. was born in Cleveland, Ohio, November 24, 1945. She lives at a mission on Skid Row. She says the Bible has kept her alive. (1/21/18)

I WILL BE BURIED IN CANOGA PARK

DAN MURPHY

The heat inside the house matches the heat outside
and now they lay me down on my childhood bed
at five in the afternoon, and everyone takes Librium

lying down in the red shag carpet with Algebra book for pillow
(its grocery bag cover) and listen to Side Two of Bowie's *Low*.
It always skipped between the seventh and eighth measure

and the deep trilling sadness that ensued. I always thought
of *1984* and its gloomy interiors. It's almost twilight,
summer's first person singular. They leave me alone

to think new thoughts. Ted comes back from the liquor store
with three cases of Michelob, a couple of sixes of Schlitz Malt Liquor.
All for old times. Now they're out by the pool and everyone is seventeen,

everyone forty, skinny and fat, pimply and shy, but beer and sedatives
win the day and full of bravado and stories shirts come off—
thrown on the ice plants—girls strip down to bikini underwear,

T-shirts and bras, pants are hung on the bougainvillea and bottlebrush.
Some fall. Some are thrown. Shouting and splashing. The music
gets louder in the dining room, one speaker is dragged onto the back porch—

the first Clash album, *Survival*, then *Babylon by Bus*. Zeppelin *Houses of the Holy*.
Someone wants a little Motown. They fight for my legacy. The political, the personal
Like in life. Everyone knew me best. Like in life. Now my dead mother

can slip into my bedroom and tell me it's alright: *You just pass from one room*
into another. She cups my face in two hands like she's gathering water.
Just lie here a little while longer—a few of them will remember you and come

back before they leave. When it's dark, wait. I'll come for you.

FATHER PRESCRIPTION

DAN MURPHY

My mother died when my father
should have. My friend, my good
good friend and my cousin both
died—they all died—brain tumors
all—and my father swallowed
his blue and white pills, his green
pills. He ate oatmeal and turkey,
he had two heart surgeries,
he got better, he convalesced,
he had good family and terrible
friends, a photogenic face,
he drank coffee, he paid bills,
he swallowed his thirteen pills
and went to AA meetings, he ate
grand salads with stirred-in premade
dressing, he grew thin, his pants rose
on hipless hips, we saw more of his socks,
he read and reread Shakespeare and smart
mysteries, he read bad mysteries and
in his last two months a romance or two,
his children found him a new home
and paid his bills, sold his house, he
stayed death until finally
no one else could die unjustly. No one.
To die for himself and not another,
caught by an effeminate nurse

he had scorned, who held him, sorry
stick of a man, sores on his hands, deep
bruises on his arms, forgetting
to breathe at the end, and he died,
he died. All that quiet fighting done.

Dan Murphy's poetry has been published in The Los Angeles Review, Field, The Beloit Poetry Journal, *and other publications. He lives in Los Angeles.*

DOLORES DE LA VIDA

HENRY LARA

"I'm not sure how to explain my life. Too much to say. I often think of my childhood. I was born in Quito, Ecuador, on April 9, 1938. It's a very beautiful place. It's up in the Andes. Recently, I was thinking about how much I loved the way the mountains in Quito looked in the winter. I used to tell my parents that the Cotopaxi [a 19,347-foot active volcano] was covered in azúcar. I called it La Montaña Dulce. It got so white in the winter, it was beautiful. My parents owned a small oil company and made enough to support us all. I liked school, but as a teen I fell in love with volleyball. My last year in high school we won the volleyball championship; it made me happy. I married young, my husband beat me all the time. My love wasn't enough. He always found his way to domestic violence. It's what he did best. We were killing each other, so I left him. He gave me three beautiful kids. It's the only good thing he ever did. I wasn't making it financially, so in 1985 I decided to move here. Some cousins living here told me work was plentiful. I arrived here with a tourist visa and started cleaning homes in Los Feliz and Hollywood. I was also a niñera. I took care of kids. I love business, I learned it in Ecuador but never practiced it. My cousins and I don't see eye to eye, so I'm out here now. I haven't seen them for two years. I lived at the Norbon Hotel but that only lasted two months. I've always lived in South L.A. but in the past year, things changed. I've been assaulted four times and landed in the hospital a few times. But somehow the universe tends to take care of me. To make a little extra money now, I sell flowers. Todavia tengo apetito para la vida. Amo la vida. I want to see my kids. I haven't seen them in fifteen years. Lately I've had this strong urge to go back home to feel them. They don't know the condition I'm in. I like the feel of the sun but now I want to feel my kids' touch. It's time to go back home. I have to figure it out somehow."

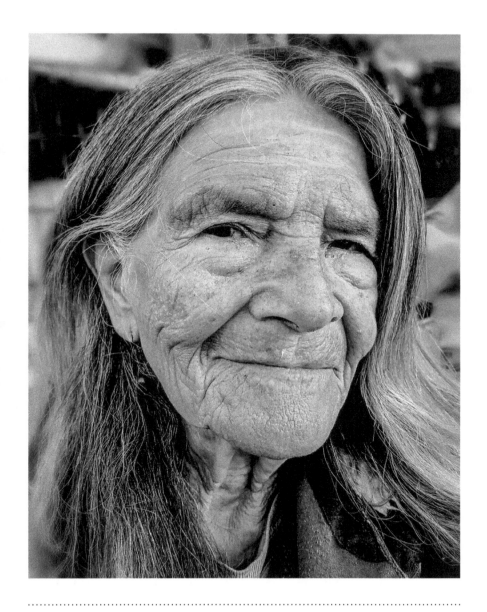

Dolores S. is currently living on the streets of Skid Row. She loves liberty. The indoors make her sad. She misses seco de chivo and tortillas de papa. (1/29/18)

WINTER DISCOUNTED

MICHELLE LATIOLAIS

I'm in the shop. The seasons are changing. Not out the window, not leaves and flowers. I mean, the spring line is here, hanging on racks in the back in plastic. Winter's on sale. Woolens, knits, velvets, all on sale. Out there, out the window, everything is expensive, real estate, the cars, parking, sunlight, expensive. Los Angeles. Inside my small shop, a lot is on sale. I don't advertise this in any big way, a small sign in the calligraphy I do is propped against the vase of lilies on the round table near the front window. *Winter Discounted*, the sign reads. That's quiet, I think to myself, looking at the vase aglow in sunlight, an opaque amphora I found in a junk store years ago. I buy flowers whether I can afford them or not. I can't afford them, actually, let's just be clear on that, but I afford them anyway. It can't all be on the meter, I say to myself, but it all is, no matter what I think or do. It's all costing someone somewhere something. *Winter Discounted*, I say softly to myself, feeling at least at peace with that phrasing.

My shop's not inexpensive, but the three independent designers I carry are not off the charts, either. The clothing is architectural, is perhaps a good way to say it, clean lines, perfect fabrics, and simple, too, and so they look more expensive than they actually are. I love the designs, the care taken with the designs, all made here in Los Angeles, and so it's hard for me to have people coming into the shop just because they think they're going to save money. Nor do I really want them coming

in because they're just dying to spend money. It's hard for me to love these inclinations, just because I own a shop and am in business. I'm supposed to encourage buying, buying, buying, but I have lived too many hours watching women spend money. It's not going to help her feel better for very long, or change her body's fuller shape or draw the eye of a man who no longer sees her. When she's slovenly and pushing a rocket ship of a baby carriage, then it's difficult to observe the index finger through the hangers, through clothes that might remind her of a former self, or perhaps some self put on hold. Maybe these are the women I have the most trouble with, too, the sloppily dressed mothers with designed-to-the-nines baby carriages, the ones to whom I actually would like to sell something, the ones who really do need this good dress, this striking coat, but it feels aggressive to me to prey upon their need, to take advantage of their maternal deprivations. Sometimes I'm just a mixed up ball of necessary actions dragged into hesitancy by thoughtfulness. Ugh, I say to myself, ugh in the morning quiet.

A woman and another woman, younger and following, come through the front door. So, one older, a mother perhaps, and one younger, a daughter, a niece, or I suppose friends. Possible. Women are sometimes friends. Rarely. But sometimes. They don't speak to each other, or at least they haven't yet, and the older woman nods at me standing mid-shop, smiles, and seemingly without looking pulls a dark blue gabardine dress from the rack along the north wall and holds it behind her. The younger woman looks, takes the hanger into her fingers, turns it. She sees the voided velvet insert at its back, a square plane, like a frieze at the top of a wall. Acquiescence seems to emerge in her face, which might be lovely, pretty, if she weren't so quietly worried.

"She'd like to try that on," the older woman says. "Would that be possible?" The older woman hasn't looked behind her, hasn't seen the

98 acquiescence on the younger woman's face.

"I would like to try this on?" the younger woman says, her long brown hair falling across her face as she tilts her head in inquiry. "I would?" she asks again.

"You would."

"Of course," I say. "My fitting room is here," and I walk to them and take the dress before I walk to the back and draw the pocket door aside. It makes a low trundling sound. I realize they haven't followed me, and are quietly speaking. "Please," I hear the older woman say, "not to worry so much about it. You'll feel better . . . or you'll feel just the way you always feel and then in that case, all will be familiar but you will look so much better feeling it."

The younger woman laughs quietly. She is perhaps thirty-five, maybe younger, maybe older, I can't always tell how old a woman is when she's actually taken care of herself, taken care of her skin, stayed out of the sun. She wears pants off the rack, so pants that fit her only in places, not in others, and a pale blue sweater, hand-knit beneath a leather jacket. Her boots are very old and worn rather wonderfully, the old in this case surprising and thus new, the detail that matters. The dress that I'm holding will be too big on her, I think, but I'm not saying anything because too big is perhaps the only way she'll appear comfortable—perhaps the only way she'll even wear it. I think the older woman knows this even better than I can surmise and I'm taking my cues from her. These dresses hang as straight planes rather than as fitted garments. Hannavee Kim is the designer and she herself is a perfect squat pear. I've never seen her wear anything but cheap jeans and sweatshirts, but she designs like an angel. Funny.

"You don't even need to try anything else on," says the older woman. "That is a fantastic dress. You're tall enough for it. You need some shoes, a small bag, done. It won't be cold. You'll be fine." Her voice is bemused, kind, stern, I like her, but feel some aspect of her ajar, off center, perhaps just missing. Something?

I hang the blue dress on a thin mounted rail in the fitting room, wondering as I turn how high the younger woman's boots rise up her leg. This dress hits mid-calf and a part of me thinks she might just wear her boots and that leather jacket with this dress. It might work, her hair up, done professionally, but her boots, her jacket, her personality wearing it all. Maybe? I suppose it depends on the event. Something tells me not to ask.

She is now walking toward me, her long hair falling on both sides of her narrow face. She will look quite stunning with her hair drawn back from her face. "There's a chaise in the room," I say. "You can sit down, pull your boots off, but I'm wondering if you might then put your boots back on. I'm wondering if you can't just wear those great boots with this dress?"

"I like the thought," she says, laughing again. "Halloran, did you hear that?"

"I did ... and I'll think about whether or not I wanted to hear that."

I pull the pocket door closed after the young woman. Halloran and I have the shop to ourselves. It's strangely awkward for a few seconds. Then I realize I haven't put any music on. It's Saturday, and almost noon and the street's been hopping for two hours already, and I've not thought to put on Pandora or Sirius. I have it all and sometimes I thumb through the various affects or moods and can't decide what to select. Sometimes I want to see the clientele before I type in the selection. Plus I resist the product formation the minute I choose something, like a bee sting that swells me into a potted plant they know precisely what to feed and water. Fuck you, I want to say always, and I don't care that the simile doesn't quite work either. Fuck them on that, too.

"Winter Discounted," the woman named Halloran says. "I like

100   that." She is not looking at the sign, is mid-shop and I realize she has seen it coming in, has remembered it. "Now is the winter of our discontent," she adds.

"Something for you?" I ask her. "For this same event perhaps?" Everything is in place in her save one significant aspect, and I look, stupidly, at the shorthand called jewelry, ring finger, left hand, nothing. I look at her bag, because there are purses women will buy for themselves, and others that only men buy ... and still others men buy if they're well instructed or advised. It's a huge woven Bottega Veneta, which is money, yes, but not five figures, and she bought it herself, no question on that, this subdued shade of green, not enough of a statement.

She can feel me looking at her, and so I dip my head to the silver sliver of a laptop I've pulled from the drawer beneath my table. I'm cleaving it open, thinking the younger woman is a part of her life, but not a relation, not a daughter, and then I tumble. She's her agent. Of course. The older woman turns to me and speaks across the shop, "a wrap," she inquires, "something as a covering perhaps, a thin coat even?"

A wrap. Old phrasing, I think. A wrap in this town is an end, a finish. *Strike the set—it's a wrap,* but there is a coat, with a dropped back, to show the voided velvet panel, and so it's almost a dress itself, or is in conversation with the dress, such that they belong together. The one coat I have is saved for Constance Boll. She'd called, instructed me to put it aside, she'd be in, and yet I know from experience that she might or she might not be in, that she might or she might not remember, that she might or she might not really want it in the end? Too many times I've been left with something I could have sold several times over, a beautiful dress left hanging on the back rack because Constance—anything but constant—had thought she'd wanted it, couldn't live without it, so happy "it is finally on sale," and money bags herself, what the hell did she need a sale for? I type in Thomas Adès and up comes *The Exterminating*

Angel, The Tempest, and I scroll down to violin concerti, then *Polaris*, and I point the pointer and push my finger down and the shop slowly fills with a cool trickling piano, and low haunting horns.

"The quiet was actually nice," the woman named Halloran says, and I'm not sure what to do with that, but after a measure or two I ask if she wants me to turn it off.

"No, no. Just saying the quiet was nice. I've never been in here."

"Yes," I say, "where have you been?"

She smiles. "Wrap, coat. Not a shawl, not anything that entails fussing."

"Sure. Excuse me." The coat is in the back, but it takes me a minute to think where I put it because the spring collection is on several hanging racks all lined up and permitting only a narrow passage. Finally, I remember I put it under plastic and suspended it from the hook on the back door. Even still, it's behind three dresses waiting to be sent out. All three the same dress, the same size, black, three-quarter length sleeves, their skirts six gores of fabric asymmetrically assembled, their only interesting detail, but interest nonetheless. She's a judge, the woman I had them made for. I reach up behind the dresses and grab the sleeve of the coat, hiking it up, working to get the hanger unhooked, and then the coat is crumpling down across my face and chest, my breath moistening the plastic it is encased within. As I pull it off my face and secure it in my hands, the plastic is already starting to be worked off, and I continue extracting the coat, ruching the plastic up and off. I hold the long fluid gabardine coat before me, its traditional monochromatic front, a narrow collar and covered buttons, but then the collar continues over the shoulders and down the sides of the coat, dropping to frame the voided velvet back of the dress. How much money is this woman going to spend, I wonder, because the dress, and then this, puts her over fifteen hundred. Who's the one paying out there? Will I have to

102 deal with Constance Boll, or will she forget she's ever had me lay the coat aside? I sidle my way out of the backroom, holding the coat before me, and then sweeping it up over my arm to keep it from dragging on the floor.

The shop is empty, and I turn back to see the dressing room door open just enough to allow a body through. The dress is not there on the rack. I don't particularly hurry to the front of the shop, but I go and stand beside the table and the flowers and gaze out the window. The women are across the street, the dress wadded up in the younger woman's hands, and they are getting into a small BMW, the older woman on the driver's side. I note the license plate, and even get a clearer read on it as they pull out of their parking place and drive north on Beverly Drive.

There is the protocol of what one does in the face of shoplifting, but because it's been happening so much recently, all up and down the street, I feel slowed by what is expected of me in this call and response, this tired procedural. I do have a license plate number, and that will interest the police a little more than the usual description of a face seen only once, and too quickly taken in to provide much detail. What was stolen? its value? and the report number will be written down and handed over by the policeman. I have a few of these numbers, but it's just understood to be hopeless pretty much, too small fry to merit the expenditure of police time and attention. At least, if Constance Boll ever comes in to buy this coat, it will be here for her. I won't have to navigate that bit of searing desert landscape, no good excuse in sight. I hold the coat up before me. I'm still standing in the window, and I shimmy the plastic sheath down over the coat's dark blue shoulders and as I turn, I see hundred-dollar bills on the table beside the vase. *Winter Discounted* is gone, the sign I've done in calligraphy. What had the woman said, "the winter of our discontent," wasn't that it? "Now is the winter of our discontent."

I look at the bills scattered about the base of the vase. There are **103**
five of them I count with my eye, and of course I want it all to mean
something, to somehow be more important than it probably is. I fold
the coat back over my arm, and gather the bills and walk to my desk. So
rarely does one have cash these days I almost don't know where to put
it, what to do with it. The face of my iPhone is lighting up as I lay the
coat across the end of my desk. I pay less attention to my phone than
perhaps I should. It's never the person I want it to be, can't ever be, and
now it's just a number I don't recognize. Two women are coming into
the shop, two girls, really, early twenties, talking, and I wait for them
to turn toward me, to recognize me before I say hello. They continue
talking, never turning or looking up. I never exactly know what to do
in these instances, whether to just call out "hello," overriding their
conversation? or to let the moment go. Not even when one of the young
women is standing at the desk, holding two silken shirts out, telling me
she'd like to try these on, does she say hello, or acknowledge me. ✄

Michelle Latiolais is the award-winning author of Even Now *(FSG),* A Proper Knowledge *(Bellevue Literary Press),* Widow *(Bellevue Literary Press), and* She *(Norton). She is a Professor of English at the University of California at Irvine.*

CHARLES AND GIZZY

HENRY LARA

"Today has been a decent day. I had an eleven-dollar hamburger from someplace on Spring Street. I got to talking with a nice lady who lives up here in one of these lofts. She spoke, I spoke, and it landed me a flavorful meal. I grew up in Fresno and Anaheim. I did twelve years in the military and had some runs up in Afghanistan, Fallujah, and Iran. I suffer from tinnitus after a bomb went off about twenty yards away from me. I had a handyman business with eight employees but while out at war my business partner threw the whole thing away. I lost trust in most people but I know good people, and it gives me hope for the world. Anyhow, this is Gizzy. It's just her and me. Although she was only supposed to live for eight years, I've had her for eleven. I give her much love, I talk to her and give her vitamins. I love small towns. I wish I was in Butte, Montana, or somewhere in Kansas listening to John Cougar Mellencamp. I don't like L.A. much but many of us veterans end up here. That whole putting your hand over your heart thing is a big lie. I lost faith in our government a long time ago. Anyhow, I do like the architecture here in downtown but that's about it. Live your life and love your children. Do what you must."

Charles was born in Fresno, California, 1962. He was listening to K-Earth 101 FM and rubbing Gizzy's head. Freedom makes him happy. (8/15/18)

PANDA EXPRESS

FRANCISCO GONZÁLEZ

Alone at night in his dorm room, Mateo typed "STD" into a search field. Distance was crucial. The student health center was not an option. If he should run into an acquaintance, he might face questions, and he was in too much pain to work out the right answers. Information could make its way back to his parents in Mexico. His life would be ruined.

Mateo was a finance major at Stanford University. The nearest Planned Parenthood clinic was up the block in Palo Alto, unacceptably close to campus, so he decided to visit the far-flung San José branch instead. He could reach it by public transit. Although the round trip would eat his entire Saturday, it seemed to him this was a small price to pay.

The next morning, on an eastbound bus, he used his iPhone to browse the clinic's positive Yelp reviews. All of the reviewers appeared to be female. One woman boasted of having gone "in and out in less than an hour" for her combined hormone patch. The recovery room, wrote another, was equipped with cushy recliners and stomach heating pads. She went on to praise the nurse practitioner who "treated me like a person, not just another patient." The clinic's average rating was a respectable three-and-a-half stars out of five.

Traffic was bumper-to-bumper, and it took ninety minutes for the bus to stammer its way to San José. When Mateo disembarked, the sun was out in force. To disguise himself, he had worn an Oakland Athletics cap, a pair of Ray Ban aviators, and a yellow fleece jacket that made him sweat profusely. He glanced this way and that, surveying the street, at every moment worried about being seen.

The brick-and-concrete clinic resembled a parking structure. Its exterior was not as discreet as Mateo had hoped. The organization's blue logo was embossed on the side of the building, with upper-case Ps as tall as grown men. His apprehension diminished somewhat as he saw that there were no protesters nearby. He had read about groups that gathered outside these facilities to wave signs and chant slogans, which often involved the words "Christ" and "murder." He reflected that their absence would make this episode easier to forget.

The lobby was a dull shade of ivory. Gray plastic chairs hugged the walls; many were already filled by patients, none of whom showed obvious symptoms of illness. Mateo approached the receptionist, who slid a sheaf of intake forms through a deal-drawer. He asked her how long it might take to see a doctor.

"For a walk-in it'll be two, maybe three hours," she replied, her voice soft behind the bulletproof glass.

Mateo cringed. He removed his Ray Bans in order to negotiate. "I can pay extra if the wait is shorter," he suggested, but the woman rolled her eyes, shook her head, and Mateo remembered how hard it was to grease the palms of clerks, guards, and bureaucrats in the United States. He turned away and slumped in a chair in the corner of the room, next to a ficus plant.

Almost immediately, Mateo's iPhone died in the palm of his hand. He wished he had brought a charger, or at least a book, a crossword puzzle. Near him, a pair of stone-faced women sat together, holding hands in silence. Farther down was a heavily wrinkled man, who whispered in the ear of a girl beside him—his grandchild, perhaps. "Yeah, well there's a reason," the girl snapped. "You really want to know it? Right now? You might not like it." Mateo heard nothing more.

Losing all sense of time, he began to fidget. He paged through the clinic's Notice of Privacy Practices, reading and re-reading until he felt himself going mad. A buffet of informational brochures lay within reach on a low, rectangular table. He snatched the nearest one. Its title was, *Are you safe in your relationship?*

Mateo rarely missed his hometown. He was from Ciudad Victoria, the capital of Tamaulipas—a war-weary border state. At the age of seventeen, he saw a severed head for the first time. It belonged to a sergeant in the municipal police force, and the men responsible had used a length of baling wire. They had suspended the officer's head from a flagpole in the middle of a busy roundabout, not far from Mateo's high school.

He walked to class that morning, peered skyward, and felt the shudder of something indelible etching itself in his mind. He wanted to look away, but was unable to do so. Vehicles passed by, their incredulous drivers lingering, panicking, zooming off. Its mouth was wide open, its hair disheveled, its eyes rolled back; this made the head appear lazy. Around that time, Mateo's parents forced him to apply to American universities.

He was the only child of two only children, and his family ran several textile mills across northern Mexico. His parents and grandparents had always emphasized his duty to marry and produce offspring. They were fond of reminding him that he who takes a wife receives favor from the Lord. But Mateo was a quiet, studious boy who showed little interest in romantic entanglements. As he remained indifferent to females into his teens, his clan began to fear the worst. They made it clear that he should one day find a girl, woo her, and wed her if he expected to inherit the family fortune. His responsibility, they said, was too great 109 for him to do any less.

Mateo dreaded all the talk of dating and matrimony, which seemed to plague him on a daily basis. He was happy to escape it, if only temporarily, by going abroad.

On a hot and humid late-August evening, his relatives gathered for a farewell meal at the family villa, near Reynosa. Servants roasted a wild boar in the courtyard; its flesh was sweet and nutty. A six-piece norteño band played cumbias, and there was much two-step dancing and gifting. Mateo's grandmother brought a barrel of date-palm liquor.

"Remember your people. Remember where you come from," she admonished, as if he had already forsaken them. And then she murmured, "You are not what you feel, my child. You are what you *do*."

Later, Mateo's great-uncle—a respected army colonel who had killed three men in Chiapas—clapped him on the back, gave him an envelope full of thousand-peso notes, and said, "You're lucky. I was in Santa Clara for a few weeks in the '90s. They have many beautiful women. A little bit of everything."

Mateo's grandfather chimed in between mouthfuls of carnitas, "Blondes, m'ijito. Give the blondes a try, if you can."

Mateo promised that he would.

That was three years ago. In a tiny examination room at Planned Parenthood, a doctor gave him a ceftriaxone injection, an amber vial of doxycycline, and a speech on the importance of prophylactics. Mateo was then instructed to remain celibate for at least one week.

On the return journey, he told himself that things could be worse, that he was not as ill as he could be. He had the promise of wellness a few short days away. And beyond that, an expanse of youth not yet depleted. There was nothing wrong with going to Planned Parenthood; there was nothing wrong with contracting a disease through anonymous,

110 unprotected sex.

He lost himself in this mantra until the bus struck an enormous pothole somewhere in Mountain View, and his genitals throbbed. He gnashed his teeth all the way back to Stanford.

Mateo blamed the strip clubs for his troubles. There were many in San Francisco, but Twisted Nob was the one he had liked best. It was a place he went to make himself happy, when books, exams, and problem sets were too much to endure. He often took the Stanford CalTrain to King Street in the city. From there, the club was a ten-minute walk. He would visit on Fridays, Saturdays, or Sundays. Or anytime he got the urge.

He discovered Twisted Nob through Yelp on his twenty-first birthday. It was wedged between two high-rises on a disreputable block of the Tenderloin. The club's façade looked as though it belonged in a different decade, with a yellow rock-and-plaster veneer so ugly that Mateo nearly turned back at the sight of it. But he had traveled the entire length of the Bay to reach this destination, and he was determined to see his adventure to its conclusion.

The bouncer was a thirtyish woman in a patent leather jacket, her head shaved bald, two meters tall if not more. When asked for identification, Mateo handed over his green passport.

"Mek-see-co, huh?"

"Yes, that is my country." He played up his accent in order to sound more exotic.

The bouncer inspected the passport and smiled, revealing rows of crooked teeth.

"Happy birthday, you're in for a treat. I bet you guys don't have anything this good south of the border." She returned Mateo's passport before adding, "There's a two-drink minimum. And a hundred-dollar entry fee for VIP rooms."

The main stage at Twisted Nob was a violet half-moon that glittered under muted lamps or spotlights, disco balls or strobes. It was large enough for five or six dancers to do floorwork at any given time. At its center, a brass pole reached up to the high ceiling.

Rainbow-hued neon lights snaked their way around the semi-dark lounge, which was crammed with shouting, laughing, inebriated men. As Mateo squeezed through the crowd and its mingle of deodorants, he felt that he had entered a parallel world of color, pleasure, beauty—a world where he would be in his element. The club had two dozen or so vinyl armchairs with acrylic endtables, but they were all taken, and he had to wait for a place to sit. All the while, he was so giddy that he could not stop his limbs from trembling.

Once he was seated, Mateo paid nine dollars for a Keystone Ice— his first legal drink in the United States. He took a gulp; it smacked of piss and seawater.

Strippers came forward and offered their bodies to him. On subsequent visits, this would turn out to be his favorite part: they were young men—brawny, hairy, waif-like, fat-bottomed, now and then a slight pot belly—and the act of choosing gave him a sense of elevated importance. They introduced themselves with names that sounded oddly tailored to their appearances: Kilo, Deco, Aston, Diesel. Always, they shook hands with him, as if doing so was a prerequisite for the grinding that followed.

Mateo's early lap dances were learning experiences. As a rule, the music was bassy, thumping, generic, and contact lasted the length of a song—three minutes, if that. More than once, he instinctively tried to caress a stripper in mid-session, only to be told, "Sorry, honey. I can touch you, but you can't touch me. Okay?" When he heard this for the first time, Mateo felt deceived and heartbroken in equal measure.

Women seldom appeared at Twisted Nob. When they did, they

usually arrived in overdressed phalanxes of five or more. By and large, they did not enjoy physical interactions with strippers. Few of them approached the stage rail, and only the bravest among them dared to thrust banknotes into waiting palms, waistbands, cracks. Sometimes the female patrons danced with each other. Mostly, they preferred to pose for selfies, applaud politely, and sip cocktails through bendy straws. Mateo found their conduct ridiculous. They seemed to disrespect the club by misunderstanding its purpose and rejecting its benefits.

Visitors were typically older males, and they could be rowdy. One night in September, Mateo witnessed an ejection. It happened when a silver-haired man staggered out from the velvet curtains of a VIP room, obviously intoxicated. The man began to shout incoherent threats at one of the strippers, and the bouncer was on him in a flash. Trapped in a headlock, the patron kicked his legs in every direction, overturning tables and drinks.

"You've lost your mind this time, Earl," the bouncer snarled, as she dragged her captive past Mateo's armchair, toward the exit. "Completely lost your mind."

Mateo watched the scene unfold and felt embarrassed. He vowed that, no matter what, he would never disgrace himself like that. The DJ turned up the music—something by Lil Jon—to drown out the uproar, but one could still hear the man wailing, "I want my money back! I didn't pay a hundred dollars for a fucking air-dance!"

The stripper in question, a fine-boned redhead in leopard-print boots, shouted, "I'm not teabagging for tips, sweetheart!"

Mateo thought the ill-behaved patron had been banished. And yet he was astonished a week later: he arrived to see the middle-aged man standing beside the main stage, catcalling a pole-artist as if nothing had happened. When Mateo asked how this could be permitted, the bouncer sighed and told him, "Earl's been a regular for years, and—

believe me—he's put some of these boys through college. Management gave him a pass."

By then Mateo was himself a regular. He discovered that he, too, could break certain rules. One night during a lap dance, he slipped an arm around his dancer's gyrating pelvis; he was elated when the young man did not push him away. This fellow was leaner than most, with a buzz cut and large gray eyes. He was so smooth that his body, from the neck down, seemed as though it had never sprouted hair and never would. The amenable stripper wore nothing but a golden thong. He rocked to and fro atop Mateo, whose hand probed, wandered, and came to rest on backbone. Mateo closed his eyes and savored the weight of a warm body against his, until the song ended and the stripper dismounted.

Before leaving the club that night, Mateo wrote his number on a white napkin and folded it twice. He gave it to the stripper, who held it to his heart, winked. For days afterward, Mateo watched his phone. He waited for unfamiliar digits to light the screen, but received no call, no text. He cursed the name of the club.

Finally Mateo went back to Twisted Nob. When he waved at the stripper who had taken his number, the man did not appear to remember him. Mateo simmered, then balked at the absurdity of a glamorous, scantily clad individual wielding such power over him. He had to think clearly, and it was getting harder to do that lately. The lights, flesh, and alcoholic aura of Twisted Nob were distracting him from his goals. Mateo excoriated himself. He was a grown man, and these outings to San Francisco were beneath him. He needed to find a girlfriend; he had put it off for far too long. The more he thought about this, the more he felt proud of having reached such a sensible conclusion on his own.

But then it struck him that he had already put himself in danger: his parents had promised to visit in April or May. If they should find out where he was spending so much time and treasure, he would end up

114 disinherited, cast out for his sins. Or perhaps they would simply have him murdered. In a way, that would be preferable to the slow demise he would face, cut off in a foreign country.

Mateo pondered these eventualities. Overcome with terror, he got up and left without finishing his banana daiquiri.

Valeria was a first-year math major. She was an employee at the Panda Express in Tressider Union, in the same food court where Mateo liked to eat a few times a week. Because she came from a poor family—and because she regarded idleness as a source of shame—she worked as many hours as she could. Sometimes young men would flirt with Valeria while they stood in line; this made an impression on Mateo. He considered that perhaps the answer to his problems had been hiding in plain sight all along.

At first, Mateo did not feel prepared to ask Valeria out on a date, but he started dining at Panda Express as a way of exchanging pleasantries with her. Every so often, he would ask for her guidance on what to eat, so as to appear vulnerable and thoughtful. He would compliment her choice of earrings, necklace, or bracelet, to make his attraction understood.

Valeria was bilingual like Mateo, but spoke with an accent in both languages. He tried to remember the things she told him in passing. Gradually, he pieced together that she was American-born and had never been to Mexico. Her parents were immigrants from Quintana Roo, but she had grown up in El Dorado, California—a rural town so obscure that she preferred to tell people she was from Sacramento.

Following each encounter, Mateo took notes on his phone. In this way, he accumulated dozens of miscellaneous details about Valeria's life. She enjoyed running outdoors on cloudy mornings. Her favorite telenovela was *Rubí*. She did not like bamboo shoots, partly because she had not tasted them until her mid-teens. But she loved sushi—she said she would eat it all day if she could.

Valeria began to smile whenever he approached. On days when she was serving, she would ladle extra food onto Mateo's styrofoam plate. She would stop by his table.

"How is everything?" she would ask. Or, "Are you doing alright?" Mateo took this as proof of her affection.

By mid-October, Panda Express became a daily ritual. At the end of each day, when he shambled up the stairs to his third-floor room, he felt the weight of an anchor in his gut. He was racked by diarrhea at unpredictable intervals; one bout was so severe that he had to bolt mid-lecture from his Debt Markets class. After that, he bought Imodium in bulk. He kept a few eight-ounce bottles in his backpack as insurance. Valeria did not work on Mondays or Wednesdays, and he was grateful that he did not have to eat at Panda Express on those days.

One afternoon when Valeria was cashiering, Mateo spurred himself on to decisive action. As he reached the register, he was aware of the people in line behind him, and of Valeria's three coworkers watching him. He looked Valeria up and down, struggling to dislodge words from his throat. She had long black hair and large breasts. Her face was squarish, with pouty lips. She reminded Mateo of the Olmec colossal heads he had seen years prior, on a family vacation to Tabasco.

Despite his mental preparation for this encounter, it was a leap into darkness. He inhaled deeply and told himself to concentrate on his mission. Before Valeria had a chance to greet him, Mateo blurted, "Would you like to get together? For coffee?"

"What?"

"Not right now. I meant, at a different time."

Valeria did not immediately respond. Mateo forgot to breathe. For a moment, he was certain that she viewed him as a clown. Then she smirked.

116   "So. At last you grew some balls," she said. "I'm done at five. Will that be alright?"

They met at Starbucks, next to Panda Express. Over caramel macchiatos, they fumbled for things to talk about. Mateo asked Valeria about her family, and learned that she had three younger brothers and two younger sisters. She said that, as the elder sibling, she was under constant pressure to set positive examples. Her family's trailer had only two bedrooms: one for the children, the other for her parents. In high school Valeria had often sat awake until early morning, working on the bathroom floor. She studied linear algebra and French beneath a flickering incandescent bulb, while everybody slept.

Mateo told her that he, too, felt responsible for his family's happiness; his fulfillment had always been secondary. He told Valeria about his own college preparatory years, when his father made him study English for three hours a day. His tutor was an American expatriate who had been denied tenure at a liberal arts college, and whose breath always reeked of tobacco. Mateo's hatred toward English had crystallized instantly. Vowels rarely produced the same sound twice, which made the language seem deceitful.

Mateo and Valeria started having coffee or tea on a regular basis, and then the occasional meal in town. Mateo got used to Valeria's quirky north-of-the-border accent; he even came to find it endearing. They talked about their hometowns. Valeria told him about the ranch her parents worked on, a winery famous for its Zinfandel grapes. Her father had been the vintner's right-hand man for more than twenty years. She told Mateo about herds of deer invading the vineyards, her father rising before dawn to shoot them from the crook of an oak. She was used to hearing gunfire, she said, especially in springtime. She was also used to eating venison.

In an effort to make himself more relatable, Mateo remarked that his family owned some farms in Chihuahua state. He did not specify that they **117** were cotton plantations spanning more than a thousand hectares each. He also omitted the fact that his people would not dream of involving themselves in manual labor; the actual farming was done by peasants.

Mateo and Valeria spent more time together, and their stories became increasingly personal. One day, as they drank tea, Valeria told Mateo how the vintner had assaulted her when she was sixteen. She had been home alone one Sunday, too sick with fever to join her family at Mass. The vintner stopped by, looking for Valeria's father, and let himself into the trailer. Valeria woke to find him undressed on the bed beside her, his hand in her pajamas. A scuffle ensued. Somehow she managed to flee to the bathroom and lock herself in.

Days later, the vintner brought her parents a Toyota Tundra—a vehicle worth tens of thousands of dollars. He gave it to them in the guise of an extravagant Christmas present, when it was clearly meant to buy her family's silence. Valeria had already told her parents about the assault, and yet they did not reject their employer's gift. Nor did they attempt to bring him to justice.

"If he throws us off his land, we will be ruined," they had pleaded.

Now Valeria only spoke to them when she absolutely had to. As she told the story, her eyes misted. "It taught me that anyone can sell you out, anytime."

Mateo reached out and clasped Valeria's hand in both of his, as if to assure her that he would do no such thing. She squeezed back, smiled through her tears, and he understood that he need not say anything more, because they were living a moment of shared consciousness and trust. This form of intimacy was new to Mateo; with it came an intuitive sense of responsibility. Although he had never been involved in a physical altercation, he imagined himself punching the vintner in front of Valeria and her family, knocking him unconscious, standing

118 over him. Thinking this made Mateo feel heroic. He decided that Valeria was lucky to have him, that he was fulfilling her unmet needs.

That evening, they went to the library and studied side by side, holding hands. Mateo was happy to intertwine his fingers with Valeria's, especially in public. The more people who saw them together, the better.

The week before Thanksgiving Break, Mateo took Valeria to a French-sounding restaurant in Palo Alto. She had mentioned visiting France someday, and he viewed this as an opportunity to harness her attraction to a faraway place, transmuting it to sexual attraction toward him. The restaurant had a seaside-chic decorative approach. Its dining room featured faux-driftwood tables. Near the entrance, a jazz quartet performed downtempo muzak.

"Wear something nice," he had told her. "Because I'm going to dress up for you." He settled on a navy micro-check suit with a gray shirt. Valeria wore an ankle-length, strapless black dress, with ribbon trim. She had borrowed the outfit from her roommate.

Mateo had chosen the restaurant because of its four-point-five star average on Yelp. It also boasted a four-dollar-sign price designation. These were important details. He reasoned that by spoiling Valeria, he would induce her to associate him with positive things. If he persisted, she would eventually come to rely on him for happiness. Valeria stared out the restaurant's window-wall, with its generous view of the Bay.

"You're really pulling out all the stops, aren't you?" she asked him, in English.

"What does that mean?"

"Come on. Don't play dumb."

Their waiter was a man with a Costa Rican flag tattooed on his wrist, and Valeria addressed herself to him in Spanish. To Mateo's chagrin, she did so in the informal "tú." The waiter engaged Valeria in conversation. Later, when he brought drinks to the table, he appeared to smile too boldly at her. Mateo found it difficult to keep his eyes off the broad-chested, smooth-talking man. All the same, he was frustrated that his date's attention should be siphoned away.

Valeria ordered a quinoa salad and pan-seared Pacific salmon. Mateo chose the blood-orange-marinated grilled rack of lamb. He ate slowly, sulking. When the waiter returned to check on them, Mateo glowered until he left.

"Alright, what's wrong?" Valeria asked.

"Nothing. The food is excellent."

"I'm not allowed to talk to anyone else. Is that it?"

They chewed in silence. At the end of the meal, Mateo did not leave a tip.

"I'll walk you home," he grumbled, still smarting with jealousy.

She scowled. "I'll be fine. Don't trouble yourself."

But Mateo insisted out of mechanical politeness, and Valeria did not protest again.

Her apartment was six blocks away, on a street lined with hawthorn trees. With every step, Mateo felt berries squishing underfoot. He did not speak to Valeria, look at her, or slide his hand into hers. The evening was a failure, and he wanted nothing more than to put it behind him.

They reached Valeria's building—a garden-style apartment complex owned by the university.

"Well, this is my stop," she told him.

Without the slightest warning she grabbed his shirt collar and pulled him to her, kissing him so aggressively that he almost lost his balance. Mateo was dizzy; he was pleased. He felt silly for having been upset moments before. Valeria was a good kisser. She toyed with him, adapting to his movements, easing up and pushing back.

When they paused to catch their breath, Valeria slapped the back of his head. It hurt.

"Fuckin' crybaby," she scolded. "You know, you really need to lighten up. You're lucky you're hot enough to get away with the kind of shit you pulled at dinner."

Mateo shrugged. "Sorry."

"Yeah, whatever. I'll see you next week. Absence makes the heart grow fonder, right?"

She walked into her building without looking back.

In his dorm before bed, Mateo stared into a mirror. Valeria had worn purple lipstick. He used a clump of tissue to wipe it from his mouth.

Valeria spent Thanksgiving break with her aunt in Stockton. Mateo texted back and forth with her every few hours. Sometimes they joked about how dull life had gotten without each other's company, and Mateo wanted to believe that Valeria actually missed him, but he imagined himself becoming less important to her over time. She was probably enjoying the holiday.

Mateo went to Panda Express, in hopes that it would help him focus on Valeria. With students mostly gone, the food court was so desolate that one could hear its working parts: steam wands, hot oil, spatulas, mops. Employees stood around, looking bored in their caps and gloves and aprons. There were intermittent bursts of small talk. Otherwise, the air was dense with silence.

Mateo ordered broccoli beef with two egg rolls on the side. His appetite vanished a few bites in. Adrift in thought, he stared at his red tray, fiddled with the too-small utensils, and examined his reflection in a cup of Sierra Mist. Several minutes went by. His food cooled. The broccoli sagged, and grease began to jell at the margins of his plate. Coming here felt like a mistake. He rubbed his temples and groaned as a familiar impulse shook itself loose within him. All at once, he was overwhelmed by recollections of male bodies, their dexterous maneuvers.

Dazed, he opened a fortune cookie. He squinted at the band of paper between his thumb and index finger. It read:

"Be mischievous and you will always be happy."

At last he acknowledged that the cure for his cravings was only a train ride away.

For the most part, Mateo found Twisted Nob just as he had left it. The bouncer smiled at him. She looked smug, as though she had been expecting him all along. She did not ask for Mateo's identification, but told him, "You know the rules."

Mateo took a seat. The loud music hurt his ears. A rap track was playing; its lyrics explained the importance of dividends, bitches, and making it rain. Some of the strippers were new. One of them put a hand inside Mateo's thigh and said, "This is my favorite song! How about a dance, sweetie?" Mateo was not impressed, having heard that line a thousand times. "No thanks," he replied. The stripper would have to try harder.

Hours passed. People went in and out the door. It was the night before Thanksgiving—a Wednesday. Mateo figured that the club patrons were like him: individuals who could not go home or see their romantic partners. Lonely, misunderstood men. Every time he remembered Valeria, he signaled for another drink.

The barkeep that night was a recent hire: a short, mustachioed man in a half-open button-down. Sometime around midnight, he struck up a conversation with Mateo, who was nursing his tenth beer. The music got louder, faster, uglier, and they talked about anime, politics, the weak Mexican peso. They did not exchange names. Eventually, they snuck into the empty women's restroom, stumbling into a stall. At close quarters, the barkeep seemed dirty. His shirt was blotched with perspiration, his skin and hair were oily. With the barkeep's mouth against his, Mateo thought he tasted something deep-fried. Somehow this did not matter.

The lock in their stall was broken.

"Don't worry," the barkeep panted. "We've got the place to ourselves."

The next morning, Mateo woke up with a new kind of burning sensation in his groin.

Mateo did not tell Valeria about his trip to San José. He did not mention Planned Parenthood. When she returned to campus, they agreed to have sex for the first time.

They decided that her apartment would be the most suitable venue. Partly this was because Valeria's roommate was out working late that night. Also, her full-size platform bed was more comfortable than Mateo's frameless twin mattress. Less than a week had elapsed since Mateo's injection, but he had been pain-free for two days, and that seemed good enough to him.

Valeria's room was unassailably tidy. It smelled of citrus and verbena. The bookshelf, above her small desk, contained math textbooks and science-fiction novels, ordered from tallest to shortest. Mateo watched as Valeria slipped out of her skirt, folded it into a perfect square, and placed it in a wicker hamper. He saw a trio of stuffed animals atop her dresser: a bear, a pig, a squirrel. The animals' beady eyes made him strangely self-conscious, so he switched off the floor lamp in the corner of the room.

They removed the last of their garments beneath Valeria's wool duvet. Mateo released her bra hook, while she in turn unbuckled his belt. The room was dark, but the night outside was clear, and stripes of moonlight pierced the window's horizontal blinds.

"Give me a sec," Valeria said. She got a scrunchie from the bedside table, gathered her hair into a ponytail, and wound it into a loose bun. "There we go—all set."

As he unwrapped a condom, Mateo was afraid that Valeria might notice something not quite right about him, that he would fail to satisfy her. It occurred to him that, in the act of sex, she would assimilate his **123** innermost feelings. Valeria would grasp that he had visited strip clubs in San Francisco, exposing at last his enormous misdeeds. He imagined her outrage, a denunciation in a public place, loud enough for all to hear, with him cowering and begging.

Mateo was trapped in these premonitions while Valeria moaned and the bedsprings creaked. He had only been at work for a minute or two or three, and his forehead already glistened—not from exertion, but from runaway anxiety. She licked him, kissed him, urged him on, and yet he could feel himself going soft.

Valeria lay supine underneath him. Her eyes were closed, her lips parted, her breath raspy. She betrayed no sign of noticing his ongoing collapse. Even so, Mateo's own thoughts continued to infuse him with raw panic, and he wondered how long he could go on. He forgot why he was having sex in the first place.

Desperate, he shut his eyes and thought back to his hands on the barkeep's buttocks in the women's restroom of Twisted Nob, pants around ankles, the pulse of electronic music racing at 150 beats per minute. Mateo conjured up his memory of the man's outstretched arms, palms flat against the filthy green wall-tiles, and within a few moments his erection was firm.

Five minutes later, he came.

"You finished?" Valeria asked.

"Yes. And you?"

She nodded.

Mateo felt unburdened. Having sex with a woman made his past seem small and ludicrous. Although they had not yet introduced the word "relationship" into their conversations, he was certain that Valeria was now his girlfriend. She slept beside Mateo, drooling on his chest, while he remained wide awake. He envisioned a lavish wedding, a home

124 full of children, his family's suspicions quelled forever. He basked in those details until night sky gave way to scarlet and opened up bigger, bluer than he remembered it could be.

That same day, he strolled through the University Arboretum and FaceTimed his father to report that he was no longer single. When his father answered the call, he was wearing a shoulder belt in the backseat of the family's Cadillac Escalade. The chauffeur was driving him somewhere, but Mateo had no way of discerning their location.

"Wonderful, m'ijito!" his father shouted. "Where did you meet her?"

"At a restaurant."

Along with excitement, Mateo sensed impatience, ambitions sprinting to the distant future.

"I hope she's fluent—I want grandsons who can speak to me!"

Mateo smiled. He texted his father a headshot of Valeria, pulled from Facebook.

"I see. She is dark, isn't she? Quite dark. But beautiful, also. How serious is it? Do you love her?"

As he met these questions, Mateo perceived himself to be in hazardous territory. He believed that falsehoods become truths if you repeat them enough, that they can take shape if you will them to do so. He replied that he loved Valeria, and yet it sounded like a phrase for another man, perhaps a different version of himself. Regret laid waste to him. It was hard to breathe. He was pinned beneath the weight of his own words.

Mateo's mother had been off-screen, eavesdropping, and just then her face popped into view. She was a dour, soft-spoken woman who rarely showed enthusiasm for anything but business. Now she was laughing, diabolical with joy. She shook her fists triumphantly.

"Give her a dozen roses! Treat her to breakfast in bed! Don't let her get away!"

PANDA EXPRESS

Mateo knew that his parents would celebrate. They would probably open a bottle of mezcal and get drunk.

A week later, Mateo and Valeria attended a men's soccer match. It was now December. Stanford was playing its rival, UC Berkeley, in the national tournament semifinal. This outing was Valeria's idea, and Mateo readily consented. He had no liking for sports, but regarded the shared spectacle as a way of reinforcing their attachment. If nothing else, he could refer to it later as evidence that their partnership was built on good times. The tickets he bought were the most expensive ones available: first-row seats along the western sideline.

They arrived at nightfall. The stands were a crush of red-apparelled Stanford fans, with a smattering of blue-and-gold Berkeley supporters struggling to make themselves heard. Mateo and Valeria settled in beneath the glare of stadium lights. From where they sat, they could make out the strained expressions on players' faces, their damp hair, shadows trailing them in artificial day. Not long after halftime, a freezing gale howled across the field, and the twenty-two athletes lurched in a movement that appeared almost choreographed. Valeria, in her cutoff jeans and white blouse, shivered. She hugged herself.

Mateo had studied the forecast. From his backpack, he produced the same jacket he had worn to Planned Parenthood.

"Here, this should help."

"Well played, sir," she said, through chattering teeth, and Mateo was not sure if he detected sarcasm in her voice. In any case, Valeria took the jacket, put it on. A minute later, she lifted the metallic armrest between their seats. She scooted closer to Mateo and kissed his cheek.

The game went on. When the Stanford fans cheered, Mateo cheered too. Blood rushed to his head. A new life seemed to expand around him. He conceded that perhaps sporting events were more enjoyable than he had realized. The cold air was harsh, but it tingled on the moist spot where Valeria had kissed him, and he felt safe.

Mateo could not stop himself from staring at the blond, long-limbed captain of the visiting team. The young man was an intrepid forward. Late in the match, he eluded three opponents to unleash a well-timed strike—the tie-breaking goal—and the ocean of spectators churned and groaned. In the wake of scoring, the captain appeared to lose himself. He hollered at no one in particular, pounded his chest. Then he removed his number-nine jersey and sprinted to midfield, arms flailing, as though attempting to extinguish invisible flames. The referee displayed a yellow card.

For the longest time Mateo looked on in wonder, and thoughts escaped his control in the way that boiling water overspills a lidded vessel. He pictured the fair-haired athlete dancing on a stage, shorts discarded, bare flesh drenched in crimson light. A surge of music faded, bloomed again, as the vision gained in clarity, and Mateo could imagine reaching out to slip a wad of cash into the young man's briefs. ✄

. . . .

Francisco González's fiction has appeared in The Southern Review *and his poetry in* Arts & Letters. *He is the winner of the 2020 Gulf Coast Prize in Fiction. He lives in East Los Angeles.*

BODILY

MARY OTIS

the landlord ripped
the roof off the house
with us in it napping, still
renting, always renting
from land baron bluffers
peekers and cheats, the one who
disappeared and her daughter said
send your rent to the parrot rescue
they were all before this one who
did cleave the brain of our house
with his axe and finding
a kewpie doll tucked in the rafters
flung her into the blue

HUMAN SOUND STATION

MARY OTIS

I rented an office where the words
of long dead writers swirled in the air
like prehistoric ash, so said management
and not only that they said
you'll sit where famous sat and
think better thoughts because
everyone knows great writing
shoots from ass to brain

I tried to write and I did I wrote
in my office by the kitchen by the
microwave minute every second of the day
snack wraps to mouths like oxygen masks
everyone so ding ding hungry

the hallway a human sound station
for coughers cranks and stomps and
downstairs the drag race show, not to
mention the next-door masturbator
and his private hullabaloo

every day I couldn't take
the clank of the belt buckle
the felt fuckle film, ejecting men and
many, mute luminaries evanesced
all good thinks forsaken

back to the roofless house

blue tarp flapping a broken sky

where I began my book

in the laundry room

back to the beginning

when my mother said

why can't you just stay put?

Mary Otis is the award-winning author of the story collection Yes, Yes, Cherries *(Tin House Books).*
She is a fiction professor in the UCR Palm Desert Low Residency MFA Program.

BÁNH MÌS AND A DREAM

HENRY LARA

"I am from Ho Chi Minh City. I moved to the United States seven years ago. I spent my first two months in Michigan, but I didn't like the weather. It was too cold. I soon got an opportunity to move to Los Angeles and help manage MỸ-DUNG here in Chinatown. My father knew the owner. They were both in the Vietnamese military. He was tired and needed a reliable person to run it for him. We arranged for me to move here to help manage the place and I've been here ever since. I didn't know what to expect when I arrived, but it didn't take long to feel comfortable here. At times, Chinatown reminds me of home. There's a lot of Asian people here and I have made a few Vietnamese friends. The only difference is that there is a lot of poverty in Vietnam. Los Angeles is even better than I thought. We have everything here including the best weather. It's better than the weather back in Ho Chi Minh City. I don't leave the area much. I'm too busy with work and other parts of L.A. are much different than here. My work has always involved food, so I know the business of the báhn mì sandwich. Three dollars is cheap, my friend! The bánh mì' I sell here are as good as the ones in Vietnam. They are tasty, try it, my friend, you try it! We also sell both the Vietnamese and Chinese newspapers like the *Zhong Guo Daily News* and *The Vîet Tide*. We have good strong Vietnamese coffee and fresh fruit. I arrive at 6:30 A.M. and prep for my 7:30 A.M. opening. My life is work; I like work. I'm happy in Los Angeles and this is where I will retire, my friend."

Chinh Le said he's living a dream and is happy with his pay. Bánh Mì MỸ-DUNG is family-operated and is located near the corner of Ord and Broadway in Chinatown. Try the Special Sandwich for $3. He wishes everyone a Happy Chinese New Year. He also sells seasonal kumquats and said they bring good luck. (3/15/18)

MESSIAH WOLF

JOE DONNELLY

When I was a boy, my imagination was ripe for wolves. But, it wasn't the usual folktales and fables that got to me, or the scenes of wolf packs airbrushed onto the panel vans of my suburban youth. At six years old, my wolf was a companion, not a cautionary tale or a signifier of being born to be wild. As far as I can recall, some of my first (and last) unencumbered moments were spent on the porch of our South New Jersey home on rainy summer afternoons, watching big drops chase little drops down the screen while *Peter and the Wolf* played in the background and those French horns signaled the arrival of something as wild and doomed as any six-year-old boy. There, I daydreamed of adventures to be had and redemptions to be won by my wolf and me.

Of course, my wolf sidekick was a construct. One formed of the reams of mostly fanciful received knowledge about wolves our psyches start getting fed at an early age, accelerated in my case, no doubt, by the suggestiveness of my German shepherd and the trick of music on my child's brain. What creature other than the wolf has been such a big part of our lives and such a small part of our experiences?

That I would daydream in some abstract idea of *wolf* is not all that surprising. The abstract is where Americans have been most comfortable with wolves ever since we brutally purged them, along with Native

Americans, from most of our lands. In the abstract, they are usefully 133
totemic. In the abstract, we can call on them when we want to summon
a little nostalgia for the primal past or a bit of remorse for burying it in
mass graves. There, they don't demand too much of us, nothing that
requires any sacrifice.

More recently, though, wolves have been gaining ground on terra
firma. Once relegated to bands of holdouts in northern Michigan,
Minnesota, and Wisconsin, the number of gray wolves in the lower
forty-eight states has more than doubled to about 6,000 following their
mid-'90s reintroduction to the Rocky Mountain West. They are getting
closer all the time. At least fifteen now live in Northern California after
being absent for nearly a century.

The current wolf population is still just a tiny fraction of its historical
numbers distributed across a tiny fraction of its historical habitat. Even
so, the growing presence of wolves in a landscape that is much messier
than a six-year-old boy's imagination is forcing a long-overdue reckoning
that, like so many others, we might still not be ready for.

Nobody said salvation was going to be easy.

It certainly doesn't seem so when I find myself waking up dry-
mouthed and dizzy next to a woman in a room in a fancy hotel neither
of us could afford.

It's the winter of 1989 and I am two decades and thousands of miles
from Prokofiev and that screened in porch in South Jersey, on a ski trip
in Lake Louise, Alberta, Canada. In a few years, a lanky Iowan by the
name of Carter Niemeyer will venture into the frozen tundra north
of here, trap a few dozen wolves, and bring them back to the remote
mountain wildernesses of Wyoming and Idaho where they will quickly
set the aforementioned reckoning in motion.

I've been wandering around a different kind of wilderness, that of
an unmoored early adulthood lacking any sense of direction or purpose.

134 I'm on this ski trip with a bunch of fathers and sons from Pittsburgh, the city where my family eventually settled. Pittsburgh isn't known for skiing because the skiing in Pittsburgh sucks. But the *going skiing* signifies.

See, by 1989, the last of the big steel mills had shuttered and the city's nosedive from third-largest corporate headquarters in the U.S. to one of its suicide capitals was complete. Even the once-eternal Steelers dynasty had been gathering dust for nearly a decade. For these fathers and sons of Pittsburgh, this ski trip to Lake Louise, Alberta, signals they've made it through the initial wave of Rust-Belt regression with some of their bourgeois aspirations intact. They are here to celebrate that.

They are also mostly too young for their marriages and their children and the conventional lives they've struggled to attain. So, when the celebration moves to the fancy hotel's disco bar—picture a well-appointed Holiday Inn lounge from a Boston suburb somehow transplanted into the bowels of a gorgeous Victorian chateau in the middle of the Canadian Rockies—they take an overbearing interest in my flirtations with a cocktail waitress. Right around last call, the men pass a hat, literally, to get us a room.

In the morning, I stumble outside for a scheduled group photo, leaving the girl dreaming in a high thread count. The men greet me with cheers and slaps on the back. Still woozy, I take a gulp of cold, clean air and wonder if thrills are always going to be this cheap. The air, though, is something else. It tastes ancient and unspoiled at the same time, a brand new sensation. I take another gulp and smile for the photo op, the snow-covered Canadian Rockies in the background.

Next, we board a bus for a tour of the glaciers around Banff National Park. I sit by myself, doing my best to take in the scenery while pondering my hangover and run-of-the mill malaise. The men don't seem to be similarly burdened. They are drinking and growing restless. After looking at a couple of glaciers, they demand the bus return to the hotel—the disco bar calls. Someone says, "You've seen one giant hunk of blue ice, you've seen them all," and everyone laughs.

Those were the days.

On the way back to the hotel, the bus crosses a low bridge over a train track that runs through a narrow valley separating two peaks. An easement girds each side of the tracks before it's overtaken by tree and slope. The bus moves slowly across the bridge—maybe there is ice. As it creeps along, I stare out the window, pondering how the tracks look like a lazy creek. Then, something catches my eye: a large, dark figure about fifty yards away, sauntering alongside the tracks.

I watch it move. It seems so at home, so devoid of neuroses ... so unlike us. I'm mesmerized. When it stops for a moment to look back toward the bus, a jolt of recognition, maybe even connection, shoots through me. I must have said it in my head a few times before the words make it out of my mouth. "Wolf, wolf, WOLF!"

My fellow travelers are unmoved. I point out the window and say it again: "Wolf!"

But, it's gone.

The guy who'd had enough of looking at glaciers says it was probably just a coyote and everyone agrees and that's that. Who could blame them, what did we know of wolves then, other than as cartoons characters and team mascots?

I can't summon the faces from that trip, but I can still see those blazing, imperious eyes looking through me with something innate and fierce. My first encounter with a real wolf was more than I'd ever imagined as a boy.

I like to think that wolf could have been OR-7's great, great, great, great grandfather.

More than twenty years later, summer is turning to fall and no one yet knows of OR-7 when a woman and her husband set out from McCall,

136 Idaho, on motorcycles. They are going to visit relatives in Weaverville, California, just west of Redding. It's a long ride, traversing more than 600 miles and a time zone.

They probably start out on Route 95 South, which shadows the Snake River as it cuts through Hells Canyon, the deepest river gorge in North America, and drains the steep mountains between Idaho and Oregon. I say probably because I'm piecing things together from a sketch of the trip the woman felt compelled to share in the form of a letter to the editor of an environmental magazine.

Having visited this area, though, I can assure you it is a sparsely populated land of intense beauty. The iconic Snake and its tributaries carve through deep canyons and meander past high meadows abutted by 9,000-foot peaks that are often compared to the Alps. The topography can be vibrant and verdant with lodgepole and larch, speckled with mountain lakes and wildflowers, or it can be rugged and barren depending on elevation and slope angle.

The speed limits are higher in Idaho, so the couple slips by the southern reaches of the Wallowa-Whitman National Forest and makes it to the border town of Ontario in less than two hours. Ontario, with about 11,000 inhabitants, is the biggest city in Malheur County, and one of the biggest cities in all of eastern Oregon. Here, they pick up Route 20 going west and glide between the southern edge of Malheur National Forest and the northern boundary of the Malheur National Wildlife Refuge.

This is high-desert scrubland, big buttes under big skies, a hard land fit for coyotes, cougars, and cattle grazing. Most of it is federally owned and operated by the Bureau of Land Management. The refuge is where, in 2016, Ammon Bundy's well-armed brigade of ranchers, sovereign-staters and tinfoil-hat wearers seized the park's headquarters in hopes of fanning the anti-government conflagration Ammon's father, Cliven, had set off at his Nevada ranch two years earlier. The flashpoint,

ostensibly, was the $1 million in back fees Cliven owed for twenty years' 137
worth of grazing cattle on public lands.

The real beef, though, is with what the refuge represents—the idea
that the land is something other than a strictly utilitarian proposition,
that the public has a stake in a region where cattle is king and public
resources, nature even, have traditionally served special interests. There
were probably better targets for the Bundy bunch's ire—Teddy Roosevelt
created the Malheur Refuge to protect waterfowl from hunters—but in
this one, and in other more recent conservation projects throughout the
West, they could discern a growing threat to the generations of Manifest
Destiny-salted entitlement around which their culture has cohered.

Four weeks into the Malheur occupation, one of the Bundy gang
tries to run a roadblock and is shot and killed by federal officers. Ammon
Bundy's brother, Ryan, suffers shrapnel wounds. The Bundy militants
eventually surrender. Criminal charges, indictments, and trials follow.
A handful—along with their beliefs that the government was spraying
chemtrails on citizens, that President Obama was not one of those citizens,
that homosexuality was a disease, and that the southern counties of
Oregon should be an independent country—go to prison.

Not that long ago, this nonsense retained the whiff of the exotic. Now,
we're inured to images of bearded men wielding unfortunate tattoos and
long rifles at state houses and sandwich shops, railing against the tyranny
of mask ordinances in the face of a deadly and highly communicable
disease; railing against the social contract and the common weal.

In the early fall of 2011, however, as the motorcyclists roar past a
refuge not-yet-under-siege, we don't fully grasp how much further down
the road to suicidal stupidity we are yet to travel. We don't know that
the couple enjoying Route 20 for all of its high-desert, blue-highway
beauty is navigating another tributary that is rushing toward our current
calamities.

138   Something else, though, a young wolf, is moving in the same direction, breaking path for a different destiny, one that we could still seize if we follow his lead.

At this point in his wanderings, he has gone too far to call this foray a restless walkabout. At this point, he is a disperser. One that has relinquished a sub-alpha role in the territory that his parents, OR-4 (the legendary fourth wolf captured and fitted with a GPS collar in Oregon) and B-300, had reclaimed just a few years prior by braving the Snake River and climbing into the Oregon side of the Hells Canyon Wilderness.

There, they found something wolves abhor—a bountiful and ready habitat devoid of wolves. There, they found the Zumwalt Prairie, North America's largest intact prairie grassland, a lingering remnant of the pre-cattle West teeming with elk and deer and, most importantly, lacking in humans. The pair started a pack near the confluence of the Imnaha River and Big Sheep Creek, just outside of Joseph. Wolves have been proliferating under the shadow of 9,838-foot Sacajawea Peak ever since.

By the fall of 2011, their son, OR-7, is halfway to California, stealing along a patchwork of public lands and open spaces, traveling a shadow infrastructure that has been stitched together by years of dogged environmental advocacy. This tenuous greenbelt just barely connects the Wallowa Mountains of his natal pack in the northeast of Oregon to the Cascades that run south and west down the spine of the state into California. By leaving those wild mountains and starting his trek just months before the motorcyclists start theirs, OR-7 is unwittingly proving the efficacy of linking up natural spaces into what environmentalists call wilderness corridors.

A public that becomes increasingly enamored with his lonesome wanderings will eventually give OR-7 the nickname "Journey." And though he is just the seventh Oregon wolf to be captured and fitted with a GPS collar, OR-7's lineage goes all the way back to the first few

dozen wolves Carter Niemeyer brought here from backwoods Alberta, 139
just a few years after I had been astonished by that wolf moseying along
the train tracks.

Those wolves were released into Wyoming's Yellowstone National
Park and Idaho's the Frank Church River of No Return Wilderness.
The mid-'90s return of wolves to the northern Rocky Mountains,
accomplished through a resolute application of the Endangered
Species Act, is hard to top for dramatic and undertold stories of men
and bureaucracy. It quickly turned into a proxy battle, the contours
of which are all too familiar now, in the country's larger culture wars.

The anti-wolf lobby weaponized the rhetoric of paranoia, conspiracy,
and tribalism. They depicted wolves as dangerous, wanton creatures and
called their reintroduction an act of Deep State treachery, an affront to
"traditional" Western values. They prophesized ruination and promised
retribution.

Underneath the hyperbole, they harbored deep existential anxieties.
An ocean of blood had been spilled to take this land for "Americans,"
for their cows and their saws and their drills and their insatiable desire
to subjugate. What was all that for if we were just going to return it to
the vanquished? Where would it end?

Proponents of wolf reintroduction, on the other hand, pointed to
the billions in subsidies that prop up otherwise untenable ranching and
livestock concerns—industries that have damaged the environment
more than cars ever will. In the return of wolves, they saw small but
necessary steps toward curbing our appetites, restoring some equilibrium,
and extending the ethical sequence to include the land, much as Aldo
Leopold proposed in his essay "The Land Ethic" not long after examining
his own regret for shooting a wolf on a mountain.

Leopold realized that a mountain without wolves is a dead mountain.
For some, a land without wolves is a dead land. If you squinted hard enough,

140 you could almost see in wolf reintroduction a modest pilot program for reparations aimed at amending some of the sins of Manifest Destiny.

All this baggage added up to gray wolves being brought back to the West under an unprecedented twisting of the Endangered Species Act. They were designated an experimental, nonessential species. This meant no habitat would be put aside for them (pointless in the case of wide-ranging wolves anyway) and that they'd be on their own after populations reached politically tenable, but scientifically dubious, numbers.

The ranching lobby's predictions of ruin haven't come true, of course. Wolves do kill livestock, but in statistically anomalous numbers. According to the USDA's industry-friendly stats, predators are responsible for just two percent of livestock deaths and wolves tally just a fraction of that. And while any animal loss is significant to individual ranchers, they are compensated when wolves are to blame. Negligence and disease kill the most cows by far, despite the billions of taxpayer dollars we pitch in for mending fences, clearing forests, dredging drainages, providing grazing lands, building culverts, dusting crops, enhancing pastures, and generally doing what we can to keep the cheeseburger supply chain intact.

Far from ruinous, there is evidence that returning gray wolves to the West has indeed improved the environment, setting off what is called a trophic cascade of benefits. For example, Yellowstone's ecosystem had been suffering from prolific and complacent deer and elk populations that stripped entire swaths of the park clean. This was particularly egregious in the valleys where streambeds and riparian areas suffered from lack of cover and ecosystems collapsed. When wolves returned, they brought back a so-called ecology of fear, forcing prey to be alert and to move around more naturally. They put the wild back into the wilderness and overgrazed areas recovered.

The recriminations, on the other hand, were immediate. As gray wolves proliferated and moved farther west, they were met with calls

to *shoot, shovel, and shut up* and to *smoke a pack a day*. In the spring   **141**
of 2011, just before OR-7 left his pack, federal protections for wolves in
the Northern Rockies were lifted via a budget-bill rider. Many outside
the livestock, hunting, and logging lobbies viewed the move as an act
of political expediency. As soon as they were let off the leash, states
such as Montana, Idaho, and Wyoming went back to killing wolves
with prejudice.

At Bend, Oregon, the motorcyclists pick up Route 97 going south
toward Crater Lake, where they spend the night. It's now early fall 2011
and OR-7 isn't even a rumor yet, let alone Journey, arguably the most
famous wolf in the world. But he's been moving stealthily in the same
direction as the motorcyclists, logging mile after mile along the edges
of the human world, hidden by trees and shadows and tall grasses in
open spaces.

The dangers are many—cars, crosshairs, a broken jaw—but this
wolf is young, big, and strong. He weighs more than 100 pounds and
can easily travel fifty miles a day. For food, he might take over a lion's
kill, or bring down a deer. He can make due with small mammals if
needed. He's good at being a wolf.

The woman takes the lead out of Crater Lake in the morning en
route to Upper Klamath Lake and the southern end of the Oregon
Cascades. She isn't far down the road when an apparition flashes in
front of her just as red and blue lights flash in her rearview mirror. She
had forgotten about Oregon's ridiculous 55 MPH speed limits, but that's
not what's on her mind as the sheriff writes her up. She is transfixed
by what she has just seen: a wolf crossing the road up ahead.

The deputy hands over the speeding ticket and tells her she's wrong,
there are no wolves in these parts. But the woman knows wolves. Her
hometown of McCall, Idaho, is an easy ride to the Frank Church-River
of No Return Wilderness, and she was around when wolf B-13, just

142   nine days after being repatriated from backcountry Canada to cattle country USA, trotted sixty miles north onto a rancher's spread and killed a calf. The wolf was shot through the heart and left to rot alongside the calf—the first two casualties in the wolf wars that have raged ever since.

A few months after the encounter with the cop, the woman's mother-in-law, who lives in Oregon City, sends her a newspaper clipping about a lone wolf spotted in the area where she and her husband had been riding their motorcycles. It wasn't a ghost she'd seen; it was OR-7.

Not long after that, just before Christmas 2011, OR-7 crosses into California. He dallies briefly in Siskiyou County on the state's northern border. As if to make a point, he moves on to Lassen County where the last of his California predecessors had been killed in 1924. The welcome wagon isn't exactly rolled out for the first wild gray wolf in California in eighty-seven years. The supervisor of Siskiyou County tells the *Los Angeles Times* that she'd like to see any encroaching wolves shot on sight.

After looking like he was heading for Reno, GPS readings throughout the summer of 2012 show OR-7 doubling back and lingering around Lake Almanor in northern Plumas County. It's possible a massive wildfire in the region forced animals toward the lake and the wolf found the pickings easy.

Still, it's a curious place for him to be. Young wolves disperse in search of mates and OR-7 is now more than 600 miles as the crow flies from the nearest prospect. He has logged well over a thousand miles in a quixotic quest only he seems to understand. As Journey's travels gain more attention and more admirers, the California Fish and Wildlife biologist who oversees his newly adopted territory cautions that this wolf is a goner, "a genetic dead end."

At home in Los Angeles, I have a different reaction. My imagination is still ripe and a wolf has once again captured it, filling my head with visions of a fierce-eyed dissident, a king of the forest coming to heal the land and maybe us in the bargain.

I jump in my car and head north. I'm not hoping to find OR-7 so much as I'm hoping to bear witness to the possibilities he represents—to find the map to the new world struggling to grow out of the smoldering ashes of the old one.

I follow his trail through our sclerotic arteries and into the boundaries of his new territory. I trace his steps into the hot summer timberlands of the northern counties on up through the wet, piney spine of autumnal Oregon. I go all the way to the snowcapped mountains whence he came. Nowhere in my travels do I find evidence of any great civilization that has risen from all the dammed rivers, scalped mountains, stripped valleys, and spilled blood.

Instead, lonely logging trucks on winding passes, sandwich shops in one-stop towns, vacant mining shacks, railroad tracks, and cows. I see nothing, not even in the great cities I skirt, that explains what all of the killing has been about. Nature, still insistent amid the charred husks, is the only thing.

And now, a lone wolf.

It's August 2014, an inflection point in California's epochal drought, and I'm driving north again. Somewhere, just after Interstate 5 winds through the steep rises, deep canyons, and shallow valleys that give shape to the counties of Shasta and Siskiyou, the road curves around the towering hulk of Mt. Shasta. It is here that the afternoon sun shrivels to a red dot and the sky darkens as if a thick fog is rolling in. One is not. It is smoke and ash from raging wildfires choking out the firmament, turning the landscape dull and gray.

Across the Oregon border, things start to look better. A massive dark cloud looms in the rearview mirror, but the sky ahead is blue and the late-afternoon sun is a familiar shape and color. The foothills and mountains recover a greener hue.

After ten hours of driving, I arrive at Ashland where, despite its name, I can breathe without scarring my lungs. I check into a motel and walk around a little to get my legs under me. I have an appointment in the morning to see a man about a wolf.

OR-7 isn't alone anymore. Another wolf picked up his trail out of northeast Oregon and followed his tracks along the edges of humanity to the end of the state. They found each other near the Rogue River, south and west of Crater Lake near the Sky Lakes Wilderness, a region shaped by a collision of the wet coastal ranges with the drier inland Cascades. It's rife with water and vegetation. It seems perfectly designed to support life, and at five years old, near the end of the line for most wolves in the wild, the "genetic dead end" sired a litter of three pups here. The Rogue Pack became the first pack of wolves in western Oregon in more than six decades.

Their timing was uncanny. On the same day the Oregon Fish and Wildlife Service released the photos of the new wolf family, the California Fish and Game Commission was meeting to rule on whether or not gray wolves deserved protection under the state's Endangered Species Act. The proposal, inspired by OR-7's California adventuring, had looked bound for the floor when the California Department of Fish and Wildlife recommended against protecting wolves after OR-7 appeared to have settled north of the border. If there were no wolves in California, why protect them?

OR-7, though, has a knack for pranking bureaucrats. He crossed back into California on the very day the department made that recommendation. Then, on June 4, 2014, as the Game Commission met in Fortuna to make its final decision on the matter, photos of a new wolf pack just over the state line went viral. The room, stocked with wolf advocates, erupted in cheers. OR-7 forced the commission's hand and now gray wolves are under the protection of the California Endangered Species

Act. So far, legal challenges by the California Cattlemen's Association 145 and California Farm Bureau have failed.

OR-7 would go on to sire twelve pups in five consecutive litters between 2014 and 2018. One of OR-7's male offspring returned to his old haunts and started the Lassen Pack in 2017. The Lassen Pack is the only known wild wolf pack in California, though sporadic sightings of lone wolves following in OR-7's footsteps continue. This past spring, the pack added eight new pups. There are now fifteen known wolves in California. More wolves and packs are sure to come.

Wolves are protected in these parts, for now, but they are coming under increasing attack elsewhere. Last year, a ranch in Washington that grazes cattle on public land had twenty-six gray wolves killed for livestock depredation. The rancher said he believes the reintroduction of wolves is a plot to end private-enterprise cattle grazing on public lands. "I don't feel that we have room for wolves in Washington State," the rancher told the *Los Angeles Times*. "If it's allowed to continue, it's going to drive the ranching industry out of Washington, which is what a lot of people want. We're just stubborn, and we won't leave the range."

The return of wolves to our wilder spaces is far from settled, but OR-7 has arguably done more than any other wolf to give them a fighting chance. Fittingly, a biologist and lawyer with the Center for Biological Diversity, her tongue only slightly in cheek, dubbed him Messiah Wolf.

On the morning of my appointment, evidence of the inferno I'd driven through to get to the edge of the Sky Lakes Wilderness sits ominously over the southern border. The sky to the north, though, is mostly blue and I drive a few miles in that direction to meet up with Joseph Vaile, the executive director of the Klamath-Siskiyou Wildlands Center. Vaile is tall and boyishly handsome and would be played by John Krasinki in the movie. He has agreed to take me up into OR-7's territory. I guess I'm hoping for an audience with the messiah.

Vaile, a Midwesterner, tells me of growing up in a stultifying monoculture, a landscape long ago subjected to the floristic equivalent of gentrification. He studied biology in college and came out West to be around the last remnants of wild America—biological reservoirs in unaltered states, he called them.

As we gain altitude, the sky gets bluer and the trees greener and Vaile explains that we are in a vast eco-region of profound biodiversity, a geography of varied ranges, watersheds, topographies, and microclimates that stretches west to the coast and south into the border counties that OR-7 patrolled during his years of living dangerously.

The land is great habitat and coveted for its timber production, making it a source of much conflict and some compromise between conservationists and loggers. Organizations like Vaile's throughout Oregon and California have been fighting to protect these areas and add to them as they come under mounting stress from climate change, drought, and extraction industries. By traveling from one end of Oregon to the other, and then on into California, and by establishing footholds for wolves everywhere he went, OR-7 proved the value of their efforts and fortified their arguments: land that can support wolves is land that has intrinsic worth... if for nothing else than seeding a comeback for wildlife after climate catastrophe.

We park at a trailhead and start hiking. About a mile up, past the tree farms, the forest turns thick with old-growth stands. Needles and cones cover the ground, birds chirp, and butterflies flutter. Critters scurry under fallen trees. The air feels fresh and new like it was on that morning in Alberta twenty-five years ago. Vaile says we are in the OR-7's vicinity, but wolves' territories are huge and OR-7 is not nearly as interested in me as I am in him.

I don't encounter OR-7 or any other wolves, but I might have found what I was looking for, anyway: a glimpse of a future beyond the embers that have covered my car in soot by the time we get back down to the trailhead.

I had planned to go in search of OR-7 one last time, but the wolf that has taken up a storage shed's worth of my preoccupations went off the radar earlier this year just as the pandemic started laying bare so many of our misapprehensions.

Wolves don't harbor delusions, though, and OR-7 was likely exiled after his mate took up with a younger, stronger alpha. Eleven-years old is ancient for a wolf in the wild and too old for a lone one. OR-7 is either dead or dying. It's probably just as well. A taste for cattle has turned the old wolf and his Rogue pack into outlaws in recent years. It's messy here in the real world of wolves and men.

So, now, the pine needles that once padded his huge paws pull at him like quicksand. Now, the ravens and magpies that lived on his scraps look to see if his nostrils still flare. Now, the coyotes yip excitedly as news of the end of the big gray wolf from up north, the great disruptor, the great restorer, travels through the forest in the language of the forest.

He leaves as he came, a spectral figure tracing the liminal terrain between worlds, haunting us with the idea that we can either live with wolves, or die without them. ✂

Joe Donnelly is an award-winning journalist, writer and editor, and the author of L.A. Man: Profiles From a Big City and a Small World *(Rarebird Books). He is currently Visiting Assistant Professor of English and Journalism at Whittier College.*

A FEW WORDS FROM PEPPER

HENRY LARA

"The outdoor life ain't for everybody. And I ain't talkin' bout camping out in the wilderness for recreation. I'm talkin' bout street life. This out here ain't no joke. You have a better chance of surviving a bear attack than you do out here in the cold, ruthless streets. You think you bad? You think you a quick gunslinger? There's always someone bigger, worse, and with a quicker gun that's smoking around every corner out here. You gonna look for problems you gonna get problems. But things have taken a turn. The time is in the past for gang-banging and fighting. Now, it's time for peace and love. It's time for unity, okay! This is all we got left. I'm proud of some of the good changes that have been happening out here on Skid Row. Along with countless unselfish people, we're creating a better Gladys Park, which we now call Home of Champions. There's five, six different kingdoms right here united in love. It's time to pop a few love pills and make more love. We need more babies and more unity. Fuck the badasses cuz we gonna eat them up every day, we hungry for them! We need love, we need the word of the Father [pointing up]. We need people like OG, like Frank, like Pauly's Project. People who make a difference, people that bring light into these dark streets. We all don't live under blue skies. I live a living death with only half my immune system working. I can lay out and die tonight! But that don't stop me. Live every day like it's the Last Supper, homie! Every minute! Love your brother, the war is over, baby. All the heroes in our lives are dead. We don't need more heroes, baby, we need more lovers, fewer fighters! Now go get that heart checked, homie. I'm out!"

Pepper is well known in the Skid Row community. He gives countless hours to his community through different projects. This year will mark his fifth year of sobriety. He is as passionate and energetic as ever. (2/6/19)

PEOPLE SAY THEY WANT SOMETHING

SIEL JU

The first girl I dated in L.A. was my first match on Tinder. We met up at a strip mall at noon and ate shawarma pita wraps. They were about what I could afford on my budget then, but she seemed fine with that, even grateful. The rushed, desperate way she attacked her food really got me. I thought, here's a woman I can take care of. Bony thin and quirky, she was an actress who worked as a barista at Coffee Bean. Afterward we went to her messy one-bedroom and had sex on her twin bed while her roommate watched COPS in the living room. It was the best date of my life.

I left her messages for weeks afterward, and she never called back.

I did meet one other girl from Tinder. I was surprised when we matched; in her profile she'd said she was just looking for something casual, and these kinds of girls never swiped right for me. Not because I'm hideous or anything. I'm an average guy, just not anyone's fantasy. This girl though, after drinks at Daddy's, took me to her place. It was a dark loft in the basement of an old Hollywood apartment complex, the air slightly dank and musty. She initiated everything. Her skin was bluish-pale. Afterward, she started crying. She said she'd had it with guys using her then throwing her away like she was some broken toy. I told her I thought she was pretty, we could do this again if she wanted. I even meant it. But at that she started yelling, really screaming at me, about every guy she'd slept with who'd said they'd call then didn't. I was petrified the neighbors would call the cops. She seemed the type to claim I'd raped her. I ran out with my shoes in my hands.

That was it for me, with Tinder. I focused instead on settling into the city, physically and professionally. I moved out of my Airbnb and found a place in Van Nuys. I got a desk at a cheap co-working space and met other web programmers, developers, would-be entrepreneurs. Like me, they were freelancers with big dreams. Separately we'd decided L.A. was the best environment to incubate something new. We tossed a lot of ideas around between writing lines of code. I joined a gym and started spinning. In the evenings I scanned Craigslist's used furniture listings. I wanted my place to look livable, but like I said, funds were low.

It was because of a couch that I met Cellie. The couch was ugly and listed under free stuff. I figured I could use it until I found one I actually wanted. The photo showed a cheap, boxy thing that looked to be made of Styrofoam. "It's got some stains on it. It can be cleaned, but I haven't gotten around to it," read the description. This seemed very honest. I texted the number on the ad.

She called me back immediately. "Can you get it tonight?" she said.

"Tonight?"

"I really need to get it out of the house tonight."

"Oh, is a new one being delivered tomorrow?"

"No, I just want it gone."

I demurred. "Tonight is difficult...."

At that she went at me: "See, this is the problem. People say they want something, but then they just flake on you. I don't get it. Why do you go through the trouble of reading Craigslist and contacting people when you have no intention of actually getting the stuff? I really want to know. Why?"

"No, I really want the couch," I said.

"Why?"

"Why do I want the couch?"

"Yeah, why," she said, then laughed hysterically. The laughter went on for a while, long enough that she started making me laugh, incredulously, and a little curiously too. I wondered if it would ever stop. Then she was back. "Seriously, why do you want it? It's disgusting."

"I just moved out here with nothing," I said. I sat down with my back against the wall and put the phone on speaker. "I'm literally sitting on the floor right now."

"So then why can't you get it tonight?"

I thought about this. There was no particular reason I was putting it off, aside from the fact that I was more of a planner, I wasn't in the habit of doing anything right then and there, on the fly. But maybe it was time to change. "Okay, I'm coming," I decided. "Where are you?"

She was the one who sounded taken back this time. "Wait," she said. "How will you move it?"

"It didn't look that big in the picture. It'll be fine. I have an SUV."

"Really?" she said. She turned quiet, then sedate. She gave me her address. "The buzzer isn't working, so I'll come out and get you."

"What's your name?"

"Cellie. I'm wearing like a green dress."

"Okay."

"I'm not very strong. I can't help that much with the couch."

In spite of myself, I started fantasizing about Cellie while driving to Mar Vista. I guess I was pretty lonely. I had an image of her, dark eyes and a mass of dark hair, a sultry, sensitive girl with a few hard edges waiting to be smoothed out. I imagined aggressive, flirty banter. I imagined her offering me a drink, the two of us on the couch, slowly moving closer to touch each other until her hair brushed my face and things blurred.

Of course I was disappointed when I met the real life Cellie, though there was nothing wrong with her. She was just a normal girl in her late twenties: average height, average weight, with slightly frizzy hair and soft, heavy thighs. Not that I thought her entirely unattractive. She did have those dark eyes. If I'd met her close to last call at a bar, I wouldn't have been opposed to taking her home. She had that slightly caustic vibe of sad, easy girls. I smelled an open bottle of wine as soon as I walked into her studio and pegged her as the type who spent most nights drinking by herself. I turned out to be right about that, although this night, her manner was cordial and business-like, almost efficient. She quickly picked up one end of the couch and showed me how to tilt it to get it out the door.

After we loaded it in the car, she shook my hand. "Welcome to L.A.," she said, and met my eyes for the first time. Her face looked a little loose.

"Thanks," I said, then out of habit added, "Let's keep in touch."

"Sure!" she said cheerily. She said she was going to be getting rid of a lot of stuff, that she could call to see if I wanted any of it. I thanked her again.

I didn't think about her again until that Saturday, when she called to ask if I wanted an iPod charger. Cellie said the first Craigslist guy who was supposed to pick it up didn't show, then stopped picking up her angry calls. Then the second guy tried to get her to mail it to him in Long Beach. "He was like, 'God help me, I will pay you back!' about the postage. Fucking loser."

Her histrionics were entertaining. I was glad she'd interrupted my work; I'd been spending all my waking hours coding in an anxious cloud of self-pity, determined to be disciplined about my money and my time, but feeling increasingly beaten down by the city. I asked, "Why don't

154   you just donate this stuff to Goodwill?" and she said a lot of things got lost in the shuffle at Goodwill and never got reused.

She suddenly said she had to go then, but a few nights later, called again, this time about an old rice cooker. We had a good, long conversation that time, making fun of L.A. people and their weird grain-free diets. I told her about a guy at my gym who tried to get me into offal.

After that, we started talking a couple times a week. She had a petulant but enthusiastic manner I liked, and more than anything, it was nice to have a girl who wanted to talk to me. She said she was an urban environmental activist. She grew herbs on her windowsill and biked to the farmers market. She thrifted her clothes. For money, she worked at a chain yoga studio in Santa Monica. She wasn't an instructor; she just checked people in and out. She complained that the studio kept cutting her hours because of work-exchangers—people who watched the desk for free in exchange for yoga classes. "They act like it's some community-oriented, barter-exchange, alternative currency type thing, but really the owners are just miserly corporate suits. Free classes should be a perk that's just given to the employees, not payment in and of itself."

I agreed. She rambled a lot, obviously tipsy, but her voice was warm and breathy, always like she was letting me in on some secret. As a few weeks went by, she grew prettier in my mind, a little closer to the girl I'd imagined when she'd called the first time. I even suggested getting off the phone and talking over drinks instead. I said I'd come to her. But she declined. She said she was already in her pajamas, plus we lived so far away from each other, she'd be asleep by the time I got to the westside. She said this in a slightly panicked way, which gave me the sense she was ashamed of something. Her drinking maybe. Maybe she was under the illusion that she was keeping that well-masked.

So we just talked on the phone. One night she went on a rant about

how the green movement had been co-opted by greedy MBA grads that
wanted to exploit environmentalists. Then she said, "I bet you have
an MBA," in this coy voice.

I didn't, but I was flattered enough by her comment that I didn't
contradict her. "Don't people need to work to change the system from
the inside?" I asked.

She snorted. "Well, that's a cop-out," she said. Then she sighed.
"Maybe you're right though, about the work. My permaculture teacher
says stop complaining about The Man, whining The Man did this, The
Man did that. My teacher says The Man gets up early in the morning
and works hard all day to get what he wants. Are you doing that?"

"Am I?"

"No, the collective you. Are any of us, who want to change the system."

I thought about this. "These days, I'd say I am. It's probably unhealthy,
but aside from going to the gym, I'm basically at my computer from
when I wake up until I go to sleep." Suddenly I felt exhausted, wrung
out by the all-work-no-pleasure of my startup dreams. I had nothing
yet to show for my labors. I thought, right now, no one here would miss
me if I disappeared. No one except Cellie. "I have no social life," I said.

"I bet you go out to the bars with your friends all the time, and pick
up girls," she said in that teasing voice again.

I was drawn in by how she saw me—as some confident guy on the
up and up, smooth, outgoing. The kind of guy I was intent on becoming.
"I just moved here," I said. "I don't have any friends except you."

I don't know why I said that. It just slipped out. But once it did, I
could tell my words pleased her. She was quiet for a moment. I heard
her take a slurp of her wine.

She asked me what I was working on. I told her I was building a
Groupon-like phone app, except all the deals would be socially progressive
in some way, like for TOMS shoes or Honest Tea. I went on for a while

156 until I realized she was only half-listening, she was thinking about something else. "It's a good idea," she said distractedly.

"What do you like about it?" I said, testing her.

"What?"

"What are you thinking about?"

"This Groupon I bought," she said. I heard her clicking around on her laptop, her phone pressed to her face so her breathing sounded muffled. "Sorry."

"No need to be sorry. I use Groupon all the time. Our app hasn't even launched yet."

"It's for two nights at this spa hotel in Desert Hot Springs. I forgot all about it until now. Shit." She sighed. "It expires this month."

"So use it," I said. "Go tomorrow."

"Well, I don't want to go alone," she said. "And all my friends have, like, regular jobs. This Groupon's only good for Sunday through Thursday." She sighed again. "I've never been to Desert Hot Springs."

"Me neither," I said.

"Oh, so you're—" She paused, then started babbling. "The mineral water is supposed to—fix a lot of things. Make you calmer. Less stressed."

It dawned on me, what she was getting at. "Are you inviting me to go with you?" I asked.

"I hadn't thought about it," she said, her words belied by the apprehensive, eager lilt of her voice. "Are you saying you want to go?"

What did I have to lose? If I went with her, I'd see once and for all if this thing was going to go anywhere. And even if it wasn't, there was a good chance we'd have sex at some point over the three days. At worst, I'd get away from the city for a bit, soak in the pools, relax. I really needed to start having more fun. "Sure," I said, before I could change my mind. "Why let it go to waste?"

She pretended to think about it for a minute. "I mean, we *are* friends, right?" she said, then giggled.

Driving over late Sunday morning, I was tense with anxiety and anticipation. I'd never gone on vacation with a girl before. Mostly I pictured good things, a hot, lazy time in the desert, soaking and lounging and a lot of fucking. But what did I actually know about this girl? A part of me feared she might suddenly yell at me, or start crying, or do some other crazy thing. That had been my experience so far with L.A. women, these sexually aggressive and thin-skinned creatures.

I told myself everything would be fine. This wasn't some Tinder date with a stranger. I'd been talking to Cellie for over a month.

She was standing in front of the gate to her apartment complex when I pulled up. As soon as I spotted her, my mood sunk a little, the reality of her clashing again with my re-idealized image of her. I felt bad about that. In my mind I'd come to picture a lively, teasing girl, bold about her sensual curves. In broad daylight, the real Cellie gave off this inured, acquiescent vibe, like she knew she was a disappointment, everyone she'd met in life had already let her know it. Her posture had an apologetic quality, shoulders slightly hunched, head tilted so her hair hung over her face. She was holding an old duffel bag and a Trader Joe's bag full of snacks. There was a dowdiness to her, though once I got up close, I could see she'd put in some effort; she wore a red halter and a loose white skirt that swept the ground. Her face was made up, a pink shimmer on her lips and cheeks. I was touched.

We hugged awkwardly in greeting. She gave me a big, uncomfortable grin. "Can you believe we're doing this?" she said.

"What do you mean?"

"I'm finally going to Desert Hot Springs."

As soon as we got in the car, she started chattering the way she did when she was nervous, listing the environmental features of the hotel we were going to while readjusting her seat, fiddling with the air vents.

158 Her eyes kept darting away from me. I tried to calm her by agreeing with pretty much everything she said, nodding along and laughing. This worked. We soon relaxed into being together, more like when we were on the phone. I told her about the other guys at the coworking space, how we were friends there but never hung out outside the place, everyone else already had their own lives. She nodded understandingly. "People are so like that in L.A.," she said. She pulled out a jar from her bag, this new Trader Joe's spread she'd bought. "It's insane. It's basically crushed up cookies mixed with peanut butter," she said. She insisted I try some, feeding it to me on round crackers. This felt oddly intimate; a couple times, her fingers touched my lips. She ate a few too, chewing daintily, like she was afraid of getting crumbs in the car. When I said I didn't want anymore, she reluctantly put the snacks away. Once we got on the freeway, she nodded off and napped.

The road was calm, no traffic, the only sounds the whoosh of the road and Cellie's even breathing. Everything was going to be fine, I told myself. Maybe it wasn't going to be some sexy weekend, but it would be a decent time, two friends getting away from the city for a few days, just shooting the breeze and relaxing with each other, laughing. Or maybe we would end up having sex after all, become friends with benefits, some fun without all the fuss. That would be good too.

The hotel was actually more of a bed and breakfast, the clean, modern kind with organic granola and fair trade coffee. The stocky, gray-haired woman who checked us in said the Groupon came with a complimentary bottle of wine. "Red or white?" she asked. "White," Cellie said. The woman got a bottle from the fridge and Cellie immediately tucked it under her arm. We got a small tour of the place, six flat units arranged in a semicircle around the mineral water pools, one warm and one hot. I was disappointed to discover the pools just looked like normal tiled swimming pools; they weren't the undeveloped, rock-bottomed affairs I'd imagined. Our room looked like a page out of an IKEA catalog, complete with plastic gooseneck lamps. The stocky woman showed us the cinnamon-infused water in the mini-fridge and taught us how to work the remote control for the air conditioning, which she discouraged us from using, as the fan was more natural and usually adequate. Then she left.

Cellie and I stood quiet for a moment. The bright yellow bed shone in the sunlit room, waiting to be addressed. I could tell she was attracted to me at some level, but I didn't know how exactly it would play out. She skipped to the bed and turned down a corner. "Look, organic sheets," she said. Then she went to the kitchen area and started rummaging.

"What are you looking for?"

"A corkscrew. We can drink while we soak in the pools."

"Now?"

"We're on vacation."

"What about lunch?"

"We still have the snacks."

We sat at the white plastic table. Cellie alternated bites of banana bread with small sips of wine. I ate chips with hummus, and little mandarins. We didn't talk much over our little meal; Cellie seemed entirely focused on her food. After the fifth mandarin I started drinking the glass she'd poured me. It was already warm. Cellie kept the bottle at the table, for easy access. Once she finished her glass she abruptly poured herself a second, like if she did it quickly I wouldn't notice. I didn't drink much those days, and with the heat, the first few sips of wine hit me immediately. When Cellie went to the bathroom I lay down on the bed. I felt my body sink down, anesthetized.

"I think I need a nap," I said when she came out.

"Okay," she said. "I'll be in the pool."

I fell asleep immediately. I woke up right at sunset, its orange glowing through the sheer curtains. Cellie was lying next to me, feigning sleep. Her hair was damp and her halter clung to her. I watched her braless chest move up and down with her slow breathing.

"Your hair looks good like this," I said.

"My hair?" she said without opening her eyes. "I haven't done anything with it."

"You don't need to."

"Guys say stuff like that, but they don't mean it."

"Stuff like what?"

She sighed, shifting her body slightly towards me.

"Stuff like what?"

"You should drink some water," she said. "The heat dehydrates you, even if you're not sweating. That's why you're tired."

She shifted again, and I stroked her hair. We started kissing. Her skin tasted faintly of chlorine and wine. She was enthusiastic but in a slow, heavy manner, like her desire was coming from a deep, murky place. The desire was there though. She moved heatedly against my hands, pressing in. Once I was inside her she moaned a lot, these long, low moans that hinted at some profound, primal wounding.

Afterwards she turned shy again. She moved away and pulled the blanket over her naked body, despite the heat. "Sorry, they don't have TVs here," she said.

"I don't want to watch TV," I said.

"You would turn it on if there was one."

Her tone had turned cold. After that it got uncomfortable, because she was right. I did want something else to focus on so I wouldn't have to focus on her. If I could have left right then without leaving her stranded and feeling like a total asshole, I would have. I guess a part of me had known it would get this way, even before I'd agreed to go on this trip with her. But the knowing always came after the fact.

We finished the wine in order to fall asleep.

I woke up groggy and bloated the next day. I drank cinnamon water and refilled the pitcher from the sink. I tapped on Cellie's shoulder so we wouldn't miss the brunch. She opened her eyes, then buried her face under the covers. "Don't look at me," she said. She shrouded herself with a sheet in a sort of burka and shuffled into the bathroom. Ten minutes later, she came back out wearing a sundress and eyeliner. "Okay, I'm ready now," she said.

Her weird caginess about her body irritated me. Maybe I should have addressed it, said, "Hey, I've already seen you naked." But I didn't know that she could handle it.

The brunch was better than I'd imagined. Hard-boiled eggs, fresh fruit, tangy yogurt. We were the only people in the dining cabin; the hotel was far from full. The stocky woman came in and made a fresh pot of coffee, then mentioned we could buy ice cream sandwiches for four dollars.

"You're not having one?" Cellie said.

"I'm too full right now. Why, do you want one?"

"I'm not having one if you're not having one," she said testily.

I figured getting the ice cream would help ease the tension. We took them to our room. After I finished mine, I plugged in my phone, which had died overnight. I checked my messages facing the wall.

"I don't text," Cellie said, licking her fingers.

"Why? Are you charged per text?" I asked.

"No, I'm against it from a moral standpoint. It's dehumanizing."

That's how it was for the rest of the day, her acting passive-aggressive and caustic, but in an injured way, like I'd mistreated her and needed to make up for it. I did hold myself responsible to some extent. I'd known she had problems before I'd agreed to the trip. Why else would she drink so much? All morning I spent a lot of mental energy finding ways to

162 mellow her out. I gave her lots of compliments about her sundress, the snacks she'd picked, her environmental ideals. Her mood would slowly ease into something more pliable, then suddenly I'd hit a hard edge again.

Around noon I decided it would be easier if we just started drinking. We drove to a Ralph's and I sprang for the six bottles ten percent off deal, which pleased her. So we wouldn't have to get in the car again later, we drove another two miles to a Mexican restaurant to get burritos to go. Cellie said it was supposed to be the best in the area according to Yelp, but the big, dank interior was empty, save for two teenage waitresses. Desert Hot Springs was a rather sorry place, a tourist town that no longer drew tourists, decayed with slow-dying resorts.

Back at the hotel, we got into the small, shallow pool with glasses of wine. Cellie wore a black tankini; she didn't take her cover-up sarong off until she was already in the water, up to her waist. After a couple glasses, she loosened up. She sidled up to me and I put my arm around her. We made out intensely for a long time, the heat of the water and wine combining to create a hazy, haloed feel to her skin, my skin, the air softly caressing us. Eventually we went back to the room, the bed. She was even more passive this time. I enjoyed it, moving her the way I wanted. I liked the visceral way she moaned.

"I feel really dizzy," she said afterward. "I can't feel my legs."

"You can't feel your legs?"

"It's okay, it happens sometimes, with Valium."

"You took Valium? When? Why?"

She saw my look of alarm, and laughed drowsily. "To relax." She turned her eyes to stare up at the ceiling. "It's normal," she said. "I have a prescription. I used to get these panic attacks."

I sat up, and my head spun too. At the pool Cellie had kept topping off our glasses, so I wasn't sure how much either of us had drunk. A lot, for me. I got up and got the pitcher of water, then propped her up to drink it. She obeyed, suddenly docile. Then she lay back and closed 163 her eyes. She seemed to fall asleep, breathing shallowly at first, then more deeply. I drank some water too.

I watched her sleep for a while. I couldn't imagine myself ever getting into the habit of drinking every day like she did, but I could understand on a theoretical level the appeal of it, wanting to stay in that blur.

I paced around, wishing there was a TV. I lifted the curtain to look out at the pool. There were two women there, middle-aged, one fat, one thin. The fat one turned to see me, then both of them floated a little in the other direction, like they were getting away from a peeper. I turned the air conditioner on full blast. The sudden cool air made me feel like I'd finally crossed some sort of finish line, after going through a long and arduous trial.

I checked on Cellie. Her breathing was really slow now, slow enough that I put my finger under her nose to check for an exhale. I touched my hand to her forehead; it was warm and a bit clammy. I tapped her shoulder like I had that morning, but she didn't wake up. At this I shook her shoulder, and she simpered a little, without opening her eyes. When I stopped she went back to her slow breathing.

After a while I lifted the sheet off her body, first her chest, then the rest of her. She didn't protest. I touched her breasts, tentatively, then with more force, until I was pressing on them pretty hard. There was no reaction. I tickled her armpits. I patted her public hair like I would a small pet. I wedged a hand between her legs. It was sweaty and slick; the room was a sauna. I pulled it back out, smelled it. I studied her face for signs of wakefulness, but if she was faking sleep this time, she was doing it well. The breathing continued, slow and rhythmic. Otherwise her body looked dead to the world.

She looked relaxed and content. Her lips were turned up in a slight smile. Her nipples were soft. I thought, she doesn't even need me here. She's having a better time all by herself.

I pulled the sheet back over her.

I went outside and walked circles around the pool. I looked at the stars, perfectly beautiful and perfectly boring. I thought about what rating I would give this place on Groupon, out of five stars. Five, I decided. I'd gotten about what I had expected, I really had nothing to complain about. It wasn't what I would have considered an ideal vacation, but it gave me an odd presentiment about the future—that something like this was about what I could reasonably expect from vacations, from women, from life. The knowledge was disappointing, and also calming. My hopes were diminished, but I'd learned something, and I could handle what was coming.

Back in the stuffy bed, it took me a long time to fall asleep.

She woke up before me the next morning, in a groggy but cheerier mood. We drove back, an easy, friendly two hours, like nothing had happened. When I dropped her off I handed her the four remaining bottles of wine, and she took them gleefully.

We never talked or saw each other again. Life went back to normal. The app launched, failed, and I found a job as a medical coder for a billing company in downtown L.A. ✄

Siel Ju is the author of the novel-in-stories Cake Time, *which won the 2015 Red Hen Press Fiction Award, as well as two poetry chapbooks. Her stories and poems have appeared in* ZYZZYVA, The Missouri Review, *and* Denver Quarterly.

SHOW LOVE TO POLAR BEARS AND EARN 1,000 POINTS

GENEVIEVE KAPLAN

The difference between you and everybody else, or one and everyone

else, is maybe very slight. Everyone knows what a cat is; everyone knows

what a child is, everyone knows what a prank is, everyone knows a rose. Within this

almost formulaic impression of the softened everyday, I had

a misunderstanding with myself. What was seen, and what was touched,

and which items meant something different when set by the sea. What, from the island,

was given an advantage? What about ants? I want for the cups, the plates, to last,

to outlast me.

Genevieve Kaplan is the author of In the ice house *(Red Hen Press), winner of the A Room of Her Own Foundation's poetry publication prize, and most recently,* (aviary) *(Veliz Books), as well as three chapbooks. She edits the Toad Press International chapbook series.*

MI VIDA LIBRE

HENRY LARA

"I was eight when I fell in love with Lucha Libre back in Jalisco, Mexico. My favorite wrestler was Ramon 'Ray' Mejia. He was very acrobatic. I also liked El Rayo de Jalisco. I used to go watch them at the local arena. My aunt sold tacos there and always snuck me in. I was a happy chamaco. I remember them flying in slow motion. Era una bellesa. In '74 my wife and I moved to L.A. to better our lives. The following year I heard a commercial on a Spanish radio station. They were looking for luchadores. I immediately called. They asked me how big I was. I told them I was a big guy. When they saw me, they immediately took me in. After three years of training, I made my debut in '78 at a dance hall on Main and 25th St. A good friend billed me as Doctor Muerte. I was living a dream. I became a tag team wrestler and started slamming in churches, dance halls, and school gyms. After a few years, I was put on cards at the Olympic Auditorium. To have matches in a venue where many greats fought felt unreal. I was proud to get my ass beat there. I began traveling and had many matches in cities such as Hermosillo, Ensenada, Tijuana, and Bakersfield. I was paid an average of $125 per match. Sometimes all they provided was room and board, but I did it for the love of it, never for the money. I rubbed shoulders with greats such as Mil Mascaras and Rey Misterio Sr. I fought in over two thousand matches including fifteen Royal Rumbles winning a little over half of my matches. I became the CLLP (Club Latino de Luchadores Profesionales) tag team champ in '83. In '90 I broke my pelvic area, my knee, and messed up my neck. It was ugly. Pero soy terco. After a year of rehab, I was back at it again. My wife and I began having issues due to my passion to wrestle. Luckily, she hung in there and became my biggest supporter. In 2006 I was unmasked. My head was sliced, and I began to cry. My daughter was next to me. It was dramatic. It's a big deal when you get unmasked. It was basically the end for me. In 2012 I was honored by both the FMLL (Fuerza Mexicana de Lucha Libre) and CLLP for my contributions to Lucha Libre Mexicana. Todavia puedo! Come, I'll show you."

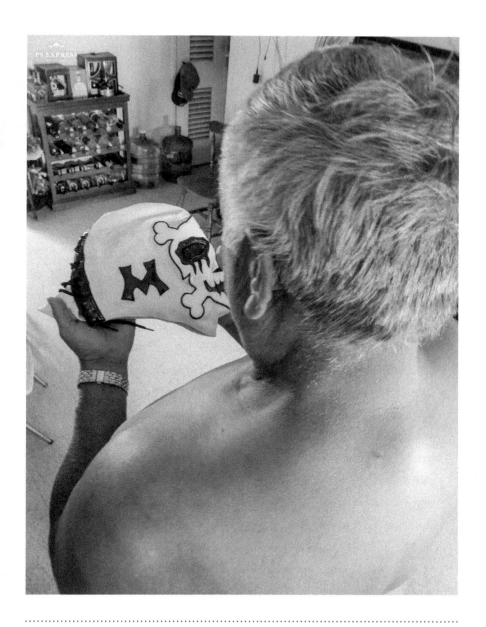

Lorenzo Sierra works part-time delivering building materials throughout L.A. At sixty-nine, he can still somersault.
(10/28/19)

THIS IS GOING TO HURT

PERRY JANES

Observation: Children, before their more fully developed adolescent stages, can be incredibly difficult to see through, the way a body of water—when murky and churned by wind—can be impossible to tell the depth of without simply diving in.

The subject of children comes up while Dwayne and I row a crate of Kiwi birds across Michigan's Lake St. Clair at two in the morning. I watch Dwayne angle each oar before dipping it in the water, careful to make as little noise as possible, and I marvel, again, at how his gawky arms can sustain the motion hour after hour. The teak wood boat is wide enough for twelve passengers, no light vessel, and the last two aisles are taken up by metal crates complete with ventilation shafts for oxygen. I don't subscribe to gender roles but I'm happy to let Dwayne shoulder the load just now.

"I'm only saying." Dwayne has a baritone voice that reminds me of old Frank Sinatra tunes. Even his whisper carries across the open water. To counteract this effect, he's tied a bandana around his face, a brown paisley thing that only makes him look like more of a criminal. "What if these weren't Kiwis?"

"So what if they weren't?" I say.

"You remember Jason?"

I nod.

"Jason got a tiger a few months back."

"A tiger."

"That's right. A Bengal, from the southern tip of India. Wouldn't you be concerned, then? I mean, how old is that kid you hired, huh? Twelve? Thirteen?"

I concede: Dwayne has a point, here. I had recently hired an underage sentry to help keep lookout back on shore. After all, who suspects a twelve-year-old of international animal trafficking? The truth is I normally avoid children, but not all encounters require our consent. Two months back I'd nearly lost a crated capybara from the flatbed of our hardtop pickup in a crowded parking lot and thought I'd gone unseen until a twelve-year-old girl sporting afro-puffs approached the passenger side door with a sly smile on her face.

I needed to keep her quiet. She didn't want a bribe. She wanted to come on board. Her name is Gabby. Despite my initial skepticism, she's proven to have a real flair for the job. In only a few short weeks, she has become an invaluable asset. Dwayne likes to joke that she's my duckling, imitating my each and every move. I prefer to think of her as an apprentice. My Oliver Twist, my Pied Pipee.

At the ship's prow, a fish flips into the air, its splash knocking spray against my teeth. I turn, spit. I eye the metal crates. Through the nearest cage's aperture, a slender beak pokes into the open air.

"It's no tiger," I say.

I didn't start illegally smuggling animals into the States until Rhode Island was sinking underwater. By that point half the population of Bangladesh, Chad, Indonesia, and The Netherlands had been assigned refugee status by the UN, the rest of the known world either opening its borders in support or building walls to keep them out. In all the crisis and confusion, no one seemed to think about the animals. It started with zoos, handlers smuggling creatures left for dead into the

170   backs of tow trucks or passenger vans. But there were others, pseudo-conservationists trapping and hauling wildlife by the truckload out of distressed coastal zones. Suddenly, there was nothing more fashionable to the wealthy or elite than using their spare garage as a makeshift habitat for orphaned beasts. I sensed a profit to be made. And—I flatter myself—a difference.

Observation: When Dwayne has a bone to pick, but wants to avoid real conflict, he glances off the subject like a light off water. I know this talk of responsibility to our youth is just Dwayne's way of bringing up children. Again. Because he wants them. And I don't.

I watch him chew his lip, warming up for round two.

"Let's just get these birds to shore before they freeze," I say.

*   *   *

Smuggling animals started off easy but quickly became a good deal more complicated than either Dwayne or I anticipated. For instance: our former colleagues—a husband-and-wife duo—had been stopped at the Canadian border several months back, where a K-9 unit tasked with sniffing out cocaine turned up, instead, a box filled with African land snails each the size of a wrestler's fist. Whipped to a frenzy by the unfamiliar creatures, the dog in question left our female colleague with bite-mark souvenirs along her arms and legs. When her husband went to intervene, border patrol put two bullets in his lower intestine.

Worse, though, are the drones. National Security recently mobilized a fleet of two-thousand-plus, complete with infrared sensors that can distinguish between a human's thermal readout and an animal's. Now, we keep each cage stacked with packages of ice—to mask the creature's heat signature—but the truth is all we can do is pray.

I've explained all this to Gabby a dozen times. The risks, that is. Death, imprisonment, etcetera. Nothing will deter her.

Back on shore, Gabby waits near the water's edge. She tucks behind an oak tree, poking her head occasionally toward the road, such that I can only make out her silhouette by the tufts of hair bobbing above her ears. When we make landfall, she nods to give the all clear.

After loading our crates inside the truck, we wind around Detroit's backstreets to avoid unsolicited attention. In Dwayne's rearview mirror, I watch while Gabby rides in the flatbed cooing to our stolen Kiwis. She wears a violet-colored hoodie at least two sizes too large with cigarette burns around the wrists and a pair of flats that remind me of ballet slippers. In the corner of the mirror I catch my own reflection staring back: hair tied in a threadbare shawl, utility jacket adding bulk to my narrow shoulders.

When we round the corner toward our condo, I peer at the clouds overhead. In Detroit, particulate ash blown into the air means even a drone's faint ON light refracts like a lens flare in the sky, giving away its position. Above, I'm comforted to see only a millstone stretch of dark.

Once parked, Gabby hops from the truck to keep lookout on the street while Dwayne and I heave our metal crates inside the freight elevator. Our building, which used to be a car factory before being rebranded as luxury lofts and promptly abandoned by its developer, offers all the amenities of any industrial warehouse without the pesky oversight. Once we have the elevator loaded, I whistle. Gabby joins us in the compartment and shuts the loading bay's grillwork door.

Observation: Living in Detroit is a little like occupying a virtual reality that every person plugs into differently. Penthouse suites abutting refugee camps. Rehabbed warehouses concealing smuggled rations. The fact is, when disaster struck, Detroit became the perfect oasis. Perpetually in decline, perpetually reinventing. There was space here, and infrastructure to spare. To the rest of the country, we had already endured our own apocalypse. If we could do it, couldn't they?

172 Dwayne and I have long hated these people. As Dwayne likes to say: With opportunity comes opportunists. We prefer not to turn this examination back upon ourselves.

When we arrive at the thirteenth floor—bad omens be damned—Gabby wrinkles her nose at the threshold. "Did something take a shit in here?"

"Lots of somethings, probably," I say.

Together, Dwayne and I occupy the top floor. Because the building's developer had turned tail before finishing construction, there is only one wall in our unit, a thick plaster partition running down its middle. On either side, concrete pillars slope out of the floor in trunk-like shapes before fanning into the ceiling's canopy of tile.

After stowing our crates in a far corner of the room, I go to our kitchen and pull a pot of cold grains from the fridge. When I hand a bowl to Gabby and Dwayne, they consider the murky soup before settling in to eat. Ensconced in our silence, I watch Gabby wolf the food with gusto. Flecks of tomato water dot the sleeves of her hoodie. I wonder, not for the first time, where she comes from. It's a question I've never bothered to ask.

Before we've finished, Dwayne's cell phone breaks the silence with a ping.

"Shit," he says. "The buyer wants to move our meeting up. Tomorrow afternoon."

"So?"

"I have a shift."

To legitimize our income, Dwayne and I each work part-time day jobs: Dwayne as a stock boy at Army Supplies General where he receives a discount on basic gear, me as a ticket-taker at the bus stop perpetually swarmed with new hopefuls arriving in search of salvation. Neither of us likes our respective jobs, but neither of us wants to lose them.

"I'll go," I say. When we first began smuggling, we decided Dwayne **173** would be the front man for our little outfit. I would be the administrator, coordinating payments and managing accounts. Every so often, though, we're forced to reverse roles.

"Bring Gabby," he says, which means one of two things: he doesn't trust our buyer, or he hopes proximity to Gabby will overwhelm my hormonal system with maternal instincts.

I hesitate. Dwayne stares, unwilling to take no for an answer.

I relent. "How about it, Gabby?"

She shrugs. "Is it cool if I crash here tonight?"

"Don't you have someone waiting on you?" I ask.

Gabby breathes a cloud on the window, draws a penis with her thumb. "So?"

I look to Dwayne, who shrugs.

Without a proper bed to speak of, Dwayne stacks his collection of wetsuits on the floor—artifacts from his survivalist collection, should the floods ever reach us in Detroit—to form a makeshift mattress. I unroll a sleeping bag over top.

"Sweet dreams," I say.

"Right." Gabby stretches, not bothering to conceal a smirk.

On the other side of the room's divide, I climb into bed with Dwayne. He hooks an arm around my ribs and scoots me across the mattress.

"You okay?" he asks.

"I'm not sure I like her staying here," I say. "What if someone starts asking questions?"

"Maybe she needs our help."

"I'm just being careful."

Behind me, I can hear Dwayne smile, that faint pop as his lips un-suction at the corners. "We make a good team, you and me. Good cop, bad cop."

"You calling me the bad cop?"

Observation: When Dwayne wants me to suck his dick, he runs his fingers through the slats on my neck's vertebrae. Tracing his finger's path in my mind, I imagine a skier from way overhead, alone on a mountainside, slaloming between obstacles. This gesture is so distinctive that, without asking, I know exactly what he wants.

In this instance I don't give it to him.

Instead, I barrel roll in bed and kiss him so hard I can feel his teeth pressing on the inside of his lips. I desire Dwayne most when I want to shut him up. When he pokes at my pet peeves, or lapses into one of his sentimental rants, I pull the lever of his silence with a simple kiss or touch. So what if it's a power thing? Dwayne sans voice is a different man altogether: confident, instinctive. On his worst nights, he opines about the pull of male desire. He even goes so far as to compare it to the moon, the way it pulls the tides of impulse with unseen gravitational forces, much like a woman's ovulation—and here I typically stop him, because there's only so much bullshit any one woman can endure.

We get down to work quietly. Discretion is new for us, having only the occasional caged animal to listen in on our lovemaking. The wall separating our room from Gabby's is thick, floor-to-ceiling, but we've never tested it for soundproofing. To ease things along, I reach down to touch myself. Dwayne doesn't like it when I do this. He says it makes him feel excluded from the enacting of my pleasure. I don't like it when he speaks like a professor. I tell him it makes me feel like I'm studying for a test. It's difficult for us to orgasm at the same time, but Dwayne remains thoughtful, attentive even, dutifully following my cues until I feel the quake in my thighs.

Once I finish, Dwayne powers up, fast in-outs that remind me how differently our bodies function. I lie underneath him and admire the way his head melts into the dark of our ceiling. I often do my best thinking at times like this.

Observation: In feature films across the decades, mothers are portrayed as altruistic henchmen willing to self-immolate at the altar of their children. In the rare instance they appear otherwise, they play either (A) bipolar victims of their own fragility or (B) latent psychopaths threatening to break.

Observation: Dwayne is terrified of burning to death. Every lighter in our disaster kit comes with a two-step safety mechanism. He's banished matches from the condo. Unlike Dwayne, I live in abject fear of drowning. Our nighttime boat rides terrify me.

Observation: There is a photo of The Great Rhode Island Flood made popular by newspapers and online message boards. The carefully cropped snapshot shows a mother standing three steps behind— presumably—her infant child. The young boy toddles on the lawn of a New England bungalow as a crash of water sluices down Newport's cobblestone walkways, lifting brickwork from the road. From the frame's edge, his mother lunges forward as though to shield him from harm, to lift him toward shelter, and I sometimes wonder: what hope does she have, really? Does she believe she can buoy her child to safety while the tide crushes her to bits? Would she not be better served leaping for high ground? Grabbing the shingles with both fists and biting on the gutter, just in case? If it were me, and my child, the solution seems clear: jump, grasp, chomp.

Dwayne finishes with a final grunt. Outside, the whip-poor-wills squatting in our gutters chirrup in response.

✻   ✻   ✻

When we first started out, I thought we were doing a good thing.

It was August, late afternoon. Dwayne and I had just arrived in Grosse Pointe outside one of those giant gated mansions that remind me of old Fitzgerald novels. We had an Arctic Fox penned in a plastic dog crate that used to belong to Dwayne's parents, and I could hear the creature whine as we drove along the gravel drive. Outside, a private security guard waved us toward a six-door garage at the back of the estate where a man in camouflaged overalls so pristine I knew they had never seen a day of work waited in the shade.

The transaction was quick: a pre-paid money card we scanned for tracking devices using a hacked app on Dwayne's cell phone. When we handed over the crate, the buyer rolled his garage door halfway open and wordlessly disappeared beneath.

We stood there, waiting. The garage interior was damp. I could feel the dank air wafting from its open door. And a smell, too: stale with sharp, sour notes that made me clench my jaw to breathe between my teeth.

Eventually, Dwayne and I loaded back inside the car to make our exit.

At the estate's locked gate, the guard waited with his hands clasped behind his back. He did this in a way that made me wonder if he had a gun tucked in his waistband. As we rolled to a stop, Dwayne hand-cranked the driver side window.

"What's he do with them?" Dwayne asked, point blank.

The guard surveyed us with that particular strain of condescension reserved for servants of the wealthy. After a brief pause, he pressed a button on the gate and waved us to the road without reply.

❊   ❊   ❊

In the morning, I wake before Dwayne—nothing unusual there—and roll out of bed as quietly as possible. The condo is cold. In the corner, the Kiwis make faint peeping noises that remind me of a malfunctioning fire alarm. When I pad into the kitchen, there's Gabby, wearing a dirty tank top above a pair of neon blue panties with the anti-theft tag still clipped to the butt. Her legs are mossed in a fine down that stands rigid in the chill.

I eye the security clip.

"Yeah?" she says.

I take the hint and shuffle to the coffee machine. When I open the black metal pot, two eyes peer up at me from the container, lids rimmed in purple mascara, blinking.

Observation: The antidepressants I'm prescribed often make me loopy. With the rise of Climate Affective Disorder, the drug market worldwide has more than tripled. I sometimes wonder if the pharmaceutical companies don't sneak "extras" into the highly proprietary mix. When I began to experience these side effects, my therapist suggested I keep a running list of observations. To chart my own reality.

"You okay?" Gabby asks.

Inside the coffee pot, the kitchen light bulbs reflect back at me.

"Let's get a move on," I say.

In many ways—most ways—life in Michigan hasn't changed much. The larger paradigm shifts, the biggies, are more abstract. Twenty-two percent of all animal species on planet Earth have gone extinct in the last ten years. Our summers are hotter, our winters are colder. There's a lot of panic on the news. But practically? Urban centers have become more crowded, basic utilities more expensive. No one, and I mean no one, is taking a family vacation to see the ocean. Most important, the grocery store has smaller inventory, including in their dairy section, where I find myself with Gabby making breakfast selections. I choose a box of sliced cheddar cheese and crackers, on sale. Gabby, on the other hand, seems stumped.

"You could try eenie meenie minie moe," I tell her.

"How old are you?" she asks.

"Thirty-two."

"You ever want kids?"

As she waits for my response, she begins to load the shopping cart with strawberry-swirl yogurt. The squeeze-tube kind. She lowers each tube in slowly, never breaking eye contact, and—intentional or not—it feels like a challenge.

"That's good," I say, sidestepping the subject. "You're going to buy them out of dairy."

"I've got growing bones."

"They can't be growing that fast."

She crosses her arms, causing her thumbs to poke from two particularly large holes in her hoodie's worn cuffs. I don't have a seamstress bone in my body but goddamned if I don't want to sew those stupid holes together.

"If you don't want me around, you can just say," she tells me.

I may have underestimated this girl.

"Get the fucking yogurt."

After making it through checkout, Gabby and I eat in the parking lot. We sit on the asphalt with our backs to the pickup truck's tires. Across the street, I stare at the industrial compound where I'm scheduled to meet our buyer. The landscape is barren in a way that both reassures and worries me.

"Is this what it's like?" Gabby asks.

"What?"

"Being a criminal." She says the word with crisp pronunciation, like an elocution student, and I realize that this is how she thinks of me. Of herself, maybe. A criminal.

"Yes," I say.

She considers this. "It's boring," she says finally.

"So are all jobs." In my lap, crumbs of salted cracker gleam in the sun. Overhead, a sparrow flits back and forth. Spying, I'm sure of it. I collect the crumbs in my palm and sprinkle them near the truck's back bumper. The bird descends on them with gusto.

"Did you know Native Americans used to have a dance to call the rain?" Gabby says, fidgeting.

"I did indeed."

"I've been practicing," she says.

"A rain dance?"

"Sort of, except for animals." She lets this pronouncement hang in the air. "You want to see?"

I check my phone. Thirty minutes until the buyer makes contact. At least.

"Sure," I say.

Gabby leaps to her feet and hurls into motion. She opens her mouth and waddles to-and-fro, like a hippo. She thrusts her neck out and kicks straight-legged at the air—a crane. She locks her arms at her side and undulates in wave-like motions, an eel in the ocean. With each twist of her body she becomes a different kind of creature. Land, sea, air. In this way, there is nowhere she can't escape.

When I was Gabby's age, my mother liked to play a very specific game. Before each kiss goodnight, with each lunch she handed me for school, before unwrapping gifts on Christmas morning, she would say: "This is going to hurt." Over and over. It was her favorite inside joke. "This is going to hurt," she'd say, and hug me. "This is going to hurt," as she served us ice cream sundaes. When, later, a friend of my father's arrived to babysit one Saturday evening, his hand on my shoulder as my parents headed for the car, his fingers playing at the collar of my dinosaur patterned pajamas, working a determined circle beneath the seam, around my nape, she said, again: "This is going to hurt." Eventually, this became a guessing game, of sorts. Would it, or wouldn't it? In this way, I learned not to trust a word my mother spoke.

Today, I'm the one my mother isn't certain she can trust.

My parents know what I do for work but typically refuse to mention it, avoidance being my family's greatest power. They live in Wyoming somewhere, now. I've never been. Once the floods began in earnest, they packed up their suburban Tudor in Bloomfield Hills and hightailed it to the very center of the country. I had pointed out to them, before moving, that Michigan is the ideal stronghold for this new world order: lots of unsettled space, the largest domestic supply of fresh water reservoirs, and gun-happy mid-state militias training to protect us from encroachers on our resource bank.

If you ask me, the refugees spooked them away. Detroit, Kalamazoo, Flint, they'd all been inundated with staggering numbers of settlers. When they expressed dissatisfaction with these new communities—immigrants, they called them, refugees, I reminded them—I said: "That thinking's for the dinosaurs."

"Well that's exactly the way we're headed," they replied.

Observation: Gabby has parents. I know because on the rare occasion they come up, she refers to them in present tense. My mom is a cunt or my dad doesn't need to know my every move.

In the parking lot, Gabby looks like a drawing from a sketchbook. A cartoon of some kind. Humongous eyes, broad lips, that purple fucking hoodie. When she finishes her final dance, as a penguin with stiff arms flapping near her hips, she collapses on the asphalt.

"Wouldn't that be cool?" she says.

"Wouldn't what be cool?"

"Being able to call any animal you want across the world? Right to you?" She sucks wind, catching her breath. "Think of how many we could sell."

And here I'd been thinking Gabby's dance was a form of childish make-believe. A fantasy reflection of some utopian animal kingdom.

Criminal indeed.

"What are your parents like?" I ask.

The question seems to catch her off-guard. "Why?"

I shrug, not wanting to push her on the subject. "Just wondering who taught you how to dance—maybe I can get some lessons."

"I'll teach you," she says, as a faint blush reddens the corners of her lips. "You don't need them."

When she finishes the last few drops of yogurt, she tosses the messy foil down a nearby sewage drain. She yawns. One by one she sticks her fingers in her mouth to lick them clean.

Observation: Childhood is the loneliest place on earth.

✻　✻　✻

At one o'clock, I get a text from an unknown number.

is this menagerie

I pause at the code name. Really? I write back:

affirmative

A moment passes before I receive, simply:

;-)

Another moment while I ponder this bizarre response. And then, as though this were all a matter of course, the buyer writes:

water tower

off grand

eight minutes

I drive the truck around the block, where I turn down a narrow shipping alley. Posted bills line the corridor. NO SLEEPING. NO TENTS. TRESPASSERS WILL BE PROSECUTED. When we emerge from the other end of the passage, I park in a small annex between buildings, a weedy courtyard with a miniature water tower leaning in its center.

"Out of the car," I say.

182   *"Please,"* Gabby adds, like I've forgotten my manners. "Where do you want me?"

When people assume that I'm a mother, they become more receptive to negotiating. Gabby seems to understand this without my needing to explain it.

"Over there." I point to a nearby wall, far enough to be just out of earshot.

"And I should do what?"

"I don't know. Play a game or something."

Gabby plucks at the two puffs of hair tied atop her head as though to say, "whatever." She takes her position twelve paces away, picks up a rock, gives me a fake smile, and pretends to juggle.

Exactly thirty seconds later, a burgundy Honda minivan emerges from the alley. Not what I expected. Most buyers come in one of two iterations: wealthy clientele flaunting their luxuries—a Porsche, typically, despite the Midwestern winters that are only getting worse—or some less savory family member used as a surrogate to complete the transaction, some rural cousin driving his mud-stained all-wheel-drive whose life spent hunting white-tailed deer has inured him to the suffering of animals.

The car rolls to stop and out steps a man, short, maybe five-foot-six, warm smile dimpling his cheeks, a literal bounce in his step. I peg him as the paternal type, overindulgent, talked into buying his daughters some exotic pet to prove that daddy cares.

"Morning," he says. Even in the dim-lit annex I can see his teeth are a dark yellow shade with stripes of residue blooming near the gum line.

"Morning," I say.

He puts his hands in his pockets and rocks on the balls of his feet, surveying me, Gabby, the truck—everything. I take his hesitance for inexperience.

"If you'd like, you can see the birds before wiring me the money."

He chews his tongue. There are those teeth again. "I'm afraid I've got some bad news."

183

"Uh-huh."

"I'm not going to be able to complete our purchase."

I stare at him, processing. "You mean you don't want them?" I ask.

"We had a second buyer," he says. "We only recently lost his account."

"What does that have to do with our arrangement?"

He holds his hands up in a gesture of surrender. "Trickle down economics."

"You could have phoned," I say, flattening my voice.

He shrugs again. "I wanted to see what else you might have to offer."

In the nearby shade, Gabby kicks rocks at the wall. She passes the stone from foot to foot, like a soccer player. She somehow makes this charming.

The man follows my gaze. I can feel his head swivel almost theatrically in her direction, as though he's been waiting all this time and only now allows himself to look.

"What about her," he says.

"What about her?" I ask.

"I can pay seventy-five thousand."

He's a sterile looking man. I'm not sure how else to say that. He has the neatly manicured hair and modest wardrobe of a schoolteacher. His minivan is newly cleaned, with automatic side doors, as suburban-chic as anything I've seen in years. It seems to pop faintly, the same noise of Dwayne smiling in the dark.

I hear myself say, "Seventy-five thousand."

"More," he adds, "if there are others."

Another faint pop from the minivan. I dig a finger in my ears, thinking it's the drugs again, the anti-depressants muddling my senses. But then I squint and see, in the backseat's tinted cab, a girl blowing bubble gum

184 against the window. Ten, maybe. She wears headphones, the antique over-the-head kind made of bulky plastic with felt cushions on the earpiece. I can't hear what she's playing, but her head bops in time to the beat as she stares from the window. An oily haze of fingerprints clouds the glass around her face. When she raises a hand to scratch her nose, she flips me the middle finger—so fast I can't be sure it happened. She stares me right in the eye as she sucks in, blows, and pops a second bubble on the windowpane. Shreds of gum stick to the glass.

"Is she yours?" I ask, even though we both know.

"Think about it," he says.

❋ ❋ ❋

Nobody regulates how much illegally traded animals cost. I keep a ledger of the creatures Dwayne and I have sold. For posterity, yes, but also to track the relative worth of smuggle and sale for each exotic genus. It includes:

Birds of Paradise (2); Origin: Papua New Guinea; $1,200.00/unit.
Sugar Glider (4), Origin: Indonesia; $3,400.00/unit.
Fennec Fox (2), Origin: Morocco; $5,500.00/unit.
Emperor Tamarin Monkey (1), Origin: Peru; $9,600.00/unit.
Hyacinth Macaw (1), Origin: Brazil; $18,000.00/unit.

In some ways, moving humans is easier than moving animals. Machines can only pinpoint the thermal imprint of a creature. To a drone, a bus full of families on their way to the movie theater reads the same as a truck full of teens zip-tied to their car seats.

Seventy-five thousand buys us a shack in the U.P. with its own backyard well and wood splitter. Outright. We wouldn't need to see another starving animal again.

❋ ❋ ❋

THIS IS GOING TO HURT

"So?" Gabby asks.

I drive circles around Interstate 75, doing ten under the speed limit to spare the Kiwis stowed in back any undesired bumps. If Dwayne were here, he'd say I'm just begging to get caught.

"We hit a snag in our deal," I say.

I signal for the exit and bank onto Jefferson Ave through Delray. A scrim of smog veils the sky, almost scenic. Gabby picks her nose, thinking I can't see, as I wind along the riverfront drive before pulling off-road onto a vast stretch of overgrown weeds. Before us, huge electric pylons march into the distance.

When Dwayne and I first began to see each other, this was our equivalent of Lover's Lane. There's something magic about the weeds here. No king devil or razor grass. Only dandelions. In June, when the wildflowers budded yellow, I would lay on my back and let my eyes unfocus, where the weeds began to look like sunflowers. Fields and fields of sunflowers. Today, it is one of the few spaces in Detroit not yet claimed for population overflow.

"So?" Gabby says again.

"You ever look at the stars?" I ask.

I can almost feel Gabby roll her eyes. "What are you talking about?"

"I'm just curious," I say.

"Why?" she asks. "What's so great about the stars?"

I peer through the windshield at the slate gray sky above. "When I was a kid, we thought the stars were our big shot. Once we fucked it all up here, away we'd go."

Gabby sucks air through the gap in her front teeth. "That makes you sound really, really old," she says.

Observation: Dwayne has a theory about scarcity. He does not believe, as the professionals do, that the world is crumbling into abject criminality. A few coastal cities have disappeared, and an abundance of crop fields, but we still have cell phones, grocery markets, live music venues, *Saturday Night Live!* He believes, instead, that the anticipation of scarcity gives us permission to simulate different modes of being. That's how he puts it. Dwayne, a once and always aspiring academic. What he means is—we choose: good guy or bad guy.

"What are you going to do now?" she asks.

"About what?"

Gabby jerks her head toward the flatbed where the Kiwis are their usual quiet selves.

"I haven't decided yet," I say.

Outside, the electric towers begin to move, their metal posts bending from beneath their vines like knees beneath a dress, dancing, and I know it's the drugs again, but I want to see it, and I do, I see it, their lumbering choreography causing wires to snap where they fall into the grass, sparking, a family of rabbits sent leaping for the fence line, I fucking see it, until Gabby coughs, a wet spray of saliva hitting the windshield, and the thrall, if that's what you can call it, breaks.

"Sorry," she says.

I have no idea how to talk to Gabby but I'm surprised to find I want to. As our breath begins to fog the windows, she leans forward to wipe her spit from the dashboard with her sleeves. The security tag still clipped to her underwear comes loose from beneath her jeans and raps against the belt buckle.

"How would you like some new clothes?" I ask her.

She takes a moment to process this proposal before smiling.

"Okay then," I say.

Good guy, bad guy.

Later that night, Dwayne paces in the parking lot.

"What the fuck are we supposed to do with a crate full of Kiwis?"

"I'll take care of it," I say.

He pulls a pack of smokes from his pocket, purely symbolic, and
tugs a cigarette with bite marks on its filter from the carton. He sticks
the pale cylinder between his lips, where it sits, limp. Dwayne refuses
to light up or inhale, but he claims to like the feel of it. Some nights,
he flicks the cigarette with his tongue, disaffected, like Bogie in some
whodunit. Other nights—the bad nights—he chews through the paper
to the tobacco underneath.

Tonight, he chews.

"Is Gabby upstairs?" he asks.

"For now," I say.

"How's she doing?"

I consider the question. "We should send her back."

"To where?"

I shrug. "Her parents, I guess."

Dwayne shakes his head. "We don't know them. I mean, think
about it. A girl shows up, out of nowhere, attaches herself to you like
a barnacle—that's a kid with problems. How do we know they're good
to her?"

"We can call social services," I say.

Dwayne gapes. "Are you fucking nuts? After all she's seen? You
want to, what? Put her in government custody? Oh, and by the way, that
couple I was staying with, you should see the pets they keep around."

All I want in this moment is for Dwayne to agree with me. To send
Gabby away.

"Please," I say.

"Hey," he says, softening. "You're doing great. She looks up to you."

I let Dwayne run his fingers through my hair.

"You're doing great," he says again, "really great," and again I want
to shut him up.

"We're never having children," I tell him.

His lips go thin as a wire. The flesh above his cheekbones seems to literally fall, a cascade of muscle that slackens his face, pronounces the bags beneath his eyes.

"You can be a real bitch sometimes," he says.

The reality is you don't have to be some exotic animal caught between flood lands and rustlers to know what it's like to feel trapped. Here's my mea culpa: I used to want very particular things. I wanted a vintage Dodge Challenger, 1970, white. I wanted a spice rack filled with turmeric and coriander and ras el hanout. I wanted a sex life that bordered on the criminal, with Dwayne and I sneaking into this empty warehouse or that dark alley where I would shove his boxers to his knees and he would bend me next to some dumpster dripping with grease and we would hold our noses for the forty-seven seconds flat it took us each to cum, and the shame of this would be thrilling enough not to be boring. If we had a child, this was how she would be conceived. No rote missionary in the bedroom or faux-romantic tryst on the beach. Dwayne didn't fully understand but he went along. This was our compromise.

That I don't want these things any longer has rightly confused Dwayne's compass. It isn't always easy between us. But there are no more empty warehouses, fewer dark alleys not home to one tent city or another, and no matter how much we might claim to miss that solitude, the truth is neither one of us can face this world alone.

You tell me who the fucking captive is.

❊　❊　❊

Five blocks over, I pull the pickup off the road onto a patch of grass bordering the river. During daylight hours, the park is popular with fishermen hoping to catch their dinner. After dark, the riverfront is strictly off limits. On the dashboard, my police radio murmurs quietly. Even when I step outside the car, open the trunk, and unload the crates, its purr calms me.

Sometimes the corpses of dead animals wash up on shore. When this happens, news stations blanket the airwaves with gruesome snapshots. Rare Snow Leopard / Endangered Reptile / Near-Extinct Breed of Canine Found Drowned in Detroit. They bemoan the wanton death of our rarest and most beautiful creatures. Like these animals wouldn't have drowned in their natural habitat, anyway. To the public's credit, they only assign us smugglers half the blame. They assume the dead animal must have leapt from its constraints while being ferried across the water, or else the boat must have capsized, perhaps drowning everyone on board. Wrong wrong wrong. When an animal doesn't sell, it becomes a liability to its handler. Tell me, how else would you dispose of a Ring-tailed Lemur on the eastside of Detroit?

When I kneel on the grass, the damp dirt soaks my knees.

And—look. I'm careful with them. Of course I am. I open the cage and pull the first Kiwi from its pen. Surprisingly large but lightweight, its feathers slick my palms with perspiration. It wriggles, but only slightly, subdued by weeks of unknown handlers, cross-continental travel, and malnutrition. Beneath its oily down I run my thumb against the creature's fretwork ribs.

When I lower it to the river, it doesn't make a sound. Just plunks below the surface. It goes like this. One by one, down they go. Overhead, in the distance, a drone's green ON light flares across the sky.

When I arrive back at the condo, Dwayne is gone. I know by the silence, his incessant need to leave his radio on low at all hours of the day.

Silhouetted by a jury-rigged floodlight taped to our fridge, Gabby sits in the kitchen. She slumps against the countertop in the ostentatious way children sometimes do, sighing heavily, projecting discontent. She cradles a cup of two-day-old coffee between her palms. When she lifts the mug, I can tell she doesn't drink, just lets the lukewarm sludge bump against her lips.

Gabby sees me in the corner of her eye but keeps staring straight ahead. In that same theatrical way, she asks: "What happened to the birds?"

I'm ready for this question. "We gave them away," I say.

"For free?"

"For free."

From a distance, I notice Gabby wears her brand new dark-rinse jeans, black sneakers, and cotton tee. She still sports her dirty purple hoodie over top.

I slip out of my shoes and shuffle into the kitchen. The concrete floors are cool against my toes.

"Did you and Dwayne have a fight?" she asks.

"We're thinking we might take a break," I say. "From work, I mean."

"Yeah," she says, as though with the weight of understanding.

"Unfortunately, that means you're out of a job for a while." I touch her lightly on both shoulders, like a knight, and with an air of authority intone: "I release you from your duty."

"Free as a bird," she says.

Though I stare into her coffee mug, I can sense every tremor of Gabby's movement. Her outline in the dark apartment. Her sniffling, which she wipes with a shirtsleeve. How shallow and young her breathing sounds.

"I don't want to go home," she says.

I'd been expecting this, too.

"Where do you want to go?" I ask.

She stares into space as though weighing some unseen list of options. "I'm not sure."

"You could stay here for a while," I say. "If you want."

Gabby turns. With the floodlight just behind me, she's forced to squint to look into my eyes.

Observation: I omitted a crucial detail. In the photo I referenced earlier, from The Great Rhode Island Flood, the toddler on the lawn isn't facing the water. He's facing the camera. Behind him, it all rushes forward. But the boy—he knows what's about to happen to him. Maybe he'd seen the waves and just turned as the photograph was taken. Maybe he only sensed it. What I know is the look in his eyes: that something beyond his scope of understanding has just come into view and all he can do is brace.

Observation: I cannot be sure the woman in this photograph is anybody's mother.

And here's the truth: I dream about this photo. I'm standing on the lawn of somebody's condo, not ours, and there's Gabby, staring at me like she knows something is about to happen, something terrible and—if not terrible—large and incomprehensible. Behind her, the flood approaches, but I don't jump for the roof. We stand there regarding each other until, finally, I reach out both my hands for her to take. I'm rooted to the spot but I'm shouting something, like come on or let's go or we can still make it out of here. But she doesn't move, and neither do I. She just sways there, considering my open hands, unsure if she should take them. ✄

Perry Janes is a writer and filmmaker. His work has appeared in The Indiana Review, Tupelo Quarterly, The Michigan Quarterly Review, *and other publications. He lives in Los Angeles.*

JUXTAPOSITION

HENRY LARA

"I'm John Fogelman, born and raised in Little Rock, Arkansas. Came to the area in the early '60s to work the railroads—Union Pacific over in Commerce to be specific. Things have changed and it's just part of the process called life. Either you take it, or you drown. I've forcefully taken it with restrictions. I've never married. I've shacked up but never saw the reason to pull the trigger on myself. Marriage is death, and even though I've never gone through with it, I personally think a piece of you dies. I've seen the picture of my friends lose their color because of it. But who am I to say? Some may become better because of it. All the beautiful whores are gone now and those are the women that gave me company when I needed it. I may have a few kids out there, but no one has claimed me as their father yet. Well, I'll tell you, I arrived to work the railroads, you see. I enjoyed that part of my life. I have a great pension but really, there ain't much to do with it but eat and be human. I was a regular at all these bars, which I don't visit anymore. The Hard Rock Cafe, El Corino, Crabby Joe's, and King Eddy here next to me. I've also probably slept at every hotel and motel in the area. They've now become SROs. They were a big part of my life for many years. I live on memory and although I see a different movement now, I'm blind to the present. I'm just riding it out. I'm not depressed by any means; I just don't see the point sometimes. People overplay life, it's human nature. I'm a lover of great conversations, kind of like what I'm having with you. That's where the steak is. Life gave us each other for that; to ricochet our triumphs and problems back and forth to each other. But the person must be in juxtaposition or north of me or the conversation is null. Electronics have ruined plenty. I stick around the area for the nostalgia part of it and alcohol is an old story. I drink warm milk now. I survived the beatings of life and now I get to see people take theirs. I can talk all day and I wouldn't want to waste your day. You take care now."

John Fogelman has thick white hair and a red moustache. He has lived for more than 35 years in the Historic Core in downtown Los Angeles. (3/21/17)

JELLO SEES

KATHLEEN MACKAY

J ello, late from lunch, opened the fire door to the bay of cubicles, and sped, her nylons whistling down the corridor toward her cube, tracking the path over purple carpet fluffy like Muppet fur to the north corner by the secretaries. She passed co-worker head after co-worker head, faces turned to scribbly white screens. Here was a last break of space in the bank of cubes, a straight row that led to the manager offices along the windowed wall. Supervisor Kathie's door was open, and possibly vacant. Jello loosened her step a little. But no—here was Jello's cube, and pacing before it, Kathie, with her tiny stilettos and insecticide perfume, her arms crossed below her breast, popping her xylitol gum at the hidden secretary and laughing…? She swayed toward Jello, and regarded her, uncrossed her arms and pointed at her.

"Jello, have you—"

Jello shook her bangs a little hoping they'd fall over her eyes more. Seemed that Kathie at times like this looked at Jello like she was sinisterly germy, like she had sneezed into her own hair. Kathie disliked Jello like the moms of her elementary school friends had always disliked Jello. Suspiciously. When Jello told third grade Stephanie that at night she turned into a fairy, Mrs. Ory stuck her head out the minivan in the carpool line and called her a liar.

She considered intriguing diversions, questions she could ask Kathie about a project, anything to not bring up her morning lateness and lunch lateness, the sick kitten. She had once tried to explain tardiness with sick kitten problems and had seemed very ridiculous even though a few women her age, like her friend Rana, always had baby problems that resulted in lateness.

Finally, something cloudy that had been before Kathie dispersed, and objects regained their sharpness, and Jello could now fully observe and hear Kathie and the copy machine behind her, the potted plants, the purple carpet under her genie-ish heels. She heard that she was not being lectured about her late lunch return, but another mistake she had made about a show she had encoded several months ago and forgot…this being even worse than lateness, but still, relieved Jello of the previous terror for a moment.

"It must be like, 2 or 3 A.M. in Portugal, but I will leave a voicemail, and send an email," Jello said.

"Send an email now, and make sure you follow it up with a phone call," Kathie said.

"Yes." A pit, low in her. "I'm sorry."

"That's okay." Kathie studied Jello. Sometimes, walking past her cube, Jello's hands would hover above the keyboard, her head turned to the gray modular wall like she had seen something out a window.

"I just really lost track."

"It happens," Kathie said, her eyes widening, "it's okay." She uncrossed her arms and shrugged her shoulders to show Jello this was true. The girl's eyes looked red, like she was about to cry. Kathie smiled with no teeth and nodded at Jello before walking away.

Jello pouffed into the leather captain's chair and wriggled her mouse to bring her computer to life. She felt sick, the rush of her lunch and cat, now this Kathie guilt and need for absolution. This shifted soon enough reading through her emails. She was of course, better than all this. She was too good, too smart for her cubicle, and the other people in their cubicles, on her floor and all over the world. She scrolled through the laziness and incompetence of everyone, emails passed like trash down a chute waiting for someone at the bottom to deal with, and Jello was somewhere in the middle, lazily forwarding and responding to forwards, trusting somewhere down the line a physical action would result from the slurry of computer words, and she wished she would die tonight—a car accident—at least get injured enough that she wouldn't have to return to this scary and boring gray and purple forever-place. How did she get here?

In the parking garage, Jello had forgotten which level again. She often lost her car when she left work at lunch and moved from her morning spot, and she often left for lunch. If not for kittens, then to shop. Thrifting in North Hollywood, or one of the markdown fashion stores on Ventura Boulevard. Out the windows of the garage, sunset, peach smog slipping into blue. Across the Valley, yellow windows lit in low buildings, tall buildings topped in red plane lights. Garage floor thick with dirty rainbows of oil and exhaust from the cars, their headlights coming around the bend at Jello as she walked, level after level, and depressed the button on the little remote, hoping to hear her car return the sound. She was wrung from the half-day of work versus the quarter-day of work she was accustomed to. For the remaining four-and-a-half hours after lunch, she bent at her cubicle trying to fix her project, drank machine coffee with hazelnut creamer until her tongue browned and her lips cracked. She hadn't slept much because of the kitten. Now walking, her thin ballet flats feeling the grit and stone of the parking garage, almost to her car, she could almost daydream. She was teasing herself, thinking about a man she sort of knew, though tainted from the day, she couldn't quite think of him, either.

They had only met once. Jello had a hyper-physical awareness of

Whitney. He sat beside her at a dinner party and every time he moved his fork to his lips, scratched his chin, clapped his hands together in appreciation of a joke, she had seen all of it, one eye on him throughout the meal. At one point a shift in his position caused the fabric of his shirt to buckle, rendering a sliver of firm belly visible in between buttons, and she wasn't able to speak until the shirt resealed itself. She had been wearing a dress she conjured and found—one like her mother wore in 1989. Burgundy, crossed at the bust in an almost wrap, bell sleeves, a tulip skirt. Her mother would wear it with a cigar amethyst pendant set in silver filigree tree branches. Hot metal and grass smell of her mother's hair set with rollers, White Shoulders powder before she rolled on nude pantyhose, readying for a party with her father, or, if Jello was with them, a Christening, a wedding, Jello sitting on her mother's lap, rolling the amethyst between her fingers. When she was older, during a period of cleansing, she had insisted the dress, which her mother could no longer wear, be given to the Salvation Army. Now, this kept Jello up at night. The replacement dress was almost-good. Whitney had sat close to her in the new dress. When the plates had been cleared, he leaned back in his chair, carelessly draping his arm across her chair back, his fingertips just brushing her shoulders, but to Jello it felt as if he chose her. Tapped her like a sugar maple, he sucked out part of her essence and in turn, filled her with some of his. After the dinner party, home again in her apartment, she realized in the water spots on her bathroom mirror what he could do for her. What together, they could be.

Up another level, this one with purple poles. Jello depressed the remote button, the little red light flickered, and her car horn responded down the row. Yes! She raced to it, good little thing. Stepped around the scraped silver bumper, the taillights flashing as she unlocked it with the remote to the driver's seat. Inside, dark, cozy cabin light, familiar smelling like dust, syrup, cardboard. Happy beeps and bells as she

198 turned the key in the ignition, and then descended the garage, this time in the safety of her car.

If Whitney were to take her to the pier. If he were to suggest they meet in the early afternoon on a spring weekend among the boardwalk crowd. And waiting for him, she would see in the breaks of the waves white horses. She wears an off-shoulder sundress, white linen crackles against her skin. He grabs her in an embrace around her neck, the other arm around her waist. Rakes his lips across the back of her head. This would be the first he has touched her fully. And it lasts only a moment before he releases her and spins away, and rests his back on the splintered wooden railing of the pier. He lifts his gaze to the sun, a white whorl twinned in his sunglasses. She would see he's just shaved, the follicles cut deep, his pores erect, his jawbone a knife. She, like hot pavement, and he, like a glass of water, a snowdrift, an empty porcelain bowl. Hard to look at him directly, and he would know this and like this in her. Unable to not-look any longer, she might step away from him, down the weather-warped planks of the pier.

She would come to the fisherman sitting where wood rail met metal rail. Red sun-browned men, the base of their poles secured to the pier beside their sandaled feet filthy with sunflower seeds and fish guts and flies. If she were to have gone to meet Whitney in the early afternoon, she would not have eaten that day, and in seeing this, guts and seeds, she swoons. She needs some air, away from this … And so she perches on the metal rail sidesaddle, eyes closed, breathing deeply, wind in her face. (Whitney watches from somewhere). But, she tips, she loses her balance on the rail.

Her vision is blue sky when the back of her head hits the water. Down, turned in the sea, her arms and legs tread until her head breaches the waves. Pedaling toward shore, she watches Whitney, his white T-shirt blazing, push through the crowds of the Ferris Wheel and arcade games,

down the wooden steps of the pier. The shore patrol buggy a wailing
blur in the distance, she met Whitney on the beach, linen plastered
against her skin, hair in dripping ringlets, trailing a strand of kelp
wrapped around her ankle. He wouldn't say anything. If anything, he
tilts his head to one side, and grabs her shoulder with one hand, shaking
her slightly, a smile shudders over his lips before he hid it, and steers
her away from the beach, while together they ignored the concern of
the beachcombers.

At his apartment, she unbuckles off her sandals, her feet opossum
grippy on the white marble floors. He watches her undress from the
bedroom doorway, takes her wet things. She lies on his bed, the gray
sheets unstable beneath her. Through the venetian blinds of his bedroom
window she sees the tops of two date palms, black shadow spiders from
the angle of the sun. Window blinds tap against each other in the breeze.
Whitney places a bag of frozen peas beneath her head, cradling her
skull, and he kisses the freckles between her breasts, and tongues her
cunt while the hairs at the nape of her neck freeze.

Red brake lights. Jello's heel slipping over the floormat to catch
the brake and crush the pedal because now she was speeding toward
the line of stopped cars just ahead. Her car lurched to stop, rear tires
skidding. She would surely crash into this blue car just before her. Shit
shit shit so she wrenched the wheel to right to slide onto the shoulder,
her front bumper inches from blue. Sweaty, she pulled her car back in
the highway lines. And then, the realization she was on the arroyo of
the 101 freeway now, the next exit was home.

At the white tooth gate, she pushed the button of the garage opener
clipped to her sun visor. The passenger sun visor had another garage
remote, the one that opened her boyfriend Phillip's garage door. In
the garage, she sat for a minute, tired or fried but zoomy, not sleepy,
content in the dark. She wanted to be home and have the cozy evening

she was preparing, but also something seemed frightening about that, too. Like if she did that—check on the kittens, make a healthy dinner, watch TV, go to bed early and alone—she'd be agreeing to something. She'd be doomed.

Her purse buzzed as she lifted it from the passenger seat onto her hip; Phillip, her mother. Someone she would have to call tonight, or not. Car beeped locked, she stepped across the parking garage, half below ground, half sea level, always smelling like damp clothes. She passed the wall of cement block patterned with starburst, crumbling at the edge, the stars collapsed near the walkway. Outside, blue dusk, sun down, but light enough to still feel like the very last of the day. Parrots screeched like shapeshifters, Jello craned her neck to see from where, to glimpse the flock of green feathers, but saw only faint stars, the moon hidden. Walking past the center courtyard, oxblood-colored stone, overgrown fern and giant scarab skeleton leaves, a graying Christmas cactus, a miniature stone pagoda, and seemingly random landscape lights on shaggy and shadowed hunks of volcanic rock and limestone. Down the path to her apartment door, apartments in a row closed and mysterious to her, the path prehistoric with banana leaf, elephant ears, and lantana she called "butterfly bush." Her neighbor's wind chimes, hollow wood, creaked and knocked as she passed. She unlocked her front door, and flipped the light switch as she stepped into her apartment.

Poe and Silky Boy blinking their eyes sleepily, their pupils shrunk in the new light to diamond slits, stepped across the laminate wood to her. Poe broke into a trot. He was black as a bat, with bat-like ears and black whiskers. He yawned, a shock of pink inside. Silky Boy kept his jungle cat gait, a sashay to her, until Jello collapsed in the doorway, her back against the front door, purse still elbow hooked, and the Siamese narrowed his eyes and ran. She dropped her keys as Poe hopped into her lap, Silky Boy gathering speed and leapt onto her, tackling his brother.

She pet them, murmuring sweet things about their ears, their good nature, their grace. Poe closed his eyes blissfully, his body rumbling, buzzing, she used her forefinger and thumb to stroke his forehead, around his ears, his throat. Silky Boy purred, arched, climbed over the uneven terrain of her lap, pulling loose threads from her skirt, his tail licking her upper arm, until he flopped onto his back and bit above her elbow.

"Ah!"

She jerked her arm, and the kitten fell down the hill of her leg, closer to his brother, and bit his ear. The pair rolled, a blur of cream and black, tails like lashing serpents, ears flat, they rolled off Jello's lap, chasing each other onto her sofa, past all she bought—the catnip mice, the rope and carpet scratching post, the feathers on sticks, the ferret ball.

She sat for a moment, pleased in her space, in how she'd decorated in the same spirit of its '60s ('70s?) construction—the blue-green sofa and fuzzy white rug, sunburst mirror over the whitewood mantle of the un-working fireplace. Dining room with the white square table, an empty green globe vase in its center, the wall of window jalousies—a lovely feature—in the dining room that looked out to the apartment walkway so she hid from her neighbors with sheer white curtains. If someone were to look in, walk up the path past her neighbors, and press their face to her living room window, to the break in curtain by the glass slats of blinds, they might see all this. Thrilling and terrifying to consider. Rarely had another person entered her apartment. Why? She could invite someone. She might, maybe, after kitten season, have her own dinner party. She dug for her phone and stood to check on Seraph in the bathroom.

Kitten season ran from early spring to late fall. March now, Los Angeles was lousy with kittens. Feral mothers dropping litters under parked car wheels, in toolsheds, in basement dugouts, feral mothers imbuing their young with intestinal problems, parasites, or worse, FKS

202   or Fading Kitten Syndrome. Jello had seen it once, personally last week. Not her kitten but while picking up her ration of Royal Canin and extra blankets from the shelter, she saw Judy, a fellow foster mother, wiping tears from her glasses on her sweatshirt, waiting for the vet, the FKS kitten hidden in the depths of the gray plastic carrier she held. Jello didn't want to ask if it were still alive, superstitious. To speak of it would somehow transfer death into her onto her kittens. And so she panicked last night, flooring it, weeping as she drove thirty minutes to the emergency hospital in Tarzana, and stayed until 3 A.M. after she saw the tubing of pink protrusion.

"Ew," Phillip said, as Jello explained the prolapsed rectum.

"She almost *died*," Jello hissed. "If I hadn't been there, who knows what would have happened."

"Well, good, honey." And then, "So I take it we're not having dinner together."

He'd have to manage with the overboiled noodles and sweet jarred pasta sauce, or hot dogs on the George Foreman grill, whatever he made without her, frequently these days. When had she last seen Phillip? Monday. Today was Thursday. Seemed much longer. She felt a slight lift, soothed by not having to cook dinner with him tonight, or watch his TV show, or hear him and see his face and feel his body press into hers for a hug.

"I'm afraid she's not healing."

Jello was on the bathroom floor, against the cold tub, her legs bent into a V, she couldn't stretch them without disturbing the cardboard rectangle of litter plopped with peanut butter poops, the food and water dish, the nest of towels beside the toilet tank. In her lap, Seraph bit the wedge of her palm between her thumb and forefinger, her teeth sunk in as she mightily shook her head, practice to sever the flesh.

"I shouldn't have left her by herself all day. I might have to take off work tomorrow," Jello said. "I'm truly afraid to leave her for even a second. I'll most likely be at the shelter all day Saturday with the vet, and just monitoring her progress all day Sunday."

"I see," he said.

She could picture him in front of his computer, scrolling the news, scratching his dry beard. Rana wasn't at work today due to a flare-up of her rare autoimmune disease (yesterday she had come to work with her lip swollen, hidden by large sunglasses, and when she removed them at Jello's request, she was swollen all over, her jaw and forehead engorged and looked—though Jello didn't say it out loud—Neanderthal), and so Jello hadn't spoken or thought anything nice about Phillip. Rana was happily married to Aaron who worked in Sound, and she and Jello spoke of weekend plans and funny guy-things their partners did. The version of her life with Phillip that she relayed to Rana made Jello like him again, or at least, like being with him, having a boyfriend, and she could often carry that to his place for a while, feeling lovingly until that dispersed with his eyes on the TV, his cold complacency, him saying nothing of interest to her, and his complete disinterest, only comfort in her. Not that she hated him, she just wished the ties of their relationship (how long had it even been. Four years? No, five. God!) would disintegrate completely, and she would wake up in the morning unbound to him, not having to speak or do anything at all to remove him from her life.

"You probably won't be at the shelter all day Saturday—"

"Well—"

"Why don't you check in with me after you're done? I was thinking we haven't been to the westside in a while. It's supposed to be a beautiful weekend. We could go to beach."

"I mean, unlikely. I might need to take Monday off work, too…"

In her kitchen. Lit by the bubble overhead, her reflection flickering in the black glass over the kitchen sink where she worked, separating spinach leaves from the bunch. Through the window, she heard faintly the sound of her neighbor's television. *Dun Dun.* The gavel. Someone was watching *Law & Order*—her show at the studio. She scheduled encodes of dubbed language versions. English replaced by Castilian Spanish, Latin American Spanish, French, Brazilian Portuguese. The episodes always had evocative one-word titles. *Censure. Sanctuary. Breeder.* She rinsed greens, whirled them dry, and let them rest in the plastic basket on the counter while she cranked open a can of chickpeas. Silky Boy stretched up her leg, reaching as far as he could up her calf, his needly Velcro claws caught on her black nylons as he pulled to free himself and stuck behind her knee.

She tried to return to the daydream, the date, but it was different somehow. The pier, Whitney, the same images but without taste, without prickling all over her skull. She considered the images, read them like one of her delivery spreadsheets. Whitney touching her. Jello over the rail. A flash of it—embarrassing. Shameful. She wanted it off her now, away from her. She rinsed the chickpeas, loose skin like condoms pulled off the beads under the stream of water. She rubbed her left eye—it itched. Why the change, the disgust? Phillip. As if he'd sensed her mental pull toward Santa Monica lately. It was, after all, where Whitney lived. Everyone knew that.

She ate dinner on the sofa, Silky Boy and Poe pawing over her crossed legs, and sniffing her plate. She looked at her phone. A week after the dinner party she had messaged Whitney. Casually, normally. She asked about a campsite he had mentioned. A brief flirtatious back-and-forth after that. And then a few days later he sent a link and a semi-related comment that spawned another brief, flirtatious rally. She reread both interactions, eating dinner. She could message again, come up with something related or another question. She could message him late night tonight, and maybe in bed, he would respond. She was good at saying things Whitney—or men like Whitney—would respond to. He didn't bring a girlfriend to the dinner party, though maybe he had a girlfriend. That hardly mattered, he had met Phillip. She had cringed watching them interact in the kitchen while helping clear the table. Like a friend meeting her father, some bumbling, brusque old fogey that everyone must be polite to, and breathed easier once he was out of the room. Thankfully, Jello had to only endure this in childhood, her father gone by the time she was eleven.

Seraph was at the door trying to slip out, and Jello swooped her with one hand, closing the door behind them. In the bathroom mirror, she regarded herself, the kitten at her breast. Her hair a little mussed from the day instead of the stiff blow-dry of the morning, green chiffon blouse untucked from her black skirt. For a moment, she looked like a woman who had lived, not wildly, but with a secret that carried her, a pulse. She winked her left eye unintentionally, and rubbed it with her wrist knuckle.

Now seated back against the tub, she parted the kitten jaws, and squirted 10 ccs of antibiotic down her throat. Freed, Seraph shook her head, her tongue lapping the air, while Jello replaced the dropper inside the brown medicine glass. Jello kissed between her smoky gray ears, a gradient of silver to downy fawn. Her eyes half-closed, she had been purring since Jello picked her up, not stopping even with the medicine. Seraph had a particularly beautiful face—like if Botticelli painted kittens, Jello thought, and that's how she named her. She was good with names. All her kittens were cute, of course, but Seraph was exquisite. It would be difficult to part with her, especially after all they had been through. She should probably just keep Seraph. She'd miss her brothers, but maybe not much. She was more solitary. When Seraph was healthy, she'd try to join the games, but was more often off by herself battling a plastic wrapper, leaping in and out of a paper bag,

206 in the dark of Jello's closet, startled when Jello turned on the light. If Jello could find an adopter to take Poe and Silky Boy—together of course, they were bonded, it would be traumatic to separate them—she could keep Seraph, make sure she healed. Allow her the space and quiet and love that nourished her. Maybe. She had feelings of adoption for past kittens, too. The shelter discouraged this. Most of the foster moms had several grown cats at home, and the shelter didn't want to promote bad habits. Unspeakable, the danger. *Hoarding.* Jello was safe from all that. Her space disturbed only litter-by-litter, sanitized in between, and completely kitten-free by the end of the season. She must. After all, Phillip was allergic to cats.

Her legs cramped, ached when she stood. She was in the habit of taking most the afternoon following lunch to walk down the path that flanked the L.A. River. When she was first at her job years ago, she had wandered the paths between soundstages on the lot, but now she preferred this isolated strip where rarely she came across another person. From her building near Gate 3, along the corridor of cement, along the chain link fence, behind which was a paved inverse trapezoid, sides sloped down to a flat flooded plateau, mossy with green algae, cattails in the narrow trough that ran the channel. She would walk the whole lot this way—landscape of hedges, dogwoods, building dumpsters separating the path from the rest of the lot, though Jello could see the tower of the theme park rollercoaster on the hillside above, the studio buildings changing from Venetian village to midcentury glass and birch to little white Golden Age bungalows. She walked, watching her shadow. Jello could admire herself this way, her shadow, not in mirrors. She could admire herself in window reflections, in pavement best, in motion best, and as she walked, she adjusted her carriage to complement her figure. There had been no time for this today.

Seraph, still purring, winding through Jello's legs. She wouldn't sleep until Jello left, and she must rest, recover. Jello thumbed the switch of the nightlight, pink glow of the seashell making the laminate cool-warm, heavy like marble, casting everything dark but soft pink when she switched off the overhead light. She opened the bathroom door, and Seraph darted through the crack. Jello caught her, kissed her head twice, and shut her back inside the bathroom.

She had unfortunately seen once last glimpse herself in the mirror before the overhead light went off. Jello pulled the blouse over her head walking to her bedroom. Sap green chiffon, cheapy gold-painted plastic buttons, ruffled bib. An ugly shirt she knew was ugly when she bought it, yet somehow convinced herself was Edwardian, ladylike. All her clothes were like this, she could wear them everyday not thinking, and then one time, she'd touch them, hold them up to the light and the dream of them against what they were in material form would come at her, shocking, painful. Betrayed by the blouse, she would hide it in the back of her closet to dispose of later, drop it at the Goodwill and look for something better, something that didn't shatter in the light. In her bedroom, walls she had painted Tiffany blue, glossy laminate faux-wood headboard in Deco half circle crossed and diamonded with silver, she sat on the bed in her bra, immobile for a moment. The lamp on her nightstand was too bright. She tossed the green blouse over the shade, the lamp a beer bottle through the chiffon.

In an old T-shirt, leggings, thick socks, she searched for a cardigan squatting in the closet, hoping the one she wanted had fallen off a hanger. She pulled stray skirts and blouses, dresses heaped in the dusty back corners with no luck. She had noticed Phillip once or twice eye the sagging rod, bowed from weight of her clothes as she dressed in his presence. She would need to clean her closet, yes, get rid of things. Hard unless she hated the item, until she must remove it from her life. The cardigan she wanted was from eighth grade, a Gap splurge she had made shakily with her own money. She settled for another cardigan. Moving to plug her phone in near her bed, she got a call from her mother.

"Well, I moved that armoire—"

"By yourself?"

"Dolores came over. And as soon as we wrestled it, you wouldn't believe."

"What?"

"Black mold. I'm sure I've been coughing and sick because of it. Yuck!"

Now a fight with the landlord. Now, she was sleeping on the foldout couch in the living room. Inadequate repairs and re-repairs. Jello asked why not just sleep in her old bedroom, her teenage bed still covered in its quilts, her desk and drawers painted black and pencil scraped with her name.

"I was until I moved your armoire. Black mold! They said it was the black paint on the wall, but I knew better, I'd seen it before."

"And are they fixing that, too?"

"They better be."

She spoke of the fumes from the paint, the smell of mold still clinging to the bedroom walls as she checked daily, hourly. And there was probably more mold. In the garage. Jello pictured it, stacked with boxes, everything stacked around the covered car body of her father's red Chrysler LeBaron convertible that her mother was sure would sell for lots of money when she found the time to sell it. All things stacked around and on top of the old car. Old science textbooks, encyclopedias from her mother's teaching days before she was married. Old exercise equipment, her father's tools, laundry baskets with broken hairdryers, pink foam curlers, a black leather barber's chair, thin black combs, capless lipsticks, diaper pins, wire drycleaner hangers, marbles, naked Barbies, vacuum parts, a lone sock. Stuff.

"Why not move for a bit, somewhere smaller, somewhere that won't make you sick?"

"Not with Rosie like this."

Jello didn't want to talk about the dog. Golden retriever that once hopped the backyard fence over high weeds and the upturned wheels of Jello's old scooters, ran to the marsh, and returned midnight frosted with ice, ticks in the tub when Jello and her mother bathed her. Now, white on her muzzle, thick-necked, weeping brown eyes, hip dysplasia.

"She's still good when I walk her in the back on her puppet strings, but alone all day. She messes her bed. She's barking as soon as she hears me home from work in the driveway. Dolores says she barks all day." And then, breathing heavily, "I need you to come home and look at her. Tell me what you think we should do."

In the mirror, she tried to see if there was a mascaraed lash turned up and into her tear duct.

"What's wrong, sweetie? Are you sad about Rosie?"

"I've just had a really long day."

"Did you see any stars?"

She did see one, but she couldn't remember his name or the show he was on. But she could have said that, described him and the television show, and it would please her mother. Now that she was retired from teaching and cutting hair again for money at her friend's beauty shop, she liked these stories from Jello. She would tell a lady in the chair, and the lady would possibly know who he was, and they'd both be happy that Jello saw him and could gossip—a story straight from the Hollywood lot.

Jello had come to hate the celebrities. Funhouse faces that looked familiar and disappointing in their ordinariness, but always beautiful, always remarkable for their familiarity. This seemed unfair.

"No."

"Well."

That "no" had come as a snarl, a black curling from her throat. If

210 she could get off the phone without becoming even more unpleasant. She felt tracked, trapped. Cornered somewhere like the garage, flowering with black mold and boxes.

"How close are you to the Santa Monica Pier?"

"What?"

She had been rubbing the corner of her left eye, but stopped, dropped her hand. She barely heard the rest of the story, about the client's daughter's stepdaughter and her gymnastic tournament.

Interrupting her, "Mom, I gotta go."

"Oh. Okay my love. I'm sorry. I didn't get a chance to hear about your bad day."

"I didn't have a bad day—" She stopped, lacing her gym shoes. It would wound her mother if she got off the phone like this, and the next time they spoke in a couple days it would have morphed, soured further. "I love you, Mama, I just haven't been outside all day and I'm feeling a little—"

"Crabby?"

"Yeah. So I'm just going to go on a little walk. To you know, clear my head."

The frosted orb of the foyer's light flickered, and then flickered out as Jello closed the glass doors behind her. Into the empty street, the pavement potholed and rocky, as if torn up from the waffle treads of her gym shoes. Seemed her mother dispersed in those pebbles, still present, but at a safe distance. What had felt so stifling now loosened from her, replaced with a light and brittle feeling. A closeness to her mother that felt safe. She had felt this before.

After her father left, during the time she attempted to renew her credential and needed money, her mother cut and colored hair at home. The laundry room converted to a mini beauty parlor: mirrors, chair, hooded hair dryer, special hose contraption on the sink. In a turquoise dress with shoulder pads, blush high on her cheeks, laughing, racing **211** around. She liked coloring best—mixing chemicals, composing formulas. After school, Jello sat under the helmet dryer, windstorm in her ears, and watched her mother in the mirror, silver scissors flashing, her mother a mime. For a moment, she threw back her head in silent laughter, the scissors motionless, her mouth gaped to show silver fillings, wet hair pulled halfway through the comb, forgotten for a moment, her mother and the lady in the barber's chair, laughing, noiseless, while Jello looked on, a hot tornado on her head.

Jello walked past the white bow of her split-level complex, pipe railings and round windows, her complex an ocean liner docking up the hill. At the top, the road leveled and curved into a circular street with Mediterranean houses and high white walls and thick landscaping obscuring the surrounding city from view. She took the left fork. Dark blue now, a night chill coming from the left, the Pacific Rim of the circle neighborhood. Low turrets with little stained glass shields. She walked, feeling the neighborhood was a citadel, heard the whisper of water from fountained courtyards behind garden walls. Porch lights on yellow stucco, white stucco, blue.

An image began to coalesce, of Whitney in a house here. She watched him walk barefoot over terracotta kitchen with a water glass in a shirt his mother bought him, out a French door onto a red stone patio draped in angel's trumpet. Hadn't he mentioned that he grew up along Mulholland Drive in a house like this? Looking down onto the spill of night city light and in the day, all smog and spiked palm trees, cars on the roads that stretched all the way to the sea on clear days? Where was he now? A Santa Monica apartment, a place to breathe before something better.

She stopped before her favorite house, her cardigan pulled around her, palms cupping the old leather elbow patches. Silent Movie house. A gate before her of white wrought iron, iced curlicues and spires secured with a chain and a padlock painted white. Behind the gate, concrete steps a pair of plaster lions guarded the stone terrace, a tri-columned archway, a shadowed recessed porch. Old Spanish, maybe. Sometimes there was a floodlight from the upper level, but all dark tonight. In the daylight, it was easier to see the two worry lines below terracotta roof tiles curled like tongues, gray fissures in the cream, the soot beneath the lintels.

There were other houses nicer than this in the neighborhood, newer or better kept, but this one felt like hers. Imagine it, crumbling and grand. Stepping out from the colonnade with her coffee in the morning as a roof tile falls and splits on the concrete inches from her feet. Yes. She wanted this one. A housewarming party. He laughs, he tells the story to friend after friend. *Out of the whole neighborhood, she only wanted this one.*

She knew what she would wear to a party at this house. Vulgar black satin. A dress to fall past her toes, backless, exposing her spine, her bird wing shoulder blades. A headdress, black appliqué crawling across her cheekbone like a spider.

There are lanterns in the acacia trees. She drinks oil slick liquor from a vessel shaped like a baby's head. She wears her black satin dress. There are women with rainbow trout sequined dresses. There are women in dresses like leaf skeletons. There are women in dresses of nothing but gold beads, they spell out the constellations.

At her door, Jello fingered her keys. She was thinking still, of that Silent Movie house, how she would look and be in that space, how the new glamorous people in her life would reflect a truer version of herself, and how Whitney, even though he saw glimpses now, would see her in full splendor. She thought the crash came from the party for a moment. A dropped glass of champagne. No—a real, heavy crash she realized now fumbling with the door, the noise materially entered her apartment.

Inside now—she had left the light on for the kittens. Poe and Silky Boy beside her white square Formica dining table, crouched, tails wobbly, looking at her curiously. On the floor before them—a whole jug of olive oil that she had left on the kitchen ledge, smashed onto the hardwood.

"Bad! Bad!"

Slamming the door behind her, she raced to the spill. Silky Boy dipped his head down, nose twitching to smell the oil, whisker tips wicking droplets of gold.

"Back!"

She pushed Silky Boy away, his little body easy to fling, and then reached over the kitchen counter for paper towels. When she turned back, Poe jerked his wet black paw up from the oil and shook, dark spots shot across the floor.

"Damnit!"

She dropped the roll, and swooped both kittens, tossed them inside her bedroom and slammed the door—regretful, as she walked away, and prayed for no glass in their paws.

On her hands and knees, almost a whole roll of paper towel to get the glass and oil into the trash. She mopped with a soapy rag, but still, the floor felt slick, and so mopped again, water shining the floor. She pushed the sheer curtains, pulled the lever to open the panel of glass-slat blinds on the windowed wall, all the way to the floor. Breeze floor-to-ceiling, hopefully to dry and not ruin her floor. She was always doing something like this—coffee on her white rug, a bleach ring on her counter top, the drawers of her bureau ruined and off the track. She admitted it—her eye was actually, really uncomfortable. She looked into the mirror above the mantle on her blocked-up fireplace.

A stye. Sickening. How? She knew how. Squirting old Visine found in her purse so her eyes looked less red and tired. Drumming on her work keyboard and picking crusted sleep. Cleaning the litter box and putting on eyeliner, masturbating with dirty hands, never, ever washing her face. She was a gross, gross, gross girl. Of course her eye was infected. She opened her bedroom door to get her laptop—Poe and Silky Boy freed, skipped between her legs in search of their amusing mess. Jello searched cures—hot tea bags, but she only drank coffee, hot compresses with clean washcloths—all her washcloths were kittened-out. Cleansing pads could be bought at any drugstore.

In the brightness of the drugstore checkout, Jello wished she had the huge saucer sunglasses of the girl before her in line, her black hair in a curly ponytail. In her basket: nail polish, remover, cotton pads, bottles of electrolyte water, a plastic clam-shell salad. *She* wouldn't have olive oil on her floor because she ate only drugstore salads. How empty her apartment must be. A month-to-month lease, perhaps. Not years like Jello, no forever job. Nice to be so pure. With that purity, the lack of earthly ties, this girl was surely closer to herself, was going to be, or already was, somebody. Somebody who would be held up, admired for her own delicious and intoxicating person. Yes, wasn't that the idea, why she came? An actress, a filmmaker, a make up artist, a set designer, a costumer. Endless, what she could become when she moved to L.A. A dream of this, a decade-old dream arose in Jello, pounded in her chest. Of course she failed. Jello never became so simply, so freely, herself. She came with a U-Haul full of her old clothes. A cubicle job for years now, the fringe of the industry she thought she'd grandly enter. Her mother's voice in her head from years ago. *But it's on the studio lot! Pretty soon, you'll be walking around and be asked to walk right onto set!*

Did her mother even say that?

A red plastic bar slapped down beside Jello's cleansing pads, and then on the conveyor belt, boxes with her own name. She was good with names. As a child, eight years old at the kitchen table, seeing

Mom mix a bowl of hot pink powder, green grapes, a Pyrex measuring glass of steaming water poured from the kettle, the box. She played with its name—why did it interest her? Ah, because it was her own. Janelle. Collapsed it, whatever her mother was making to bring to the third grade open house, at the new, good school, the one for "gifted" children like her. She brought Jello. Good to be a brand. She was very popular in third grade after that.

215

Now, she couldn't look at the face that belonged to the veined, shaky hand that put next to the boxes with Jello's name, tiny cans of cat food.

No—she didn't care about being famous anymore. In her car, she depressed the garage button on the visor, the gate pivoting up. Remember: she still could have everything that went along with that—the beautiful old house and nice things to put in it. She could have appreciation for her Jello-ness, love of millions compressed, diamonded into just one man who saw. Remember: everything now was temporary—her man, her job, her stye.

She had once messaged him—isn't that how it began, years ago? Phillip, a friend-of-a-friend. *He's a music producer.*

If she were to meet him at the studio, late night. She would have been drinking downstairs at the bar he recommended—a piano bar. Old Fashioneds, she sucks maraschino cherry after cherry, smokes cigarettes, grinds butts into a black marble, waiting. Almost midnight he texts her to come up.

The console, a bed of faders, buttons, knob and dials. Tiny red and green and yellow lights. He would be a little out of it—working day and night, his shirt creased with sweat, greasy hair, wild beard, Coke cans on the carpet. Leaning in to hug her, he smells the whiskey and ash in her hair. A stir of this, holds her a little closer. He plays for her what he's been working on, and she—free from the drinks—hums along. "Let me try something," he says, "just for fun." And she is put

216 in a glass stall, a Snow White coffin, headphones dwarf her ears, and she is insisting no, and he is insisting yes, just for fun.

Phillip's shirt—funny, horrible, she realized—the same shirt Whitney's mother bought him. Jello wanted to scrape this from her head. All this. If she could erase everything.

Plastic bag swinging on her arm, up her walkway to her apartment, almost at her door, she sees at first two pricks of light on the path, two yellow-green fairy lanterns. Eyes. And it is Silky Boy on the path before her apartment door. He sees her, and crouches to bolt. Jello throws herself on the cement, her hand slamming the kitten to the pavement. He yowls. She holds him to her chest, squirming. How?

She looks to the window, the panel with the blinds open and in the corner, the screen torn, frayed on the edge, and torn more by a kitten wriggling through. Silky Boy scrambling under her arm, the purse, the cvs bag, her knees stinging, everything awkward as she groped for her keys. Poe, the timid one, was surely inside and safe. Inside finally, slipping a little over the slick floor, she shut the blinds. All the lights on. She crawled, Silky Boy behind her, a game. Here kitty kitty kitty. Here kitty kitty kitty. She searched. She heard mewing in the hall, only to find it coming from under the bathroom door.

Her door slammed shut—no time to lock the door! She used the flashlight on her phone, trained it under giant elephant ear leaves, under webs of vine. A little black kitten could be anywhere. She traced the walkway. *Here kitty kitty kitty.* At least—the glass foyer. For a second, she relaxed with the hope he was locked in with her. But no, of course. There was the starburst garage, the toothed gate, thin slats that he could easily squeeze through. Jello made a low, guttural noise.

She wanted to message Whitney. Help me, please. Get me out of here, deliver me from all this evil that heaps around me.

Jello, past the curved rail over her apartment building. Her phone in her hand, she sent arcs of light across the pavement. In her periphery, homes, large, grand, cool stone all around her, like she is in a walled fairy-tale city. She wears, maybe, a black satin dress.

All dark now, the sky is black as it can be. Streetlights scarce on this hilltop. She found herself in front of the house.

Jello gripped the white wrought iron fence. From her phone, a thin light up concrete steps, a planter of succulents. Out of her reach was the house looming smokily up the steps. No floodlight, she could barely see anything.

She took a picture. Her camera flash jolted something. Strange birds overhead.

I think we need to buy this house.

And in a minute, a miniature image of him, a locket smaller than a stamp showed his picture, which means he'd seen the message. A thrill of this, a satin shiver across her body.

Why?

I think my kitten is in there.

Thinking bubbles, not as good as eyes, she thought, not as good, but almost as good as looking into a man's eyes when's he is trying to figure her out. She watched him think. Type, delete, wait, retype, wait, type. She was a mystery.

?

It's really beautiful, isn't it?

Yes. Where?

She sent a little map of the location.

You're there now?

Yes!

He could come. Up the 405 at this time of night, not twenty minutes.

I need to find my kitten!

On the recessed porch, she squinted to a shadow, a tiny black creature

218 that darted in the darkness, under a tri-columned archway, to maybe an open door in the back.

Jello rattled the gate. Her phone slipped from her hands and down to the cement, the light, now out, the screen black. On her knees, she reached for her phone. On her stomach to stretch, drew it to her with her claw hand. Dark, all darkness on the screen.

Keyless, she paced before the foyer glass. She could not get in the other side, through the garage, either. She knocked on the glass, her fist stinging, she knocked, if she could break the glass—she might! She looked in the landscaping for a large enough lava rock.

Creeping, along the wall of her apartment building. There are little aquarium windows of her neighbor's bedrooms like the one in her bedroom. She leapt to see into a window. Nothing—an inside flash of light but nothing she can hold onto. She crept. She hopped up to see into the next. A little black cat on a couch maybe.

Now, on the other side of the building near the garage. There, matching the garage, a fence, an entryway white gate for the residents who wish to enter this side of the complex. She climbed onto a lava rock, one hand on the gate for balance, and peered into the rectangular window of a unit this side of the building, one she had hardly noticed before.

A TV tray on precarious metal limbs was set beside a bed, '70s scratchy plaid comforter, a television on a bureau. On the bed, an old white Persian cat, drippy eyes looked up at Jello. On the TV tray, two remote controls, an empty sleeve of saltines, a jar of creamed herring. Jello thought, Silky and Poe would have knocked it all by now! Farther, beyond the bed, through the open door, Jello could see into the kitchen. The whole layout is the same as Jello's apartment, of course, though this one seems shabbier, unchanged since the building's construction. In the kitchen, a strange sight. A piece of moving furniture, creaking around. No, a person. Jello's hand burned holding the gate. She peered

in, her breath fogging the window making everything look cozy inside. **219**
An old woman strained to reach into the cupboard for another sleeve
of saltines, her housedress creeping up her lumpy legs laced with blue
veins, nude trouser socks in folds around her ankles, her feet in oversized
men's slippers.

Jello makes a fist. Her plan is to rap on the glass, to disturb whatever
has happened here. She hesitates. Close, so close to her face they could
kiss, a woman with a red eye. She shifts her vision past her reflection
to the old woman, unsure now, what she is seeing. She hopes to knock,
for the woman to see her, to let her in. And forgive her. ✄

Kathleen Mackay is a writer and teacher. She lives in Los Angeles.

A JOURNEYMAN IN LIMBO

HENRY LARA

"Life is a mystery to me. I quite don't understand the purpose of it sometimes and I probably never will, but that's for another discussion. I was born in the city of Burbank in 1947 at Providence Saint Joseph Medical Center. I grew up in the San Fernando Valley and attended San Fernando High. I never hung out with the crowd and I've always journeyed through life mostly alone. For some odd reason, I like it this way. After high school, I worked all over Southern California. I did framework for many years, then I became a journeyman painter. I enjoyed wearing that white painter's suit. I enjoyed the daily surprises work brought me; I was at peace. I've painted some beautiful homes throughout my life. One day, I think it was '72 or '73, I was having a conversation with an older man, he was probably around the same age I am now. He talked of fishing as something grand. That conversation moved me to alligator country. I moved to Gainesville, Florida, and started fishing for bluegill, catfish, and crappie at Newnans Lake just outside of Gainesville. It was the most fun I'd ever had in my life. A year later I started doing commercial fishing as a hand in the Florida seas. I also did some fishing nine miles off the coast of Cuba. Our specialty was marlin. I got into an incident that I could never fix so I came back to California and started working at a supper club. Nothing but fine dining, you know? Prime rib and filet mignon. I started drinking more and now I'm in limbo, you know, no home. I wish to fish again, but I isn't healthy no more. I believe in God and I always pray that we all stop killing each other—and I mean both mentally and physically. I also believe that $2 + 2 = 3$. Something is off in the world."

Louis says he has a heart condition—something is wrong with his aorta. He was heading to Los Angeles County +
USC Medical Center to seek care after blood poured out of his nose. (1/10/18)

THIS IS HOW IT HAPPENS

ANDRÉS RECONCO

Xiomara is the type of girl you carry in your mind like a secret, like something you shelter in the magic of your brain. She is Bladimir's sister. At fourteen years old she walks around with the type of disregard for us younger kids that is usual for people her age. She is only four years older than I am.

Bladimir doesn't know that when he and I play together and Xiomara walks by, I watch her, enjoying the warmth she leaves behind on my body. I don't tell him that I want him to call her over, that he should tell her to play with us so she can be near me and maybe talk to me. Once, he caught me watching her and he said, "She really likes those dresses but she only has two." He thinks I am criticizing her for wearing the same puffy dresses all the time. But I don't care about that. I like them. They're all identical except for the color and the print. My favorite one is the yellow one with the sunflowers. It makes her look like a garden swaying with the breeze. I don't tell Bladimir because I don't want him to think I am like the men who place their hands on her as she tries to walk to the store or who push themselves close to her as she rushes to school. Bladimir screams and throws rocks at them but the men simply laugh at him. He's only ten years old, like me.

Xiomara only talks to me if she can't find her brother and she needs me to deliver a message to him in case I see him before she does. I don't mind. When she gets close to me I can smell something like fruit on her, only not as sweet. I know that if I were to get closer to her, if I could press my nose against her dress, I would know what the scent is. But I would never do that. She paralyzes me.

One day Bladimir and I go to the beach to swim and to try to boogie board with broken pieces of Styrofoam. He comes to my house after and we play outside because Dad is inside, on the floor, asleep, drunk. My mom has already left El Salvador. She's been living in the United States for six months and Dad isn't taking it well. Most days I can smell the sour stench of liquor on his breath. Sometimes he walks unbalanced, as if on a tightrope. The square bottles with the clear pungent liquid pile up in corners of the house. The people in Acajutla call the drink *güaro* which sounds a lot like *water*. I tried it once. The last little drop inside a bottle that Dad had left under the dining table. When the liquid hit my tongue, I thought my taste buds were dissolving. I thought I would never be able to taste anything else again. My mother's abandonment must have left my father insane.

When Bladimir and I come inside the house to drink water we step carefully over my father's body. Bladimir says, "You can sell those back to the store, you know." He points at the bottles. "They'll give you fifty cents for each one you return." He and I pick up all the bottles and take them to the place that sells them full. The guy at the counter eyes us carefully and says, "You know, you shouldn't steal these from the drunks. Sometimes it's all they have." I tell him we didn't steal them, but the way his eyes narrow on us as he hands us the money tells me he doesn't believe us.

While Bladimir and I eat ice cream and two bags of mango smothered in ground sunflower seeds he says, "You should come spend the night. We can go to the river in the morning!"

I'd gone to his house before but I'd never slept there. I'm excited about being near Xiomara, about sleeping near her. I wonder if she will talk to me and what she might say. I think about telling her that I can swim farther into the ocean now, that the big waves don't scare me anymore. Maybe I can tell her I like her yellow dress.

"We can swim in the estuary," Bladimir says. "Have you ever done it? It's quiet except for all the frogs and crickets."

I don't like the idea of swimming in the estuary. A large sewage pipe empties all of the human waste from Acajutla into that water. Bladimir must see disgust in my face because he says, "It's not too bad at night. The sewer pipe doesn't flow as heavily. It's a trickle. Really."

I don't ask permission from my father. If I'd asked him, he would have definitely said no. Instead I wait until its nighttime, until he gets drunk and falls asleep. I've watched him before when he sleeps like that, the way his chest rises and falls like the waves do sometimes. He looks almost at peace, as if he has nothing to worry about, as if his only son isn't starting to hate him, as if his wife isn't thousands of miles away. Sometimes, I've wished for the strength to move him gently from his narrow bed and onto the ground so I could lie down next to him and fall asleep to the sound of his breathing.

To get to Xiomara's house you have to walk along a narrow trail surrounded by short trees and dormilonas. The entrance doesn't look like it leads to a path. Once there had been a gate but the wood rotted years ago and now only the concrete blocks remain. Someone had tried to plant rose bushes to mark the beginning of the trail but nothing ever grew, only long thorny branches.

I can't help but fantasize about what it will be like at Xiomara's house. I imagine myself sitting across from her at the dinner table. I don't know what we will eat. I wonder if she uses utensils. Maybe I can hand her a fork. Maybe I can accidentally touch her hand.

As I walk, the full moon casts its soft light all around me. The ground, the trees, the dormilonas all glow white, and it's as if I'm walking inside a lantern and I imagine I, too, must be glowing, and so I skip and jump and summersault, drunk on moonlight, drunk on the promise of looking into Xiomara's eyes.

The path goes on like that for a long time until right before you get to the estuary. The end of the trail is guarded by these old dying trees. They hug the road and throw crooked shadows on the path and on me. During the day, the sound of the rolling river and the coolness of the ground makes the place great for napping, for resting after long games of tag or fútbol. But the moonlight transforms the trees, gives them veiny hands and long crooked fingers that shudder with the wind. I know there is nothing there that can harm me but my heart beats fast and I imagine faces peeking through the branches, their eyes red like warnings. I fear that one will grab me and I run as fast as I can until the road gets wider, the river gets louder, and the little wooden houses appear.

Bladimir's neighborhood is called El Estero. That's what it looks like, a large swampy area surrounding the estuary. Bladimir calls it el culo del rio because he says everything smells like ass. It does. There must be ten slightly lopsided houses scattered along the edge of the water. I don't understand how those houses don't disappear into the mud, how they don't suck everyone down with them.

When I get to Xiomara's house it is late in the night. The houses all glow from within with the pale yellow light of candles. The shadows of people move against plastic curtains and wooden walls. The only house that is dark is Xiomara's. The moonlight squeezes in through the gaps in the walls and casts a dark shapeless shadow of something moving inside. It must be Bladimir's mom. In the distance, the screams of children playing somewhere in the forest emerge like echoes of wild animals.

Bladimir is already in the water, floating lazily on his back.

"Are you coming in?" he asks. "It's clean here."

I step around the large sewer pipe sticking out of the muddy soil. Trickles of waste empty into the water, downriver from where Bladimir is floating. Once, Bladimir and I drew eyes on big pieces of white paper and taped them to the top edge of the pipe. It had looked like a monster throwing up nonstop.

"Make sure you jump over here," he says. "Right here there's no sewage."

I strip down to my underwear and jump in. Even though the wastewater is downstream from us, the current is not strong enough to push it all away and the water still smells like shit. Bladimir disappears under the water and when he comes out he says, "How many seconds was that?"

"I wasn't counting," I tell him.

"How many seconds can you hold your breath," he asks.

"I don't know. Thirty maybe."

"Show me," he says.

"No," I say. "Not in this water. What if I swallow it? Me voy a enfermar."

"No, you won't. The worst thing that can happen is you'll get worms and you already have worms."

"I don't want to," I say.

"Fine. Count seconds for me."

He disappears into the water. I look for Xiomara in the darkness of his house, but I don't see her. I wish she would come out. I wish she would swim with us and I can show her how the moon ripples inside the water. When Bladimir splashes out of the water the moon scatters everywhere.

"I beat you," he says, gasping for air, coughing. "I counted to forty!"

We play in the water a long time before Xiomara comes out of the house and calls us inside. She's wearing the yellow puffy dress. Her hair is up in a bun. Her naked feet are caked in mud. I would clean them for her if she let me.

"Mom is working tonight," Bladimir says. "Xiomara is supposed to watch us."

I try not to smile. Xiomara is so pretty. Whenever she looks at me the green of her eyes pulls me in and they hold me there, hypnotized. She is elegant, angelic almost, floating above everything else that crawls around in Acajutla.

The inside of Bladimir's house is one big wooden rectangle. Colorful shower curtains create plastic partitions for the bedrooms. There is a little wooden stove on one side, a window that looks into the estuary and a small wooden dining table. When Bladimir and I come into the house Xiomara tells him to go rinse himself outside.

"The well water is cold," he says. "I'll do it tomorrow."

"Don't be disgusting, Bladi," she says. "You'll stink up the house. You're covered in dirty water."

He turns from her, goes behind the curtain of his room and changes into new clothes.

"Hola, Marcos," she says to me and I can't help but smile. She eyes me up and down, "Please go outside and rinse your body. Bladi says you're staying here tonight. This house will stink if both of you don't clean yourselves."

It doesn't make sense to me. It's impossible to escape the smell of the estuary. Everything smells like shit. But I don't say anything.

"Let me help you find the well," she says.

We walk outside just as clouds move in front of the moon. The night darkens. The well is behind the house. It's not like the one my father and I built. My father had taken his time putting together the brick

228 cover. He'd even built a pulley system to make it easy to pull water out of it. Xiomara's well is just a wide hole in the ground covered with a large metal sheet. I have no idea how they keep it from collapsing. She lowers the bucket and draws out clear water.

"Take your underwear off," she says.

I don't want to. "I can do this myself," I say.

"Don't be embarrassed. You're little. It doesn't matter."

I don't move so she comes to me and reaches for my underwear.

"I can do it," I say again, pulling away from her. I don't know where Bladimir is. I want to call to him but I feel silly. I can't hear the children in the forest anymore. They must have all gone home.

"Let me help you," she says and grabs my wrist. She's close to me. I can smell the estuary on her hair and her clothes.

"No," I say. "I can do it. I can do it myself."

She doesn't listen to me. Her grip tightens on my wrist. I look toward her house, looking for Bladimir. There's a soft orange light coming from the inside. A fire. He's building a fire.

I stop struggling. She's stronger than I am. I am naked now and I don't know how to move my body to cover myself. She pours water on my head and it, too, smells like shit. She rubs my back and my stomach. When she tries to go lower I pull away, but my body responds to her touch and she notices. She laughs and in a voice you use to talk to babies, she says, "Oh, little Marcos is excited!" She flicks the tip of my penis and laughs again. Then she hands me a towel and says, "It's time for bed." I don't know why I'm shaking all over. It's not cold out. I wonder if this is what excitement is. But why am I so nervous? Why do I avoid her eyes? I want to go home. I want to walk under the moonlight again.

"Ya," she says. "Go inside the house."

I can feel her watching me as I walk away. I'm still shivering. My steps are heavy and it's as if my feet sink deeper into the mud than they did before.

When I come inside the house Bladimir is warming up tortillas on the embers of a small fire. From behind me, Xiomara says, "We don't have any food left. We're eating tortillas with salt. You can have one if you'd like."

I'm not hungry but I sprinkle salt on top of a tortilla and take small bites from it.

"Do you want to tell Bladimir what happened outside?" she says, her smile crooked to one side.

My face is warm.

"He got excited when I was drying him," she says and laughs. I expect Bladimir to laugh, too, but he only looks at her as if he's worried about something. "Bladimir gets excited, too," she says. "Right, Bladimir?"

I don't know why he doesn't say something, why he looks like he wants to escape from that room. I wonder if I look the same way, too. He looks down at his tortilla and minutes pass before Xiomara says, "I'm going to bed."

When she is gone, I move my chair closer to Bladimir and I say, "Don't be mad. I didn't ask her to touch me."

"It doesn't matter," he says. "Just ignore her."

"What do I do if she tries to do it again?"

"Just ignore her," he says. He puts his tortilla down and says, "Let's go to bed."

There is something in the air, an awkwardness, something uncomfortable. In his bed, Bladimir and I talk about the games we played that day. We talk about how earlier we walked across some rocks on the shallow part of the river and he slipped and fell in and how he pretended to be dead and how I ran on the muddy soil after him screaming, "Oh no! Mi hijo! Mi hijo! I'll protect you! I'll catch you and protect you!" We break out in laughter and Xiomara yells at us

230   from behind her curtain to go to sleep. That is the last thing we laugh about that night.

Outside the frogs are really loud, and as I fall asleep, I imagine them in all their crevices and on top of all their big leaves. I picture their green skin, the thin membrane of their throat expanding and contracting. I try to distinguish the individual sounds of individual frogs, try to place their location, try to imagine myself the other frog listening, saying hello, saying goodbye, asking how they're doing.

In the morning I wake up before Xiomara and Bladimir. I walk out of their house slowly and quietly. Overnight the sky darkened with thick rain clouds. From the sewer pipe flows a torrent of dark waste. It mixes with the growing river to form a whirlwind of shit and garbage. Above me, the sky explodes and immediately after, my chest shakes with the thunder. When the rain comes it falls like waterfalls and I stand there, under it, begging it to wash away the stinging smell. ❧

Andrés Reconco is a former PEN Emerging Voices Fellow and is an English teacher at Los Angeles High School for the Arts.

DEAR FATHER

VICTORIA CHANG

Dear Father,

Jeanette Winterson in *Art Objects,* called people who love to read
exiles from actuality. If I was an exile from actuality, you were
actuality. Do you remember the Ford van that you spent a summer
converting into an RV? The wooden bed you made that fit perfectly
in the back? The small foam cushion, not soft enough, that you
measured and cut to perfect size?

I don't remember speaking to you much. Speaking to you always
felt like crossing my legs. When you spoke to me, you were
waterproofing me. Giving me advice about a world that you said
would suck the sky out of me.

Your advice was so practical, it lacked a pasture. Your advice came
from Taiwan but every other word was lost in the sea. *Just work____.*
Get _____ grades. Exercise every ____. Get a _____ job. _____ money.
Save ____. How many times I rolled my eyes at this advice.

You were always the founder and president of something. The
president of the Chinese Cultural Center in Michigan, the Carlsbad
Chinese club, this group, that group. In all the photos, you stood
at the front of a room, arms in the air. Your arms weren't wings.
They were batons. They whistled orders. You were the president of
everything. You were the president of me. Now you are the president
of no one. Now I am the president of you.

Do you remember when I began working at the investment bank
in San Francisco and never had time to call you? I can tell you now

since you no longer read, that I didn't want to call you. I didn't want my ideas to be killed. I didn't want you to know that I knew I had made the wrong choice.

Do you remember the long letter you wrote me? The only letter you've ever written to me? The small thin reeds of cursive. I still have that letter but I can't bring myself to read it again. You were too open in that letter. I could see your bones through the paper.

How did you learn how to write cursive? It must have been ten pages long back and front. I think you told me not to work so hard, to get some sleep, to call home, to make time for friends.

Now when I see you, you cup your ears to hear because you are nearly deaf. You respond in shivers, not words. When you speak, it's no longer splendid or backlit. Your hands are no longer batons. Your brain is like an empty shirtsleeve. You make no sense at all. Earlier this year, you began speaking Chinese to everyone.

I have so many questions I need to ask you. What time did you wake up each morning? Did you floss your teeth at night? How did you meet Mother? How did you handle Mother's moods? Anxiety? What were your deepest fears? What hopes did you have? Disappointments? What is your shoe size? Why do you like your eye glass frames so big? Can you see when you take your glasses off? Do you dream about Mother? I don't. I've shut the door on her so many times that her body is flat.

I want to tell you so many things. There are so many words in my mouth that my mouth is stretched out. Do you know I am forty-eight-years-old? Do you know I wake up tired every single day? Do you know that I am mostly unhappy? Do you know that I am occasionally punctuated with joy? Do you know the moments of joy for me are the same as moments of language? Do you know

that my words are not practical? Do you know that my words walk? **233**
Mostly away from me? Do you know that I spend my days catching
words with my hands? That I can't catch them because my hands
are batons? That I open my mouth and hope I can swallow words
without breaking them?

Do you know that I spent my life transforming myself into
the practical person you made me, one that has life insurance,
homeowner's insurance, umbrella insurance, auto insurance, short-
term disability insurance, long-term disability insurance, accidental
death insurance ...

But what am I supposed to do with the skunk I run into each night
during my walk? The fact that it can slip under a gate just one inch
from the ground. The dead birds I find next to the office building?

Despite all the insurance, our neighbor is suing us. This is the kind
of stuff I would have told you before, would have asked you for
advice on before. She filed a complaint filled with eighty-four items
of lies. I want to tell you about her swearing at my family. How she is
broke and wants money from us. How her fist broke a hole in my sky.
The sewing kit I bought to try to mend the sky. The nights I wake up
and I am only water.

Do you remember how we used to talk about stocks all the time?
Now all the words go the wrong way. Now all your words look like
stock symbols.

Today I will visit you. Today I do not want to visit you. Next week I
will not want to visit you. Next week I will visit you. I will not want
to listen to the feathers coming out of your mouth. The rocks. The
little busy rabbits that complain. Sometimes the ferrets come out too.
That skunk. Always that skunk. Today I will worry. Tomorrow I will
worry. Yesterday I will worry.

234   I will bring you some lunch and help you figure out how to eat. I will take you for a walk around the building. You will fall and I will catch your body that feels heavy as a country. I will grab you just in time so that your glasses are one centimeter from the pavement. Then I will hear Mother scolding me for taking you out in the cold and letting you fall. Then I will find a caretaker to distract you. Then I will sneak toward the side door when you are not looking. Then I will leave and bury you all over again.

DEAR MOTHER

VICTORIA CHANG

Dear Mother,

Do you remember the Chinese restaurant we owned in Michigan? I wish I could ask you more about it. *Dragon Inn.* I think in Rochester? I wish I could ask you where it actually was. I wish I could Google it and look at its aerial view. I wish I could remember what else was around it. I wish I could see what is in its place now. Another Chinese restaurant? A hair salon? Ghosts?

Memory is everything, yet it is nothing. Memory is mine, but it is also clinging to the memory of others. Some of these others are dead. Or unable to speak, like Father.

Finding memories is a bit like free diving, although I've never free-dived before. You jump in the water and hold your breath as long as you can without dying and hope you come up with a memory or two. Then there's the problem of opening the memory.

I have a memory or two of Dragon Inn. That everything was red. The vinyl booths, the wallpaper, the lanterns, the sign. The sign in *chop suey* font with a dragon at the side. The front of the restaurant with its big bowl of mints, the kind that tasted like toothpaste.

This past week, I was in the Hudson Valley in New York. I walked out of the hotel and smelled familiar smells of garlic and sesame oil. The sign above said *Buddha Asian Bistro.* A new restaurant in 2019. Still the *chop suey* font. I couldn't turn my head to look inside in the same way that I often turn my head away from Asian people on the street. If I don't look at them, I won't have to see myself as different.

236 I remember how crowded Dragon Inn was on Sundays when we had an all-you-can-eat brunch for $4.99. The line went out the door and everything was frenzied and nameless—the waitresses getting the tables set up, the chef shoveling huge amounts of fried rice into large metal containers, my mother setting up the buffet containers, the little blue flame below them, my father organizing the customers that began to rush in.

We offered fried rice, egg rolls, fried noodles, and maybe orange chicken at this brunch. I don't remember all the dishes. But people came from all over town. Many of the patrons were vastly overweight, swaying side to side as they walked in slowly, as if in pain. *Hao pong!* my mother would always say, or *so fat*.

Eventually the brunch disappeared. I never asked why but I imagine customers ate too much and/or it was too much work. These are the kinds of questions that absolutely don't matter. These are my most urgent questions. The poet Rachel Zucker and I talked about this recently. We both yearn to ask our dead mothers when they went through menopause.

After the brunch disappeared, I remember the quiet restaurant with the handful of customers who came in occasionally for their egg foo young or their moo shu pork, none of the foods we normally ate. I later learned that many Chinese restaurants had a *Chinese menu*, or one that only Chinese people asked for. This makes me think about how Chinese people perpetuate our own stereotypes, our own disappearance. How we are all resolved.

Resolve isn't inactive though. Resolve is a live animal. We perpetuate the narrative that is given to us. We opened restaurants because of the labor restrictions placed on Chinese immigrants in the nineteenth century. What was the alternative? Change the font. Go out of business.

VICTORIA CHANG

So much of our identity is based on how *others* expect us to be, how **237** others want us to behave, to dress, to talk, how others perceived Chinese food to be. All the expectations, all the way down to the font.

Once the $4.99 brunch disappeared, I spent my Sundays going back and forth to the liquor store next door. I remember having the urge to see if I could slip a small chunky chocolate square into my pocket without the owners noticing. I was so bored that I even missed the white people who lined up to not see us. Who lined up to eat us alive.

I remember the restaurant and then it just disappeared. It may have had something to do with my father having a full-time job at Ford Motor Company. Or that the restaurant didn't make money. Or that the chefs (always male) were always fighting with the waitresses (always female). Always intentionally and stereotypically Chinese. Because that's what customers wanted. Expected.

Much later, my mother said they had bought the restaurant for her brother, whom they had sponsored from Taiwan, but he didn't want it or want to live in Michigan. I don't know which brother or where he is now.

When I googled *Dragon Inn Rochester Michigan,* another *Dragon Inn* came up and a link to Yelp for the *10 best Chinese restaurants in Rochester* with other names such as *Panda House, Pings, China Town*.... I wondered about all the Chinese American children wandering around those restaurants. I imagined the mother yelling *chi fan,* time to eat. And then all the kids gathering at the back table to eat dinner, a dinner that the chef made just for Chinese people.

Once a photographer asked me if I had a *Mao outfit* that I could wear for the alumni magazine's shoot. *No,* I said. *Can you wear all black then?* I thought about it, *sure.* Because I thought a Chinese person should always try to say *yes.*

238 Now when I go to a Chinese restaurant, sometimes I ask for the Chinese menu, something my mother always did. I always feel a bit nervous doing so though, since I'm not a native Chinese speaker. And I look for any kids in the back slipping fortune cookies into small wax bags.

Now I yearn to be around Chinese people, the way plants have companions too. The way garlic plants improve the growth and flavor of the beets next to them. And dearest Mother, when I am seated at a Chinese restaurant, a real one where Chinese people eat, and I see an old Chinese woman at the table with her daughter, I see you, your garlic personality, my beet cheeks, and order everything you taught me how to order.

Victoria Chang's poetry books include Barbie Chang *(Copper Canyon Press),* The Boss *(McSweeney's),* Salvinia Molesta *(University of Georgia Press), and* Circle *(Southern Illinois University Press). Her most recent book is* Obit *(Copper Canyon Press). She lives in Los Angeles.*

BUT MAYBE I SAVE A LIFE:
A CONVERSATION WITH WANDA COLEMAN

STEVE RYFLE

The intensity of an encounter with the late Wanda Coleman
was not soon forgotten. Whether in person or on the page, in
conversation or in poetry and prose, Coleman used words as
weapons in a lifelong war against the racist systems conspiring against
African American life and art. Born in 1946 to a poor family in the
South Central Los Angeles community of Watts, Coleman underwent
a long, gradual process of self-education, life experience, and political
and artistic activism en route to becoming one of the most influential
and controversial West Coast writers of the 1990s and 2000s, and the
unofficial "poet laureate of Los Angeles."

Coleman was fascinated by literature and showed promise as a
writer from a young age, but without a college degree she developed
her craft amid the Los Angeles arts scenes of the 1960s, taking part
in the writing and performing arts programs that blossomed after the
Watts rebellion, and attending poetry workshops, readings, and parties
with the likes of Charles Bukowski in the creative circles of Hollywood,
Silver Lake, and Echo Park. Moving—often uneasily—in both the Black
and white worlds, Coleman supported herself by working jobs ranging

240 from waitress to screenwriter, medical transcriber to magazine editor, and struggled through the tumult of relationships and motherhood all the while, until her creative writing career officially began with a chapbook of her poems from Black Sparrow Press in 1977.

Over the next thirty-six years Coleman would publish thirteen books of poetry, two short story collections, a novel, and two essay collections, plus innumerable pieces of short fiction, journalism, columns, and criticism. She experimented with form, incorporating jazz- and blues-like riffs into her verse and surrealism into her sonnets. And always there was the intensity, the dark cloud of racism and the anger and despair it wrought, fueling her stories of life against a backdrop of poverty and violence, love and longing. In hundreds of readings and public appearances, Coleman's anger and despair were just beneath the surface; often, they burst forth.

Coleman warred not only against white supremacism but also Black elites, whom she believed tolerated and encouraged mediocrity and passivity in African American art while leaving no room for her uncompromising, blunt-force work. She received fellowships from the Guggenheim Foundation and the National Endowment for the Arts; her sweeping book of poetry, *Bathwater Wine* (1998), won the prestigious Lenore Marshall Prize from the Academy of American Poets; *Mecurochrome* (2001) was a National Book Award finalist; and in 2003-04 she was named the first literary fellow of the Los Angeles Department of Cultural Affairs. There were other awards, but Coleman continued to work on the literary fringes, striving for recognition but refusing to temper her writing in order to receive it. Though she held teaching gigs at a few universities, Coleman felt shunned by academia and the critical establishment, especially after her scathing 2002 *Los Angeles Times* review of Maya Angelou's *A Song Flung Up to Heaven* made her something of a pariah in those circles.

Wanda Coleman (1988)

242   Given Coleman's prolific writing and accomplishments, there were relatively few critical studies of her work and only a handful of interviews with the writer published during her lifetime. The following interview, one of Coleman's last, took place in April 2011 in Glendale, California, and was conducted as part of a project on the Civil Rights movement and its influence on the film and television industries. The wide-ranging conversation focuses on several little-known aspects of Coleman's career: her brief but significant gig, at age twenty-four in 1970, as the first African American female writer for a prime-time network television series, penning "The Time is Now," an episode of NBC's mystery-thriller series *The Name of the Game*; her trailblazing stint in 1973-74 as the founding editor of *Players*, an iconic African American softcore men's magazine created by the same white publishers whose Holloway House imprint had struck gold with the novels of Iceberg Slim, Donald Goines, and other Black pulp authors; and her work as a staff writer on the NBC soap opera *Days of Our Lives*, winning an Emmy for its 1975-76 season.

The fire of her unending battles had not dimmed; several times during this talk, Coleman took a quiet pause to allow her anger or sadness to subside. More often, the restaurant where this conversation took place echoed with her raucous laughter; somehow, she could still find humor in the absurdity of America's racism. Coleman's third husband, the poet and artist Austin Straus, was present during the interview; at the time, she was collaborating on a collection of love poems with Straus, as well as a new poetry book, *The World Falls Away*, both of which would be published posthumously. Back in April 2020, Black Sparrow Press published a collection of her selected poems, *Wicked Enchantment*, edited by Terrance Hayes. Coleman died in Los Angeles in 2013. The interview is condensed and edited for continuity.

STEVE RYFLE: In the mid-'60s you were part of Studio Watts, one of the earliest Los Angeles collectives to champion the performing arts and writing in the inner city. How did that shape your later writing?

WANDA COLEMAN: This was post-riot L.A., and there were a lot of organizations that sprang up to deal with the creative energy, to mine the post-riot energy. I had read a *Los Angeles Times* article talking about [screenwriter and novelist] Budd Schulberg's Watts Writers Workshop. I had already been going to a Saturday workshop occasionally, run by a playwright named Frank Greenwood. But this really sounded exciting and more like what I was looking for. I hadn't seen Schulberg's movies at that point, so it didn't really compute. The idea that people were paying attention to Black writers and trying to develop them, that's what excited

"I was dying to be able to tell my story, and I was serious about being a poet."

me. I was dying to be able to tell my story, and I was serious about being a poet. So, I hitchhiked part of the way down there and I took the bus the rest. I was living over off 81st and Broadway in the city then. When I got off the bus, I made the wrong turn; I should have turned left but I turned right. And I ended up at Studio Watts; I got involved at Studio Watts and I ended up being the only writer there. My involvement with Studio Watts was fairly deep.

The next time I went down there, I found the Budd Schulberg workshop and the old House of Respect [a collective of writers and artists who broke away from the Schulberg group]. At Studio Watts I was the only writer; I was taking a graphic arts workshop there, and I got involved in dance and other things, but I still wanted to be in a writing workshop. So, I did finally end up in Budd Schulberg's writers' workshop. But I didn't stay

244 very long; I must have gone about five or six times before I finally said screw you, wrote them a nasty letter, which they posted on the bulletin board, and left.

SR: Were you the only female member of the Watts Writers Workshop?

WC: No, there were several other female writers, but they were all older women, and they would all defer to the men; they wouldn't speak up. I would speak up and then get bashed for it, you know, for being the upstart. There were women who were mature; I was still in my mid-twenties. After the riot, the fellows, they were really full of it. People don't understand, but when those riots happened it was the first time in the history of the United States that African Americans could speak openly about their condition, in the way Malcolm X had been already doing. He had sort of set the pattern for whatever discourse was going to come about; he was the only African American who was really, truly vocal [about] the way that people

had been suppressed. So, after the Watts riot, there was this burst of energy, especially among the men. It was the first time in their lives, and in their daddies' lives and their granddaddies' lives, that they could say what they wanted to say without fear. People used to whisper in their houses, they were so afraid of whites. And so, this energy would overwhelm the workshop activity. You couldn't really ever get down to the business of writing because these fellows were so full of their new-found freedom of expression. And the workshop director could not handle it. Ted Simmons, a white writer, was running it and he could not handle it. These people would just run over him like he was nothing. People would bring in stories, poems, essays, what have you, just like any writers' workshop. But when it would come to critiquing and going around the room, that's when things got out of control. [Simmons] was sputtering a lot. (*Laughs*) He had to be careful how he critiqued them because they were very sensitive and could take offense easily. And they were feeling super macho.

SR: Why did you leave the group?

WC: I met Schulberg a couple of times. The last time I saw him all the media was there; they were having some sort of special to-do and they were taping. And when the door opened, Schulberg came in, in white robes, like Jesus floating on the water. My eyes got big; I was frozen in disgust. And then this old guy who I did not like because he was so, how do you put it? Old-timey deferential, obsequious. He went and bent down and touched the hem of his garment. And I bolted; I detested the whole thing. I don't know what it was supposed to be, but I couldn't stand it.

This corresponds to the period where I was going into Hollywood, going up to Echo Park. I was all over the place. I was even in another workshop called Hollywood Writers West, which was short stories. I was interested in short stories, too. So, I was all over town. Then I started going to Beyond

Baroque [a Venice Beach literary arts hub, opened in 1968] when they first opened their doors. I was in Hollywood, Venice, Watts. (*Laughs*) I'd get in my car and I was everywhere at once.

SR: Some of the writers in Schulberg's workshop got television writing gigs. Is that how you broke into TV writing?

WC: No, I was at Studio Watts. The phone rang, and I answered it. It was Universal City Studios looking for writers. The word had gotten out. I had had some plays produced at Studio Watts; in fact, I met [Christopher] Isherwood, who came down there, and a few other people had come down the night one of my plays was scheduled to debut. Ida Lupino and Howard Duff were there. They were like my heroes. I had been going to the Open Door program at the Writers Guild [a minority writer-training program, launched in 1969]. I was also involved with a group of Black writers who called themselves the Black Writers Committee. And they were angry

246 because they couldn't get into the Writers Guild; the WGA would not help them or support them to get work in Hollywood. I was going to their meetings, too. They had script writing workshops at the Guild, and I was studying with Lois Peyser, who was a successful script writer. I met Octavia Butler at that time, because she was also in the Open Door program. But the committee was outside of the Open Door program, and they were angry at the racism, and they were planning to be very militant and disrupt things. I left that meeting where they were planning their strategy, and the next thing I know they were going to meet with the Guild honchos. Next thing I know, the Black Writers Committee was part of the WGA West. We were like, "What? What happened here?" You know, it kind of felt like we got sold out. We went from being militant to being neutralized, neutered.

SR: The subject matter of your *Name of the Game* episode is interesting. This was around the time that Black Studies programs were coming into their own in universities and they were controversial; in Detroit and other cities there were campus protests. There's a big debate at the beginning of the episode between Roscoe Lee Browne and Yaphet Kotto, between the old school and the new school of thought, and some of the rhetoric is kind of fiery there; it's different than most television images of African Americans during that time. Did you face resistance from the network about the material?

WC: It's straight out of my political underground activities. *(Laughs)* I didn't have any trouble. They didn't censor me. I told them what the sources were. I had been in these groups, I had been in the political underground. That's how they spoke, these were things they said, and this is how it went. I was the authority; they couldn't say no to that. They said they wanted something that reflected reality. I'm writing out of my experience, right? Like all writers are supposed to do, right? (Laughs)

SR: As a writer who was young, female, and a person of color, how much leverage did you have?

WC: I got a cut-rate deal. If I could execute the script, I got a bonus. And I executed it. They felt that most Black writers couldn't write a script, and women of course can't write action. So that was their justification for giving me less money than if I had been a young white man. You don't get the full monty when you're Black. (Laughs)

SR: Some of the great African American actors of the day were in the episode: Yaphet Kotto, Roscoe Lee Browne, Max Julien. That must have been exciting to see.

WC: No, I goofed there. I was invited to come onto the set. And I didn't realize how early these people work, or how hard they work. So, I recall myself getting up about seven o'clock, getting ready, get the kids off to school, and then driving out to the Universal Studios, and they said, "Sorry, they're gone already. You've got to be here at five o'clock in the morning." I

said. "Whaaat?" (Laughs) So I missed my opportunity. I didn't meet any of the people on the show until years later I met the young man, who's Cuban, actually, who played the sympathetic character. Georg Stanford Brown. I used to wonder about him. You can kind of sense the differences between Blacks who are islanders and Blacks who are homegrown. There's a difference in the sensibility. These people from the islands, they grow up a majority. They don't feel like a minority. So, their whole mindset is different. And I have more in common with them than I do most of my African American peers because I was raised in the west. And even though I was a minority, my parents would tell me you're as good as anybody; you're anybody's equal. And I believed it. I always thought I was every bit as good as my white peers and I expected to have all the privileges that they did. So, the L.A. school system sort of beat me upside the head, telling me otherwise.

248   **SR:** Why didn't your TV writing career take off at the time?

WC: The fact that I got the bonus handicapped me. See, I didn't get the full monty, and it was kind of like saying, "You only went halfway; you've got to go the whole way before you can work for us." In other words, there's always a reason we can't use you. Then one day

Days, she searched for me and found me. I was working out in the Valley in the porno business. And I was sitting there thinking, "If I have to look at another tit, I'm gonna scream!" And my mother called me and said, "Wanda, you've got a letter forwarded from the Writers Guild. And it looks like money!" [Falken Smith] was doing a project

> *"... even though I was a minority, my parents would tell me you're as good as anybody; you're anybody's equal. And I believed it."*

I went in to pitch to a [producer] and he kicked back in his lovely suit, sitting on his real leather chair, and he told me, "You know Wanda, the Civil Rights movement is gonna be over soon. And we won't have to hire you people anymore." *(Laughs)*

SR: How on earth did you end up writing for *Days of Our Lives?*

WC: Pat Falken Smith [1926-2001, a prolific soap opera writer] met me during that time. And when she ended up as head writer for

with Howard Hughes, just before he died. In fact, his death ended the project, because I was about to be hired to help develop this film that she wanted to produce about an interracially married couple. She knew from our interview that I had been interracially married and that I had a background for it. She wanted to develop the first major film about interracial marriage, and Howard Hughes was going to produce it. I was going around and pitching through the pitch dens at that time, and that's how I met her, and that led to *Days*.

SR: You were actively pitching ideas for films and TV. What sort of stories?

WC: I had one based on my father. He was the sparring partner of "The Old Mongoose," the boxer Archie Moore. My father was a graphic artist. He did beautiful work. He tried desperately in the '50s to get a Black *Playboy* going, a Black *Esquire*, really; I think it was before *Playboy* came out. He and his partners managed to get interest in their "bronze beauty" project but they couldn't get a distributor. Johnson Publications [publisher of *Ebony* and *Jet* magazines] was killing anything anywhere in the U.S. that was African American that might threaten them or cut into to their little pie. They would go to the distributors and stop it. When they were trying to do the magazine, Archie Moore was a part of that. In fact, I actually got to hold a couple of his [championship] belts. He used to bring them by the house to show all the guys. They worked out of the garage then. They used to come by and hang out in the garage all hours of the night. I could look out the back bedroom, and they would shoo me out, me and my brother, they would shoo us into the house if he wasn't by himself working. When the fellas would start to come around and hang out, then we had to go in the house and watch TV or something.

These were bright guys, bright Black men who were forced to be boxers, in a sense, because that was the only way they could make money. Most of them were creative, and they wanted to be something else. In fact, I wrote a piece recently about Ira Hayes. He was the American Indian who was one of the group that raised the flag at Iwo Jima. And he used to come by. He was an alcoholic. And before he went back to the reservation and died, he used to hang out with my father and his pals. In the Tony Curtis movie that they made of his life they show Tony Curtis hanging out with some Blacks in a very

250 kind of negative way, a night club, going crazy, jazz and all jived up, you know. Because those were the zoot suit days, the tail end of that energy. I used to like that man, he was really nice to me and he would always talk to me. He'd come to our house all hours of the morning, before sunrise, drunk as a skunk. He would ring the doorbell and beat on the doorbell until my father got up, and I got out of bed, and my mother would put on a pot of coffee. And my father would sit there and read the Bible to him.

SR: Few TV shows had Black writers on staff in the early 1970s, apart from the Norman Lear comedies.

WC: I met Norman Lear. I went in with St. Clair Bourne [1943-2007, a documentary filmmaker]. He had a project, and he decided I would be one of his staff writers. We were going to pitch what they call now a dramedy, a dramatic show with comic overtones to it. It was gonna be about a Black family. And we got knocked out by *The Cosby Show* [1984-1992]. We were going to bring it upscale,

you know, middle class. But Bill Cosby came along with his show and that was the end of the story. Also, before that, I went into partnership with two white men and another Black woman by the name of Barbara White Morgan [a Los Angeles playwright]. The four of us teamed up and we came up with a series that would take place in a Black neighborhood, about people aspiring to get out of the ghetto. We went in to pitch at Universal, and the day we had the big meeting with the suits, I was wearing— in those days the vogue was the dashiki. And I had my little yellow head wrap on. I got pulled over by the cops on the way to the meeting. I pulled up in the [studio] parking lot. Barbara had just pulled up. I gave that woman my purse and said, "You'll find an address book in there. Call my mother." The suits, at the same time, they were arriving and they saw me being handcuffed from behind. I was on my way to Sybil Brand [a now-shuttered women's jail in Los Angeles], baby, and that was the end of that project.

We [also] went in to pitch at NBC. At that time, the head of programming was a Black man at NBC.

SR: Stanley Robertson, who was the first African American network TV vice president.

WC: That's right. When I went in, I had on my little mini-dress, my big 'fro, and my hoop earrings. Mama was hot, grandma was hot back in the day, okay? (*Laughs*) So I go in there with Barbara Morgan and my two partners. And they've already cautioned me about my big mouth, being so frank. "Please don't say anything, Wanda! Please don't say anything!" When we went in, Robertson's [hair] just about stood up on his head when he saw me. I was like a visual indictment of everything he was. And so, my partners started talking. Everyone was talking but me. I'm sitting there and things are going well, and all of a sudden Robertson said something and I missed it. And I asked the man to repeat it. He said, "You can't say that to me!" And he waved his

arms and he ordered everybody out of his office.

SR: Most all African American primetime shows of the '70s were comedies: *Sanford and Son, The Jeffersons, Good Times, That's My Mama, What's Happening!!,* and so on. Were you trying to do something closer to your later poetry and prose?

WC: A lot of my stories are about ghetto life, how you survive in that environment and how cruel and horrible it is. Just the opposite of something like, you know, "We're movin' on up." I recently had neighbors evicted, and it sent me into chaos when the landlady evicted them and she put the notice on the window. And there were a few kitchen items outside the door. And I saw this, and even though I detested these people and was glad to see them go, it still set off something in me, and I realized that it had taken me back forty years to when the sheriffs were the ones who came. On a beautiful spring day like this, with the sun shining here in

252 beautiful California with the nice little lawns and everything, you'd look down the street and see the sheriffs moving up and down the street, evicting people and setting their belongings just on the lawn or on the sidewalk or in the street. And anybody could come along and help themselves if they were thieves. One time, man, they carried an old woman in her sick bed out and set her on the sidewalk. And I used to look at that and I'd be terrified, wondering if I'm gonna be next. You know, living that kind of life where, you know, they say "on the edge" is the expression? And you work so hard to earn something only to have some thieves come in and steal it from you and you can't afford to replace it. That kind of life, where people are going to siphon gas out of your car or put sugar in your gas tank or put paint remover on your finish if you come up with a car that they are jealous of. The nightmare of trying to survive in that kind of environment. And there's no place for that on TV, you know? There's no place for that in the world of entertainment because it ain't entertaining. Racism is not entertaining, and the people who have to suffer it, or the consequences of it, the residuals of slavery, it ain't entertaining. You have to be a fool or an asshole and put some shit out there and you can make beaucoup bucks. And it's always been that way.

> *"Racism is not entertaining, and the people who have to suffer it, or the consequences of it, the residuals of slavery, it ain't entertaining."*

SR: And a brilliant filmmaker like Charles Burnett toils in obscurity because he makes stories about human beings.

WC: That's right, human beings. That's what Hollywood doesn't want to see. When my son was dying of AIDS, and I knew it was coming, in the 1990s, I decided I was going to give Hollywood one more run. I was going to get out there and pitch. Found me an agent by chance, who heard me read some poems and said they wanted to represent me. She had studied with one of the "dream team" members in the O.J. Simpson trial; she had been one of [Robert] Shapiro's students and she had become an agent. And she started sending me to do the pitch dance again. It hadn't changed. Generationally it had changed but the process was still the same. And now I was meeting younger people; I had nothing in common with them. Especially the white bread. I went from pitching to sixty-year-olds to twenty-five-year-olds, and it was the same. I went over to [John] Singleton's outfit and pitched. His right-hand man looked at me like granny had just come in, or great aunt so-and-so. So, age became a serious factor. I was too young then, now I'm too old. Besides the Blackness. (*Laughs*) Couldn't win for losing!

SR: A couple of soap operas in the mid-'70s were notable for hav-ing prominent African American characters. Is that why you were hired, to bring the dreaded word "authenticity" to the writing?

WC: I was a political move from the get-go anyway. Because Pat Falken Smith wanted a mixed-race family in the script. So, it became that *Days of Our Lives* presented the first marriage between a Black woman and a white man on television, and I was the political justification for that, being on staff. Because they knew ahead of time that people were going to jump up and down and say, "Where are your Black writers?" So there I was.

SR: Did you have full status as a writer this time?

WC: No, that was a bargain basement deal also. I was not getting paid what the other writers were getting paid. I had some sort of union deal, when you go to the union and they say, "Well, we'll let this person work for less money, because at least they're working." That kind of thing. So, it was more money than I had ever made in my

253

254 life at that point, but it was still less than what the other writers were being paid. And I was never allowed on the set.

SR: Why not?

WC: Granny was pretty cute. Granny was hot. You should have seen granny in toreador pants. With pinstripes! She stopped traffic. "You might hook up with somebody." And the only person they wanted me to hook up with, and they actually arranged for us to date, was one of the Black stars on the show. And we were not each other's taste at all. He was an islander; we didn't have anything in common but a certain pallor to the skin. But they didn't know that, because they didn't understand the difference. I can't even remember the poor man's name. Al something.

SR: Al Freeman Jr.? No, that's not right. He was on another soap opera, *One Life To Live.*

WC: It wasn't Al Freeman; the best thing Al Freeman ever did was *Dutchman* [1966]. I teach that film in school because it's still valid, it's still true. That's what's so spooky about it. You know, [playwright Amiri] Baraka should've gotten the Nobel Prize in Literature lightning years before Toni Morrison. That's what this nation does to us! That's what these motherfuckers do to us! Oh, God! That's what they do to us!

[Here the interview pauses for several minutes to allow an emotional Coleman to regain her composure.]

WC: They only reward the safe. I'm so sick of it! Oh God, man, I'm so sick of it. I wish I had the courage of that man in Tunisia. [Mohammed Bouazizi, a street vendor who self-immolated in protest against the Tunisian government in 2011, inspiring the Arab Spring revolts.] How many dictators has he brought down? How has he changed the shape of the future? But he had to set fire to himself to do it. And who was the Buddhist priest? [Thich Quang Duc, a Buddhist monk who set himself on fire to protest the persecution of Buddhists by the

South Vietnamese government in 1963.] I wrote a poem for the priest who set himself on fire in 1965. I was in high school. And I sat and I looked at that photo, and I looked at it, and I looked at it, and I looked at it, and I looked at it. Could I have that kind of courage? Oh, could I have that kind of courage? Could I set fire to myself and change the world? Is that what it takes? Do I have what it takes? Oh God, do I have what it takes? I say that prayer every morning when I wake up. And here I am, a poet, about as valueless as anyone in this nation can be. But maybe I save a life. Maybe I save the life of the soul who set themselves on fire.

[Coleman pauses to catch her breath.]

SR: Before you achieved visibility as a writer, you got a bit of press for your work as the first editor of *Players* magazine, a men's bi-monthly. Along with the nude

> *"And here I am, a poet, about as valueless as anyone in this nation can be. But maybe I save a life."*

photo spreads, you cultivated some very good content including fiction, journalism, photography, and graphic design. How did you end up working there, and were you at all conflicted about being a woman, albeit a powerful one, editing a men's adult magazine?

WC: They found me by chance. I went in there [to Holloway House, the publishing firm] with a novel, you know, to hustle my novel, and I told them what my background was, that my father had also taught me to be a graphic artist; he had taught me how to put together magazines. I already knew what to do. I had the ability and the talent but no money. *(Laughs)* Like my dad. I had already worked for porno magazines. So, being a men's magazine editor? I had seen it all, so it was no problem.

SR: Looking back, the circulation was about half a million per issue, amazing for an upstart publication

256 of its type.

WC: [*Players*] was the happening thing; all sorts of actors and movie stars wanted to be in it. It was staggering. Anyone who had Black product, because the opportunities were so rare, the marketing opportunities were so rare. *Players* was, like, it—for adults, and for people who halfway had a brain. One of the largest responses I got were from Black intellectuals who said, "We've been waiting for this." Madison Avenue was hungry for the magazine; they had been waiting over a decade for a magazine like *Players*. Everybody wanted a piece of the action.

SR: You left after the first six issues.

WC: I couldn't go anywhere. I was starting to get recognized when I was going down the aisle of Ralph's, trying to shop for my dinner on Sunday. People knew who I was. I couldn't go anyplace; it was becoming my whole existence. I had always been able to separate myself; I always had that little place where the poet could live and thrive. And that space was being gobbled up. I couldn't connect to the people who were closest to me; I couldn't talk to them anymore because I was suddenly famous. I was experiencing fame on the level that destroys most people. And it was starting to get to me. I needed people close to me who I could trust, and I couldn't trust anyone anymore. I was doing the work of ten people. I was the only employee who had a key to the building. I could come in any time of day I wanted to. I'd come in at five o'clock in the morning and get on the phone to Europe. I had stringers, I had people working for me in New York, Chicago, New Orleans, D.C., San Francisco, all the major cities. When you're moving on the Black hand side, you hear all the good shit first. You get all the good gossip first, before it gets into the white media, including the *Enquirer*. So I was getting the dirt firsthand; I would know what was going to happen before the white media ever got it.

I was there six months before

the first issue hit the stands, because I had to set it up. I got my ass to cracking, man. My kid was just going from babysitter to babysitter. I'd pick him up and drop him off and pick him up and drop him off. "Mommy, where are you?" I got to the point to where I had to find me a boyfriend who I could take places with me, you know, a beard. I had to find me an escort, straight off the streets. That was protection, because people were constantly trying to seduce me with either dope or sex. If I hadn't quit, I would have been in the first issue of *People* magazine. They were going to have a layout on me in the first issue, but I quit.

SR: A number of the Holloway House authors had fiction published in the magazine. Did you edit any of them?

WC: Only Donald Goines. He was murdered. That was while I was there. I had warned him. I told him they were going to get him killed. I knew that the gangsters he was fucking with weren't stupid, and I knew he was stealing his material from people who were still out there, who had gotten away with other killings. As long as he could keep those novels flying, he could stay in pocket. He was writing them as fast as he could. When he started using the pseudonym [Al C. Clark], when I realized what was happening, I went to [the publishers] and I said, "Please, this man's work needs better editing." What I was advocating was not for him to stop writing the novels or stealing the material, but to write it in a way that was different enough so [the gangsters] wouldn't necessarily kill him or hurt him, because they wouldn't know who the source of the material was. He wasn't smart enough; he wasn't enough of a writer. He was a good storyteller, which is different from being a writer.

SR: You mentioned hanging out with artists and writers on the other side of town. Presumably this was a white crowd. How did that come about?

WC: My first husband was Charlie Jerome Coleman, and he was

258 in Martin Luther King Jr.'s inner circle. When he came to L.A., he came with Jessie Jackson, Vernon Jordan, and Stokely Carmichael, and they were all staying with the friends of SNNC at sort of a crash pad over on 54th and Normandy. He was a political activist and an itinerant Baptist preacher, and a musician. He played the mandolin, spent a lot of time in Topanga Canyon. We were wild children out there, wild and young and doing it, man. So, half the time we were in the Black political underground, and the other time we were with the hippies in the parks. It was quite a time. And if you read my bio you know I hung out with Manson up at Griffith Park in the

> "We were wild children out there, wild and young and doing it, man. So, half the time we were in the Black political underground, and the other time we were with the hippies in the parks."

the guitar, and the banjo, and the mouth harp. In those days, after the riots, L.A. became an open city. I mean, I was at Frank Zappa's house. We were just all over the planet, constantly going to parties, and he used to entertain a lot of times at the party, and I would back him up. I had a repertoire of about 100 folk songs and civil rights songs. One time we danced for twelve hours at Eddie Albert's, at his pad. Wore out his floors. We days of the love-ins and the be-ins and the happenings.

My brother George, the oldest boy, the second child, went to Otis Parsons [College of Art and Design] and his professor there, a woman by the name of Rose Idlet, was married to John Thomas [1930-2002, an influential Venice West scene beat poet], who was one of the ringleaders of this crazy pack of white guys. George started telling me about these dudes he was running with, that he would go out carousing with them, drinking and doing whatever they did. Drinking and fighting in alleys. "Wanda, you gotta meet these guys! You gotta see it to believe it!" [George] was living in John Thomas's basement, up in Echo Park. I used to drive up there sometimes. I had just separated from my first husband but on the weekends or after work I still went to a lot of the hangouts in Hollywood, Echo Park, and the Mt. Washington area where we had frequented. I would stop by and see my brother and he introduced me to John Thomas. I knew about Charles Bukowski at that point, but Thomas started introducing me to his work. He took a lot of pleasure in nourishing me, teaching me. I had asked him to critique my first fledgling manuscript, and he told me the truth, how bad I was as a poet. (*Laughs*) And he started

"I was at Bukowski's first reading. I was the only female in the room."

to educate me, giving me Pound's *Cantos*, and he had all these beautifully printed books of poetry, first editions that he had collected. And some of them were Bukowski. He loaned them to me and made me promise to bring them back without roach eggs. So, I'd take them home to the ghetto and read them and we'd discuss them. In a way, it was part of my education.

I was at Bukowski's first reading. I was the only female in the room. That happened frequently in those days. Suddenly I'd look around and I was the only thing Black and the only thing female. I would sit there, and I wouldn't say anything, I would just watch Charles Bukowski for the evening, and the people who collected and gathered around him, his girlfriends. We usually got there early. Neeli Cherkovski [poet and Bukowski biographer] would usually be first or second.

And I would just listen to them talk, and mainly they talked about poetry and different poets, the local scene, that was usually the extent of the conversation until the party got started. When other people started coming in, then the party got started and about two thirds of the way through the evening when the old man got drunk, it was kind of like that's what everybody was waiting for. Then the show would begin, and Hank would go into his thing.

SR: He was known for his public persona as much as his writing.

WC: It was sad, let me tell you. The sadism, the pleasure people got watching this man destroy himself. I reached a point where I couldn't stand it and I quit going. The last one I went to, his girlfriend was flirting outrageously with a good-looking guy and, in fact, it was funny because Hank was staring at me. I was sitting across from him on the floor; he was on the couch and there was a coffee table. He went into sort of a slump and he was staring at me. I was sort of squirming and looking away, and his girlfriend, she had come over and stepped on my boot to let me know that—"Hands off"—Bukowski was hers. Then she turns around, about forty minutes later, and she's flirting with this young guy. And he starts roaring and snorting and gets into an uproar, and starts throwing bottles up against the wall, to everyone's delight. And I'm watching all of this and I just said, "I don't need this shit." I went outside. I had parked crossways in the driveway, behind his Volkswagen. When I went out to get in my car, he was behind the wheel of that Volkswagen, crying. Yup. With the engine running. I said, "You can't get out, old man. I'll let you out." And I got in the car and drove off. And that was the last Bukowski party I went to. ✂

Steve Ryfle is the co-author of Ishiro Honda: A Life in Film, From Godzilla to Kurosawa *(Wesleyan University Press) and author of* Godzilla vs. the World: The Politics of Japan's Disaster Monster, *forthcoming from University of Texas Press. He lives in Los Angeles.*

UNCERTAIN FRONTIER

DAVID HERNANDEZ

Although I would prefer another mood, this one
I'll take. This one I'll choose over yesterday's

       black ash passing through my body
       or Thursday's darker flurries.

But now I'm standing before my modest
orange tree, slumped in the corner of the yard.

       Its six humble suns. The brightest I twist
       off its stem, feel my hand prickling

with ants and quickly toss the fruit—
It thumps the earth, once, then tumbles over

       wet grass, collecting the morning's rain
       inside the pores of its rind.

Against my thigh I smack my hand, both
sides, flipping fast, as if cursed with flames.

       This hour I'll recall. This sun I kick
       across the lawn. These stunned ants

escaping from the stigma's puckered knot
as they navigate the orange, maneuvering

       around the jewels of rainwater.
       Strange time, is it not, to live

while the fire grows in the eyes of civilization?
This day I'll take. This fruit I'll taste, despite.

A LIFE THAT DOUBLES-BACK ON ITSELF

DAVID HERNANDEZ

circle a Walmart parking lot in a pickup stuck recalling the thunderous light that lifts the armored vehicle in front of his then a limb in flames bounces off his hood while police watch at a safe distance a man

David Hernandez is the award-winning author of the poetry collections Dear, Sincerely (University of Pittsburgh Press), Hoodwinked (Sarabande Books), Always Danger (SIU Press), and A House Waiting for Music (Tupelo Press). He teaches creative writing at California State University, Long Beach.

NABOKOV'S ROCKING CHAIR: *LOLITA* AT THE MOVIES

TOM BISSELL

L ate in Vladimir Nabokov's *Lolita*, Humbert Humbert—liar, child rapist, soon-to-be murderer—looks upon the book's titular heroine (Dolores Haze on the dotted line) and ponders how "hopelessly worn" his obsession has become. She is all of seventeen—and pregnant with another man's child. Humbert then casts back to Lolita's one-time ambitions of movie stardom, wondering if the baby inside her is not "dreaming already ... of becoming a big shot and retiring around 2020 A.D." Well, child, here we are at the appointed year, and sorry to say: Mother Lolita remains the biggest star in the room.

"No matter how many times we reopen 'King Lear,'" Humbert says elsewhere in the novel, "never shall we find the good king banging his tankard in high revelry, all woes forgotten.... Whatever evolution this or that popular character has gone through between book covers, his fate is fixed in our minds." This perception of dramatic fixity has come to affect Humbert and Lolita as well. Nabokov was perfectly aware that, with this uniquely incendiary novel, he was creating characters, and a situation, that were iconic.[1] Dramatic fixity is also the core problem of *Lolita*. As a story, it comes to our minds preheated by cultural osmosis; it cannot be read cold. Maybe it never could.

In Stanley Kubrick's 1962 film adaptation (the screenplay nominally—and only nominally—by Nabokov himself), Dolores/Lolita (played by Sue Lyon) finds Humbert (James Mason) scribbling in the diary he uses to record his growing preoccupation with the nymphet. When Humbert notices Lo he squirrels away his infernal, incriminating notes. In a line that appears neither in Nabokov's novel nor his published screenplay, Lolita laughs and says, "Afraid someone's gonna steal your ideas and sell 'em to Hollywood?" A good joke, as a middle-age French poetry professor's annihilating sexual obsession with a twelve-year-old girl could hardly be imagined, then or now, as promising cinematic material. When Kubrick's troubled adaptation finally premiered, it came festooned with a Hollywood adman's curiously defeatist tagline: "How did they ever make a movie of *Lolita*?"

If I were writing about another novel, this sentence would be the lapidary transition where I backfill the themes, motifs, and characters of the book under examination. If you really require a summary of *Lolita*, head for Amazon Prime and click the story description tab on Adrian Lyne's equally troubled 1997 adaptation of *Lolita* (screenplay by Stephen Schiff), whereupon you will find this: "A man marries his landlady so he can take advantage of her daughter." Well, yes, but whether in print or on film *Lolita* tells a story no summary can approximate—much less disinfect. In the mid-1950s, when Nabokov was struggling to publish *Lolita*, even some of his closest friends judged the book to be "repulsive." (Privately, Nabokov referred to *Lolita* as a "time bomb" and kept the

---

1   Strange to think that the name Nabokov gave his nymphet, which has passed so deep into the culture that it founded an entire genre of *pornography*, was originally not Lolita at all. Virginia she was, and Virginia she stayed, until relatively late in the novel's gestation.

manuscript locked in his office.) His longtime *New Yorker* editor, and **265** literary champion, Katherine White, couldn't finish the book, she said, because she kept thinking about her granddaughters. No one could have imagined what a sensation it would become when it was finally published in the United States in 1958, much less that Nabokov would answer his door on Halloween to find a little girl dressed up as Dolores Haze.

In Kubrick's *Lolita*, Humbert Humbert somehow became an avatar of situational comedy. In the Clintonian 1990s, Lyne's film worked hard to transform Humbert into a figure of wanly eerie tragedy. These days, though, Humbert seems more familiar—and more insidious. He's now the emblem of a much wider cultural nightmare in which any number of urbane, feted, sophisticated child rapists walk free among us.

✻ ✻ ✻

In interviews, Nabokov was always happy to discuss his antipathies. For instance: "I happen to have a morbid dislike for restaurants and cafés. I detest crowds." He also detested music, driving, hotel-room noise, and talking on the phone. He could be a bully. When one of Nabokov's Cornell students confronted him in class about his frequent dismissals of Dostoevsky, Nabokov tried (and failed) to have the lad expelled. With his fervid butterfly collecting, his frequently bizarre literary opinions, and his (justified) egotism, Nabokov was a deeply strange man. But then, many gifted people are strange. Nabokov's gifts were of such magnitude that they *dwarfed* his strangeness. That's how a novel with such appalling subject matter can stand today as a monument to adamantine artistic control.

But he liked pop culture more than he let on. He and his wife Véra were fans of *The Ed Sullivan Show* and Nabokov sneaked in the occasional soap opera, at least according to one of his colleagues at Cornell. Nabokov's student Alfred Appel Jr., who later compiled *The*

266 *Annotated Lolita*, once sat behind his professor during a showing of the 1953 John Huston comedy *Beat the Devil*, which Huston co-wrote with Truman Capote. According to Appel, Nabokov laughed so hard during the film that "it became clear that two comic fields of force had been established in the theater: those who were laughing at the movie, and those who were laughing at (nameless) Nabokov laughing at the movie." Nabokov's son Dmitri often went to the movies with his father; the Three Stooges and Abbott and Costello were particular favorites, which Dmitri claimed his father "seemed to love as much as I did." This is clearly not the forbidding aesthete of Nabokov's interviews and letters.

Many have remarked that *Lolita* is a novel haunted by death. One begins the book proper knowing Humbert is dead and when one rereads it's with the shock of encountering Lolita's death—or rather, the death of "Mrs. Richard F. Schiller"—on page four. Charlotte, Lolita's hapless mother: run down by a car. Clare Quilty, Lolita's abductor and Humbert's tormentor: executed. And look, there's poor Charlie Holmes, the young man to whom Lolita loses her virginity, shot dead in Korea, on page 290. But *Lolita* is haunted by something arguably more powerful than death. *Lolita* is a novel that's haunted by the movies.

Nabokov's cinematic style has been much remarked upon. Typically, prose judged to be "cinematic" feels thin and rushed, like stage direction amputated from its dialogue. Nabokov's cinematic style, on the other hand, is anything but rushed. Instead, it creates a visionary, heightened reality in which the most vivid details have a somehow extra-sensory power. His paragraphs are the all-seeing lens, his sentences the calibrated camera cuts. This is not an accidental effect. One of his earlier Russian novels, translated into English in 1936 as *Laughter in the Dark* and written while Nabokov was living in the penury of Berlin exile, was expressly conceived as a project likely to score its author a film sale— which it did, albeit three decades later, when he and Véra no longer needed the money.

In this highly particular sense, *Lolita* might be Nabokov's most "cinematic" novel. Consider his wizardly observation that the shadows thrown down by bamboo are "thrifty, practical." How perfectly one sees them! Or listen to the sound of a distant train when it's described as "mingling power and hysteria in one desperate scream." The speakers of your inner skull practically vibrate. But *Lolita*'s movie-hauntedness goes beyond the descriptive overload of its prose. Lolita herself is obsessed with movie star magazines. According to Charlotte, Lo "sees herself as a starlet," whereas Charlotte sees her daughter "as a sturdy, healthy, but decidedly homely kid." Charlotte tells Humbert this in confidence, making its casual cruelty even more startling. Kubrick and James B. Harris, who co-produced the film with Kubrick and helped him rewrite Nabokov's script, retained this line, but turned it into something that Charlotte (Shelley Winters) shouts at her daughter in a moment of anger. In Nabokov's novel, Humbert tells us of the lie he concocts to explain his and Lolita's frequent absences from school: Humbert's "Hollywood engagement" as "chief consultant in the production of a film dealing with 'existentialism,' still a hot thing at the time." Both Humbert and Nabokov intend this lie to be ridiculous, but certainly it's no less ridiculous than a film about a man sexually obsessed with his twelve-year-old stepdaughter. That is probably why Kubrick and Harris impishly retained this line, too, as voiceover, even though Nabokov left it out of his script. At one point in the novel, when Humbert and Lolita are on the run, Lolita stops to stare at WANTED posters on the wall of some anonymous post office. Here's how Humbert describes the rogues' gallery:

Handsome Bryan Bryanski, alias Anthony Bryan, alias Tony Brown, eyes hazel, complexion fair, was wanted for kidnaping [sic]. A sad-eyed old gentleman's faux-pas was mail fraud, and, as if that were not enough, he was cursed with deformed arches. Sullen Sullivan came with a caution: Is believed armed, and should be considered extremely dangerous. If you want to make a movie out of my book, have one of these faces gently melt into my own, while I look.

Almost certainly, this is not the voice of Humbert, a man so immune to the popular culture of his time that he doesn't know the names of any of Lolita's matinee idol favorites.[2] What this prosody-inflected passage gives us is the voice of Vladimir Nabokov himself, a writer thinking in cinematic terms and seduced by cinematic devices, but ultimately scornful of their heavy-handed obviousness.

On his way to murder Clare Quilty, the novel's Humbert passes a drive-in movie theater, which results in one of *Lolita*'s most haunting passages:

In a selenian glow, truly mystical in its contrast with the moonless and massive night, on a gigantic screen slanting away among dark drowsy fields, a thin phantom raised a gun, both he and his arm reduced to tremulous dishwater by the oblique angle of that receding world,—and the next moment a row of trees shut off the gesticulation.

Yes, that is indeed a commash, a punctuational artifact considered antique even by the 1940s, and which appears nowhere else in *Lolita*. It would seem this commash is part of an elaborate private joke, for the scene Nabokov is describing apparently derives from the book he dearly hoped would score him a handsome film sale: *Laughter in the Dark*. We're

---

2   Not that Nabokov was much better in this respect. At a party at producer David O. Selznick's house in 1960, he met and failed to recognize both John Wayne and Gina Lollobrigida—one of the stars of *Beat the Devil*, the movie at which he guffawed a decade before.

deep in the Nabokoverse here, a world as internally complicated and
self-affirming as the Marvel Cinematic Universe. So just as a thriving,
happy Timofey Pnin is said to be heading the Russian Department at
Wordsmith University in *Pale Fire*, *Lolita* gives us a bloody-minded
Humbert driving past a late-night, alternate-reality screening of his
creator's most noirish novel.

In his screenplay, Nabokov moved Humbert's murder of Quilty to
the front of the film—one of his few narrative choices that Kubrick left
unaltered—so we never encounter the moonlit drive-in. In his *Lolita*
screenplay, Stephen Schiff retains Nabokov's original ending and closely
follows its intended imagistic logic:

HUMBERT'S CAR—DRIVING—NIGHT

Moths in the headlights. Dark barns. A drive-in with a gigantic
screen, slanting away among the fields. A figure on the screen
raises a film-noir gun, prepares to shoot—and then passing
trees obscure the view.

Or consider another subtly vital image from Nabokov's bravura
finale: the rocking chair that Humbert accidentally shoots while
attempting to murder his rival. In the novel this chair responds to the
impact by "rocking in a panic all by itself," which is a typically observant
image. In Nabokov's published script, Humbert's shot "sets a rocking
chair performing on the landing," which is evocative enough—especially
that "performing"—but nowhere near as good as the language in the
novel. And here's how Schiff's stage direction describes it: "Humbert
fires. The bullet hits a black rocking chair, causing it to rock madly."

Now, not even Nabokov bothered to precisely re-create the gorgeous
image from the novel, even though he fought for the inclusion of the
rocking chair itself. Schiff, too, fights for the rocking chair, but doesn't
do anything with it. At first blush, it feels like a screenwriter's sad

capitulation. But is it? More likely, Schiff believed that while the rocking chair itself was worth it, the reader's mental effort in visualizing it the way Nabokov intended was not. Stage direction needs no more than minimum vividness—but also, crucially, no less.

*　*　*

Books and screenplays are not remotely comparable. A screenplay is a map, a blueprint, a starting point, whereas a book is the X, the edifice, the destination itself. Years before I began writing screenplays, when I was still firmly a prose supremacist, I chuckled whenever prose writers I admired inveighed against the sordidness of screenplay writing. The thing is, if you judge a screenplay by the same standards you'd use to judge a finished work of literary prose, screenplay writing *is* pretty sordid. Pick up Quentin Tarantino's shooting script for *Pulp Fiction* and you'll notice the most acclaimed, "literary" screenwriter of our time believes plurals take an apostrophe. Now that I've written screenplays myself, heard actors perform them, and withdrawn from set to slam my head against the nearest catering table, I've come to understand that questionable grammar has no bearing upon Tarantino's real talent, which is composing the kind of dialogue actors spend their careers waiting to perform. Knowing instinctively how to get the best from actors is not a negligible talent. Neither is an unerring ear for interesting verbal tics and turns of phrase. Doing both at the same time, while also creating characters that feel distinct, explosive, and alive? Not negligible. For what it's worth, William Faulkner was a terrible screenwriter.

Many novelists write screenplays on the sly. In my experience, the writer of prose who first tries his or her hand at screenwriting can be relied upon to operate under the mistaken assumption that a script is centered on dialogue. Read a prose writer's first (or second) script and you can count another mistake: the over-attribution of mood-explaining parentheticals. So instead of this:

TOM Where are you going?

TRISHA Yoga. Why do you ask?

You get this:

TOM *(suspiciously)* Where are you going?

TRISHA *(angrily)* Yoga. Why do you ask?

As the nascent screenwriter quickly learns, few actors want their inflections pre-supplied. Although it may seem to the writer of prose sheer negligence *not* to give actors a sense of moment-by-moment authorial intent, it's simply not the actor's job to be the screenwriter's emotional stenographer. What the seasoned screenwriter understands is that screenplays are primarily about character and transitions. Character doesn't have to emanate from what people say. Oftentimes, it's better when it doesn't. As for transitions, they're the building blocks of structure, and structure is what allows a director to begin to assemble a film or television show in his or her mind. A screenplay is first and foremost a tool of enabled envisioning. This doesn't mean your screenplay can't—or shouldn't—be fun to read, but if it's *only* fun to read, congratulations: you've succeeded in creating a document of perfect uselessness.

This speaks to the core tragedy of screenwriting and the not-so-hidden shame of its practitioners, for much of what makes a film or television show successful exists beyond the parameters of a script. Unlike a work of prose, visual entertainment has no single author. A film is first envisioned by a screenwriter but performed by actors under directorial guidance, shaped by hundreds of technical artists across a dozen disciplines, and finally assembled by an editor. Every visual entertainment is constructed out of myriad sensibilities and misruled by all manner of real-world volatility. So yes, a good screenplay provides a blueprint, a map—but a blueprint for something that will not be precisely built and a map for a destination that will never be exactly found.

Adapting a literary work for the screen would seem to make the collaborative, unpredictable process of filmmaking somewhat less fraught, as all the roughneck work—story, structure, character—has already been completed. Unfortunately, storytelling methodologies don't easily transfer across mediums. The more faithful a filmed adaptation tries to be to its source material, the more strangely paralyzed it can often feel. The great film editor Walter Murch once described the core problem of adaptation as "abundance," given that the "amount of story in a novel is so much more than a film can present.... If the filmmakers are overly respectful of the way the novel tells itself and of every novelistic detail, it's a recipe for filmic trouble."

Every adaptation thus pits two works against each other in a kind of useless battle—and when it's all over down there in the sandpit, there's always a perceived winner and loser. But how could it be any other way? The practice of adaptation is hinged upon competitive destruction. Characters are eliminated, events are compressed, narrative threads are combined. Whenever I'm adapting a book, I place the text on my left and maintain an open notepad on my right. I read and take notes simultaneously, as though doing double-entry bookkeeping. Yet it's not quite reading I'm doing on the left; it's more like reinterpretive pruning. And they're not quite notes I'm taking on the right; they're mostly page numbers, character names, swooping arrows. After a few hours, the book on my left looks to have been angrily stabbed to death with a blue pen. The notepad on my right? A skein of hieroglyphics.

Adaptation involves becoming a kind of stealth- or demi-author, creating through reshaping. Which brings us back to *Lolita*'s endgame rocking chair. Despite its presence in Nabokov's script, there's no errantly shot, madly performing rocking chair in Stanley Kubrick's *Lolita*. Yet that chair *is* present in Adrian Lyne's *Lolita*. There, Jeremy Irons's

Humbert fires at Frank Langella's Clare Quilty. The rocking chair is hit, the rocking chair rocks, and the camera moves on. It's just another prop—an object present for no apparent reason other than as an Easter egg for unusually close readers of the novel. Nabokov's rocking chair manages to encapsulate the principal conundrum of adaptation, whereby you retain things out of love and disfigure them out of necessity.

❉ ❉ ❉

In his introduction to the published screenplay of *Lolita*, Nabokov admits, "I am no dramatist." But that's not quite true. As a young man he wrote plays for the Russian theater in Paris while living in Berlin, which was his first stop on the long, traumatic journey that took him from the Bolshevik Revolution, through the inaugural fires of World War II (he left Paris a week before German tanks rolled into the city), and into the groves of American academia. What Nabokov wasn't was a particularly good dramatist. Like many failed practitioners of a difficult and exacting art, he turned angrily on the form, which, in *Lolita*, he allows Humbert to describe as "primitive and putrid." At the same time, he admitted to having enjoyed the experience of writing the *Lolita* screenplay, describing the final push to finish it as "exhilarating."

Shortly after the Nabokovs arrived in America in 1940, they settled briefly in California, as Stanford was the first institution to offer Vladimir employment. (His later, more permanent academic appointments brought him back east to Wellesley, Harvard, and finally Cornell.) Véra loved California, if only for its "illusion of European life," as she later described it. When they returned in 1960 so Vladimir could write the *Lolita* script, she was thrilled. There's a conceivable version of Nabokov's career in which, after he finishes the *Lolita* screenplay, he and Véra remain in California rather than move to Europe. (The only reason this didn't happen was due to their son, Dmitri, who was pursuing an opera career

in Milan; they wanted to stay close to him, so to Europe they returned.)
So what happens when our alt Nabokovs forsake Europe and decide to
call California home? Easy. Vladimir continues writing novels while
moonlighting as a professional screenwriter. And why not? Consider
how the 1950s treated him. The first edition of *Speak, Memory* sold
poorly. *Lolita* was rejected everywhere. So was *Pnin*, which was written
after *Lolita* but published before its American debut. (Think about
that: Nabokov, standing atop the Everest of his creative powers, had
a consistently hard time getting published. It has never been a good
time to be an American prose writer.) It's now known that Nabokov's
interest in screenwriting went deeper than one might suppose. In 1964,
he responded to Alfred Hitchcock's request for a story pitch with a cloud-
cuckoo précis about a young actress "of not quite the first magnitude....
[being] courted by a budding astronaut." The astronaut returns from
space a hero, but "soon she realizes that he is not the same as he was
before his flight.... Time goes on, and she becomes concerned, then
frightened, then panicky." (Oddly, this is basically the plot of the 1999
thriller *The Astronaut's Wife*, which starred Johnny Depp and Charlize
Theron.) Hitchcock did not "move forward" with the pitch, as they say
in the industry, but it sparked Nabokov's interest in an aborted sci-fi
project called *Letters from Terra*, which ultimately became the story-
within-the-story of his late novel *Ada*. At another point, Nabokov was
asked to adapt Proust's *In Search of Lost Time* for the screen, which he
was apparently keen to do. Once again, the project never came to fruition.

Even if he'd kept up the endeavor and entered the ranks of the
WGA, there's good reason to suspect that Nabokov would have never
become a first-rate screenwriter. His entire conception of how fiction
works was antithetical to what most of us would describe as the goals of
commercial filmmaking. Perhaps more than any other author, Nabokov
is a ghostly but detectable presence in his books. The peerless Nabokov

scholar Brian Boyd has referred to the "secret communion of the author and reader behind the narrator's back" that takes place in virtually all Nabokov's work. But it's less a "secret communion" than a raucous cocktail party of author-audience chatter that Nabokov's narrators, ears plugged with haughty pride, somehow refuse to hear. Humbert is often referred to as an unreliable narrator, but he's not—at least not traditionally. He tells us he's irresistible to women ("I could obtain at the snap of my fingers any adult female I chose") and everything that happens in the novel bears out the boast: Charlotte falls for him, as does (in her initially innocent way) Lolita herself, to say nothing of Jean Farlow, Lolita's friend Mona, and the late-appearing lush Rita. Nabokov made his unreliable narrators more mysterious than transmitters of sketchy information. He made them intellectual antiheroes who miss the point of their own existence. You laugh at them, but you're also terrified of them. Their blindness—moral, political, ethical—is entirely recognizable today. What are Charles Kinbote and Humbert Humbert if not the progenitors of "alternate facts"?

Nabokov playfully referred to himself as both a "prison director" and "an anthropomorphic deity" when writing, while dismissing his characters as "galley slaves." *Reality* was a word Nabokov distrusted, especially with regard to literature. "To be sure," he tells us in his commentary to *Eugene Onegin*, "there is an average reality, perceived by all of us, but that is not true reality; it is only the reality of general ideas." This so-called reality of general ideas "begins to rot and stink as soon as the act of individual creation ceases to animate a subjectively perceived texture." Nabokov thus creates entirely closed narrative systems in which not even the weather feels incidental. His worlds tend to be so singular, so one-man-bandified, that few directors in their right minds

276 would *want* to film them.[3] All of which is to say the collision between Vladimir Nabokov and Stanley Kubrick—demanding, impractical men partial to writing the unwritable and filming the unfilmable—seemed fated to result in either a perfect creative match or a welter of duels and lawsuits. The reality would be, as reality often proves to be, far more mundane.

✿   ✿   ✿

In 1958, in the midst of the life-changing tremors attendant to *Lolita*'s success, Nabokov received a letter from Kubrick and producer James B. Harris, seeking the film rights to *Lolita*, a book that remained banned in several countries and whose American publisher was still sweating the potential legal ramifications of having released it. Nabokov likely doubted much would come of the offer. The film industry was still subject to a notorious censorship regime in the form of the Production Code. Nevertheless, Nabokov retained the legendary Hollywood deal-maker Irving Lazar and negotiations began. Weeks later, Nabokov was sitting down for lunch with reporters from *Life* magazine when the phone rang. *Lolita*'s film rights had gone to Kubrick and Harris for $150,000, the equivalent of $1.3 million today. Nabokov quickly recalled a dream he had had four decades before, in 1916, shortly after his wealthy Uncle Vasya died. In Nabokov's dream, Vasya came to him and promised two men named Harry and Kurvykrin would resuscitate his lost fortune. And now here were Harris and Kubrick making him as rich as a writer in

---

3   And yet a few dauntless souls have persisted. Other than *Lolita* and *Laughter in the Dark*, his novels *The Defense*; *King, Queen, Knave* (starring Gina Lollobrigida!); and *Despair* (with a screenplay by Tom Stoppard) have all been filmed, with results that could be politely described as mixed. *Laughter in the Dark*—which was updated to take place in the swinging '60s, and whose making was, predictably, a fiasco—is not commercially available in any way and missing from most rare-film archives, which is probably the most Nabokovian thing about it.

mid-century America could hope to be. It's a wonderfully Nabokovian story, which is why it's almost certainly not true. To friends and relatives Nabokov's reaction was more embittered; he complained to his sister Elena that "all this should have happened thirty years ago."

Kubrick had first been given *Lolita* by novelist and screenwriter Calder Willingham, with whom Kubrick had collaborated on *Paths of Glory* and what became (once Kubrick and Willingham left the project) the only film Marlon Brando ever directed, *One-Eyed Jacks*. *Lolita* hit Kubrick with full force. When he first read it, he was still at work on *Spartacus*, a film he later wrote off as having had "everything but a good story." Thirty years old, and with only one proper Hollywood film under his belt, Kubrick had been press-ganged into directing *Spartacus* by Universal when the original director, Anthony Mann, was fired. By all accounts Kubrick successfully acquitted himself, but the sword-and-sandal epic was not his film. Moreover, he knew his involvement with it had placed him at a vexing career crossroads. He and Harris were determined to go back to smaller-scale filmmaking, but—and blink three times if any of this sounds familiar—the Hollywood of 1959 was focused almost entirely on epic-scale pictures due to competition from television, where "human interest" storytelling reigned. *Lolita* gave Kubrick the perfect opportunity to shoot a small, high-profile, ferociously psychological film, potential controversy be damned.

In 1959, Kubrick formally asked Nabokov to write the screenplay for *Lolita*. Nabokov received the invitation in Arizona, while he and Véra were in the middle of one of their cross-country Lepidoptera hunts. Intrigued, the Nabokovs drove on to Los Angeles to meet Kubrick. Things got off to a poor start when Nabokov was told that the film version of *Lolita* would have to end with Humbert and Dolores getting married— with the blessing of a relative, preferably. (In the novel, Dolores *has* no other living relatives. That's kind of the point.) Of course, this suggestion struck Nabokov as the height of inanity. But Harris[4] had already sat down for initial meetings with the MPAA, the trade association that represents film studios, to discuss ways to maneuver around the Production Code. When the MPAA argued that Humbert and Dolores's relationship was too immoral to depict, Harris pointed out that it was perfectly legal in several states for a man of Humbert's age to marry a twelve-year-old girl, provided she had her parents' blessing. (Horrifyingly, it still is.) The MPAA agreed that Harris had identified a potential checkmate against inevitable Production Code complaints. Nabokov might have appreciated the irony. In the novel, Humbert himself ridicules the obvious madness of "a civilization which allows a man of twenty-five to court a girl of sixteen but not a girl of twelve." Promising he'd think about a way to turn *Lolita* into a screenplay that wouldn't get them all thrown in jail, Nabokov left Los Angeles. A month later he quit the project, deciding he wanted no part of what Kubrick and Harris were creating.

Kubrick consequently turned to Calder Willingham, whose efforts proved unsatisfying to the famously demanding director. In late 1959, when the Nabokovs were still traveling around Europe in search of a suitable place to settle, Vladimir received a telegram from Kubrick: "CONVINCED YOU WERE CORRECT DISLIKING MARRIAGE STOP BOOK A MASTERPIECE AND SHOULD BE FOLLOWED EVEN IF LEGION AND CODE DISAPPROVE STOP STILL BELIEVE YOU ARE ONLY ONE FOR SCREENPLAY STOP IF FINANCIAL DETAILS CAN BE AGREED WOULD YOU BE AVAILABLE." Soon after, in Sicily, Nabokov had what he later

---

4   James B. Harris is still alive. Following his association with Kubrick, he went on to produce and direct a number of films, including an adaptation of James Ellroy's novel Blood on the Moon. His most recent credit was for producing Brian De Palma's 2006 The Black Dahlia—a credit that stemmed from a contractual attachment to an earlier, abandoned Dahlia adaptation. Hollywood fun fact: Harris's brother, Robert, wrote the bubonically catchy theme song for the 1960s-era Spider-Man cartoon show.

described as "a small nocturnal illumination of diabolical origin."
Somewhere within his mind he saw the novel's Enchanted Hunters sequence—in which Lolita and Humbert first have sex—broadcast in full color, as though in a Kodachrome vision. Suddenly, he had a way to adapt the novel that would both tiptoe past the Production Code and honor his artistic intentions.

Véra sprang formidably into action. According to Stacey Schiff, she "negotiated a comfortable arrangement with Kubrick. Her husband was to be granted every creative freedom in his work; he was not to be paid for fewer than twenty-six weeks or detained in Hollywood for longer than thirty-four; he was to be entitled to a vacation. In exchange he granted Kubrick his exclusive attention"—at a time when Nabokov's attention was, quite literally, the world's most valuable literary commodity— "and agreed to participate in the film's publicity." Nabokov later disingenuously referred to the "honorarium" he'd been paid to adapt *Lolita*, but he was awarded (in inflation-adjusted numbers) $280,000 for his script, with another (inflation-adjusted) $244,000 thrown in if he received sole credit, which he did. That's today's equivalent of half a million dollars for a script that, in large part, wasn't even used— proving that, then as now, the film industry is structured to function as welfare for already wealthy people.

By March the Nabokovs were back in Los Angeles. Soon Vladimir was meeting with Kubrick regularly about how to (as Nabokov put it) "cinematize" the novel. Their first meetings were held in Kubrick's bungalow on the Universal lot, where he was overseeing the *Spartacus* edit. In his introduction to the *Lolita* screenplay, Nabokov describes these early conversations as "an amiable battle of suggestion and countersuggestion.... [Kubrick] accepted all my vital points. I accepted some of his less significant ones." Nabokov's recollections were almost always reframed to show him at maximum favorability,[5] but here, especially, Kubrick—one of the greatest artists in the history of cinema—comes off like some nodding junior camera operator.

Once he and Kubrick settled on a first-act outline, Nabokov and Véra moved into a rented home in Brentwood, which was helpfully buffeted by miles of thick scrub Nabokov avidly scoured for butterflies once his morning writing session was complete. He scratched out the script on his famed note cards, his reliance on which had intensified during his work on the novel version of *Lolita*. (He drafted much of the book in a car, either while Véra drove him from one butterfly-laden canyon to another or sitting in his driveway—the quietest spot the audiophobic author could find during Ithaca's summers, which were always agrowl with neighborhood lawn mowers. He loved the cards because they were like small, portable desks.) Nabokov's qualms about working in the screenplay format "dissolved in the pleasure of the task," he later wrote. He even invented several new scenes that, as he put it, "were now produced as naturally as if the core of the novel was evolving a new life of its own."

This toil took him from March to June, whereupon Nabokov's stay in Los Angeles was extended beyond the terms Véra had negotiated. Kubrick needed more from him, and anyway Nabokov liked the nearby public library, which was helpful for his early research on *Pale Fire*.

---

5 In the afterward to Lolita, Nabokov mockingly paraphrases the various rejections he claims he received from publishers, along with their suggestions to make the book palatable: change Lolita into a boy, make Humbert a farmer, etc. Several scholars and biographers have read every rejection Lolita received and in not one of them do such suggestions appear. Nabokov is actually citing a letter he wrote Graham Greene in 1956: "The pity is that if I had made [Lolita] a boy, or a cow, or a bicycle, Philistines might never have flinched." Most writers reshape their memories into self-flattering mirrors; likely every person does this. But Nabokov was always crowing about his superlative gift for recollection—a trait he shares, incidentally, with one H. Humbert.

By summer's end, a thousand note cards had been filled. Typed up **281** by Véra, the *Lolita* script's first draft came in at 400 pages, leading Harris to famously remark, "You couldn't film it. You couldn't *lift* it." Once Kubrick had a read, he dropped by the Nabokovs' house and told Vladimir that, if filmed, his script would take seven hours to run. Nabokov spent the next three months chopping the pages down to a cinematically feasible length. While this was the most enjoyable part of the process for Nabokov creatively, he'd also begun to recognize that something was amiss between him and Kubrick. Anyone who's written for a studio or director will squirm in recognition at the slow freeze out Nabokov describes here: "During the next months we met rather seldom.... [C]riticism and advice got briefer and briefer.... I did not feel quite sure whether Kubrick was serenely accepting whatever I did or silently rejecting everything." Know that, if you have to ask, they're silently rejecting everything. For once, the puppet master himself was forced to look up for signs of the telltale strings.

Why Kubrick gradually soured on Nabokov isn't a great mystery. The answer can be located in something Nabokov declaims in his introduction to the *Lolita* screenplay: "[T]here is nothing in the world that I loathe more than group activity, that communal bath where the hairy and slippery mix in a multiplication of mediocrity." If you view mediocrity as the predestined result of collaboration, you probably shouldn't be writing screenplays. At the same time, the bitterness Nabokov felt about writing an unused *Lolita* script—which took him a decade to fully admit, even as his view of the film itself mellowed[6]—is more understandable when you learn that both Kubrick and Harris professed to the man's face that he'd turned in the best screenplay ever written in Hollywood.

---

6   This loop had closed by the time Lolita: A Screenplay *was published in 1974, allowing Nabokov to end his introduction by describing the work as not a "pettish refutation of a munificent film" but rather as "a vivacious variant of an old novel."*

NABOKOV'S ROCKING CHAIR: LOLITA AT THE MOVIES

282 The pair then spent the next few months completely rewriting it—only to rewrite it again days before *Lolita*'s filming commenced in England. Interestingly, Nabokov and Kubrick's greatest disagreement while the writing was underway was whether Nabokov would reserve the right to publish his own version of the screenplay. Kubrick probably feared this because he already knew his and Nabokov's visions for the film were not at all complementary. Also, who would *welcome* a readily available source of comparison with Vladimir Nabokov? As it turned out, though, Kubrick had little to fear.

❋   ❋   ❋

From page one of his screenplay, Nabokov struggles to make the transfigured story of *Lolita* appropriately "cinematic," as when he painstakingly describes the camera's journey around the dilapidated mansion of Clare Quilty. The camera "slides down" a gutter pipe, for instance, "glides around" a turret, and even withdraws from one object "with a shudder." It's impossible to guess how seriously Kubrick took any of Nabokov's cinematographical suggestions, but it's worth noting he used precisely none of them. On the second page of the script, you learn something truly fascinating, which is that Nabokov intended to frame the story of the filmic *Lolita* as a parody of a public service announcement about the dangers posed by Humbertian perverts. The host of this PSA is none other than John Ray Jr., PhD., who provides the novel's fatuous forward. As Nabokov's stage direction has it, Dr. Ray, looking over a manuscript on his desk, "swings around toward us in his swivel chair" and proceeds to unleash a page of dialogue. (A sample: "As a case history, his autobiography will no doubt become a classic in psychiatric circles.") Out of curiosity, I asked a professional actor to perform Ray's speech, which took more than two minutes to get through. Needless to say, stranding an unmoving actor on an uninvolving set and asking him to speak for two minutes directly into camera at the very beginning of a film is not the wisest use of screen time. Nabokov's published screenplay version of *Lolita* was a heavy rewrite of what he once believed would be the shooting script, and as such it's clearly intended more to be read than performed. It nevertheless illustrates how curiously uncinematic Nabokov's otherwise highly visual imagination could be.[7]

Early on, Humbert's voiceover plays atop diffracted vignettes from his early life. A question thus emerges. If the film is supposed to be framed as a Ray-hosted anti-pervert PSA, why does Humbert even have a voiceover? Does that not break the narrative logic of the intended frame? Nabokov's script can't even agree who should be doing the voiceover, for sometimes it's Humbert and sometimes it's Ray. Later on, the screenplay dons another ill-fitting parodic mask. When Humbert bolts outside to find his wife Charlotte dead in the street, the stage direction suddenly relocates the viewer to, of all places, a police department projection room. A character called the Instructor coldly narrates Charlotte's fatal accident, replete with Nabokov's descriptions of diagrams, dotted lines, and impact markers. An amusing bit, but good directors will ask their excitable screenwriters to justify *why* such a reality-breaking device is being introduced. Nabokov might have argued that the sequence suggests Humbert's clinical distance from his wife's death. Surely, though, there were other, less abstract methods to indicate the same thing. These sequences—and there are several more

---

7   *Screenwriter Nabokov is also more literal-minded than his prose-writing brother. In the novel, Humbert's childhood love Annabel becomes the ur-nymphet—the source, we're told, of the deranged man's later attraction to children. This leads the novel's Humbert to famously conclude that he has willed Lolita into existence by "incarnating" Annabel in her. In the script, Nabokov has Humbert and Lolita together look at an old picture of Annabel, whom the stage direction tells us should be "the same actress as the one that plays Lolita but wearing her hair differently, etc."*

like it—present a version of Nabokov that we rarely encounter in the fiction: a stylist who seems to be gloating rather than illuminating.

Flights of fancy are the least of the script's problems. Generally speaking, Nabokov's characters say three times more than necessary with half the poetry and artistry they need. And while there are some very good bits of writing in Nabokov's screenplay, it's amusing to see how often the twentieth century's greatest prose writer is defeated by the labored mannequin posing of stage direction: "Charlotte transposes jar of skin scream from farther mat (mat 2) to nearer mat (mat 1) and sits down on mat 1. Lolita yanks the comics section, and the family section, and the magazine section, out of Humbert's paper and makes herself comfortable on mat 2." Got all that, director? Good. Now let's block it.

The script does contain some genuinely delightful Nabokovian flourishes, the most literal of which involves Humbert and Lolita getting lost in a godforsaken canyon. Lolita, spotting a stranger, suggests they ask for directions from "that nut with the net over there." I'll let the stage direction take it from here: "The Butterfly Hunter. His name is Vladimir Nabokov." Nabokov the character proceeds to be a pedantic jackass to Humbert about the distinction between a "rare specimen" and a "rare species" of butterfly, which shows us the real Nabokov having fun with his reputation for infuriating meticulousness. Probably the funniest moment in the script occurs (oddly enough) when Humbert shows up at the home of Lolita's husband, Richard Schiller, with a handgun in his pocket and revenge on his mind. A nearby dog begins barking at Humbert's approach. Nabokov cheerfully lends this beast the dignity of a line, complete with a parenthetical:

DOG (*perfunctorily*) Woof.

Nabokov's script is at its best whenever Humbert and Lolita get a chance to talk. In the book, of course, we see Lolita only from Humbert's perspective, which is necessarily blurred by his obsession; we hear only what he wants us to hear. When the novel's Humbert tells us, "Mentally, I found her to be a disgustingly conventional little girl," you have to read between the lines to understand that Lolita has begun to resist her captor. Many readers of the novel don't bother to do that, leading them to conclude that Lolita is exactly how Humbert describes her: "a most exasperating brat." The screenplay presents a different Lolita. She's funnier and more playful, especially during her and Humbert's increasingly perilous flirtation—that is, before their fateful congregation in room 342 of the Enchanted Hunters hotel.[8] Here's a fine example of how spritely—even charming—the screenplay's pre-assaulted Lolita can be:

LOLITA Tell it to Mom.

HUMBERT Why?

LOLITA Oh, I guess you tell her everything.

HUMBERT Wait a minute, Lolita. Don't waltz. A great poet said: Stop, moment————. You are beautiful.

LOLITA (feigning to call) Mother!

HUMBERT Even when you play the fool.

LOLITA That's not English.

HUMBERT It's English enough for me.

LOLITA D'you think this dress will make Kenny gulp?

HUMBERT Who's Kenny?

---

8   How Nabokov proposes handling the tricky sequence of Lolita and Humbert's first sexual encounter is fairly ingenious: a series of cutaway inserts to show what's going on elsewhere in the hotel. Thus, in Room 180: "Dr. and Mrs. Braddock—he snoring lustily; she is awakened by two pigeons on the window sill." The image of innocent misapprehension within Room 344—i.e., next door to Humbert and Lolita—is especially disturbing: "The laughter of a child in the neighboring room rouses Dr. Boyd, who looks at his watch and smiles." When we finally cut back to Room 342, Lolita is said to be "messily consuming a peach."

LOLITA He's my date for tonight. Jealous?

HUMBERT In fact, yes.

LOLITA Delirious? Dolly-mad?

HUMBERT Yes, yes. Oh, wait!

LOLITA And she flew away.

She flies away.

Later in the script, Lolita requests a dime for the jukebox. Humbert refuses; he wants to talk to her about something. Okay, Lolita says. She'll talk. "If you give me a dime. From now on I am coin operated." You come to understand what Humbert actually sees in Lolita in a way you don't while reading the novel, which is doubly strange given how often Humbert obsesses about her. The novel shows us a monster's erasure of a girl. The screenplay shows us a girl fighting off her erasure.

But as much as Nabokov's script elevates Lolita, it also fails her—at what is perhaps the story's most emotionally pivotal moment. In the novel, as in Kubrick's film, it occurs the day after Lolita and Humbert's first sexual encounter, when Lo believes they're on their way to visit Charlotte in the hospital. It's clear by now that Lolita's "seduction" of Humbert (his word) is clearly some kind of Electra-complex power play, for Lo resents her mother at least as much as her mother resented her. Humbert has cruelly kept Charlotte's gruesome fate from Lolita, who until this point in the novel is the very picture of playful, outrageous precocity. When Lo's impatience to see her mother ruptures, Humbert finally snaps and tells her the truth, which is followed by a space-break relocation to a nearby hotel. There, in the middle of the night, while both recline in separate rooms, Humbert tells us, "she came sobbing into mine." They proceed to have sex—followed by Humbert's despicable, marrow-chilling assurance: "You see, she had absolutely nowhere else to go."

Lolita's horror of the future that awaits her with Humbert is palpable, but to escape her own crushing loss, she flees into the arms of her 287 abuser. Before she learns of Charlotte's death, Lolita likely believed she could have some fun with her weak-willed stepfather, perhaps even manipulate him, but now that the man has her in his talons, she knows how dearly she's miscalculated. This is Dolores Haze at her most heartrending and Humbert at his most damnable. Nothing about this scene is particularly uncinematic or "literary," which is what allows Kubrick's film to re-create it more or less as it's written in the novel. But Nabokov's screenplay, for some reason, leaps from Humbert's announcement of Charlotte's death to a "thick crayon smear" tracing Humbert and Lo's passage across "three or four mountain states." A few scenes later, Humbert begs Lolita never to leave him. Her answer: "Leave you? You know perfectly well I have nowhere to go." It's the same line, the same sentiment, but this is no longer tragedy. This is itinerary.

Véra Nabokov was adamant that Kubrick's *Lolita* "would have been much more brilliant" if only he'd used her husband's script. Yet at one of the most crucial and revealing points of the story, her husband lacked the dramatic sense to use his own novel.

✻   ✻   ✻

Kubrick apparently went to his grave regarding *Lolita* as his only complete cinematic failure. "Had I realized how severe the limitations were going to be," he once said, "I probably wouldn't have made the film."

There's no question *Lolita* is a strange, handcuffed movie. It's a story about child abuse that doesn't—can't—depict any child abuse. It's based on one of modern literature's most famous road novels but excises 90 percent of its road-novel material. Kubrick's *Lolita* is generally a very funny film, but whenever it tries to be funny in the way the novel is funny, it isn't funny at all. Throughout the film, the ratios—whether dramatic, comic, or scenic—feel somehow misaligned. The crucial

288 scenes following Humbert's installation within the Haze household, for instance, with him and Lolita warily eyeballing each other, barely register. The film then plants us in the middle of an eight-minute-long summer dance sequence that establishes little and muddles surprisingly much.[9] For those who love the book, the general rule of thumb for Kubrick's *Lolita* is this: all the scenes you regard as important will sail carelessly by while all the obviously unimportant scenes are turned into set-piece extravaganzas.

One explanation for the imbalances has to do with the narrative dilemma posed by the wicked playwright Clare Quilty. In the novel, Quilty is a phantasmic shadow whose intermittent appearances become apparent only when rereading. When Lolita finally runs off with Quilty, the first-time reader has no idea where she's gone or with whom. For his part, Humbert spends three fruitless years trying to piece together the identity of Lolita's abductor. When Humbert finally catches up to Lolita in the novel, he demands to learn the name of the man who stole her. "There was no shock," Humbert says, when Lo tells him, "no surprise. Quietly the fusion took place, and everything fell into order, into the pattern of branches that I have woven throughout this memoir with the express purpose of having the ripe fruit fall at the right moment." Yet Quilty's name remains undisclosed to the reader for several pages more. Humbert explains this delay by claiming "the astute reader" has figured it out already, but this is one of Nabokov's sly jokes. No first-time reader of *Lolita*, not even the most astute, has been prepped to identify this "ripe fruit." In a novel, a character doesn't have to be seen to make an impression and can reappear again and again without his identity being disclosed. The novel's Quilty, at once everywhere and

---

9   Among other things, the dance sequence strongly insinuates that Charlotte Haze and Clare Quilty had a previous sexual encounter and hints that Jean and John Fowler, largely inoffensive suburbanites in the novel, are swingers interested in Humbert's company.

NABOKOV'S ROCKING CHAIR: LOLITA AT THE MOVIES

nowhere, is a uniquely literary character because the delayed revelation of his identity is a uniquely literary conceit.

In Kubrick's film, Quilty serves a different purpose, and that is to be a character played by Peter Sellers. The role was actually enlarged to accommodate Sellers, which irritated Nabokov, as did the fact that Kubrick let Sellers invent most of his dialogue. (It didn't much please Sellers's costar James Mason either, who later complained Kubrick "was so besotted with the genius of Peter Sellers that he seemed never to have enough of him.") From the moment Quilty appears in the film's prologue—drunk and peeking out from under a white slipcover, which he quickly fashions into a toga—we know whose picture this is going to be. "Are you Quilty?" Humbert asks him. "No," Quilty says. "I'm Spartacus. You come to free the slaves or something?" By taking a shot at the film he just directed, Kubrick is establishing rule over this fictional realm, and you can understand why Nabokov later likened the experience of watching Kubrick's Lolita to "a scenic drive as perceived by the horizontal passenger of an ambulance."[10]

To be sure, something happens to the story of Lolita at a cellular level when Quilty trades Nabokov's existential mystery for Sellers's exquisite buffoonery. In the novel, Humbert's ignorance of Quilty's machinations feels blameless, even vaguely sympathetic, because we're as lost as he is. But when in the back half of Kubrick's Lolita a disguised Quilty shows up and taunts Humbert in a thick German accent about Lolita's "acute suppression of ze libido," our primary source of entertainment is Peter Sellers dissolving into yet another

---

10 Kubrick has Humbert present an accusatory poem he's written, which (as in the novel) he demands Quilty read before he shoots him. While this works quite well in the novel, even Nabokov had the sense to leave it out of his script. Sellers's Quilty dutifully reads a few lines of Humbert's poem before stopping to smirk. "Kinda getting repetitious there," he says. It feels like an unambiguous, if gentle, dig at Nabokov himself.

290 persona—and unwittingly auditioning for *Dr. Strangelove.*

In the novel (and Nabokov's script follows the scene closely), Quilty first appears in person on the pillared porch of the Enchanted Hunters hotel. Lolita is upstairs. Humbert has pumped sleeping pills into the girl and now awaits his chance to molest her without resistance. As Humbert turns to leave the porch, a man's voice says, "Where the devil did you get her?" Humbert, startled, asks the man to repeat what he just said. The man does: "I said: the weather is getting better." The sinister roundelay goes on like this ("You lie—she's not"/"I said: July was hot") until Humbert extricates himself. The encounter occupies a page in the novel and less than a minute of screen time in Nabokov's script.

The porch scene in Kubrick's film is nearly five minutes long. At this point, we've already met the filmic Quilty twice, as a disheveled madman in the prologue and as a dapper, tuxedoed smoothie during Dolores's school dance. Here on the porch of the Enchanted Hunters, however, he's a stammering wreck. Sellers's performance, largely ad libbed and based on Kubrick's outer-borough voice and mannerisms, is so casually virtuosic it feels like a transmission from some small, troubled asteroid adrift deep within Peter Sellers's mind. Claiming to be a police officer, his Quilty speaks with minimal interruption on the theme of what "normal guys" he and Humbert are:

> I couldn't help noticing when you checked in tonight—it's part of my job—I notice human individuals—I noticed your face. I said to myself when I saw you, I said, "There's a guy with the most normal looking face I ever saw in my life." ... It's great to see a normal face, because I'm a normal guy. It'd be great for two normal guys like us to get together and talk about world events, you know, in a normal sort of way.... May I say one other thing to you? It's really on my mind. I've been thinking about it quite a lot. I noticed when you was checking in you

had a lovely pretty little girl with you. She was really lovely.
As a matter of fact she wasn't so little, come to think of it. She
was a fairly tall little—what I mean—I mean, taller than little,
you know what I mean? But, uh—she was really lovely. I wish
I had a lovely pretty tall lovely little girl like that.

Many critics of Kubrick's *Lolita*, even some who've admired Sellers's performance, have complained that by letting Quilty hijack the film, Kubrick squandered the chance to properly adapt *Lolita*. That is probably true, but it was also the best option Kubrick had, given the reality of the Production Code.

It's not as though Kubrick's film tries to hide what's going on between Humbert and Lolita. In fact, *Lolita* is a racier film than it's given credit for. "What was the decisive factor?" Charlotte asks Humbert, after he announces his intention to lodge with her and her daughter. Humbert replies, looking askance at Lolita, "Your cherry pies." While Charlotte and Humbert play chess, she worries aloud about Humbert taking her queen—just as Lolita gives Humbert a too-long kiss on the cheek. The scene in which Lolita teases Humbert about the "real good games" she learned at camp, which leads to their first sexual encounter, is unmistakably about what it's about. Late in the film, one of Humbert's neighbors informs him that people "are getting a little curious" about his relationship with his daughter. (This is to say nothing of Quilty's same-sex flirtation with Mr. Swine, the concierge at the Enchanted Hunters hotel, which is shockingly overt for a film of its era.) But Kubrick had a real problem whether Humbert's relationship to Lolita was mostly inferred or blurted over a megaphone. Without knowing what Humbert is thinking, without the novel's sustained access to his mind, his behavior is virtually impossible to understand. Imagine the first-time viewer of Kubrick's *Lolita* who has not read the novel—who has no idea what the novel is about. They'd likely regard Humbert as a bumbling incompetent, barely cognizant that the story they're watching details his wanton destruction of a child. The part of Kubrick's film Nabokov hated most was the Buster Keaton antics his cultured antihero has with a foldable cot while Lolita sleeps. It's a genuinely funny sequence, but you get why Nabokov reacted so negatively: it's neither here nor there, rather like Kubrick's film, which has a *here* (Lolita) but no real *there*.

Except it does. Its *there* is Clare Quilty. In the novel Humbert frequently admits he's insane ("soon after my return to civilization I had another bout with insanity"), which is not how readers typically remember him. They remember Humbert as intelligent, witty, and a monster, but not as a lunatic. James Mason, despite his uncanny physical resemblance to Nabokov's description of Humbert ("pseudo-Celtic, attractively simian"), is an actor of such decency that part of you winds up rooting for Lolita to stay with him. Kubrick takes the madness of the novel's Humbert and embeds it in the film's Quilty because Humbert's insanity *is* Quilty, clammily embodied. This is truer to Nabokov's vision than most readers might realize, as there are hints throughout the novel that Quilty, a playwright, is wholly in control of Humbert's story.[11] How else can he know so many private things about Humbert and Lolita?

Kubrick also grasps a deep-cut secret hidden within Nabokov's novel: The tragic hero of *Lolita* isn't only Lolita. It is, also, her mother. Yes, Charlotte Haze is bathetic and needy. Yes, she is an exemplar of Dwight Macdonald's "midcult" taste, with her bad French and fondness for Mexican tchotchkes. Yes, she's cruel to her daughter. But Nabokov accounts for why Charlotte is this way. I speak of the letter she leaves

---

11 This is a recurring theme in Nabokov. Krug, the main character of *Bend Sinister*—one of Nabokov's greatest, most underrated novels—is driven insane when, after witnessing his son's murder, he realizes he's a character trapped inside a story.

for Humbert before driving Lolita to camp. There, Charlotte puts her heart on the line, telling her lodger he must leave the house because she's hopelessly in love with him. If, however, Humbert's still there when Charlotte returns, well, then she'll know "that you want me as much as I do you: as a lifelong mate; and that you are ready to link up your life with mine forever and ever and be a father to my little girl."

Because Humbert is incarcerated while he "writes" the text of *Lolita*, he lets us know he's recounting Charlotte's letter from memory. He then admits to having "left out a lyrical passage which I more or less skipped at the time, concerning Lolita's brother who died at two when she was four, and how much I would have liked him." And there it is: the explanation for Charlotte's keening desperation, the peculiar emotional intensity of Lolita, and the rancor that persists between daughter and mother. These are survivors who lost a father and husband, that we know—but also a brother, a *child*? There can be no pain more profound, and yet Humbert skips past it. It's a perfect demonstration of his cruelty and one of Nabokov's more cunning reminders of how malevolent his mind really is. Kubrick and Harris gleaned the importance of this backstory, though they retrofit it. When the film's Charlotte and Humbert look upon a picture of her late husband, Charlotte remarks how much Humbert would have "liked" Harold Haze—exactly what the novel's Charlotte says to Humbert about her dead, unnamed son.

Shelley Winters, who plays Charlotte, had a difficult relationship with Kubrick, which mirrors the experience of several other female actors—Shelley Duvall especially—Kubrick later worked with. After one argument, Kubrick tried to sack Winters in the middle of filming. We should be glad he didn't, for Winters's performance is in many ways equal to that of Peter Sellers. She does not condescend to Charlotte. She plays her exactly as she is—an endlessly heartbroken but stubbornly optimistic woman trying to better herself and relieve her loneliness.

294 When Charlotte learns the truth about Humbert—when her world has fallen utterly apart—she flees upstairs to embrace her husband's urn. "Harold, look what happened!" she cries. "I've been disloyal to you." She begs for her dead husband's forgiveness, demands to know why he left her: "I didn't know anything about life!" Then, the awful kicker: "Next time it's going to be someone you'll be very proud of!"

None of this is in the novel. Neither is the kidney disease Kubrick and Harris give Charlotte, which is revealed after her death and, we're told, would have left her with very little time to live had the car swerved to avoid her, thereby explaining something else the novel doesn't. Mrs. Harold Hayes has obviously tricked herself into ignoring the danger signs emitted by Humbert, but why? Because Humbert is, quite literally, Charlotte's last chance for human happiness. Stanley Kubrick's *Lolita* might not be a faithful adaptation, but it understands the novel better than many who've read it.

❊   ❊   ❊

Adrian Lyne's 1997 adaptation of *Lolita* has been described by its screenwriter, Stephen Schiff, as "the most famous unreleased film in history." Unable to secure traditional distribution, this *Lolita*, which had a production budget of $60 million, finally premiered on Showtime in August 1998, giving it what Schiff describes as "the very dubious honor of being the most expensive movie ever to have its U.S. premiere on television." The issue preventing *Lolita*'s release stemmed from a 1996 law that passed while Lyne's film was docked in the editing bay. The Child Pornography Prevention Act—attached by Orrin Hatch as a rider to an otherwise unremarkable spending bill—was intended to combat deviants who used computer graphics and other forms of digital manipulation to simulate sexual acts with and between children. Problem one with the rider was that its legal applications were far too broad. With its passage, it suddenly became a crime to depict *any* activity involving children that "appeared to be" sexual in nature, even if the actors were adults playing children. Thus, anyone who distributed or broadcast Lyne's *Lolita* would be, technically speaking, breaking the law.[12]

Schiff was a film critic and literary journalist before he turned his hand to adapting the novel he describes as "a difficult and convoluted masterpiece," a phrase sure to have raised Nabokov's hackles. In 1990, Irving Lazar, Nabokov's now-ancient Hollywood rainmaker, was pushing to "cinematize" a suite of Nabokov novels, including *Lolita*. Schiff was lured into adapting the book by his friend Lili Zanuck, whose husband Richard was then *Lolita*'s principal producer. (The film's eventual producers were Mario Kassar and Joel Michaels.) Schiff wrote a number of pages, but when the ardor for a new version of *Lolita* died down, he abandoned them. Two years later, Adrian Lyne, the director of *Fatal Attraction*, signed on to *Lolita*, which had long been his dream project, and brought aboard *Fatal Attraction* screenwriter James Dearden to begin work on the script. What Dearden ultimately came up with is an abomination worthy of spinning several generations of Nabokovs in their luxurious graves.

All you need to know about Dearden's *Lolita* script, which takes place in the 1980s, is that it opens with Humbert in prison, handing out Stephen King and Norman Mailer novels to his cellmates. Lyne needed little prodding to move on to the playwright Harold Pinter, whose *Lolita* script is reputed to be superb but commercially untenable, largely due to Pinter's refusal to shrink from depicting Humbert's depravity. Carolco, the studio that initially financed Lyne's *Lolita*, was going bankrupt by the time Pinter's script was rejected, and so Schiff was once again floated as

---

12 No action was taken against Showtime after *Lolita*'s premiere and the Child Pornography Prevention Act was struck down by the Supreme Court in 2002, after an adult entertainment lobbying group and a nudist-lifestyle magazine consortium came together to challenge it.

a possible option, largely because, as an unknown, he was cheap. Lyne balked, however, and instead hired David Mamet[13] to write a new draft, which used as its narrative frame an ongoing conversation Humbert has with a prison psychiatrist. Schiff had a reasonable intuition Mamet's script would not work out, so he returned to his abandoned pages, kept writing, and eventually sent a sample batch to Lyne. Soon enough, as he writes in the introduction to his screenplay, he was ensconced at the Four Seasons in Beverly Hills and "living a satire of Hollywood." While neither Schiff nor Lyne disliked Kubrick's version of *Lolita*, they nevertheless regarded it as an example of what not to do. "My source material," Schiff writes, "was the novel itself."

Schiff's *Lolita* screenplay is an admirable adaptation, not to mention more economical than Nabokov's. What takes Nabokov thirty pages to set up—who Humbert is, why Annabel is important, why Humbert flees to the United States—Schiff accomplishes in five. In a bit cut from the final film, Schiff's Humbert even gets to explain his strangely twinned name to Charlotte: "My father had rather an odd sense of humor." (Schiff is of course nodding to Humbert's real father, Vladimir Nabokov.) The way the film handles Quilty is especially interesting, with a final confrontation between him and Humbert that's arguably weirder and more terrifying than the novel.[14] As strong as Schiff's script often is, however, Lyne, as the director, is responsible for some ludicrous choices, such as when Humbert first strolls into the backyard of the Haze home, which Charlotte insists on calling the "piazza." In the novel, Humbert is reaching for the train schedule in his pocket, already concocting

---

13 What's amusing about this is that Mamet is exactly the breed of leathery American naturalist whose dialogue Nabokov parodies in his *Lolita* afterword while imagining ways the novel could have been rewritten to ensure publication: "He acts crazy. We all act crazy, I guess. I guess God acts crazy."

14 Not only is Humbert's final battle with Quilty the best thing in Lyne's *Lolita*, it's the reason to see Lyne's *Lolita*. At one point, Frank Langella's Quilty casually eats a cigarette.

his excuse to flee, when, "without the least warning, a blue sea-wave 297
swelled under my heart and, from a mat in a pool of sun, half-naked,
kneeling," there is young Dolores Haze staring back at him over her
dark sunglasses. I'm not a filmmaker, but I can nevertheless imagine
being tasked with staging this moment and not embarrassing myself.
Lyne, however, decides to place his Lolita (played by Dominique Swain)
beside an active sprinkler. You understand that choice when the light
and water droplets combine into a globular constellation of liquid gold,
when the airborne moisture allows Swain's sundress to cling to her
body—a lascivious observation to make about a fourteen-year-old actor,
yes, but we're seeing her through Humbert's eyes: rapture at the sight of
this young body is the point, however dismaying that is. Yet Lyne also
has his water-sprayed Lolita casually reading a movie-star magazine.
At no point in history has a person in possession of a magazine—even
a magazine she disliked and actively sought to damage—looked around
her immediate surroundings, spotted an active source of spraying water,
and decided, "I think I'll read over there." It's a small bafflement but
a revealing one. Freed up (or so they thought) to make a more graphic
film than Kubrick could, Lyne and Schiff commit to a lovely but often
wrongheaded lyricism in an attempt to visually approximate Nabokov's
prose. In numerous ways this *Lolita* is a better adaptation than Kubrick's,
but it's also a weaker film.

One of the problems comes down to Humbert, which requires us
to backtrack to the novel itself. As Nabokov said to the *Paris Review*,
"*Lolita* has no moral in tow. For me a work of fiction exists only insofar
as it affords me what I shall bluntly call aesthetic bliss." In his famously
rebarbative "Reply to My Critics," Nabokov claimed that his *Eugene
Onegin* translation, unlike his novels, "possesses an ethical side, moral
and human elements." The larger point he's making—that depiction
is not endorsement; that it's silly to apply one's private morality to

the behavior of imaginary people—is surely correct. But to insinuate that a novel's status as fiction should protect its author's decisions, which have real-world implications and embody actual ethical values, is surely wrong.

Contra its creator, Nabokov's *Lolita* very much has a moral in tow. To discover it, all you need to do is scan the plain meaning of its ending—a meaning helpfully telegraphed at the beginning of the novel by (of all people) John Ray Jr., PhD.: "[Humbert] is abnormal. He is not a gentleman. But how magically his singing violin can conjure up a tendresse, a compassion for Lolita that makes us entranced with the book while abhorring its author!" Compassion ... for *Lolita*? Whom he rapes repeatedly? Whose arm she pulls away from him "so violently that I feared her wrist might snap, and all the while she stared at me with those unforgettable eyes where cold anger and hot tears struggled"? Neither Ray nor Nabokov are joking. Instead, they're pointing the reader to the end of Humbert's journey, when he visits the seventeen-year-old Lolita after not having seen her for years. She is, of course, pregnant and married to an inoffensive laborer named Richard Schiller. Humbert is here because Lolita has written him a letter: she and "Dick" need money. But he's come also to murder Richard Schiller, the man he believes took Lolita from him. Once that matter is cleared up, and Dick's innocence established, Humbert puts away his revolver and the scene coheres into what can only be described as Humbert's moral awakening—his realization that "a North American girl-child named Dolores Haze had been deprived of her childhood by a maniac." As he writes in direct address to the girl-child: "I loved you. I was a pentapod monster, but I loved you."

Nabokov reportedly wept while writing this scene, and there's no question that parts of it are extraordinarily moving. Humbert takes note of Dick Schiller's "black and broken" fingernails, for instance, before noticing, more generously, the man's "strong shapely wrist," which was "far, far finer than mine. I have hurt too much too many bodies with my twisted poor hands to be proud of them." What's most striking about the scene is the superhuman grace and composure displayed by Lolita herself. She's been through a series of experiences more harrowing than most of us could endure, but she doesn't feel sorry for herself or seek the revenge upon Humbert she is very much entitled to. In fact, she pities him. Humbert hands over to her quite a lot more money than she requested, after which he asks her to run away with him. Lolita misunderstands the offer. "You mean," she asks, "you mean you will give us that money only if I go with you to a motel." She can't imagine Humbert having higher aspirations than prostituting her. She can't, with eminently good reason, imagine a *selfless* Humbert. Even so, her apparent willingness to go with Humbert proves *her* selflessness. To secure her child's future, she'll suffer one final indignity. Humbert assures her that's not what he means. He wants them to have a life together, a real life that's not a "parody of incest," as he calls it. Lolita turns him down ("No, honey, no")[15] and takes the money. She is at last free to display the attribute Humbert denied her: an autonomous self.

After the murder of Quilty, the novel comes to an end with Humbert awaiting the arrival of the police and listening to the laughter of children emanating from a nearby playground. Of this laughter, Humbert reflects, "I knew that the hopelessly poignant thing was not Lolita's absence from my side, but the absence of her voice from that concord." These are the passages, I believe, that well-meaning readers have in mind when they misguidedly describe *Lolita* as a love story. These are also the

---

15 *Schiff's screenplay tacks a brutal addition onto Lolita's refusal from the novel: "No, honey. I'd almost rather go back with Clare [Quilty]." And when Humbert asks Lolita if she can ever forgive him— something he does not do in the novel—Schiff's Lolita says nothing. Finally, after nudging her dog, she replies coldly: "Say goodbye, Molly. Say goodbye to my dad." Both adds are extremely effective.*

passages that critics, almost all of them men, cite in support of Humbert's redemptive qualities, however scant they may be. Opinion: Humbert has no redemptive qualities. He's the story's hero only because it's told through his eyes. Nabokov wanted his "pentapod monster" to be moved and changed by his experience with Lolita, but in the age of Trump, Epstein, and Weinstein (which sounds like Lucifer's personal law firm) it's fair to ask whether falling into true love with your victim provides an appropriate moral apotheosis. Because, Vladimir Vladimirovich, *love conquers all* very much appears to be your moral in tow.

It's not as though the ending of Nabokov's *Lolita* offends me. Humbert isn't real, and Nabokov—a man with predictable generational peccadillos, especially regarding women—is long dead. By any measure, though, it's a bizarre ending, especially for a Nabokov novel, whose final pages usually delight in revealing the outer workings of another exquisitely imagined sham world. It's also the type of ending Nabokov otherwise loathed: straightforward, driven by epiphany. True, Nabokov succeeds in making us empathize with a monster and his portrait of Lolita's growth and maturity is exceptionally well drawn. If you take two steps back from the end of *Lolita*, however, you realize something. This is a novel that begins with a thirty-something scholar who recognizes he shouldn't rape a child but does and ends with him deciding he could love a pregnant seventeen-year-old. In this sense, the ending of *Lolita*—a novel I love, written by an author I revere—is an ethical oil spill even when viewed through the cleansing filter of Nabokov's prose. Which brings us back to the onscreen Humbert, that potentially even-more-terrible tyrant, whose appalling actions must, by dramatic necessity, be *seen*. Maybe Stanley Kubrick had it figured out sixty years ago—that onscreen Humbert is best visualized not as a tragic figure but rather as a comic one.

The most frustrating aspect of Schiff and Lyne's *Lolita* is how close they come to suggesting otherwise. In the novel, Humbert has his first flicker of tragic conscience while he and Dolores drive away from the Enchanted Hunters hotel. Here's how Schiff realizes the moment in his screenplay, which closely mirrors the language of Nabokov's novel:

> HUMBERT (*voiceover*) I felt more and more uncomfortable.
> It was something quite special, that feeling:
> an oppressive, hideous constraint—as if I were sitting
> with the small ghost of somebody I had just killed.

This admission is astonishing—one of the few times Humbert expresses regret while Lolita is still in his hideous care. It's also accurate: Humbert *has* effectively killed someone and *is* sitting beside her ghost. Whereas Nabokov's script uses its voiceover like an indiscriminate paint gun, Schiff has an excellent sense of which of the novel's lines to isolate and emphasize. The problem is, in the film, Humbert's voice, when divided into discreet units, rarely lands with the fluency, much less the audacity, that it needs. (In Kubrick's film, this issue is just as pronounced.) As a viewer, you hear lines that register as convincingly Nabokovian and then you sit there staring at Jeremy Irons's face. When as a screenwriter you're free to pick lines from the novel's absurdly bountiful garden, there's the danger of inadvertently ennobling Humbert—a danger Schiff's screenplay does not always evade. Early in the film, we watch as Humbert writes in his journal shortly after his and Lolita's first instance of not-quite-innocent physical contact. "A normal man," Humbert's voice intones, "given a group photograph of schoolgirls, and asked to point out the loveliest one, will not necessarily choose the nymphet among them. You have to be an artist, a madman, full of shame and melancholy and despair, in order to recognize the little deadly demon among the others." It all sounds rather lovely, doesn't it, coming from this handsome, acceptably wretched older man who just happens to be attracted to little girls. The corresponding passage in Nabokov's novel is longer, crazier, and more unhinged. It's not easy or polished or fluent. It doesn't make loving children seem just a little too reasonable.

❊ ❊ ❊

Before I began this essay, I hadn't read *Lolita* in twenty years. It's the rare Nabokov novel I'd never reread. I can't remember to what degree *Lolita* shocked or disturbed me when I first read it as a young man, but I do remember being surprised, given its reputation, that it wasn't a particularly graphic book. (Humbert: "I am not concerned with so-called 'sex' at all. Anybody can imagine those elements of animality.") As I reread *Lolita*, though, one scene affected me to the point of physical discomfort. It is when, late in the novel, Lolita comes down with the flu. "I undressed her," Humbert says.

> Her breath was bittersweet. Her brown rose tasted of blood.
> She was shaking from head to toe. She complained of a painful
> stiffness in the upper vertebrae—and I thought of poliomyelitis
> as any American parent would. Giving up all hope of intercourse,
> I wrapped her up in a laprobe and carried her into the car.

I am now forty-five. I have a five-year-old daughter. I find, perhaps not surprisingly, that the latter fact greatly intensifies my rage for what Humbert makes unspeakable claim to: the sacred bond between parent and child. I have held my daughter while she trembled with a high fever. I know of no experience more scouring than a child clinging to you in search of answers you do not have, aid you cannot give. That a human being could think to poison a comfort-seeking child with "intercourse" whisks my mind past the civilized checkpoints of bureaucratic justice and sets in my hand a hard, hot stone I would gladly heave at the skull of every real-life Humbert unfortunate enough to be placed before me.

"I am now faced with the distasteful task of recording a definite drop in Lolita's morals." This is one of Humbert's—and *Lolita*'s—most diabolically funny lines, or so it once seemed to me. What follows is Humbert's recounting of Lolita's successful weaponization of what he elsewhere calls "her morning duty." Stripped of euphemism, Humbert begins paying Lolita for sex. Those of us familiar with Nabokov's novel, before we press play on Adrian Lyne's *Lolita*, could not be blamed for thinking, *They won't* possibly *go there.* Go there they do. We watch as Dominique Swain—Malibu born, fourteen years old at the time of filming, cast after six grueling months of open calls, and whom Stephen Schiff describes as "enormously gifted—at once a seductress and a little girl"— moves her hand up Humbert's thigh. "You like that?" she asks. "You want more, don't you? I want things, too." Elsewhere we watch as she kisses Humbert, first with an open mouth, eventually with full tongue. Here is some of Schiff's stage direction: "She sits astraddle him, gazing down knowingly. Then she leans down and begins to undo his pajama bottoms. As he watches—astonished, hypnotized, mad with desire—she slowly takes out her retainer and tosses it on the nightstand." I am now faced with the distasteful task of recording my feelings as I watched a brave and estimable young actor named Dominque Swain scream at Humbert Humbert that she earned her money, she wants her money, which gains her a hard smack across the face. Because that's the thing about Humbert. He's not only a child rapist, he's a child hitter—an abuser in every way available to him. "Murder me!" the film's Lolita cries out to Humbert at one point, her eyes inky with madness. "I'm asking you to murder me!" She means it. Our Lolita wants to die, so depraved has she become. In these moments, Adrian Lyne's *Lolita* is as unnerving as any movie I've ever seen. "If this film didn't from time to time make an audience acutely uncomfortable," Stephen Schiff writes, "we weren't doing our job." So I guess they did it. I guess they did their job.

304 When Lyne's *Lolita* was being edited and reedited to appease the lawyers who swooped down upon it while the producers sought not only a distribution deal but a way to avoid federal prison, one scene proved especially troublous. Schiff calls it the Comics Scene. In it, a reclining Lolita reads the funny papers. Humbert is behind her. Little by little, the viewer gradually realizes they are in fact having sex. The lawyers wanted the scene out, as it was almost certainly going to run afoul of the Child Pornography Prevention Act. Schiff argued to keep the scene in. It showed not explicit but implied sex, and implied sex, Schiff pointed out to the lawyers, wasn't part of the statute. Schiff won that argument. The Comics Scene stayed. It's followed by a shot of Lolita crying inconsolably on her bed at the Sandman Hotel.

"*Lolita* has a built-in condemnation of what it describes." Or so one of the novel's defenders once argued. This is true. It does. But it's also not that simple. A novel's virtue is its privacy; it depicts without pictures—and pictures will always be the hard problem for the eager adaptor of *Lolita*. In his introduction to his screenplay, Schiff affects annoyance with such questions. "During the shoot," he writes,

> we played by the strictest rules the film's lawyers could devise. Any nudity required an adult body double for Dominique. If Dominique sat on Jeremy's lap, a board was inserted between them. Dominique's mother and tutor were on the set whenever she was. I often found myself in the position of reassuring everyone: We're not going to be arrested, for Chrissake. This isn't the Fifties. We're not making a pornographic film. We're adapting one of the acknowledged great works of twentieth century literature.

While I assembled my notes for this essay, I found myself thinking about the twin Lolitas, Sue Lyon and Dominique Swain, quite a lot. I tried to imagine being fourteen years old and put into the position of portraying a character whose very name has become synonymous with jailbait. I attempted to contact both, to ask them how portraying Dolores Haze had affected their lives, but neither responded. Only weeks later, Sue Lyon died. Stanley Kubrick selected Lyon for his *Lolita* partially because she looked older than fourteen. The moment Nabokov saw her, during his final meeting with Kubrick, he exclaimed, "No doubt about it: she is the one."

Although her career initially surged in the wake of *Lolita*, Lyon eventually struggled to find roles. For years she refused to give interviews, but I found one online from more than three decades ago. It's a fascinating conversation. When asked if she was familiar with Nabokov's novel before she auditioned, Lyon reveals that an older girlfriend read parts of the book aloud to her before she went in. "We thought it was very risqué," she says. For what it's worth, Lyon claims to have loved the experience of making *Lolita*: "I didn't have to have an affair with an old man. I only had to make a movie about it. They took care of me in every way. They were exceptional. See, after my contract was over, and I worked with other people, I was shocked. I thought everybody in the movie business was nice.... When I found out how terrible it was, I was so hurt. I remember being hurt, that people were so mean." How mean? Here's Stephen Schiff in the introduction to his screenplay: "[Lolita] was an enormous, difficult role, and we wanted to avoid, above all, the mistake that we felt Kubrick had made in casting Sue Lyon, a fifteen-year-old who nevertheless looked like a twenty-year-old hooker." When Sue Lyon was sixteen years old and still doing publicity for Kubrick's film, her older brother committed suicide. Naturally, Lyon was asked by one curious interviewer if her brother had killed himself because his sister played Lolita. "I didn't say a thing," she says in the online interview. "I got up and I walked off. I couldn't even dignify that.... I had no words. That's typical of the reason why I couldn't be a movie star. I never could."

A great, though appropriate, irony of filming a story about a young girl whose life is ruined is knowing you could ruin some young girl's life by filming it. You could tell yourself, "We'll be great to her, we'll make her comfortable, we'll be exceptional, we'll stuff a board between her and every middle-age erection on set." In literature, no one gets hurt, because literature is not real. Yet film and television sort of *are* real when you're talking about children being tasked with roles whose impact on their lives they are in no position to understand.

Had I been asked to adapt *Lolita*—if I were asked tomorrow to adapt *Lolita*—I know what I would do. What I would do would be no different from what any other striving literary man would do. I would work hard to be true to a book that I love. I would ignore my conscience about putting a young woman in the position our production had put her in. I would tell myself that great art is worth the risk. What I wonder—what I truly don't know—is exactly how many days would go by before I realized that this was Humbert's logic, too, when he decided to destroy Dolores Haze. ❧

From *Lolita in the Afterlife: On Beauty, Risk, and Reckoning with the Most Indelible and Shocking Novel of the Twentieth Century*, edited by Jenny Minton Quigley, to be published by Vintage Books on March 16, 2021. Compilation copyright © 2021 by Jenny Minton Quigley. Essay copyright © 2021 by Thomas Carlisle Bissell.

Tom Bissell was born in Escanaba, Michigan, in 1974, and is the author of numerous books, the latest of which is Creative Types and Other Stories *(Pantheon). Several films have derived from his work, including James Franco's* The Disaster Artist *and Werner Herzog's* Salt and Fire. *As a screenwriter he co-wrote the pilot episode of* The Mosquito Coast, *based on Paul Theroux's novel, for Apple, and wrote the pilot episode of* Masters of Doom, *by David Kushner, for NBC Universal. He lives in Los Angeles with his partner, Trisha Miller, and daughter, Mina.*

COMMUNITY SUPPORT
FOR LITERATURE & THE ARTS

Bird & Beckett Books & Records

The Booksmith

City Lights Bookstore

David R. Godine /
   Black Sparrow Press

Humboldt Distillery

Pacific Review / SDSU

Rare Bird Books

Sarabande

Skylight Books

Stanford Continuing Studies

University of San Francisco MFA

ADDITIONAL SUPPORT PROVIDED BY

ART WORKS.

**National
Endowment
for the Arts**
arts.gov

CPSIA information can be obtained
at www.ICGtesting.com
Printed in the USA
FSHW021853271220
77138FS